Praise for
Cloak of the Light

"The invisible world gets a makeover in Chuck Black's *Cloak of the Light*. Often reading like a thriller, this fresh take on the unseen inspires and entertains in equal measure. Readers of all ages will enjoy this one."
—SHANNON DITTEMORE, author of the Angel Eyes trilogy

"Bring on the battle! *Cloak of Light* is a journey you won't quickly forget. Angels and demons clash in an epic story line laden with spiritual warfare. I loved this book."
—HEATHER BURCH, author of Halfling series

"Over the last several years, my family and I have come to appreciate Chuck Black's works, and *Cloak of Light* is no different. *Cloak of Light* is set in the modern world rather than the ancient times of the Kingdom Series. We have come to expect two features from a Chuck Black work: allegory based in spiritual matters and illumination of the spiritual warfare that happens around us every day. Many young people long for adventure, and this book has it. What I appreciate most is that adventure and spiritual battle are presented as common rather than special. As Christians, our adventure is in living for our Lord, and this is what Chuck Black brings out so deftly in his allegories. This is a great book for all young people, especially young men."
—DAVID NUNNERY, Teach Them Diligently

CLOAK OF THE LIGHT

BOOKS BY CHUCK BLACK

The Knights of Arrethtrae

Sir Kendrick and the Castle of Bel Lione

Sir Bentley and Holbrook Court

Sir Dalton and the Shadow Heart

Lady Carliss and the Waters of Moorue

Sir Quinlan and the Swords of Valor

Sir Rowan and the Camerian Conquest

The Kingdom Series

Kingdom's Dawn

Kingdom's Hope

Kingdom's Edge

Kingdom's Call

Kingdom's Quest

Kingdom's Reign

CLOAK OF THE LIGHT

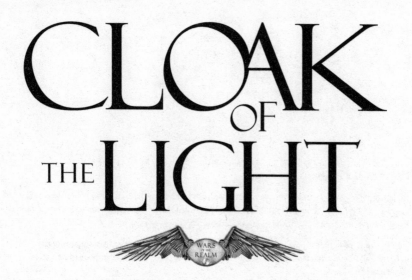

WARS OF THE REALM

CHUCK BLACK

MULTNOMAH
BOOKS

CLOAK OF THE LIGHT

All Scripture quotations, unless otherwise indicated, are taken from the New King James Version®. Copyright © 1982 by Thomas Nelson Inc. Used by permission. All rights reserved. Scripture quotations marked (KJV) are taken from the King James Version.

This is a work of fiction. Apart from well-known people, events, and locales that figure into the narrative, all names, characters, places, and incidents are the products of the author's imagination or are used fictitiously.

Trade Paperback ISBN 978-1-60142-502-7
eBook ISBN 978-1-60142-503-4

Cover design and photography by Kristopher K. Orr

Published in the United States by Multnomah, an imprint of the Crown Publishing Group, a division of Penguin Random House LLC, New York.

MULTNOMAH® and its mountain colophon are registered trademarks of Penguin Random House LLC.

The Library of Congress has catalogued the original edition as follows:
Library of Congress Cataloging-in-Publication Data
 Black, Chuck.
 Cloak of the light / Chuck Black. — First edition.
     pages cm. — (Wars of the realm ; book 1)
   ISBN 978-1-60142-502-7 (pbk.) — ISBN 978-1-60142-503-4 (electronic) 1. Adventure and adventurers—Fiction. 2. Good and evil—Fiction. 3. Angels—Fiction. 4. Christian life—Fiction. 5. Single-parent families—Fiction. 6. Family life—South Carolina—Fiction. I. Title.
   PZ7.B528676Clo 2014
   [Fic]—dc23

                                                                    2013041035

Printed in the United States of America
2017

10 9 8 7 6 5 4

Thanks to my lovely wife, Andrea, and my wonderful children, who sacrificed many hours of family time to allow this story to be written.

CONTENTS

1 Four Notes 1
2 Rivercrest High 7
3 The Curious Mind of Benjamin Berg 24
4 Mystery Girl 31
5 Carter's Curse 41
6 Redirection and Resurrection 48
7 Irreconcilable Beliefs 56
8 Evidence of a Stranger 67
9 Cloak of the Light 76
10 Darkness 85
11 Missing a Friend 95
12 Eyes of Another World 109
13 Betrayed! 116
14 The Invader War 130
15 Escape and Evasion 150
16 Off the Grid 158
17 The Guardian 169
18 Mr. Lee 177
19 Dodging Bullets 183
20 Battle of the Beast 189
21 Impossible Love 198
22 A Mission for Two 205
23 A Desperate Move 212
24 Saving Ben 220
25 The Plan 232
26 A Second Chance 241
27 Fugitive 249
28 Into the Dragon 264

29 Secret Agent of the Invader Realm 275
30 The Final Encounter. 283

A Note from Chuck Black 287
Readers Guide 289

FOUR NOTES

His dad was gone.
Forever.

Drew might only be twelve, but he knew the sting of his father's death would last a very long time—a lifetime. The pain of loss was a fresh wound to his young, unscarred heart. There were no life calluses to impede the searing ache of death.

He sat there, staring at the casket, sorrow hanging heavy on his soul, threatening to pull him down to where he could not breathe. Though the sun darted between the clouds, trying to peek down from time to time, the day was a dark one. Long faces, black dresses, tears, tissues, and "Taps"—the four loneliest notes ever played on a trumpet.

Drew tensed up when the colonel knelt down in front of him. He struggled to look the man in the eye. He had quelled his tears, letting them spill only in the privacy of his bedroom. Here, in front of military statues made of flesh and blood, he wanted to be brave for his dad. He stared at the colonel's white-gloved hand covering the perfectly folded flag being offered to him. His mother had asked that the flag be given to Drew, not to her. He wasn't sure if the gesture was for her, for Drew, or for his dad. It didn't matter.

He just wanted it over.

The colonel's deep and sober voice resonated through Drew.

"This flag is presented on behalf of a grateful nation and the United States

Army as a token of appreciation for your father's honorable and faithful service."

As Drew reached for the flag, he looked into the man's eyes—and saw there the same sorrow crushing his own heart. And though he knew the words had been spoken thousands and thousands of times, Drew believed the colonel meant them.

Tears brimmed his eyes as he took the flag. He pursed his lips to restrain his hurt, but it didn't help. He felt his mother's hand on his shoulder and knew that the pain they each bore was additive in a vicious cycle that provided no escape. He leaned in to her. He had heard that time was the salve for such a wound. If that were true, Drew wished a million years could pass in an instant to separate him and his mother from the pain of his father's death, but instead the seconds took an eternity to pass.

The day lasted forever. Drew didn't want to feel the pain, but he didn't want to forget his father either.

So he walked through it all, painfully aware that his life was forever, irrevocably changed.

And there was nothing he could do about it.

A FEW DAYS LATER, Drew and his mother, Kathryn, received a visit from Jake Blanchard. He had attended the funeral but was silent through its entirety. Kathryn invited him in and offered an iced tea. The raw emotions of the week were still evident as the odd trio sat in the living room in silence. Jake held his glass with both hands, either to keep it from falling or to give his hands something to do while he worked up the courage to speak.

How ironic that a Special Forces soldier of Jake's caliber, with years of combat training and experience, could be reduced to a hesitant, irresolute man struggling to say a few meaningful words.

Drew had seen his mother have this effect on other men, for she was a beautiful woman, the kind of pretty that could not be diminished with dirt, sweat, or sorrow. In fact, the worse the condition, the more resolute her beauty shone in defiance. Her dark-brown hair usually fell loose across the right side of her olive-toned face. Deep-blue eyes framed by high brows and accentuated cheekbones captured the gaze of both men and women. Drew remembered how he'd blush when his dad talked about how beautiful she was, but he was right.

As Drew looked across the room at Jake, he realized that his mother's beauty was not what was causing the man's unsettled beginning. Jake finally set the sweating glass of tea on the coffee table before him.

"Ma'am, I'm not very good with words, but I do have a few I need to speak." Jake dropped his gaze to the untouched tea and the ice still circling to find a resting place. His left hand massaged his right as he continued. He glanced at Drew and then back at Kathryn.

"Ryan and I were on a lot of missions together. We became good friends. In fact, he was the best friend I've ever had." He stopped and swallowed hard.

Kathryn teared up. "He wrote of you, Jake." She spoke with a sweet compassion. "I know Ryan considered you the same."

"What I'm sure he didn't tell you was that he saved my life in Iraq. I owe him everything."

Kathryn dabbed her eyes with a Kleenex.

Jake reached into his shirt pocket and removed a folded piece of paper. "I'm sure he would have wanted you to have this. It was a letter he was writing as we got called on our last duty together. He gave it to me just before—"

Drew's mother gasped, and tears streamed down her face. Jake leaned across to her, and she took the letter as though it were as precious as gold. She looked at Jake and mouthed the words *thank you*.

Jake turned to Drew. "And this is for you." He held out his father's Army Special Forces pin and green beret. "I know he would have wanted you to have these. He was very proud of you."

Drew held the pin in one hand and the beret in the other. Despite all the pain that came flooding back, these things helped. They were one more connection to his dad.

Drew sniffed. "Thank you, sir."

Jake smiled through wet eyes and nodded. He took a deep breath, as if to prep for a mission. "I don't mean to make this difficult, ma'am, but I need you to know one more thing before I leave. I was with Ryan at the end, and he asked me to make sure that you and Drew were taken care of."

"You've done that for us today. We will be all right."

Jake shook his head. "I promised him, ma'am, and I intend on keeping that promise." He leaned forward and handed Kathryn another paper. "This is my address and phone number. I will be stationed here in Fort Bragg for the next six months. No matter where you are, if you need anything, call me and I will be there for you and your son."

Kathryn took the paper. "Thank you. That means a lot, Jake."

He nodded, then stood up. Drew walked with his mother to the door to see Jake out.

On the porch, Jake turned. "It was an honor to serve with your husband, ma'am. He was one of those rare men of true honor and integrity." Jake put a hand on Drew's shoulder. "You can be very proud of your father." He looked as if he wanted to say something else, but instead turned and left.

When the door closed, Drew and his mother retreated to their rooms to spend time with their new treasures. Later, Drew's mother read the letter to him. One part stated that Drew's dad had some exciting news to share but that it was too important to share in a letter. He wanted to tell them in person. Whatever it was, it was news that was lost forever. Worse than that was how the letter ended…

"Please tell Drew that I miss him and that…"

That was it.

News untold and a message undelivered. The letter hurt more than it helped, but it was worth it because it was a final memory of his dad. The ache in Drew's heart was the painful tutor teaching Drew a new law that was as unbreakable as all the laws of the universe: life isn't fair.

ONCE ALL THEIR AFFAIRS were in order, Drew and his mother moved back to Columbia, South Carolina, to live with her mother. Although Drew had always done well in school, the loss of his father and the move to another city in the middle of his sixth-grade year were too much. He struggled in school and did not pass some of his classes. The next fall, his mother landed a teaching job at the same school Drew attended, so she decided to have him repeat sixth grade to help him get back on track.

Through it all, Drew struggled to be happy. But it was Jake who helped him smile again.

The summer before Drew started his second sixth-grade year, Jake finished his tour with the Army. He found a job with a security company in Charlotte, North Carolina, less than one hundred miles from Columbia. He invited Drew on a camping trip before school started, and Kathryn was grateful beyond words.

"Are you excited to go camping with Jake tomorrow?" Drew's mother asked as they ate supper.

"I guess." Drew poked at his potatoes with his fork. Then a thought lit up his eyes. "Do you think he'll let me shoot his 9 mm?"

"This is a camping trip, not a gun-shooting trip."

Drew's eyes saddened and Kathryn winced. "But if you ask him politely, and you're respectful, and you're very, *very* careful—"

"Really?" Drew got excited just thinking about it, even though he knew his mother wasn't really for it.

That night his mother helped Drew pack for the trip, and when she tucked him into bed, a little of the ache in his heart was gone.

"I'm going to miss you, but you have a wonderful time with Jake, okay?"

He nodded. His mother kissed his forehead a little longer than usual and then stood up and walked to the door. She reached for the light.

"Mom?"

She turned.

"I'm going to miss you too."

She smiled, turned off the light, and wiped her eyes. After she closed his door, Drew couldn't help but smile as he thought of the adventure the next day would bring.

The camping trip was a big hit, and for Drew, shooting the Beretta 9 mm was the highlight of the week. When they returned home five days later, Drew couldn't wait to tell his mother all about it. She thanked Jake three times, and he promised Drew he would take him on more trips as soon as he could work them into his schedule.

Throughout the year, Jake checked on Drew and Kathryn and never left without completely stocking their freezer with meat and other frozen goods. Drew looked forward to Jake's visits, and because Jake didn't have much in the way of his own family, holidays and camping trips together became commonplace.

At first the camping trips were just a distraction and an avenue for Drew to get to know Jake better. But in time the trips transformed into something much more. Drew learned survival techniques from Jake, and both the teacher and the student loved it. Though Drew was just in his early teen years, he had an aptitude for the things Jake was teaching him. He couldn't help smiling at Jake's surprise every time he did better than either of them anticipated.

Jake took Drew all over the country to expose him to different environments. When Drew had mastered the environs in the States, their trips reached beyond the borders of the US to further expand his training. That's when Jake began infusing combat training into their trips—and Drew soaked it up like a sponge.

Drew watched Jake navigate the fine line of being a mentor while not trying to replace his father. He came to admire and respect Jake, and though their bond grew strong, the pain of losing his father never completely left him.

2

RIVERCREST HIGH

Two weeks before Drew started his freshman year at Eagle View High School, Jake came to visit. After spending some time talking with Kathryn, Jake looked at Drew.

"Come with me. I've got something for you."

Drew followed Jake out to his car and waited as he reached in and pulled out a brand-new leather football.

"Go for a pass."

Drew took off down the street and Jake threw a perfect spiral just over his left shoulder, which Drew caught. They threw the ball back and forth for thirty minutes, and then Jake called him in.

"Football practice starts at Eagle View this week. Have you thought about playing?"

"Not really, I guess." Drew tossed the ball up a few feet and caught it. "You think I could?"

"You've got a knack, I think. You should give it a try."

Drew nodded. He'd have to decide soon. "I'm not so sure Mom would be okay with it. Do you think you could talk to her?"

Jake smiled. "Already done. It's up to you now."

Drew raised an eyebrow. "Cool."

Football practices were tough, but Drew loved the challenge. He discovered a real love for the game and a talent for it he didn't know he had. His adjustment to high school seemed to be going well, but three weeks into the school year his mother called him into the living room. Her expression was grave.

"Your grandmother has cancer."

Drew sank onto the sofa. "Is it bad?"

She didn't answer. She didn't need to.

Her expression said it all.

It was a difficult start to the year for everyone, and Drew found respite in football and the school library, where he escaped into a strangely mixed world of science fiction, sports, and war novels. He didn't devote much attention to his studies and was satisfied with the Cs he usually received. But the football season went well for Drew, and when it was over, he had even gained the attention of the varsity coaching staff.

At the end of the school year, his grandmother lost her fight with cancer. Another funeral and more sadness pressed hard upon Drew and his mother in the beginning days of summer.

Jake stayed close during those days and then planned two trips with Drew over the next couple of months. The trips were a welcome distraction from the gray of mourning. The cares and burdens of life melted away in the wildernesses of the earth, and Drew immersed himself in every aspect of Jake's planned adventures and training. Drew asked Jake about his father often, and Jake used those opportunities to honor his fallen friend by grafting into Drew's character the same patriotic spirit and commitment to honor and integrity that he had witnessed in the boy's father.

DREW SET THE PIN at two hundred twenty pounds for the bench press on the universal weight machine. He was shooting for a new max. Free weights were better, but he liked working out alone, and benching this much without a spotter would be foolish. It was evident that he had inherited his dad's athletic prowess and muscular physique. When most of his friends struggled for every ounce of muscle added, his workouts simply toned and defined the muscles his body naturally grew.

Drew took in a deep breath and slowly exhaled as he pushed hard against the bar. It lifted slowly at first, and then at the halfway point, Drew finished it off with no problem. He let the weights settle back down. The sense of satisfaction was gratifying. His sophomore football season had gone really well—he had dominated as a running back on his team. Midway through the season, he had gained a starting position on the varsity team. At last Drew felt like he was climbing out of the abyss of a ruthless and ill-fated life.

"Stay healthy, get stronger, be motivated, and there'll be a college football scholarship waiting for you," Coach White said at the end of the state play-offs. They were words that Drew hung on to and in which he found great motivation. Something about football inspired him. He loved everything about the game, and now he loved what the game could do for him.

IT WAS AT THE END of his sophomore year when Drew's law of life slapped him in the face once more. Kathryn's school district suffered severe cutbacks, and her teaching contract was not renewed. She had to apply for teaching positions outside of Columbia, and although she had hoped to stay close enough to commute, nothing was available.

One evening when Drew returned home after working at the pizza shop a few blocks away, he found his mother waiting for him in the living room.

Never a good sign.

"What's wrong, Mom?" Though she often tried to hide her emotions, he could see her heart through the windows of her eyes. He sat down next to her and put his arm around her. Drew remembered the first time he had felt his role shift from protected child to protecting man. It was strange at first but now felt natural. There were times his mother needed strength to help bear the world, and tonight was such a time.

His mother looked at him. Lines that had not been there earlier that year pulled at her eyes. "There are no jobs in Columbia, Drew. And I...I can't afford to make payments on grandma's house without a job."

Drew allowed his arm to drop, along with his gaze.

"I'm sorry, but we have to move. I've been offered a job in Rivercrest, Kansas. I know—"

"Kansas?" A familiar ache swelled within him. His dreams melted away, and anger swelled in his soul—anger not for his mother but for the fate of sorrow that dominated the course of his life. He had worked hard, and the next two years of football were looking to be nothing short of spectacular.

Drew saw his mother's face sadden further, and he was torn between his own anguish and his mother's. Even so, he couldn't help one plea. "The coach said I would have a good chance at a football scholarship here. I'm only a junior, and they're designing plays just for me."

His mother put a gentle hand on his leg. "If there was any other way, I would do it. I know you were really looking forward to the football season here, but I just don't know what else to do."

Drew dropped his head and rubbed his face with his hands. He was silent for a long while and finally forced his resentment back into the pit of his stomach. He looked over at his mother and then reached for her hand.

"I understand." He forced the words from his lips, even though it wasn't true. He didn't understand. And his mother didn't either. She didn't understand how much he was giving up. The pain of an unfair life swept in once more and mocked him.

Later, in the dark of his room, moon shadows journeyed across his floor as he spent a sleepless night trying hard to breathe in and accept the lot he'd been dealt once more.

What might have been sorrowful tears for a boy instead spawned bitterness in the heart of a lonely young man.

DREW AND HIS MOTHER arrived in Rivercrest, Kansas, and moved into an apartment three days after school started—just the perfect time for Drew's entrance into the high school to be as awkward as possible. Besides that, he had missed all the two-a-day football practices, so he was coming in late *and* unknown. He was in shape, but practice with pads and hitting was not something he could replicate on his own.

Rivercrest was a small city with a population of just under twenty thousand. Drew researched the high school and was consoled somewhat by the fact that it was large enough to support a football team in the state's third-highest division. Schools in the three higher divisions caught the eye of college scouts far easier than the smaller schools in the lower divisions.

"Do you want me to drop you off here?" His mother offered a smile as they approached the Rivercrest High campus. Drew had taken the test for his license and passed, but they owned just one working vehicle, and she needed it for work. His dad had a '95 Mustang in excellent condition—with the exception of the clutch, which had started to slip. Jake had promised Drew he would personally deliver the car once the work on it was complete, but until then, Drew would be chauffeured by his mother.

Drew huffed. "Naw...doesn't matter. It's going to be great no matter what happens now."

His mother fell silent, and Drew took a deep breath. "Sorry, Mom. It's going to be okay...really."

She pulled their minivan up to the front of the campus, where hundreds of students were lounging on benches and steps, waiting for the first bell. Drew felt many gazes fall on him. Oh, to be *any* place in the world except right here.

Just ahead of him, a slender girl slipped out of the passenger side of a silver car and stepped up onto the sidewalk. She flipped her light-ash hair over her shoulder and lifted her backpack into place. She leaned over and said something to the driver, then closed the door. As she turned toward the school, her eyes briefly met Drew's as he gathered the courage to exit the minivan. She shot him one quick smile, then walked confidently toward the front entrance. Drew decided that no matter what happened today, that one smile would keep him from becoming too discouraged.

"I hope your day goes well." His mother's smile was pained.

"Yours too." Drew grabbed his backpack and his sports bag and stepped into the social gauntlet.

He slammed the car door, stood straight, and made his way toward the wide double doors at the end of what seemed like a mile-long concrete walk. Four kids on his right laughed, but he couldn't tell if it was directed at him. He tried not to let his cheeks flush and pressed on to the door. He watched the girl ahead enter the school.

"Man, she's hot," commented one of three boys loitering near the steps.

"Bro, the only thing you'd get from her is some preachin'. She's a church chick."

"Who's the new tool?"

Drew knew the comment was directed at him but ignored it.

"Must be the new guy coach said was coming."

"Hey! What's your name?"

Drew hesitated, evaluating the potential of being harassed. "Carter," he replied, then looked to press on.

One of the guys peeled off from the other two and came to him. From the way he carried himself, he was an athlete. There was a large dose of ego in each stride. Probably the quarterback, or perhaps their star running back.

"That your first name or your last?"

"Drew Carter."

The guy looked at Drew, eyes narrowed. Square chin, close-cropped brown hair, a muscular build, and an attitude.

Great.

The guy looked down at Drew's bag. "You any good?"

"I can hold my own."

"We'll see." He gave Drew a piercing gaze, then stuck out his hand. "Joey Houk. Welcome to the Falcons." He nodded for the other two to join him.

"This is Spud. He's Josh."

The stocky, shorter one named Spud nodded, but the other just stared.

Just then the first bell rang.

The foursome made their way to the doors.

"Where you comin' from?" Spud asked.

"South Carolina. I was a running back for Eagle View High School in Columbia."

Joey looked at Spud with a raised eyebrow. "Cameron ain't gonna like that. Mm-mm."

It didn't really matter what position Drew played, there would be serious competition to win any spot. But quarterbacks and running backs were certainly at the top of the food chain.

Once inside, Drew stopped, trying to figure out how to get to the locker room to drop off his bag.

"You look confused, Carter."

"Yeah...ah, can you point me to the locker room?"

Joey looked over Drew's shoulder and smiled. "I can do better than that. Hey, Bergy...show Carter where the locker room is."

Drew turned around to see a slender, dark-haired boy dodging through students at a quickened pace.

"Can't...gotta get a lab—"

"Do it!"

The boy stopped and sneered, then looked at Drew. "Come on." He swiped his bangs out of his eyes, then led the way.

"See you around, Carter. Better be ready for this afternoon...or you're going to get your butt whipped."

Spud and Josh laughed as they turned and walked into a moving mass of students.

"Hey, I haven't got all day. Let's go."

Drew looked at the boy who spoke over his shoulder as he headed the opposite direction of Joey, Spud, and Josh.

Drew hurried to catch up. "Just point me in the right direction, and I can find my way."

"It's all right, I'm going that way anyway."

They walked until they were clear of most students, then turned to the right and went down a wide stairwell.

"Joey's kind of a jerk, huh?"

The boy looked up at Drew. "Aren't you all?"

Drew shrugged. "Maybe. I'm Drew. What's your name?"

They arrived at the door that said Boy's Locker Room.

"The lockers are at the end on the left. Yours is forty-two."

Drew cocked his head. How did he know that? he wondered.

"I'm Benjamin Berg. Statistician, assistant, water boy, kicking boy, and whatever else fits." He glanced at his watch and huffed, then moved back up the hallway.

"Hey!"

Benjamin stopped a few feet away, turned, and waited—probably expecting some snide comment to fly back at him.

"Thanks. And I'm not a jerk."

Benjamin just stared for a second. "Not yet...not until the pack gets to you." He turned and left.

"Okaaay..." Drew pushed the door open and was rewarded with the age-old smell of wet towels, sweat, and ripe football gear...the same smell that had occupied locker rooms since sports were invented. He dropped his bag into his locker and snapped on the combination lock he'd been told to bring. He made his way back up the stairs and found the main office. The staff directed him to his first class, Mrs. Wilson's Speech class. The second bell rang before he got there, and so he was once again a spectacle for everyone as he entered the classroom.

"Take a seat, Mr. Carter," the young teacher said.

He chose an open desk near the back of the room but couldn't help noticing the cute "church chick" sitting in the front desk two rows over. He took a deep breath, thankful he'd made it to his first class relatively event-free.

The morning classes went by all right. Since it was the beginning of the year, Drew hadn't missed much. At noon, he went to the cafeteria and was duly impressed. It had just been reworked in the style of a college cafeteria. He made his selections and looked for a place to sit.

"This way, Carter."

Joey passed by him with a full tray and walked toward a table where seven other guys were eating. Drew spotted fellow football players in an instant. The adjacent table was a mix of guys and girls—football players, cheerleaders, and the like. This was definitely the in crowd.

Drew followed Joey, glancing about the large cafeteria. He spotted skaters, drama geeks, hipsters, emos, populars, and of course, jocks.

Every school's the same.

"Guys, this is Carter. He's one of our new running backs," Joey said with a broad smile.

"Over my dead body." A stout boy in the middle of the table glared at Drew.

Great intro. He ought to smash Joey.

This glaring guy had to be Cameron, the running back. Threat number one.

"Hey," Drew said and sat down. He answered a few questions but tried to keep his talking to a minimum. He wanted to learn as much as possible about the coach, team, school, and players, so he tried to be the one asking questions.

"Just a heads-up. This school has a strict eligibility policy," said the boy they called Shooter. Then he smiled wide. "So if you get in trouble, just take Natalie out a couple of times over there and she'll do your homework for a month." Those who heard laughed. "Or you can just order Bergy to do it," said someone else, which extended the laughter.

Drew noticed that Benjamin had come in and was sitting by himself. Strangely, he didn't look lonely at all.

"He seems okay," Drew said.

"Are you kidding?" Joey stared at him. "He's a geek of the highest order. Just get him talking about computers or aliens and you'll see what I mean."

Most of the guys stayed at the table until it was time to go back to class. Drew stood and followed Joey and the others to the tray and dish return window.

"Here, Bergy, I've gotta go. Take mine." Cameron tried to place his tray, loaded with dishes, on top of Benjamin's, but Benjamin pulled away and the tray and dishes fell to the ground in a noisy clatter.

"I'm not your slave, O'Brian. Do it yourself."

Cameron's eyes burned and he looked like he was going to punch Benjamin. "Pick it up, you little weasel!"

Benjamin's face turned red, but he didn't move. By now the entire cafeteria had turned its attention toward the skirmish.

"I said pick it up, geek!"

Drew started to move toward O'Brian, but Joey grabbed his arm.

"Don't, Carter!"

Drew looked back at Joey and then at Benjamin. He could hear Benjamin's voice from earlier that day: *Not until the pack gets to you.*

Drew jerked his arm free.

"Back off, O'Brian." Drew moved between him and Benjamin. "You're the one who dropped it. You pick it up."

Hot anger flashed across Cameron's face as he glared at Drew. He smacked the bottom of Drew's tray, and everything went flying. The plastic glasses and plates crashed to the floor, and the two boys stood toe to toe, their fiery eyes just inches apart.

"You're dead meat, Carter. You must be as stupid as you look."

Drew was ready, although he would not make the first move. His response would depend on Cameron's attack. One move he considered could potentially break Cameron's arm, so he dismissed it and instead chose a second move, which, if executed correctly, would put Cameron flat on his back—

"Back away, boys." Mr. Herman's voice came from behind them.

Drew didn't budge. He glared straight into Cameron's raging eyes.

"O'Brian...Carter...I said back away." Now the voice was right beside them. The man put a hand on each of their chests and pushed until they backed off.

"Now pick up your dishes and take them to the counter. Both of you have detention. I'll see you there at three."

Cameron mouthed the words *dead meat* just before Drew broke eye contact and bent over to pick up his tray. He collected the dishes, and Benjamin joined in to help him. Mr. Herman marshaled the rest of the students out of the cafeteria.

Cameron recovered his tray and dishes, then disappeared. Drew's were spread everywhere, and a couple of the football players "accidentally" kicked a few pieces, scattering the mess even more. Drew heard a few choice words muttered as he tried to collect his dishes. As Benjamin knelt down to pick up a spoon, another football player near him bumped into him, which laid him out on the floor. Drew jumped toward the guy, who happened to be an inch taller and about fifty pounds of fat heavier. He was toe to toe again.

"Seriously?" Drew shoved the guy backward. "What is your *problem*?"

The guy looked toward Mr. Herman, who was just turning toward them again. Instead of coming at Drew, he joined the rest of the passing students to avoid getting detention. Drew walked over and put a hand out for Benjamin to grab. He easily lifted him to his feet. They set about picking up the mess again.

"You're not very smart, Carter." Benjamin knelt down next to Drew and set a couple of pieces of silverware on his tray. "You've just made an enemy of the jocks, and for what? To help a geek? Not much in it for you." Benjamin shook his head.

"Maybe," Drew said as they stood up and faced each other. "But then again, maybe I need you to do my homework."

Benjamin's face sobered, and he looked as if he had just made a deal with the devil. Drew smiled wide and winked, then slapped him on the shoulder.

Benjamin smiled just a little, and then a lot as he realized he wasn't being played. It was the first time Drew had seen him smile, which he imagined didn't happen very often.

As they left the cafeteria, Benjamin turned and looked up at Drew. "I don't get it... Why did you help me back there?"

Drew thought for a minute. "Because what they did was wrong, and it's wrong to do nothing when you have the power to do something." Those were words his dad had spoken, and he never forgot them.

Benjamin stared at Drew, then shook his head again. "There's a lot of wrong going on... I think you're in for a tough life."

Drew shrugged. "I don't get it either. Why do you help the jocks by being an assistant for the team if they treat you so lousy?"

The hall was moderately busy, and the odd couple caught the stares and whispers of many of the kids. Drew ignored them.

"Well, I am the nonathletic offspring of a very athletic father. And when I decided not to go out for sports, he decided I should pay my dues by becoming an assistant for at least one sport each year. I logically chose the shortest season with the least number of games. I'm quite certain he thought it might inspire me to one day actually join one of the teams, but it has instead solidified my position that such activities are a complete and total waste of time, energy, money, and various other school resources."

"Wow...that really stinks. Does your dad know how bad it is for you?"

"No, but I don't think he would really care anyway. He will be forever upset that I didn't try to follow in his glorious athletic footsteps. Any mocking I may receive would be considered justifiable payment for neglecting the more appropriate and respected activities."

Ben sure had sarcasm down to a fine art.

"Besides, there are only a few on the team that are real jerks. Most of the guys just ignore me, so it's not as bad as it may seem."

Drew marveled at Benjamin's attitude. "You're okay, Berg."

Benjamin shook his head as if to clear his ears.

"How come your friends weren't sitting with you at lunch?" Drew asked.

Benjamin gawked. "Friends? Are you kidding? In this zoo? Three years in this prison and I'm out of here. No one will mourn my departure—especially me!"

Drew frowned. "You don't look like the dropout type."

Benjamin laughed. "By year's end I'll have enough dual credits to graduate from this dump and enter college as a sophomore."

Drew looked around and caught a few more stares.

Benjamin noticed them too. "Look, you'd better distance yourself from me if you are going to succeed in this artificial social cesspool."

Drew looked back at Benjamin. "See you at lunch tomorrow."

"You really are trying to sabotage your chances, aren't you?"

Drew just laughed and headed off for his first afternoon class.

DETENTION WAS BEARABLE, but practice was brutal. After what happened in the lunchroom, almost every guy on the team was out to put Drew down. At the end of practice, Drew was bruised, sore, and wiped out. In the locker room, he was avoided like a contagious disease. He was slow to shower and pack his gear. Everyone else was gone, except for Joey.

"Bad move today, Carter." Joey walked by, sports bag in tow. "Little advice: watch your back. The football field isn't the only place we look out for each other."

The door closed behind Joey, and the thump echoed in the empty locker room. Drew sat in silence for a few minutes. Had he blown his chance to play football at Rivercrest?

With a sigh, he texted his mother for a ride, then finished up, hoisted his sports bag over his shoulder, and walked out of the school and into the parking lot. He looked around, fully expecting O'Brian to be waiting for him, but he was nowhere to be seen. A few minutes later, his mother pulled up and greeted him with a hopeful smile.

"How was your first day?"

Drew just grunted. He knew she hated that, so he added, "Fine, I guess."

They pulled up to the stop sign at the north end of the school and took a left onto Central. A few hundred yards later, flashing lights were reflecting off the rearview mirrors.

His mother glared at the police car. "I wasn't speeding!"

This day just gets better and better. Drew turned around and saw a sheriff's car trailing close behind them. A few moments later, an officer exited the car and sauntered up to their minivan.

Drew's mother looked up as the man came to the window. "Is there a problem, officer?"

"Driver's license and proof of insurance," came the stiff command.

Drew could see the starched, pressed tan uniform pulled tight across the officer's thickened abdomen. The man leaned over, probably so he could see into the minivan better. He glanced at Kathryn, then looked right at Drew. It was a hard glare...

Drew turned and looked out the passenger window. What was this guy's problem?

"You rolled through that stop sign, ma'am. You need to be careful around this school zone."

"I did?"

His mother sounded truly bewildered. Drew was too. He hated driving with his mother because she was such a stickler for following the rules. He looked back at the officer, read his name tag—and let out a snort.

"Do you have a problem, son?" the officer barked.

His mother's eyes grew big as she looked over at Drew.

"No sir. Just caught something in my throat."

The sheriff's eyes narrowed. "Stay in your car." With that, he returned to his cruiser.

"What was that for?" His mom's tone was stern.

"His name tag said Houk."

"And?"

"That happens to be the name of the quarterback on the football team."

"*And?*"

"Let's just say it wasn't the best day after all." Drew cringed at the interrogation he knew would follow.

His mother kept checking the rearview mirror. "We'll talk more about this when we get home."

Drew moaned. All he wanted to do was eat, watch some TV, and go to bed. Talking about anything, especially his lousy first day at school, was the last thing he wanted to do.

A few minutes passed and the officer returned with Kathryn's driver's license and registration.

"I'm going to let you go with a warning this time." He handed her driver's license back and looked right at Drew. "Be careful around this school."

"Yes, officer," Kathryn said.

The sheriff returned to his car and left, his lights flashing.

Clearly rattled, Drew's mother took a deep breath and eased back onto the road.

That evening, Drew fell into his bed feeling like gravity was pulling down with twice its normal force. He sank onto his bed and fell instantly asleep.

FIVE MINUTES LATER his mother was shaking him to wake up for school.

"The O'Brians and the Houks are tight," Ben explained that day at lunch, after Drew told him of his encounter with Sheriff Houk.

"Joey and Cameron are friends, but not like their parents—they go way back."

"Great. Now you tell me."

"I tried to warn you." Ben smirked.

"Yeah…I guess you did. I'll just have to deal with it."

As the week went on, the battering on the football field continued, but Drew did well in spite of it. In fact, the team's plot to destroy him backfired because it showed the coaches just what Drew was made of, and it allowed him to fully demonstrate his abilities. There were multiple altercations both on and off the field, but Drew worked hard and stayed tough. The coaches were impressed, and in time he even won a few of the players over. As things turned in his favor, Cameron O'Brian became more incensed with him. Twice he had to avert Cameron's attempts to fight him after practice.

Drew paid particular attention to Joey's reaction to it all, figuring that in the end Joey would have the most influence over the team. Drew learned that Joey was the quarterback for more reasons than just his athleticism—he was a smart tactician, supporting Cameron but remaining neutral enough to advantage himself no matter what the future outcome would be.

In the midst of Drew's challenging and painful week there was one bright spot: Jake arrived with his dad's '95 Mustang. Drew ran to the car and gave Jake a bear hug, grabbed the keys, and jumped in for a test drive.

"Be careful, Drew Carter," his mother commanded.

"Of course, Mom!" Drew backed the car out of the driveway.

His mother looked nervous and happy at the same time. Drew smiled wide as he felt the 5.0 liter engine rumble beneath the hood. Life was going to get good…he could feel it.

TEN DAYS LATER, Drew and Cameron faced off before the coaches to see who would win the starting fullback position. It was an all-out war as the two of them battled it out for over thirty minutes through five intense drills among the shouts and cheers of the whole team. When it was over, the coaches conferred for a few minutes, then announced Drew as the first-seat fullback. O'Brian swore, threw his helmet on the ground, and stormed off to the locker room. Half the team congratulated Drew, and the other half scorned him. He didn't envy the challenge the coaches now faced in trying to bring unity back to the team. After practice, the head coach called Drew into his office.

"Carter, I have to say, you've got guts."

"Thanks, Coach."

Coach Bruber was in his early forties and as fit as any of his players. Square shoulders, muscled arms and legs, and a vast knowledge of football had gained him the respect of every one of the players. He had been part of the coaching staff for the last fifteen years, six as the head coach.

Bruber crossed his arms, and his biceps and forearm muscles bulged. He eyed Drew while chewing on the inside of his left cheek, a habit Drew figured was the by-product of living for years under the stress of having to perform in a community where football was everything.

"Listen, Carter, you've earned the right to start at fullback, and I'm going to give you that opportunity." Coach Bruber hesitated, apparently choosing his next words carefully. "In my position there are many factors...and influences... that weigh into making such a decision."

Drew cocked his head, as if to appear uncertain what the coach was getting at. Although he was sure it had to do with the influence of certain well-known families in the school, something tempted him to force the coach to be blunt.

Coach Bruber looked unfazed. "I'm taking a chance on you, Carter. Don't let me down."

"I won't, Coach."

Coach Bruber scrutinized Drew. "Good. And keep out of trouble off the field too. Second chances are rare around here."

Drew nodded. Coach Bruber sat down at his desk and began looking over some stats. Drew left the office wondering just how strong those "influences" were. Well, he wouldn't give anyone even the slightest opportunity to ruin his chances to play the game he loved—and to gain a football scholarship when he graduated.

The next day before practice began, Drew saw a rather large, red-faced man leaving Coach Bruber's office.

"That's O'Brian's old man," Spud told him in a hushed tone. "You sure have made a ruckus around here." He punched Drew's shoulder.

Coach Bruber came out of his office with a steely-eyed glare. Practice was going to be rough.

3

THE CURIOUS MIND
OF BENJAMIN BERG

Ignoring the social boundaries between different groups in high school had its risks, but Drew had seen his dad give the same respect to a mechanic working on his car as he did to a bank president. He followed suit—and because of it, Drew was liked and despised by kids in all groups.

"So tell me about aliens, Ben." Drew gave a wide smile as he sat down across from his unlikely new friend during lunch hour.

Benjamin looked at Drew through narrowed eyes. What was Benjamin opposed to…his new nickname or the question?

"Seriously, I want to know," Drew prompted.

Benjamin looked left and right, probably to see if he was going to be the butt of another joke. Occasionally a couple of football players would join Drew at Ben's table, but today they were alone. The more Drew learned about Benjamin, the more intrigued he became. The boy was an absolute genius.

Drew had never met someone so peculiar.

"I'm going to become a physicist."

Drew laughed. "What does that have to do with aliens?"

"Everything! Physics is the study of matter and its motion through space and time." Benjamin looked at Drew as if that should answer all of his questions.

Drew held up his hands. *What* was Ben talking about? Maybe he shouldn't have asked the question.

Benjamin huffed. "Physicists analyze nature to understand the universe. If we can understand the universe, we will know where we came from and where to look for other intelligent life."

Benjamin looked around again. The kid bordered on paranoid.

"Everyone here scoffs at me for believing there are alien life forms, but think about it: NASA has some of the most brilliant minds in the world, and they are looking for other intelligent life. Why would the United States government spend billions of dollars if it wasn't a legitimate quest?"

Benjamin nodded his head toward the football players along the far wall. "Those clowns can laugh all they want at me while they get Cs and Ds in Social Studies. I hope to join the brilliant scientists of the world that are as convinced as I am that aliens do exist. It's just a matter of time before we find them. And do you want to know why?"

Drew's smile had faded. He stared at Benjamin, waiting for the answer.

"Because they are looking for us too."

The way Benjamin said it caused the hair on Drew's neck to stand up. For a moment, he considered the possible validity of that statement.

Creepy.

"I'm following the research of some of the leading physicists in the world, especially those whose work I believe will one day help us discover alien life. I think they are closer than we realize."

Drew absorbed Benjamin's strange and starry gaze. He didn't buy that aliens existed, but there was no doubt Benjamin did. Drew hadn't expected such a passionate answer.

Drew swallowed. "How close are they?"

Benjamin broke from his otherworldly gaze and allowed a subtle smile. "You *are* different from the rest."

"How's that?"

"By now others would be laughing and ridiculing me, but you ask more questions." He shook his head. "Have you ever wondered why science, Hollywood, and so many publishers are investing billions of dollars on the notion of alien life?" Benjamin's expression grew more intense. "It has become a consistent and central theme in much of our culture."

Drew realized just how right Ben was. Fully half of the movies he had seen in the last year had something to do with aliens.

"The influence is huge! I think we are being prepared."

Drew's eyes widened. Ben was too deep, too serious, too...right. Chills once again came over him. He had not expected to be affected by asking a few simple questions of a strange and quirky boy, but Ben's logic was unsettling.

"Prepared? For what?" he finally forced himself to ask.

"Hey, Carter! You ready for the Wolves?"

Alex plopped his tray down beside Drew. He was one of the two biggest linemen on the team, and he liked Drew. Ben recoiled like a sea anemone.

"Hungry for Wolf meat," Drew said and knucked it with Alex.

The conversation became exclusively football, and Drew was okay with that. He needed a little time to sort out what he thought about Ben and whether his eccentricity was still within the realm of normal—or if Ben was certifiable.

The rest of the day Drew couldn't help thinking about his conversation with Ben. He had never considered humanity's fascination—no, it was more of an obsession—with the possibility of alien life. That night, after having been plagued with Ben's bizarre perspectives, he came to the conclusion that humanity's fascination with aliens was no different than its fascination with zombies, vampires, and werewolves. No sane man alive would give *them* serious consideration. No, it was all in the name of entertainment.

So, that was settled. There were no zombies, vampires, or werewolves. Just as there were no aliens.

Good.

Drew felt much better—at least for a while—until he realized that NASA wasn't looking for zombies, vampires, or werewolves.

The next day at lunch, Drew grabbed his food from the lunch line and went to sit down.

"Hey, Carter," Joey called. "You want to talk football or computers and aliens?"

Drew glanced toward Ben, their eyes meeting for one brief moment; then he sat down next to Joey. Drew joined in the conversation, discussing the newest play the coach had given them, but the image of that lone figure three tables over gnawed on his conscience until he became indignant with it. The next two lunch hours he spent with the football players, telling his nagging conscience to go hang. After all, the team's first game was this Friday and camaraderie was an important aspect of a successful team.

THE RIVERCREST FALCONS won their first football game, but it was a tough one. Even though Joey was still loyal to Cameron, he was smart enough to not jeopardize his own position, or the potential success of the team, by undermining Drew's ability to run the ball. And run the ball he did. Drew scored two touchdowns and ran for one hundred forty yards. The coaches were pleased, and so were many of his teammates.

In the locker room, Cameron was silent amid the ruckus of a celebratory team. When the coaches finished their postgame comments, Drew grabbed his gear and headed for his locker, not planning to shower. He thanked each of the guys on the offensive line for doing a great job, which stunned them. His former coach had taught him to do that, and it paid off in team unity and yards.

Drew reached into his locker and grabbed his deodorant.

"Good game, Carter," Joey said from behind him as he walked past.

Drew turned around. "You too, Houk."

Joey stopped and looked back at Drew. "I didn't think you had it in you... Guess I was wrong."

He looked like he was going to say something else, and Drew felt the awkwardness of the moment. He gave a slight nod. "Later."

"Yeah, later." Joey joined up with three other guys and left.

Drew took a deep breath. He felt good about his life for the first time in a long time. He gathered his gear and zipped up his bag.

"Best stats this school has seen from a fullback in a long time."

Drew turned to see Ben putting a case of empty water bottles into the storage locker. "Thanks."

Ben didn't look up. He just grabbed his coat and walked to the door.

"See you around, Ben."

"Sure." Ben pushed open the door.

Drew watched the door swing shut and latch. His conscience kicked him in the stomach, but he tried to ignore it. After buttoning up his shirt, he threw on his shoes, slammed his locker door shut, grabbed his coat and bag, and headed for the door. The parking lot between the school and the football field was dark and empty. The cool, crisp night air washed across his cheeks as he looked left and right for Ben. One lone set of headlights on the street to the south was the only movement he saw.

"I guess you really are a jerk, Carter." He dropped his bag to the asphalt and then whipped on his coat. He took a deep breath and let the cool air fill the bottom half of his lungs. A sharp pain on his right side was a stark reminder of one particularly hard hit he had taken from a Wolves linebacker. He exhaled and bent down to pick up his bag. In that moment, something felt very, very wrong. An indescribable feeling of anxiety washed over him, and although it lasted just a fraction of a second, it was long enough for his consciousness to register the powerful emotion of fear.

In the darkness of the night, a blinding light smacked him.

He looked at his hand wrapped around the straps of his bag and could see the veins and hairs as though it were day. It made no sense until he processed the sounds that accompanied the light, and his stomach rose up into his throat.

Headlights!

The roar of the car's engine screamed at him. Drew looked up. With no time to react, all he could see were the blinding lights just ten feet away. He made an attempt to stand up, intending to jump backward, but it was pointless—the car was too close and coming too fast. Then he felt it. Something hit his chest, and he was thrown backward into the brick wall of the school, directly into the inside corner where the wall jutted outward ten feet.

The sound of the car smashing into the immovable brick wall was deafening.

Drew tried to cover his face with his arm as the air exploded around him. Shards of a hundred pieces of glass ripped through his hands and forehead. When would the pain of his crushed body engulf him? Surely death would follow in the next few microseconds...

But it did not.

Instead, he collapsed to the ground in a sea of shrapnel, numb, as a strange odor of fuel, antifreeze, burnt rubber, and blood filled his nostrils. It took a few seconds, but the darkness and the still of the night closed back in around him, disturbed only by a hissing sound coming from the engine of the smashed car.

How…

How was he still alive?

Drew looked to see if his body was still whole or if some major injury had put him in shock so that he couldn't feel the pain. The soft glow of the parking lot lights was not enough to make a determination. Warm blood trickled down his forehead and into his eyes. The thick, salty fluid stung, and he tried to wipe it away. His arms and legs all functioned properly.

He felt before him, and his hand came in contact with the cold, twisted form of the car's bumper just inches away from his chest. With a little more probing, he realized that he was wrapped in wreckage. That he was even still breathing was a miracle. He heard some faint voices and the sound of distant sirens.

"Is anybody hurt?"

The voice was familiar. Drew heard the quick succession of footsteps.

Drew tried to call out, but his voice failed him. He tried again. "Help!"

"Drew?" It was Ben. "Drew, is that you? Are you all right?"

"I think so."

"Stay still. I've called 911—they're on their way. Just stay still."

When the fireman pried open the driver's door, the sickly sweet smell of alcohol spilled out of the interior of the car. Drew heard the drunk man mumbling as emergency workers extracted him and placed him on a stretcher. They quickly but carefully pulled the wreckage away from the building and away from Drew. EMTs rushed in and began working on him. To their shock, the only treatment Drew needed was a few Band-Aids on his hands, forehead, and neck for minor cuts.

"You are one lucky kid," the older, bald EMT said. "It's a good thing you thought to jump into that corner, or you'd be a dead man."

"But the car hit me."

"Not possible. Did you see that brick wall? You'd have broken bones by the dozens. You must have reached that corner before the car reached you."

"Yeah...I guess you're right..."

"Stupid drunk!" the other EMT muttered beneath his breath, his words dripping with anger. Drew wondered how much of their work dealt with the consequences of drunk drivers.

Ben stayed with Drew until Drew's mother arrived, which was an event all in itself. She was not one to become hysterical, but it did take a considerable amount of time and convincing by Drew that he was okay. By the time he got home, it was one o'clock in the morning, and he was exhausted. The beating he had taken from the Wolves' defensive line coupled with the adrenaline from the accident had taken its toll, and yet sleep evaded him. He replayed that one moment in time, just before the car careened into the brick wall, over and over again...trying to convince himself that his quickness had saved him...

But he could not.

4

MYSTERY GIRL

By Monday morning, Drew felt almost normal again. After all, freak accidents and narrow misses happened all the time. He'd seen thousands on the Internet. He was just one of the fortunate "narrow misses" that so many others had experienced. But somewhere, deep inside, he couldn't shake the feeling that there was more to it than that. He certainly didn't believe in a God who cared or intervened in the affairs of men, so whatever had happened, no matter how coincidental, had to have some reasonable explanation. It had preoccupied his thoughts for most of the weekend, and Monday morning might not have been much different had it not been for Speech class.

The first round of speeches was to be given today. Drew did his best to listen, but his thoughts returned first to the football game and then to the accident. By the end of the third speech, he was struggling to even appear interested.

"Thank you, Justin," Mrs. Wilson called from the back of the room. "Our last speech today will be given by Sydney Carlyle."

Drew was still trying to learn names and perked up when the girl in the front of his row stood up.

Mystery girl.

This was the girl he had seen on his first day of school and hadn't forgotten her smile. "Church chick" was what one of the guys had called her, but from what he'd been able to tell, no one knew anything about her.

She walked to the front of the class and turned around.

Jake's voice came back to him: *"The smallest details often give the greatest information about a person."* Drew studied the girl at the front of the room.

Although Sydney was quiet, she was poised and confident. Stylish clothes with an extra touch of modesty set her apart from most of the girls. Drew had yet to see her come to class without looking her best. No drugs, no alcohol, no boyfriends… Drew was sure of that. Strong enough to go counterculture, but not rebellious. Pretty, but not obsessed with beauty. People pleaser, shy, reclusive, innocent to a fault.

Sydney faced the class and gave a nervous smile. Drew readied himself for another ten minutes of *ums*, *ahs*, and *likes*… Painful!

"My persuasive speech is on why it is important to abide by the copyright laws governing music, books, and videos. Every year, over two billion dollars are stolen from artists, authors, publishers, and producers for the work they have created to share with the world."

Drew thought about the hundreds of songs he had been given or that he himself had shared with dozens of other students. He'd thought he was immune to such petty petitions, but this girl's speech pricked his conscience like never before. Her delivery was polished and smooth. She scanned the room as she spoke, occasionally focusing on one student or another. One time, her gaze fell on him, and he felt like averting his eyes. Instead, he allowed the eye contact—and was mesmerized.

There was something different about this girl…something really different…something…

Pure.

She wrapped up her speech and received a reserved ovation. Drew found himself clapping louder and longer than he had for the previous speeches. No doubt about it, hers was the best speech given that day. Drew wanted to know more about her.

After class he hurried to catch up as she walked down the hallway. "Hey." He joined her, matching her gait.

Sydney snapped her head to look at him, and he realized he had startled her.

"Hi." She gave him a quick smile, then looked down the hallway.

"That was a really good speech you gave."

Sydney looked out of the corner of her eye at him. "Thanks."

Drew noticed that her pace had quickened. "I'm Drew."

She turned her head away from him. Was she so shy she couldn't even have a normal conversation?

When she turned back, she was laughing. "Yes, I know. You played a great game last Friday."

Drew smiled. He hadn't expected that—so she cared about football?

"You saw it?" he asked with a little too much enthusiasm.

"Yep. It felt good to finally beat the Wolves."

Drew dodged a couple of students. "Where'd you learn to give a speech like that? I mean, that was *really* good." Drew sensed her relaxing.

"My mom, actually."

Drew nodded. About then Sydney turned to go down the main staircase. Although Drew's class was in the opposite direction, he walked with her.

"So I was wondering," Drew began, but they ran into a sea of students and got separated for a few seconds. Sydney didn't make it easy for Drew to rejoin with her. When he did, she was moving to the front door to exit the building.

"Hey, where are you going? Second period is about to begin."

Sydney pushed the door open and looked back at him with a big grin. "To my next class." With that, she slipped through to the outside.

Drew stood looking out through the glass, feeling like an abandoned puppy.

"Well, she's got 'hard to catch' down." He turned to go back up the stairs to his Algebra II class.

At lunch Drew met up with Ben and thanked him for calling 911 and for staying with him Friday night. Ben seemed okay again.

"Hey, do you know anything about Sydney Carlyle?"

"Nope. Not a thing."

Drew told him about his strange but short encounter with her.

"Dual credit," Ben replied.

"Ah…sure."

"Half of my classes are at the college now. She's probably a senior and trying to get a head start on college credits."

"Makes sense. She's kind of a mystery. Nobody seems to know anything about her, although I heard one of the guys call her the 'church chick.'"

Ben shook his head. "I wouldn't do it…uh-uh."

Drew laughed. "So you're an expert on girls now?"

"Religion is a crutch for the weak minded and needy of the world. Nothing about any of it is logical or scientific. Get messed up with her and you'll be sorry." Ben didn't even look up from his food, as if he had given this advice a thousand times.

Ben was as intriguing as Sydney. What would she say about Ben? From one extreme to the other…

He was glad he lived in the comfortable middle.

EACH DAY THAT WEEK, Drew tried to get a few more bits of conversation in with Sydney. By Thursday, he didn't know much more about her than he did on Monday, and although he wasn't looking for a girlfriend, he had to admit he thought about her. A lot. Friday morning, he bolted to catch up with her again.

He started out with his usual opener. "Hey."

She turned and smiled, but it wasn't a genuine good-to-see-you smile. It was a not-again, forced smile. Something hurt just a little inside him.

"You sure make it tough for a guy to get to know you."

"I know."

"Why?"

To his surprise, she stopped and turned to face him for the first time.

"What are you looking for, Drew Carter?"

Drew hunted for an answer. Perhaps he had judged her shyness prematurely. "I…I'm looking to get to know you a little better, that's all." He gave a shoulder shrug.

She eyed him, skeptical.

"Okay…you got me. I'd like to ask you out on a date."

She shook her head. "I don't date." She turned and resumed her walk down the hallway.

Drew watched her walk away. He had never before had to try so hard with a girl—not that there had been many girlfriends, but he always succeeded in getting girls to talk to him. He considered following after her, but there wasn't much more he could say. She obviously wasn't interested.

It's just as well. Big game tonight, and I need to stay focused on football.

Drew walked on to his next class, trying to forget about the girl he barely knew...

Would she be at the game tonight?

THAT EVENING, THE RIVERCREST FALCONS took on the Bakersfield Badgers and tallied another win. Drew had another excellent game, scoring three touchdowns and running for one hundred fifty-three yards. Coach Bruber looked pleased and relieved. Evidently a couple of wins and proof of his making the right choice for fullback helped eliminate some of the pressure.

"Great game, Carter!" Joey gave him a wide grin. "Keep it up and we'll make the play-offs."

"You too, Houk. Way to throw the ball."

Joey had completed sixteen passes, and Drew loved it, because a throwing quarterback opened up a defense enough for him to run the ball well.

"Hey, a bunch of the guys and I are going out to Hansen's for a while. Why don't you come along?"

Drew hesitated, not sure what he might be getting himself into.

"Yeah, Carter," Spud chimed in. "Don't be a wimp. Hansen's place is awesome. Hot tub, pool table, cheerleaders...everything you need to celebrate a victory."

Well...he *should* make an effort to connect with these guys. Besides, he could leave if he didn't like what he saw. "Okay, I'm in."

Spud let out a yelp as if the party had already begun. "Awesome! You can give us a ride in that sweet car of yours. It's only a couple of miles out of town."

Joey swung his hand around and Drew caught it.

"Sweet," Joey said with a grin. "We can throw our gear in my car and jump in your 'Stang."

Before Drew knew it, he, Joey, Spud, and Justin, their middle linebacker, were on a dirt road traveling to the Hansens' place, a large home on four acres just three miles north of town. By the time they arrived, the party was well under way. Twenty-some other cars were parked in every orientation on the lot to the side of the home. Drew popped open his door and could hear the thump of the subwoofers pounding from the house. Laughter and yelling mixed in with the music. Drew could see why this home was chosen.

"Are Hansen's parents home?" Drew couldn't believe this guy's parents would allow something like this in their home and on their property.

"I doubt it," Joey replied. "But they wouldn't care if they were. Hansen has parties here all the time. It's awesome. Come on!"

As they entered the doorway, the music blasted at Drew's ears. There were kids everywhere—the foyer, kitchen, hallways, hot tub. The wide staircase and balcony on the second floor seemed a popular hangout too, as it afforded a perfect view of much of the activity. Drew became uncomfortable and considered doing a one-eighty to head for home.

"Carter!" Alex held a fist in the air as he yelled from the top of the balcony. The two-hundred-thirty-pound lineman pushed people aside to descend the stairs.

Drew wasn't sure what to expect. He locked hands with the large grinning fellow.

"You are the man!" Alex grabbed a random passerby. "This is the man... three touchdowns!"

"Awesome game, Carter!" The guy gave Drew a fist bump and moved on.

"It's easy to look good when you've got a great line. You played a great game too, Alex," Drew shouted above the music.

"Come here." Alex grabbed Drew's arm. "There's someone who's been wanting to meet you."

Alex cleared a path for Drew through the throng of teenagers, almost as if they were still on the field. Drew laughed. They made their way out to the back patio where the hot tub was and another thirty teens were hanging out. The music was quieter but still difficult to talk over, and the deep thump of the subwoofer somehow seemed even louder on the patio.

"Hey, Kaylee," Alex shouted over the heads of a dozen teens. "This is the cheerleader I was telling you about. She's been asking about you."

A cute girl slipped past a couple of guys and came to them.

"Drew Carter, this is Kaylee Marks. Kaylee, Drew."

Drew smiled. He had seen her practicing with the other cheerleaders but had never had a chance to talk to her. They didn't share any classes together. Kaylee's eyes sparkled, and a pure white smile spread across her flawless skin. Every blond hair was perfectly in place.

"Congrats on the game," Kaylee said.

"Thanks, and thanks for cheering."

Alex yelled somebody else's name and took off. Drew struggled to keep the conversation going.

"This party is crazy, huh?" He made a sweeping gaze across the premises.

Kaylee moved closer to hear him, and her perfume delighted him.

"Totally! The first time I went to one of Todd's parties I was blown away." Her fingers brushed Drew's arm.

They chatted for a few minutes, and then Kaylee looked at the hot tub. "So, you going in?" She lifted her shirt over her head, revealing a bright blue swimsuit.

Heat rushed to his face. "Uh…I don't think so."

"Come on… It'll be fun."

"You go ahead. I've gotta find Joey."

Kaylee put on a pretty pout. "Wait here." She bolted into the house and returned a minute later, pen in hand. She grabbed Drew's hand and began writing on his palm.

"Give me a call, okay?" She smiled up at him.

"Sure." He looked at the numbers on his hand and smiled back.

She giggled and ran off to the hot tub.

Drew returned to the house, where it seemed as though it had filled with even more teens. He roamed from room to room, hunting for Joey. He'd tell him so long and then head home.

He finally asked someone if he'd seen Joey, and the boy pointed to a door that led out to another patio on the side of the home. As he made his way there, he realized some teens were holding beer cans.

The Hansens were okay with this?

He shook his head.

He found Joey with another group of teens, most of them football players, talking about the game. Cameron was with them, so Drew approached cautiously. The flames from an open-pit fireplace danced and licked at the cool evening air.

"Hey, Carter, we were just talking about you."

Drew noticed that most of the guys and girls were holding beer cans. "Houk, I think I'm—"

"Give Carter a beer, Jayden," Cameron shouted to a teen over by a case of beer.

The boy reached for a can and threw it to Drew. He caught the can and felt the cold sweat from it splash on his neck. "I don't think so." Drew set it down on the brick landscaped wall nearby.

"No stomach for it, hey, Carter?"

Drew could tell Cameron had already downed at least a couple.

Everyone waited, as if to see what Drew would do. Technically he had an obligation to tell the coach about this, but that wasn't going to happen. He couldn't even begin to imagine the repercussions that would affect his life, and his mother's, if he ratted these guys out. Even if he didn't tell and they still were caught, he would be the most likely target as the rat.

"It's okay, Carter," Joey said. "One beer isn't going to kill you."

"Come on, Carter!" One of the other players joined in. "You deserve to celebrate after a game like that!"

Drew turned the cold aluminum can so he could see the brand. All the NFL football game commercials raced through his mind. Some of the best Super Bowl commercials were made by beer companies. They made it seem so cool.

He watched as his left hand reached for the top and snapped it open.

"That's my man!" Joey raised his beer. The rest joined in to toast Drew.

Drew's first drink of beer tasted horrible, and he tried hard not to show it. *Why would anyone want to drink this?*

He held the can and took a couple of small sips just to look the part, but he hated it. He joined in the conversation about the next game they would play against the Johnstown Giants. They were rated second in the state in their division—the game would be a tough one.

The other players bragged on Drew no small amount, pinning their hopes for taking the Giants down on his rushing and Joey's passing. An hour passed, and Drew made his way to the bathroom. He set his nearly full beer on the counter and washed his hands, then looked up into the mirror. The image seemed to scorn him.

"What are you doing, Carter?" Drew looked deep into his own eyes and was ashamed. He lifted the can of beer and dumped it down the sink, then walked back out to the patio and threw the empty can in a garbage sack specifically placed for removing any traces of alcohol.

"I'm out of here, Houk."

Joey looked at his watch. "Oh man! Cameron, we've gotta split too. My dad will be looking for me. I have to stay at your house tonight."

Cameron smiled. "I can't drive, Houk, and neither can you. Your dad would kill us twice if he knew we were drinking *and* driving."

"We're coming with you, Carter," Joey said, and grabbed Cameron. "Come on, O'Brian."

Drew grimaced, then thought about how bad he would feel if these guys ended up dead in a ditch someplace.

"Let's go." He walked around the perimeter of the house to where the cars were parked. His car was now wedged in, with no way out. It took another thirty minutes to find the drivers of the cars behind him so they could leave. Drew was getting more and more irritated by the minute. Cameron wasn't drunk, but he had certainly become stupid, which only added to Drew's frustration.

Joey sat in the front seat, and Cameron climbed in the back.

Drew studied Cameron. "You'd better not puke in my car."

Cameron laughed. "Relax, Carter, I'm not drunk. You know, Coach Bruber made the right call. You're the man, Carter...you're the man."

Drew shook his head. Why did he ever get into this situation? Never again. No matter how much Joey begged. He drove with an extra measure of caution, especially once he hit the city limits. Just a few blocks to go, and it would all be over.

They were approaching Third Street, the last busy intersection to cross. The green light ahead welcomed them through.

Psst.

Drew couldn't believe what he was hearing. A beer top snapping open, releasing the pressure inside.

"O'Brian! What are you *doing*?" Drew turned and looked behind him. Had Cameron actually opened a beer in his car?

He had.

Joey laughed, which further incensed Drew.

"You idiot, O'Brian!" Drew clenched his teeth and reached back to smack Cameron, but at that same moment the interior of the car flooded with light—

For a heartbeat, a sickening feeling filled Drew's gut.

He glanced to his right, beyond Joey, and caught a momentary image of a chrome truck grill inches away. Then glass exploded from Joey's side of the car, and Drew flew to the right. A fraction of a second later, the momentum of the car stopped and he was thrown to the left with less force. His head slammed into his side window, and he fought to stay conscious. The smell of beer filled the car. Drew opened his eyes...

And saw Joey, lying across the center console, his head resting in Drew's lap. The right side of his head was covered in blood.

"No...no...no..." It looked bad—Drew didn't know how to help him. "Joey!" Tears welled up in his eyes. He heard Cameron moaning in the backseat.

"Help!" Drew shouted. "Please *help*!"

5

CARTER'S CURSE

Drew didn't have the courage to attend Joey's funeral.

No amount of explanation could convince or compensate for what Joey's family, friends, school, and even the entire community had lost because of his mistake. That horrible night, other law enforcement officers had had to restrain Sheriff Houk from getting to Drew. The sheriff's screams were etched forever in Drew's mind.

It was all over.

In that one moment, he lost everything.

There would be no friends, no football, no college, no future...no purpose. The guilt pressed down on his soul like a mountain, and the curse of a broken life laughed at him.

The police investigation could not find enough fault with Drew to incarcerate him. He was charged with a traffic violation for running a red light, but that was all. The open container was not his nor accessible by him, and the blood alcohol test didn't register any alcohol. But it didn't matter.

It was the mistake that was unforgivable and unrecoverable.

Drew receded into himself. His mother wouldn't leave him alone, but she was just as emotionally spent as he. Jake arrived the following day and took on the burden of keeping the two of them from complete collapse. On Jake's last day with them, nine days after the accident, he coerced Drew and his mother to accompany him to the Flint Hills of Kansas, where the smooth, gentle lines of rolling hills on the horizon calmed the spirit.

"I'm planning our next camping trip." Jake leaned back against the rough bark of an elm tree as they sat on a blanket beneath its shimmering leaves. The bright sun warmed the country air to seventy-two degrees—a perfect fall day.

Normally Drew would follow with dozens of questions about the trip, but today his only response was a subtle nod. He sat across from Jake, his legs pulled up to his chest and his arms crossed in front of his knees.

"Thought we'd do some rock climbing in the Ozarks."

Jake glanced toward Kathryn. She gave him a weak thanks-for-trying smile, then gathered a few things and made a trip back to the car, just a few hundred feet away.

Jake leaned forward. "Drew."

Drew lifted his chin and his eyes just enough to see Jake.

"On one of our missions in Iraq, we were clearing a hostile-rich section of Baghdad. Another Ranger—a guy named Garret Woods—and I were to enter the back of a building while the rest of the team covered the other two entrances."

Jake hesitated. Drew could see memories surfacing that hurt.

"I thought I'd cleared a hallway to the right, while Garret cleared the one to the left. Somehow I missed a closet or recess, and Garret took a bullet because of my mistake." Jake paused. "I know what you're going through, and when I thought I should hang it up and quit life, your dad came to me and said, 'Mistakes that cost lives can't be fixed. All you can do is live the rest of your life in such a way that the fallen are honored.'"

Jake reached across and grabbed Drew's forearm. "I know it's hard, but giving up now wouldn't honor Joey—he wouldn't want that. Live so that Joey will be honored. No one in the world may know it, but you will."

Drew's eyes burned with tears that tried to spill. He swallowed hard and blinked. *How? How is that even possible?* The guilt, the pain, the injustice...it was too much to bear.

Later that afternoon, Jake returned to North Carolina, but Drew heard him tell his mother he'd be back soon. Drew sat on the couch and watched out the window as his mother and Jake exchanged a few words at the door of the rental car. She gave Jake a quick hug, and he left.

His mother came into the living room and sat next to him on the couch. The silence seemed deafening against the distant screams of a cruel world. Drew leaned over and rested his head on his mother's shoulder… He was a wounded little boy again. With a gentle hand she caressed his thick, dark hair.

"I can't go back to school, Mom… I just can't face any of them again," Drew said in a voice just above a whisper.

She didn't try to correct him. He knew he didn't really have a choice. They didn't have enough money to move again, and jobs were few and far between. Private schools were too expensive.

Drew sat straight again. "You could homeschool me." But he knew it was a futile suggestion.

His mother smiled. "I teach grade school, not algebra, government, and physics. Besides, the last I heard, the pay for homeschool teachers isn't very good."

Drew still couldn't smile. "I'm old enough to drop out and work. I could get my GED in the meantime."

Sadness darkened his mother's face. "Drew, I know this is going to be hard…very, very hard…but we will walk through it together. It will get better. I promise." She reached up and touched his cheek.

Other than getting a few hours of fitful sleep, Drew spent the rest of the time plotting how he could avoid as many students as possible, calculating doors, routes, and times—anything that would get him through the day unnoticed.

THE NEXT MORNING, Drew waited until the last possible moment to enter the school. The halls were almost clear as he slipped in the door to his speech class just as the bell rang. He avoided the stares, but his ears burned with the flames of whispers throughout the room. A couple of speeches were given, but he didn't see who gave them or hear a single word.

When the bell rang, he waited at his desk until he thought the class was empty. He looked up—and saw Sydney Carlyle sitting in her desk. She stood, then turned around and walked to the back, to Drew's desk. He pretended to read from a book he'd grabbed from home. He had prepared himself for any and all verbal abuse and in a strange way welcomed it. Perhaps it would ease his guilt through some cruel penance.

"I'm sorry for what happened." That was all she said. Then she turned and walked out of the classroom.

Drew looked up again at the empty room—even the teacher had left.

By the end of his second class, it was obvious the word was out—Drew Carter was back in school. The glares abounded like fiery arrows, and vicious comments were shot in his direction multiple times. At noon, Drew grabbed his sack lunch and found a tree on a remote corner of campus away from most of the students. The day was gray and cold, a quick turn from the warmth of yesterday. He took a bite of his tasteless sandwich. How was he going to make it through the rest of the day, let alone the rest of the year?

As he wallowed in his cold misery, the slender form of Benjamin Berg sauntered over to him, sack lunch in hand. He sat down near Drew and dug into his lunch without saying a single word. Twenty minutes later, they both got up and headed back to the school. Drew made it through the day and back home to his bedroom. He would have rather been pummeled in football practice for hours and done a thousand monkey rolls than have a day like that...but he made it.

The next day was much the same, including Ben eating a silent lunch with him on the corner of campus. The third day, Drew looked up at Ben at the end of their lunch.

"You always know just what to say."

Ben smiled.

"When did you start eating sack lunches?"

"When my friend did," Ben said without hesitation.

Drew turned away and let the cold, dry wind prick his face. "Thanks."

IT WAS A SLOW and painful transition into his new life, and it took weeks, but the whispers and glares diminished into a quiet hulking darkness that hung in every corner of the school. Occasionally it would scream and strike out at him, but those incidents became fewer and fewer as the weeks wore on. The football team struggled without their star quarterback and fullback, ending the season with a three-and-twelve record. Drew muddled his way through his classes, not caring about much of anything. His grades plummeted. It felt like he was back in sixth grade again, just waiting to fail in school.

And in life.

"So what are you going to do now?" Ben asked one day during lunch. They had been forced into the lunchroom by the drop in temperature the last few days. They picked a table in the corner, away from everyone else.

Drew looked at Ben with a blank stare.

"Now that football is done with you, what are you going to do?"

"I liked you better when you were silent. Can you go back to that?"

Ben just stared, waiting for an answer.

Drew huffed. "I'm going to finish this lousy year, drop out, get my GED, and join the Army. That's what I'm going to do. I hate school and everything about it."

"You're too intelligent to just wait for it to end. Why don't you actually try and see what happens?"

"Because I'm too far behind. I don't even get half the stuff they're talking about in math and science."

"That's because you quit. I'll help you."

"Why? Why should I try?"

"So you can go to college and do something with your life."

"I need college to do something with my life?"

Ben seemed unfazed by his belligerent responses. "No, but you should go because if you don't, you're going to end up bagging groceries and being sour at the world for how mistreated you've been."

Drew had taken a lot worse from dozens of other students and been fine, but Ben's comments made him angry. He stood up and shoved the remains of his lunch into his brown bag. "Thanks a lot, buddy!" He couldn't leave fast enough.

The next day Drew sat down across from Ben at their usual lunch table.

Ben waited in silence.

"Okay," Drew said.

Ben didn't even ask what he meant. He just nodded. "I'll get you through the tough stuff, Algebra II and Physics—you have to take care of Speech, English, and the other subjects on your own. I have class at the college until five, and then I'll be over."

Drew looked at Ben, and realization hit him...

The one thing he did right at Rivercrest High was defend the football statistician from a bully one lunch hour.

The next morning after Speech class, Drew hurried and caught up to Sydney.

"Hey," he said in his usual tone. Ben and Sydney were pretty much the only two students in the entire school that Drew talked to, although Alex did find him one day and told him he was sorry for how everything went bad on him. That meant a lot to Drew.

Sydney smiled. "Hi, Drew."

"You know, these thirty-second dates are getting pretty serious. I was thinking we should probably cool it a little."

Sydney laughed. He liked that. It was his first attempt at being lighthearted since the accident, though he did so without a smile.

Sydney angled a look at him. "I'm glad to see that you've found your sense of humor again. How about your motivation to study? Found that hiding anywhere?"

Ever since Drew started talking with her a couple of weeks after the accident, he'd noticed she wasn't in quite her usual hurry to get to the front door. He liked that too.

"Funny you should ask. Ben is forcing his help on me in math and science, and I thought maybe you might help with speech and English." They were approaching the front door and the end of their "date."

Sydney looked over at him. "Nice try. You know that wouldn't work, and besides..." She stopped and faced him with a look he hadn't seen from her before. One eyebrow was a little higher, and her blue eyes nearly glowed.

"You don't need me to help you, Drew...not with school. You're a smart guy. Your speeches are some of the best in the class, and you're a deep thinker." She smiled. "You'll be fine, and I'll be praying for you."

With that, she turned and walked out the front door.

Praying? Seriously?

Drew shook his head. Sydney was a great girl. But all she had to do was look at his life to know God didn't care about him.

Not one bit.

6

REDIRECTION AND RESURRECTION

Ben was a good teacher, even though he got frustrated from time to time when he thought Drew should understand the more obvious concepts, like the difference between static and kinetic coefficients of frictions. But once Ben figured out where Drew's conceptual breakdown points were, they discovered Drew had a knack for math. And although Drew enjoyed physics, he got more of a charge out of seeing Ben fly off on a tangent and start jabbering about photons, quarks, the Higgs boson particle, black holes, and multidimensional space. This usually led to deep and bizarre conversations about the origin of the universe and, ultimately, the existence of aliens.

Within just a few weeks, Drew was getting As and Bs in most of his classes. One side benefit, he discovered, was that studying occupied his mind and kept him from dwelling too much on the emotional pain of the accident. Whether this motivation was fabricated or genuine, he didn't care. He just knew it worked.

He also kept in physical shape by running and by lifting weights in the garage. His weight set wasn't complete, but it was enough to get a fair workout. Jake sent him a book on a workout designed by a Navy SEAL that required no weights, just common household items. After a few days of this regimen, he was sorer than if he had spent five tough days in the weight room. It became his daily routine, and he loved it.

Sydney remained elusive, and when she started talking about Jesus, church, and faith, Drew became uncomfortable and didn't join up with her as often.

By the end of the year, Drew and Ben had become close friends. With Ben's tutoring, Drew was able to finish up with four As and one B. It was the best he'd ever done, in spite of it being the worst year of his life. What really saddened him, though, was that Ben had enough credits to graduate. He was accepted into the physics program at Drayle University—three hundred twenty miles east of Rivercrest.

Drew would be on his own.

Even Sydney wouldn't be back because she'd finished up her senior year and was going to some third-world country to do missions work for a year. Drew couldn't begin to understand why she would waste a year of her life doing such a thing.

EARLY IN THE SUMMER, Jake helped Kathryn find a modest home on the edge of town sitting on two acres. It was a ranch-style farmhouse on the verge of being overtaken by the expanding city. A dirt road connected the home to the paved county road in front, and a peaceful covey of trees bordered the back. Drew and his mother were happy to be out of the apartment and into a regular home again.

Once the move was complete, Jake took Drew on the first of two ten-day camping trips that summer. The first to the Ozarks, as he had promised, and the second to the Badlands of North Dakota. Each time they went, Jake added more and more to Drew's Ranger training. By the end of the second trip, Drew was nearly himself again. It had been a long, hard year, and although he was different, he felt whole.

Near the end of summer, Drew bumped into Alex at a gas station, and Alex asked if he would consider coming out for football his senior year. Drew hadn't even considered it as an option and was taken aback by the question.

"We could sure use a good running back this year," the large lineman said.

A flood of unexpected emotions welled up in Drew, and for just a moment he found himself right back in the postaccident horror he had lived with for months. Still...something in his DNA tugged at him.

"I'm not so sure that would work, Alex." Drew imagined the uproar that would occur in the school, in the community, and especially from Sheriff Houk. It would make for an impossible situation, and Coach Bruber seemed hesitant even when everything was good. "Tell you what. You talk to Coach Bruber and some of the seniors on the team and see if they would even consider it."

Alex nodded and told him to take care. Before-school fall practices came, and Drew never heard back from Alex. It was what he expected, and it saddened and relieved him at the same time.

DURING THE FOOTBALL SEASON, Drew couldn't deny the deep ache in his gut. As therapy, he immersed himself in his studies and in working out, and he excelled in both. He took a dual-credit business and financial management class at the college the fall semester and loved it. It was a springboard into the world of finances, and he became fascinated with the mathematics of investments in stocks, bonds, mutual funds, and even commodity trading. He found a website where he could practice investing and trading with simulated currency on real-time prices and values. He lost five thousand sim dollars the first month, broke even the second, and started earning consistent profits every month after that.

After a couple of months' research on investment and trading strategies, he turned his original ten-thousand-sim-dollar investment into thirty-eight thousand in six months. It was a game that filled his spare time during what was a lonely year.

Despite Ben's intense academic load, he tried to make it home at least once each month. He and Drew would spend as much time together as possible, during which Ben convinced Drew to apply at Drayle. Drew had done very well on the ACT and had a good chance of winning a scholarship there.

Drew often thought of Sydney Carlyle, especially in the morning after his first-period class. He had lost contact with her and expected that he would likely never see her again. All he knew was that she was someplace in Indonesia wasting her life doing missions work…whatever that was.

AT GRADUATION, DREW WALKED across the stage for his mother's sake—he hated every moment and could still feel the harsh glares of the unforgiving. When he walked out the door of the school, it was like laying down a burden of immeasurable weight. He would never look back.

Despite Drew's protest, his mother couldn't resist having a cake made in celebration of his graduation. His mother, Jake, and Ben ate two pieces each just so the cake would look like it had served its purpose.

Drew opened the gift his mother had wrapped so beautifully. It was a new laptop with all the memory, drives, and other tech to take care of his college needs for at least the next few years.

"Thanks, Mom." Drew gave her a long hug. He let her hang on to him as long as she needed to. When she let loose, there were tears in her eyes.

"I'm so proud of you, Drew." She wiped away a tear that had trickled down her right cheek.

"And I am proud of you, Mom. I know it hasn't been easy. Thank you."

This made his mother's condition worse.

"So was it Ben or Jake who told you which laptop to buy?"

She laughed and punched him in the arm. Jake and Ben both held up their hands in denial.

Ben handed Drew a slender package wrapped in the best attempt of a physics major who could grasp the complexities of the universe but not the simplicity of folding paper around a box. Drew opened it and removed a dull spoon from the box.

He laughed. It had to be some kind of hoax. He held it up. "A spoon? Well, I suppose I will be needing this at college."

Ben just smiled. "It's a souvenir from Rivercrest High."

Drew still wasn't following. "The place I want to forget forever. Thanks a lot, buddy."

"It's the spoon from my tray that day you stood up for me. I kept it to remind me I had a friend who would stand by me, even when it wasn't easy. I want you to have it to remind you that you have the same."

Drew froze. A lump formed in his throat, and he grabbed Ben's hand and gave him a quick one-armed hug. "Thanks, man." Drew slapped Ben's shoulder.

Drew heard his mother sniffling again.

"Okay," Jake piped in. "I'm pretty sure this wasn't supposed to get so gushy, so now it's my turn."

Jake reached into his pocket and threw a set of keys in Drew's direction. Drew snatched the keys out of the air and looked at them. It was his old key chain from his dad's '95 Mustang, but the keys were different. He looked up.

"I don't get it."

"Come on." Jake grinned from ear to ear. They walked outside, and Jake clicked the remote in his pocket for the garage door to open. A white sheet hung over the beautiful and unmistakable form of a '67 Mustang GT.

Drew looked at Jake again. *"Really?"*

"Take a look."

Drew grabbed the white sheet near the spoiler and gave a tug. The sheet slid off the shiny deep-blue form as if gliding on air.

"Your dad was a Mustang fanatic, to say the least. This was his first Mustang. He got it cheap 'cause it was in pretty bad shape. When he wanted to get that '95, I bought it from him, planning to fix it up one day." Jake just stared at the car with a proud grin.

Drew looked at his mother, and she was as stunned as he.

"Oh, Jake. We can't… It's too much…"

"Nonsense, Kathryn. I want Drew to have it." Jake turned to him. "I think your dad would like it too."

"I…I don't know what to say."

"Don't say anything. Just get in and take it for a drive."

Drew couldn't restrain his grin. "Come on, Ben!"

"And be careful," Jake said as they climbed into the car. "There's not many of these around anymore."

Drew turned the ignition and was rewarded with the sound and feel of the deep rumble of the engine as it came to life.

Drew saw his mother grab Jake's arm and squeeze as he backed the car into the street. He eased the stick into first gear, and the machine quivered in anticipation of speed.

"Not bad," Ben said. "Old, but not bad."

Drew laughed and eased off the clutch. The blue steel form slipped through the air with ease.

For the first time in a long, long time...

Drew knew joy.

THAT SUMMER, JAKE MOVED to Rivercrest and started his own security company, specializing in the transportation of high-value assets and people. There wasn't enough population in Rivercrest to support the business, but Jake's reputation had earned him the respect of numerous corporations across the country. Being centrally located on the continent gave him quicker and easier access to those customers.

In spite of the challenges of building a company, Jake still carved out time for another trip with Drew that summer. Drew noticed a pattern in the trips Jake planned. Each one presented a different and new environment with challenges to overcome and survive. The first few days were dedicated to survival training, the next couple to combat training, and the last few to some fun adventure or activity. Of course, Drew never shared about the survival and combat sessions with his mother when she asked how it all went on their return.

Jake never missed an opportunity to share another story or a quote from Drew's dad. Somewhere during this last trip, Drew came to understand Jake's sacrifice and commitment to the promise that he had made to his father. That level of loyalty between nonblood brothers was something that could be forged only in the fire of battle. It was something Drew wanted and was drawn to. He knew that ultimately his place was in the armed forces and specifically Special Ops. Patriotism was in his blood, and he could not deny it. With Jake's training, he would be ahead of everyone else. He planned to get his degree and enter as an officer in four years. It was a goal that gave him purpose once more, and that felt good.

Ben stayed at Drayle for summer school, which made Drew's summer seem longer than usual. Ben thrived there and even had an opportunity to help a professor with some research. During a phone conversation, Drew laughed as Ben launched off on some superphysics jargon about light, plasma, and proving the existence of alternate dimensions. Amazing how the physicists of the world could become so excited about some subatomic particle that they might prove exists, even if only for a few nanoseconds.

Drew worked full days and earned as much money as he could in preparation for school. He knew his mother wasn't in any position to help him financially, so he was careful about every dollar he earned and spent. He started classes at Drayle in the fall and loved being free at last from the stigma of his past. Everything about college was better...much better.

ONE AFTERNOON A COUPLE of months into the fall semester, Drew was walking through the student union toward the bookstore when a familiar scene from his past caught his eye. A girl walked briskly toward the exit door, and Drew hurried to catch her. He popped up on her right side.

"Hey," he said with broad smile.

Sydney jumped.

"Drew!" Her face lit up, and she grabbed his arm. "It's so good to see you!"

Her face was tanned, and her smile was as captivating as ever. Her blue eyes were different though. Still bright and warm, but older...seasoned.

"I can't believe you're here, Sydney. I thought you were in Indonesia."

"My mission work is done for a while. I got back just in time to enroll here and get into a few classes." Sydney looked deep into Drew's eyes. "You're looking really good. How was the last year for you?"

"It turned out okay. Yeah...I'm okay. Life is good again." He crossed his fingers and held them up. "How do you like Drayle?"

"It's good," Sydney said with a nod. "I think I'm going to like it here."

Drew smiled. *Good.* "Yeah, me too. Ben's here too."

"I figured. Is he running the physics department yet?" She gave a quick laugh.

"Pretty much. So hey, do you want to catch up over a cup of coffee? You know, now that you're all grown up and everything."

"That's never been the issue, Drew." Sydney's expression grew serious. "It's whether or not *you've* grown up." Her lips curled up in a way that stilted Drew's breathing. No girl had ever had that effect on him.

"Touché." Drew returned the smile. "I should have seen that coming."

"I have to run to class right now, but I'll make you a deal," Sydney came back. "A few friends and I are getting together tonight in my dorm lobby at seven for some games and stuff. You come to that, and I'll go to coffee with you tomorrow."

"It's a date."

"No, it's not." Sydney turned to go, then looked over her shoulder. "I don't date, remember?"

Drew smiled. She had walked away from him a hundred times, and he still was left wishing she hadn't. She was pretty, that's for sure, but there was something else that he couldn't quite put his finger on.

What is it about you that's so different, Sydney?

But there was no answer.

7

IRRECONCILABLE BELIEFS

Drew was looking forward to the evening, even if he had to share his time with Sydney with other students. He could endure anything for a couple of hours since he knew he was going to spend at least one uninterrupted hour in conversation with her the next day. He was in no small way confused by the fact that this girl crowded into his thoughts and dominated them whenever he encountered her, and yet he knew so little about her. He was not so bold, even inwardly, to suppose that love had anything to do with it, for how could he love someone whom he knew nothing about? And yet he couldn't contain nor explain the ache he felt to be near her.

He arrived at Sydney's dorm lobby at seven and found her and a mix of ten other guys and girls waiting. One of the guys came right up to him, Sydney at his side, and stuck out his hand.

"How are you doing, Drew? I'm Devin." Devin looked like he was a senior. Light-brown hair and a matching beard framed his fair-complexioned face.

Drew stuck out his hand. "I'm good."

Devin had a solid handshake, so Drew was cool with that.

"We've got chips, Pizza Rolls, and pop if you're hungry. We'll get started in a few minutes, just hang loose." Devin left to greet someone else.

Get started? Drew looked at Sydney.

"I'm glad you came," she said with a smile. "Devin's with Campus Ministries. He's our Bible study leader."

Bible study? Drew moved to take a step back. Sydney reached forward and grabbed his arm.

"You wimp." Sydney laughed. "What are you afraid of? We're just going to read from the Bible a little, eat some snacks, and play a few games."

He looked at her through narrowed eyes. This must have been the "and stuff" she was talking about. "You're not playing fair."

Sydney's smile faded, and she looked genuinely contrite. "You're right. I'm sorry. I should have told you this was a Bible study tonight. I just thought that...well...that maybe you wouldn't mind so much."

She lifted her eyes, and his heart skipped a beat.

"I'll buy coffee tomorrow to make up for tricking you." Her timid smile almost undid him.

Oh yeah. He was in trouble. He hardly knew this girl and he was already putty in her hands. He would have stayed with her if they were going to discuss a Jane Austen novel. He jumped in on the Pizza Rolls and pop right away. If he had to listen to a bunch of religious gobbledygook, he would at least get a meal out of it. After ten minutes of small talk and introductions, everybody sat down on the chairs and couches so they could see and hear Devin. Drew made sure to sit next to Sydney just in case he needed to tell her he was going to make an emergency exit.

"I'd like to start with prayer. Does anyone have any requests we can take to the Lord?" Devin scanned the students and waited.

Drew sat and listened as four different students asked for prayer for a sick mother, a brother struggling with alcohol, a friend trapped in homosexuality, and a car that wouldn't start even with a jump and she had no extra money to get it fixed. Then everybody lowered their heads, and Devin prayed.

This was...weird!

Drew's family never talked about things like church, religion, or God. They just weren't a part of his life. Anything he knew about God came from Hollywood, and he was pretty sure they didn't have it right. He agreed with Ben, though—religion was a crutch for people who had a hard time dealing with reality. It was just a bunch of man-made, superstitious rituals and beliefs.

Drew reasoned that science refuted religion, but man's own history was also evidence against such superstitions because of all the different religions throughout the ages, from the Romans to the Greeks, the Egyptians to the Babylonians, and even on up to the hundreds of religions throughout the world today. How could any one of them even be close? The sheer number of religions both now and in ages past was a testimony to Drew as to how ludicrous it all was.

If he had to categorize himself, Drew guessed he fit best with the agnostic atheists: he didn't believe in God, but then, the existence of such a being was unknowable anyway.

He glanced around the room, allowing himself a slight shake of the head. He was uninformed where religion was concerned, and he preferred it that way. Why would he want to be part of a group of people who were so ignorant of the facts of life?

Drew spent the time Devin was praying to prepare his mind for the assault of illogical dialogue that was sure to follow. If Sydney was indeed deceived by this stuff, then perhaps he needed to move on after all.

Devin finished his prayer and looked around. He seemed hesitant. He opened his Bible and held his notes before him for a few moments, but folded them up and tucked them in the back of his Bible. He looked troubled, then relaxed.

"I'm not sure why, but the Lord is leading me in a different direction than what I've prepared today." Devin took a deep breath. "So please bear with me since none of what we will be discussing and studying is planned. The world is a confusing place today. For example, there are many religions, all claiming to teach spiritual truth. One might look at that and say this is evidence that there is no God and no truth at all."

Drew started. He looked over at Sydney—had she warned Devin about him? But no…that wasn't possible. He'd never shared any of his beliefs—or lack thereof—with her. No one other than Ben or maybe Jake knew what he thought about religion. And yet…he felt singled out, like he was the only one sitting in that room.

"Every tribe, culture, and civilization, both present and past, has had a set of religious beliefs to which they hold. I put before you that this is not evidence against the existence of God but rather evidence *for* the existence of God and His truth. It is overwhelming testimony, from one corner of the world to the other, to the fact that people are more than just physical beings. We are all on a quest to discover the creator God."

Drew sat back against his chair. This guy had to be reading his mind. It was plain freaky, and it wasn't fair...using his own argument against him.

"Listen." Devin leaned forward in his chair, almost seeming to sense Drew's retreat. "It's the unseen things of this world that are the most important. Would you agree?"

That was just ridiculous! Drew almost voiced a protest, when one of the other guys spoke up.

"How do you figure that? Most of our time and energy is spent on very real, tangible things. How can unseen things be more important than what we experience right now?"

Finally, someone else with some reasoning abilities.

Devin nodded. "Okay. Think about our men and women who serve in the armed forces. They have taken an oath to defend our nation. What are they fighting for? Why have they pledged to give their lives? What have so many before us died for?"

The room fell silent. Drew's mind filled with the picture sitting on his desk right now—his dad in military uniform, arm around Drew's twelve-year-old shoulders. Drew was so proud of his dad, and he had ached to feel his dad's strong arm across his shoulders a thousand times. He had asked his mother that very question: *"Why did my dad have to die?"*

But he knew the answer.

"Freedom."

The word escaped Drew's lips before he realized he had spoken it.

"Drew's right." Devin straightened. "The unseen, profoundly important right we call freedom. You can't touch it, see it, or feel it, and yet it is so important that the noble and the courageous are willing to lay down their lives to protect and preserve it."

Devin let his words stew for a minute; then he opened his Bible and flipped to a place near the back.

"Hebrews 11:1 says that 'faith is the substance of things hoped for, the evidence of things not seen.' You see, all the religions of the world are evidence that the unseen spiritual world does exist and that God is drawing people to Himself. The problem is that we have messed it up with false beliefs and doctrines. And in addition to that, the enemy of God, Satan, has used religion to confuse the world about God and His love for us. But God gave us an answer: there is only one true faith, and God sent His only Son to earth to show us the way. Jesus Christ said, 'I am the way, the truth, and the life. No one comes to the Father except through Me.'"

Drew fought the frustration crawling through him. His logic was breaking down, and he didn't like it.

"Just as so many have died to give us freedom on earth, Jesus Christ died to give us eternal freedom. He died to set us free from sin and death. True freedom requires sacrifice."

Drew stared at his shoes, but it felt like Devin was staring right at him. He glanced up to catch him—but that wasn't the case at all. Still, he didn't like the way he was feeling. When he had agreed to stay, he never thought he'd have to think these things and go through the sorrow over his dad again. He fidgeted. *Time for this to be over.*

He stayed silent through the rest of the study and spent most of the time trying to refute Devin's earlier statements. He saw Sydney look over at him every few minutes, probably to see how he was doing. He tried not to look too ill at ease, but not too interested either. He would catch a waft of her perfume from time to time, which reminded him why he was there.

This was about a girl. Not God.

By the time Devin finished thirty minutes later, Drew had reestablished his mind-set and logic. Devin asked if anyone had any questions. Drew didn't. What he had were rebuttals, so best to remain silent. He had to admit, though, that Devin had used some fair arguments that Drew had never thought about before. Even so, Devin was trying to move a mountain with a spoon. There was too much scientific evidence, reason, and logic to overwhelm the crafty arguments of a bright college kid. That mind-reading trick at the beginning was pretty weird, but it was nothing more than a bizarre coincidence.

Devin ended with a reminder about their Tuesday night worship and invited all to come. Then someone turned on music as they ate again and just hung out and talked. Devin made a point of talking to Drew for a bit. He'd expected to be harangued, but Devin asked questions about his family and home, talked a little about campus, thanked him for coming, and moved on.

Sydney made her way over to Drew, a Coke in one hand and a napkin with three Pizza Rolls in the other.

"How are you doing?" She studied his eyes.

"I'm all right. It wasn't too bad." He snatched one of her Pizza Rolls and popped it in his mouth.

"Aah!" He opened his mouth to cool the burning sauce that squirted out of the Pizza Roll with his first bite.

"Ooh...yeah." Sydney offered her Coke. "Those were just nuked."

"Ah cahn tahl," Drew mumbled. He accepted the Coke and took a quick drink of its cold contents. Relief came immediately.

"Ah...that's better." But he could tell his mouth was going to blister.

"Well," Sydney said, "a deal's a deal. So which coffee shop am I treating you to?" She flashed him a smile.

"Ben and I often go to the Mystic Blend, just off campus on Twelfth. It's pretty good. Would that work for you?"

"Sure. I have class until two, but then I'm free." She put her hands in her back pockets and gave a quick shrug.

She's nervous. Odd. "I have class until three. Shall we say three thirty?"

"Sounds good. I'll be there."

Drew noticed that the other students in the study were starting to leave. "I'm looking forward to it. Guess I'd better finish my calc homework."

"Yeah, I've got a paper due tomorrow, and I've put it off too long already," she said.

Drew turned to leave.

"Hey," Sydney called.

He turned back to her.

"I know it wasn't all that comfortable for you, but thanks for coming."

He gave her a crooked smile. "Thanks for the invite."

On the way back to his dorm, Drew stopped in and talked to Ben for a few minutes. He told him what had happened and about his coffee date with Sydney the next day.

"Dude, I'm telling you, she may be a nice girl and all, but she is going to mess with your mind." Ben leaned back on his chair until it rested up against his desk behind him. "That Bible study, or whatever it was you just sat in on, should have told you that already."

"Yeah, I know." Drew rubbed the back of his neck. "But I'll find out tomorrow just how...messed up she really is." Drew shook his head. "She's got some kind of magical powers or something."

Ben started laughing.

"What?" He looked for something to throw at Ben.

Ben waved his hand in front of him like a Jedi knight. "These aren't the droids you're looking for."

Drew grabbed a dirty shirt from Ben's bed and whipped it at him.

THE NEXT DAY, Drew made it to the coffee shop at 3:22, picked a table, and waited for Sydney. A few minutes later, she walked in the door, spotted him, and came directly over to take a seat. As usual she was dressed to a T, with perfect hair, makeup, and stylish clothes.

He eyed her. "How'd the paper turn out?"

"Okay, I think. I've written better, but it should be all right. How about your calculus homework?"

"Went good. It's still review material so far anyway. The Calc I took last year did a good job preparing me." Drew looked toward the counter. "Shall we?"

They ordered, and Drew refused to let Sydney pay, even after multiple petitions. They sat down, and Drew could tell Sydney was a bit nervous again. She looked at him, gave a quick smile, and then stared at her coffee.

"Drew, there are a few things I need to tell you—"

"Whoa!" Drew held up his hand. "Just one minute. Last night was your turn and today is mine."

Sydney looked at him and exchanged her serious look for a lighthearted one. "Yes…I suppose you are right. It's only fair. You're on."

Drew took a deep breath.

"Seriously, I've been trying to find out things about you for two years. You eluded me in high school until I started wondering if you belonged to some secret cult or something."

Sydney nodded and opened up her hands. "I'm here. What do you want to know?"

Drew didn't know where to start. There were a thousand things he wanted to ask her.

"Okay…do you belong to a secret cult?"

Sydney laughed out loud. "I suppose that depends on your perspective, but no…no, I don't."

"Then how come I never saw you in school except during Speech, 'cause I looked."

Sydney sighed. "I was homeschooled."

"Get out! You seem so…normal."

Sydney smirked. "Gee, thanks."

Drew tried to recover. "That's not what I mean."

"I know what you think you mean. Maybe your version of normal isn't what it ought to be. Anyway, Speech was something my parents felt was impossible to replicate at home so I took one class at the high school."

Drew tried to fit Sydney into his stereotypical homeschool mold, and she just didn't fit. Never did he ever think he would be attracted to a homeschooled girl, but that also explained some of the religious stuff. He would get to that later.

"What are you majoring in?"

"Microbiology."

"I knew you were smart. Tell me about your family."

Drew peppered her with dozens of questions. He loved hearing her voice and watching her expressions. When an hour had passed, he knew their time was running out.

"I have two more questions. Do you have a boyfriend, and will you go out with me?"

Sydney's gaze dropped to her coffee. "That's what I need to tell you." Her voice lost its cheery edge.

"Okay." This didn't sound good.

"But first may I ask you a question?"

"You can ask as many as you like," Drew said. He wasn't ready for their coffee date to be over.

"I'm sure you've figured out that my faith is important to me. I'd like to know what you believe about God, and specifically about Jesus Christ."

Drew sat back and took a sip of his coffee.

"Well, I have to admit that I'm not on board with all that stuff that Devin talked about last night at your Bible study."

He saw her eyes sadden.

"Do you really believe all that stuff, Sydney... Really?"

"Yes, Drew, I do... I really do."

Drew shook his head. "It's so...fabricated...so far-fetched. I mean, how can you believe that stuff when all of science and the scientists of the modern day refute it? Besides that, if there was a God, how come this world is in such a mess with millions of people starving and dying? That's not a god I want to have anything to do with."

Sydney flinched as if he had insulted her, so he stopped. He had a long list of reasons why he didn't believe in God, but he had never seen her so sad.

"I suppose you're going to try and convince me otherwise," Drew said in a hushed voice.

Sydney slowly shook her head. "No, that's not my job; that's the Lord's job. My job is to pray for you." She fidgeted with her coffee cup and then carved something into the Styrofoam with her thumbnail. "Drew, I'm sorry, but this is the last time I can meet with you like this."

She raised her eyes until she was staring right into his. As lovely as they were, they were serious, and his heart sank.

"Hey, people disagree about religion all the time. It doesn't mean they can't be friends or enjoy each other's company."

"It's more than that, Drew."

"I don't understand then... You just don't like me?" He tried not to sound too hurt. All this time he had convinced himself that she was just playing hard to get.

"No, that's not it at all." Sydney turned her head to look out the window for a moment, then recaptured his eyes. "It's actually just the opposite."

Drew reached across the table and touched her hand.

She smiled nervously and eased her hand away. "You may not understand this, but I am bound by my faith in Christ to not become involved with someone who doesn't share my beliefs."

Drew pulled his hand back across the table. He knew her religion was important to her, but he hadn't realized it might dictate her actions. It was rather ironic that all along he had been thinking that he might not want to date her because of her religion. He'd never considered the possibility that her religion might cause her to not date him.

"I really like you, Sydney. I was hoping we could spend some time together…at least as friends."

She blinked and turned away for a moment. "I…like you too, Drew, and that's the problem. It wouldn't stay as just friends between us, and I'd be more conflicted about this"—she pointed to the two of them—"than I already am. I have to protect my heart, and things like this make that very hard to do. You're a great guy and there are so many things about you that I really like, but…"

She didn't need to finish.

"I can't fake that I believe what you want me to believe."

"And I wouldn't want you to. You must be true to yourself, just as I must be to me."

Drew's gaze fell to the table. "From the first day you smiled at me, I've wanted to know you better, and now I know why."

Hope filled her features. "Why?"

"Because it's in our human nature to want most what we can't have. I think deep down I knew this would never work, so it was all the more tempting to try for it."

Sydney's countenance fell. "What you're really seeking isn't me, Drew. It's what's in me." Her eyes seemed to look straight into his soul.

"You say the strangest things…" Drew lifted his cup to his lips and swallowed the last bit of coffee, then sighed. Sydney looked beautifully sad. She slid out of her chair and stood up. Drew stood with her.

"I guess I'll see you around then."

She bit her lip. "Yeah…I guess so." She reached into her purse and pulled out a pen, then grabbed his hand. Her soft, warm fingers eased his palm open. He watched her sandy hair droop down as she wrote something and then closed his fingers and held them tight. She was sure making their good-bye difficult.

"What you need, Drew, is right here." She wrapped both of her hands around his closed fist, smiled…and walked away.

Drew opened his hand. "John 3:16" was written across his palm. He knew it was a reference to the Bible, but he didn't know what it said. Something dark skittered up his spine. The last time a girl wrote something on his hand…

Disaster followed.

He looked up and watched as Sydney walked by the front window of the coffee shop.

That was it.

He would never chase her again.

And it left a hole in his soul.

8

EVIDENCE OF A STRANGER

Over the next few weeks, Drew focused on school and on setting up a plan for his future. He decided to shoot for a double major in math and financial management, with an emphasis in sales and trading. When he wasn't studying or hanging out with Ben, he was lifting weights, swimming, and running at the Drayle wellness center, which was second to none. One week his eye caught a flier about triathlon training and competitions, and he decided to sign up.

Drew got to know his suitemates in his dorm well enough that they invited him on some of their outings. One day a bunch of guys and girls came over for video games and pizza. Drew struck up a conversation with a pretty, dark-haired girl named Danielle. He asked her out, but after the first date, he knew there was nothing special between them...not like there was between him and Sydney. But surely there was someone else out there who would make him feel the way Sydney did. He hated to think the only girl he was drawn to was someone he could never be with...

Drew and Ben made it a point to get together at least twice each week, sometimes more. It was an odd friendship, but they both appreciated how much they added to each other's lives. Drew loved having a personal tutor whenever he encountered difficulties in his math and especially his physics classes, and Ben loved having a friend who understood him in a way that the rest of the world did not. Were it not for their connection during high school, they probably would have never crossed paths and become close friends. Ben inspired Drew to work hard in school, and Drew kept Ben grounded in the real world.

The university environment for Ben was like giving caffeine to an already hyper chipmunk. He excelled in the physics program, and everyone in the department respected him, including the grad students. Drew was amazed at the level of genius in his friend. Even though it was only Ben's second year, Dr. Daivya Waseem chose Ben to work as a research assistant on Waseem's groundbreaking work on laser light acceleration technology. Much of the work was confidential, but even what Ben could share went right over Drew's head.

Every Friday at three o'clock, Drew and Ben met at the Mystic Blend for their weekly coffee to catch up. Today, Ben had called to meet earlier, at two o' clock, and now he was late.

Ben was never late.

Drew checked his watch. Maybe he should shoot Ben a text to see if he had misunderstood. He reached for his phone, but then through the windows that lined Twelfth Street, he saw Ben approaching the coffee shop. Strange…

Ben didn't saunter through the doors in his usual carefree style. Instead, he looked up and down the street, then slipped inside. He scanned the interior of the shop, his gaze briefly stopping at each table and its occupants. He even looked straight at Drew, then continued his scan until he'd taken in every corner of the room. Drew smirked, cocked his head, and motioned for Ben to join him.

Ben maneuvered through the tables, whose occupants seemed completely unaware of his passing, their sporadic conversations creating a comfortable floor of droning noise. Ben sat down in the chair across from Drew, and Drew just stared at him in silence. He'd learned long ago that pressing Ben to speak before he was ready was pointless, but this time it was hard to keep his tongue. Something was up. Ben's eyes continued to dart throughout the shop.

"Aren't you going to get something to drink?"

"Let's move to that booth in the corner." Ben spoke without looking at Drew.

"Really? I thought you didn't like cramped spaces."

Ben looked at Drew but didn't smile. *What* was going on?

"Okay, okay." Drew grabbed his frappé and headed to one of the only two booths in the shop.

They slid onto the seats, and Drew noticed that Ben moved all the way to the wall. Drew couldn't take it anymore. "What is up with you?"

Ben looked straight into Drew's eyes and hesitated. "Dr. Waseem is missing."

Drew leaned forward. "What do you mean, *missing*?"

"He hasn't come to the lab for two days."

"Maybe he's sick or had a family emergency."

Ben just shook his head. "No. I called his house today, and his wife has filed a missing persons report. Something is wrong...very wrong."

Drew wasn't sure how to respond. Ben admired Dr. Waseem more than anyone else he had known. "There still could be a reasonable explanation, Ben."

Ben frowned, then resumed his nervous gaze about the coffee shop. "I don't think so. Something strange happened two days ago at the lab. Do you remember how I told you that Dr. Waseem's experiment worked?"

Drew nodded.

"Before he went public, he wanted to do some additional testing to see if there were any effects in the visible spectrum, and I think it worked."

"What do you mean, *you think*? Weren't you there?"

"Yes, but just when we were getting ready to record the results, Dr. Waseem started acting weird."

"Like you? Right now?"

"Ah...yes, I guess, now that you mention it."

"What did he do?"

"He immediately shut down the LASOK and told me I could leave. When I asked to stay and help finish up, he..."

"He what?"

"He grabbed my arm and said, 'Leave!'"

Drew sat back. That *was* strange. Ben had always said that Dr. Waseem was friendly and charming, even when they were conducting serious research. It was obvious that he especially enjoyed Ben's company.

"What are you trying to say? That Dr. Waseem was successful and didn't want you or anybody else to know about it?"

Ben looked as though he could hardly contain his agitation. He actually leaned out of the booth to get a complete view of the entire shop, then ducked back in. Drew realized that Ben was more than just anxious. He was fearful. Drew couldn't help taking a quick glance around the room as well to see if he could spot whatever it was Ben was looking for.

"No. I think the doctor succeeded"—Ben lowered his voice to a whisper—"and it scared him."

Drew squinted. "Scared him? Why?"

Ben took a deep breath like he always did when he was going into explanation mode. "Dr. Waseem wasn't just trying to accelerate light. He was trying to accelerate light so that he could view into a portal and see…"

Drew frowned. "What? Another dimension?"

Ben nodded, and Drew could hardly suppress a hearty laugh. The only thing that kept him in check was the news of Dr. Waseem's disappearance. Ben had always been fascinated with the theory of alternate dimensions, which was why he was so taken with Dr. Waseem's work. It gave his theories and beliefs some semblance of legitimacy.

"Come on, Ben. Stay rational. If Waseem is truly missing, I could believe that it has something to do with corporate intellectual property thieves, not… whatever it is you are implying." Drew took a drink of his nearly forgotten coffee and began plotting how to get Ben's mind off his conspiracy theory and back into reality.

"There's more." Ben was unfazed by Drew's skepticism. He reached into his coat and slowly pulled out a manila envelope. He laid it on the table, then looked at the nearest table and back.

"Yesterday morning, when I opened my desk drawer, this was waiting for me. I was late for class so I didn't even open it. I put it in my computer case, but I forgot about it until this morning. When I figured out what it was, I called to meet you early."

He slid the envelope across the table toward Drew. Drew set his coffee down, caught up in the mystery of this new development. If Dr. Waseem had been successful in accelerating light, the ramifications throughout the scientific world would be nothing short of colossal. Drew reached for the envelope, hesitating before picking it up. He looked up at Ben, but his friend just stared at the paper enclosure that held the mystery within.

Drew unlatched the clasp, opened the flap, and eased two eight-by-ten-inch photos out of the envelope. He glanced at the photos. They looked identical. They were shots of the corner of Hawk Drive and Centennial, just across the street from the physics lab. The student union was off to the left, and one of the engineering buildings framed the right side of the photo. It had been taken during the afternoon, when people were scurrying between classes.

"This is it?" Drew looked up at Ben. "No note or drawing or secret research documents?"

Ben shook his head. "No, nothing. But look again at the photos. Look at the people near the student union doors."

Drew studied that area of one of the photos. All seemed in order. Two male students were just entering the door. Just to the left, three girls were talking. One had her hand in the air making some gesture. On a bench nearby, beneath a sprawling shade tree, a student had earbuds in. His feet were stretched out before him and his eyes were closed, apparently enjoying his music. A guy and a girl were just stepping up onto the sidewalk that led to the union. There were others farther away walking in various directions. When Ben was satisfied that Drew had studied the photo enough, he set the other photo beside it.

"Now look at this one. The time frame is only three seconds later." Ben pointed to the time signature in the upper-left corner of both photos. "However, this photo was taken through the LASOK lens."

Drew studied this one just as carefully. There were subtle differences because of the elapsed three seconds. The two students were now inside the union, as he could still see them through the glass doors. It looked like another student was just opening the door next to it to exit the union. The girls were still talking, but one girl's arm was now in a different position. The guy and girl students were now passing just in front of the student sitting on the bench, who had not changed at all.

"Okay, so it's three seconds different—it's nearly the same photo." Drew looked up at Ben. "Am I looking for Waldo or what here?"

"Look behind the guy on the bench, near the brick wall in the corner." Ben's voice almost shook.

Drew looked again—and frowned. He'd missed something. At first he thought perhaps it was a shadow from the tree behind the bench, but the closer he looked, the more he realized it wasn't just a shadow. There was a darkened area…in the shape of a man. It looked like ghosting that you might see on an old television set. But what was causing it?

He scanned the photo—and straightened in his seat.

Nothing. Absolutely nothing in the picture caused the shadowy form.

The hair on the back of Drew's neck stood up, and his arms filled with goose bumps. He transferred his gaze to the other photo and searched for the darkened shape, but it wasn't there. He expanded his search, calculating the approximate distance that one could walk in three seconds based on what he saw with the approaching couple, but there simply was no sign of the shape. He then went back to the photo with the strange figure and stared hard at it once more. The shape was out of place in more ways than one.

Drew went back and forth between the photos, trying to rationalize away what he knew Ben was implying. Finally he looked up at his friend.

"So we have a shadow where it shouldn't be. This doesn't prove much."

"Yeah, right." Ben smirked. "Dr. Waseem left these in my desk for a reason. I think he knew he was in danger, and he wanted someone to know it."

"Danger from what?" Drew was drawn once more to the image of the stranger.

Ben looked at Drew. "From him…the alien!"

"Alien? You can't be serious!" Drew's voice rose, but he squelched it for fear of sounding ludicrous in public. He shook his head. "Ben, you've wanted to believe in alien life since I first met you. Movies about aliens are one thing. Actually believing in them is over the edge. Don't lose your head and your reputation on some random photo that was probably Photoshopped. There isn't even enough clarity to determine what it *might* be."

"It's not Photoshopped."

"How do you know?"

"Because when you enlarge the photo enough to see the individual pixels, there is absolutely no discontinuity or disparity between the pixels near the figure and the surrounding pixels. This is an authentic photo, and that figure is an alien, and the only way we can see him is through the LASOK. It's as if he's cloaked by the boundaries of light. Once you break that boundary, no more cloak."

"You enlarged the image?" Drew ignored the alien theory. The prospect of getting a closer look at the figure intrigued him. "Do you have it with you?"

"Enlarged and enhanced." Ben reached into his coat pocket and unfolded another photo for Drew. This one showed just the figure enlarged to fill the entire eight-by-ten photo. The picture had been brightened and the contrast increased to clear up the image. Drew involuntarily shuddered as he studied the strange figure. It seemed to look straight at him. There was no pretending that this wasn't the shape of a man. Drew could even make out some features that looked like eyes, a mouth, and clothing.

He frowned. "Why isn't it clearer?"

"Not sure. Perhaps this was as clear as the doctor could get it. I'm guessing it has to do with the amount of light acceleration he could generate with the LASOK. Perhaps it needs some acceleration focusing, so to speak."

"What is that behind his head?" Drew pointed to a dark protrusion just above the figure's left shoulder.

"I don't know. A weapon of some sort is my guess."

Drew looked up to see if Ben was kidding—he wasn't. Drew studied the photo for a long time, then gave all three back to Ben. The two friends sat in silence.

"You have to admit that there is something strange about all of this." Ben watched Drew, as though looking for some confirmation.

Drew held up his hand. "I am not saying there are aliens, or intellectual property thieves, or any other conspiracy thing going on here. But just for argument's sake, let's assume there is"—Drew didn't like *thinking* it, let alone saying it—"a being or something. You're telling me they are invisible and could be standing right next to us…right now?"

Ben pursed his lips. "Yeah."

Drew considered the possibility of invisible secret agents…or aliens…and cringed. The power they would have over humanity would be unfathomable. Cloaked enemies in our midst. Drew shook his head as if he were recovering his senses.

"I just can't buy it, Ben. I need way more evidence than some mysterious photo to even consider anything that strange. I think the other TAs are playing a joke on you. They know your take on alien life."

As Drew said it, it made perfect sense. *Of course, this is all a big hoax.*

Ben held up a finger. "One, Dr. Waseem makes a scientific discovery that will shake the scientific world. Two, he mysteriously disappears. Three, he takes pictures of some matrix alien agent and leaves them for me to find. And you don't think anything is going on?"

"Look, you have to admit that your theory is, well, a bit bizarre. You would have to prove it to me somehow."

"What if I could?"

Drew raised his eyebrows. "How?"

"I have complete access to Dr. Waseem's lab and equipment."

"Okay…and that does what for us?"

"We could repeat the experiment."

"Ben, don't you think the university would be a little upset with two undergrad students messing with a missing doctor's high-dollar lab equipment?"

"It's Friday. By five o'clock, everybody will be gone for the weekend, and I help with Dr. Waseem's research all the time. We could set up the LASOK and see for ourselves."

Drew considered the plan…and the consequences. It felt like another bad episode waiting to happen in his life. He'd had too many of those and perhaps he was gun-shy, but he'd rather play it safe than be sorry again.

"I don't think so, Ben. Why don't you go to the dean and get approval to run the experiment?"

"You know they wouldn't give it to me."

"Then we shouldn't do it." Drew had never seen Ben so adamant about taking such a risk. His judgment was being affected by the bizarre notion that they'd discovered another dimension or aliens.

"This could be our...mankind's...one and only chance." Ben held Drew's gaze. "If something has happened to Dr. Waseem, the university will seal his research and our window of opportunity will vanish. What the dean doesn't understand is that I have been working side by side with the doctor for months, and I know his work inside and out, far beyond the other TAs. No one is more qualified to do this than I am. And if I don't, it is very possible that his work will be lost or destroyed or misunderstood forever."

Drew didn't respond. What could he say? It was all...crazy.

Ben sat back and huffed. "I have the proper clearance to enter that lab and conduct experiments, and I am going with or without you."

Drew shook his head. He could never let Ben do it alone, especially when he'd been there for Drew through the last two challenging years. The loyalty factor forced his hand.

"I'll meet you at the union at five, and we'll go from there."

Drew downed his last gulp of coffee and moved to slide out of the booth while Ben shoved the photos back in the envelope. He reached out and grabbed Drew's arm.

"Be careful."

Drew looked at his friend and tried not to smirk. "Sure."

9

CLOAK OF THE LIGHT

Drew sat down to study for an exam he would take on Monday, but Friday afternoons made for lousy study time. Besides, his thoughts kept going back to the conversation with Ben...and that picture. He couldn't shake the image of that man staring at him. He tried to push the image out of his mind, but it would not go away.

That stare was always on him.

He had the sense that the man had always been staring at him and was even now. Anxiety rose up in him, and he understood Ben's strange behavior in the coffee shop. Even if it was all a hoax or some visual anomaly, it was impossible not to think about it, and the more he thought about it, the more real it seemed.

Finally, he gave up studying and numbed his mind with some television. Then he logged online, checked his simulated investments, and played a game of *Domination*. By the time five o'clock rolled around, Drew felt like his old, grounded self.

He grabbed his backpack—which was nearly empty except for a bottle of water, his notebook, and his physics book—slung it over his right shoulder, and made his way toward the student union. He sat down on a bench and enjoyed listening to the sounds of a busy academic campus transforming into that of a weekend-hungry student body. Faint music played from one of the dorms not far away. A couple on their bicycles whizzed by, and a mixed posse of four students were talking about a party they were excited to get to as they crossed the street and journeyed on to the edge of campus.

Ben approached from the direction of his own dorm. "You ready?"

Drew stood and realized that fifty feet away was the spot where the mysterious man had been standing in the picture. He looked that direction, then across the street toward the physics building. Drew shook his head. No way Ben's theory was right.

"Sure, Ben. Let's put your mind at ease. I'd like to get a good look at Dr. Waseem's LASOK anyway."

They walked across the street and into the physics building. The student labs were on the main floor, and Dr. Waseem's research lab was on the second floor. They made their way upstairs, passing a lone student who didn't even look at them. Midway down the empty hallway, Ben used his key to open the door to a small, windowless office where four TAs shared a couple of desks. It was dark and empty now.

Drew reached for the lights.

"Don't." Ben's voice was hushed.

Drew cast a sharp glance at Ben. "Why not? I thought you said this was legit."

"It is. I've been given permission to access this office and the lab. I just think it would be wise not to draw too much attention."

They felt their way across the office. There was just enough light coming from the glowing blue computer power buttons on two systems to keep from bumping into desks and chairs.

"Does the university know how close Dr. Waseem was to successfully accelerating light?"

Ben shook his head. "I don't think so. The rest of the physics staff considered him a bit of a quack. No one ever believed it was possible. They only put up with him because of the research grant he was awarded. The Feds gave him six million to do his research."

Drew let out a low whistle. "Well, somebody in the government must have thought it possible if they gave him that kind of money."

On the other end of the small office was another door leading to the lab. Drew knew that because he had visited Ben numerous times in this cubicle of an office. Ben swiped a security access card, and a small green light illumined on the front of the reader. He pushed on the door, and they stepped inside.

The blinds were drawn on all the windows. Since it was still daylight, the room was bright enough to function in without turning on the lights. Drew felt a little apprehensive and couldn't help thinking that being discovered might not bode well for them. Was Ben trying to hide from university staff...or his imaginary aliens?

Ben made his way to the desk on the far wall and busied himself checking notes. Drew eased his backpack off his shoulder and set it on a stool near the door. He walked to the center of the lab, where a long, broad bench held the most fascinating array of electrical and optical equipment he had ever seen.

"So this is what six million can buy." His eyes were wide, soaking in the technological marvel before him. Whether it worked or not, it was just plain cool, even if he wasn't a complete physics nut. He recognized a powerful laser assembly at one end of the bench, but that was about it. The rest of the equipment was something out of a high-tech futuristic thriller movie. Mirrors, glass plates, steel rods, long cylindrical transparent tubes, electronic test equipment, power supplies, and a dozen other unknown devices were all placed at strategic locations to perform some function that Drew could only guess at.

Near the far end of the bench was what looked like an electron microscope, but there had been some obvious major modifications to it. Some of the access panels had been removed, and a network of wires and fiber optic cables were fed to the inner portions of the machine. The viewer itself looked like it had been modified too.

Ben joined him. "What do you think?"

"Do you actually understand this?" Drew felt wholly unqualified to even be in the room.

"Yes...at least in theory. I've been helping the professor conduct tests for months. The last few weeks he has had me prep all the equipment for him before he comes to the lab. It takes about thirty minutes to get it all ready. The plasma generator is what takes the longest," Ben said, pointing to one of the larger pieces of equipment near the electron microscope—or whatever it was.

Drew just shook his head. He'd known Ben was brilliant; he just never realized how brilliant. That the doctor entrusted Ben with such responsibility was a testimony to Ben's drive and intelligence. Apparently he was more than just a TA. Perhaps even more than a research assistant.

"How does it work?" Drew asked. "And remember I'm no genius like you."

Ben began flipping switches and turning dials as he watched gauges and looked at digital readouts. He talked as he went.

"The theory is quite simple, but the implementation is extremely complex, kind of like splitting the atom. LASOK stands for light accelerator by stimulated optical kinetics. A few years ago, groundbreaking research at Harvard University proved that light can actually be slowed down by passing it through a Bose-Einstein condensate. Dr. Waseem theorized that if light can be slowed down as it travels through a medium, then it should be able to be sped up as well. Einstein limits as defined by his theory of relativity are based on the speed of light. If one can increase the speed of light, the theory remains intact, but there is a new upper limit and a new point of reference. Are you following?"

Drew hesitated. "Marginally." It was enough to keep Ben going.

"In simple terms, Dr. Waseem developed a plasma-and-laser-excited optical lens that energizes photons as they pass through the lens. The increased energy state of the photons causes acceleration pretty much just opposite of the effect that a Bose-Einstein condensate would have on light, namely, slowing it down."

"And that's in simple terms?" Drew scratched his head.

Ben huffed. "Yes, it is, without getting into quantum physics."

Drew's own interest in physics was a mere hobby compared to what was happening here. He was way out of his league. Good thing he decided to study mathematics and finance instead.

Ben continued to turn on equipment and make adjustments as the machine came alive.

"How much can light be accelerated, and how do you know if it actually works?"

Ben didn't even look up as he answered. "The speed of light in a vacuum is 299,792.458 kilometers per second. We have successfully accelerated light to 299,792.693 kilometers per second."

"Let me get this right. Dr. Waseem spent six million dollars to accelerate light by .2 kilometers per second?"

Ben kept working, but a slight smile lifted his mouth. "I don't think you grasp the significance of what I just said. Until Dr. Waseem created the LASOK, nothing in the universe traveled faster than 299,792.458 kilometers per second. That was the limit for all of reality. He just broke through into another whole realm of possibilities."

"How does this relate to the photo you showed me?"

"For nearly all our tests, we only measured the increase of light speed quantitatively. It was during our last test that the doctor wanted to see if there were any visual effects resulting from the acceleration. Through a system of mirrors and lenses"—Ben pointed to five mirrors positioned around the periphery of the room that focused into the large scope machine to the right—"one can look through the LASOK lens in the optical kinetic stimulator and see a view of the outside. Take a look."

Ben pointed to the viewer. Drew went to the machine and looked through the eyepieces. He could see the same view that was captured in the pictures Ben had shown him earlier. Drew saw a person walk out of the union and knew this was a real-time viewing of just outside the physics building.

"Is this with light accelerated?"

Ben shook his head. "No. The plasma generator is not quite ready, and the laser still needs to be focused. In five minutes we will be able to see exactly what the doctor saw yesterday. By varying the phase shift of the plasma and the amplification of the laser, Dr. Waseem discovered he could vary the speed of light within a narrow limited range."

"Sort of like tuning in on a particular range of the spectrum?"

"Not really. That would mean only changing the frequency of the light, which gives you different colors. By changing the speed, you would have an infinite number of entire spectrums you could tune in on. *Comprendes?*"

Drew looked up from the viewer. He was trying hard to follow Ben, but his brain operated in a whole different way. "I think so… Can the image be adjusted to some place other than the union across the street?"

"Yes, but the doctor chose the union because it had the most activity."

Ben was focused on the plasma generator, so Drew let him concentrate without interruption. After a few minutes, Ben grabbed a notebook and compared some of the notes in it with readings on a couple of test instruments. He tweaked a few more settings, then stood and took a deep breath. The entire machine pulsed with life, as if anxious to shout to the world of its existence.

"We're set." Ben seemed satisfied. "Once I engage the plasma generator and the laser, any light passing through the optical kinetic accelerator will be moving faster than it's supposed to."

"Can I look?"

Ben grinned at Drew's excitement. "That's why we're here, isn't it?" He pushed the button that activated the laser, and a bright green light beam bounced through a series of mirrors and prisms that ended at the optical kinetic accelerator, where the viewer was. He then placed his finger on a toggle switch and snapped it up. The plasma generator purred to life, creating an orange glowing gaseous plasma that pulsed through a wavy glass tube. It also terminated at the optical kinetic accelerator.

Ben looked at Drew and nodded.

Drew shivered as he looked through the viewer. Would he see some hideous alien beast? But the view looked exactly as it had before Ben activated the LASOK. Drew waited a few seconds, but nothing changed.

He looked up from the viewer. "Looks the same to me."

Ben walked over and bent over to look through the viewer. He looked for a couple of minutes. "Maybe he or they aren't there for us to see."

"And maybe there is nothing for us to see."

Ben went back to the plasma generator. He made a few adjustments as Drew spoke.

"Look, Ben. Accelerating light is already a Nobel Prize–winning event. You don't have to do that *and* discover aliens all in the same day."

"Maybe the light needs to be tuned to a different speed… Or maybe we just need people to see. Perhaps now isn't the best time to do this."

Drew sighed. There had to be some way to satisfy Ben's requirements and end his quest, or at least postpone it. "What if instead of looking outside, we direct the mirrors to look back into the lab…at us?"

Ben looked up at the mirror near the port in the wall that allowed them to see down at the union. "That's not a bad idea."

He grabbed a chair and moved toward the mirror. He jumped up and started turning the mirror back toward the room.

"Look in the viewer until you get a good view of the lab," he called out to Drew.

Drew positioned his eyes in the viewer and watched the lab come into view.

"A little to the left…oops…other way. A little more. Hold it! Right there. I can see most of this half of the lab. It still looks normal. Everything looks a little…blurry."

"Try the eyepiece focus."

Drew found a knob near the viewer and turned it until the room became crystal clear…almost *too* clear. Something was different.

"Got it. It looks a little weird, but no aliens," he said with a laugh.

Ben went back to the laser and plasma generator. "I'm going to accelerate the light a little at a time, and you tell me if anything changes."

Drew watched as Ben came into view standing by the instruments. As Ben made adjustments, everything in the viewer shifted slightly. Drew couldn't describe it, but it made him feel queasy.

"Anything?"

"No, keep going."

"I'm nearly maxed," Ben said.

"I don't see—wait!" Just then, part of the image darkened near the door to the office. It looked strangely familiar.

"That's max, Drew."

"Go a little more." Drew tried to focus on the darker area in the viewer. It moved slightly, but he couldn't tell if that was just another shift similar to what he had been seeing all along.

"Overdriving the plasma generator is dangerous, Drew. What do you see?"

He could almost see it. "You have to go just a little more."

"Okay, but only for a few seconds."

Drew concentrated as Ben took the power level of the plasma generator into the red ever so carefully. The door area darkened more, then sharpened—and disappeared. Drew's heart nearly stopped.

"Back just a bit! Slowly." His heart raced. Either his eyes had tricked him or the darkened area was much more than just a visual shift. Shivers skittered from his neck clear to his legs and back to the top of his head.

The image in the view shifted again—

And then he saw it.

"Stop!"

Drew lost his breath, and his eyes watered. As clear as he saw Ben standing at the controls of the plasma generator, he saw a man standing near the lab doorway. He was in the room just a few feet behind Drew. He couldn't speak or move… Fear held him fast. His entire body ached with goose bumps.

The man wasn't looking at the viewer. He was glaring at Drew's back and occasionally glancing toward Ben. He was large and looked like a character straight out of an apocalyptic movie, complete with a long, dark coat, tight leather gloves, and sharp facial features. His face was fierce and his eyes were dark gray, almost black. If this was an alien…

He wasn't friendly.

Drew couldn't take it anymore. He slowly turned away from the viewer to face the door.

"What is it, Drew? What do you see?" Ben sounded as fearful as Drew felt.

Drew swallowed hard as he gazed toward the door and the ominous invisible man, knowing against all reason that he was just a few feet away. Just then, the LASOK made a strange noise. Ben turned back to the controls.

"It's overloading! I have to shut it down!"

"Wait!" Drew spun back to the viewer. The image flickered, but the man was still there. Drew watched, horrified, as the man reached behind his head and drew a sword as black as coal. Before Drew could call out, the man moved with blinding speed toward Ben—

And thrust the dark blade right through him.

"Ben!"

But Drew screamed too late. The controls Ben had been working exploded, shooting a shower of sparks in every direction. The last image Drew saw was the bright, hot-white plasma burning into his eyes. The sound of another explosion and glass shattering filled his ears as he was thrown backward.

Then the world went black.

10

DARKNESS

Drew could hear sounds pounding into his ears, but they made no sense to him. It sounded as if he were trying to listen under two feet of water. Over the next few seconds, the sounds cleared and made sense, but why were people talking so loudly right next to his head? They weren't shouting, but they might as well have been, for it hurt his ears to hear them. He tried to open his eyes, but nothing happened. As full consciousness came, so did his senses—and pain.

His head throbbed, then pounded. His eyes felt like they were on fire. He reached to touch them, but he couldn't move his hands.

"Lie still," an even louder female voice said next to him. "You've been in an accident."

"My eyes hurt." His voice boomed like it had been amped.

"Doctor, he's awake."

The woman's voice hurt his ears. "Please don't talk so loud! What's happening?"

Drew heard footsteps pounding on the floor.

"You're going to be all right, son." A man's voice. The doctor? He sounded like he was talking in a voice that could have been heard two hundred feet away.

Drew cringed. "Quit shouting," he said as loud as he dared.

Drew was aware of everything touching his body, from the IV in his hand to the bed sheet touching his legs down to his toes. And the smells of the hospital were overwhelming. Antiseptic, plastic, urine, body odor—didn't they have air filters?

"My eyes hurt. What happened…where am I?"

"You were in an accident at the university, and you are in the hospital. You hit your head and received a concussion that left you unconscious for over ten hours."

Drew's memory came rushing back—the lab, Ben, the LASOK, and…the man! His heart raced, and he could hear every beat. It made the throbbing in his head even worse. How was he even alive? What did it all mean?

"Ben…where's Ben?" There was a pause, and Drew's stomach clenched. "Where's Ben?"

The man's voice came again. It had to be the doctor. "He's being treated for burns on his neck and chest."

Burns? Drew remembered seeing the dark man run him through with a sword. "Is he…going to live?"

"Of course, the burns are minor."

"I want to see him. Can I go to him?"

"Actually you are in much worse condition, Drew. You need to just sit tight and lie still for a while. As soon as we're done with Ben, he can come see you."

"Why can't I open my eyes?" Drew tried to reach for his eyes again. He felt the touch of the nurse's hand on his arm. Her hand was warm and firm. Every nerve that was in contact with her hand was alive.

"They've been badly burned. Just leave the bandages alone for now. Okay?"

That explained the pain, but… "When will I get to take the bandages off so I can see?"

The nurse's hand left his arm. The silence gave him his answer.

"Your mother is in the waiting room," the doctor said. "I'll let her know she can see you."

He heard the doctor's footsteps fade, then a swoosh of the door. He was surprised that he could continue to hear his footsteps and realized that he could hear many things, even outside the door if he concentrated.

"Nurse?"

"Here," came the reply.

"My eyes hurt. Is there something—"

"The doctor is giving you something for the pain through the IV."

"Is the damage to my eyes permanent? Will I see again?"

"I think the doctor needs to answer that."

Drew listened and could hear more footsteps approaching, hurried footsteps this time, and he knew Jake and his mother were coming.

The door opened, and Drew could feel them enter. It was strange. Something was different. The pain kept him from concentrating, but the longer he was awake, the more aware he became of everything happening around him. Everything seemed…well…*more.*

"Drew," his mother said as she approached the bed. "I'm here, and so is Jake."

Her voice was much too loud, and it was thick with worry.

"Hi, guys." Maybe if he kept things light, it would ease their concern. "I can't see, but I can hear just fine. Please don't talk so loud."

He felt his mother's hand grab his. She squeezed way too hard. Her palm and fingers pressed into his hand in twelve places…strange.

"How are you feeling?" Jake asked.

"My head hurts, my eyes burn, and everything is way too loud. I feel strange." It must be the drugs… "What meds do they have me on? Something's wrong with my…my brain."

"Everything a little fuzzy, huh?" Jake said. "That happens coming out of—"

"No, actually. Everything is too clear. Whatever it is, it isn't a sedative."

Drew tried to lift his hand again and felt the restraints around his wrist. "Can I please have these things taken off?" He opened the palm of his empty hand.

He heard the nurse approach.

"Of course. Just don't touch your eyes, okay?"

He felt the straps release from his wrists.

"What did the doc say about my eyes, Mom?" He lifted his hands to his head and felt the bandages that encircled his head, covering his eyes and temples. "Are my eyes going to be okay?"

Once again, silence. She squeezed his hand even harder.

"It doesn't look good. The ophthalmologist said there is a lot of retina damage."

Drew could hear the quiver in her voice. She was a strong woman, she had to be, raising a son by herself. Drew squeezed her hand back.

"I'll be okay, Mom."

"What happened, Drew?" his mother asked. "The dean of the physics department was here earlier asking me a lot of questions. He seemed very upset. He spent a lot of time with Ben too."

Drew hadn't even considered what had happened to the lab and Dr. Waseem's research. The realization of what they had done and what they had discovered started to come at him like massive waves. He swallowed hard. There was so much to consider, so much to think about. He didn't even know what he dared say. Would anyone believe him? His head started to swim with questions and thoughts that went in a thousand different directions.

"I need to talk to Ben. How bad is he hurt?"

"It's not serious," Jake said. "He saved your life."

"What? What happened?" The lab accident must have been worse than he realized.

"You were thrown, unconscious, and he had to drag you out of the lab away from the fire," Jake replied.

"Fire? There was a fire?"

"The fire suppression system kicked in before it spread to the rest of the building, but the lab was pretty much destroyed. If Ben hadn't pulled you out, it would have been much worse. And he was singed pretty badly in a few places too. Plasma burns are nasty."

Drew didn't know how to respond. The lab destroyed? What would that mean for Dr. Waseem's research? What would that mean for Ben and him? "When can I see Ben?"

"Maybe the nurse can tell you." Jake turned. "Nurse?"

"She's just left," Drew said.

After a brief pause, his mother spoke. "How did you know that?"

"I heard her leave just a minute ago. I must see Ben as soon as possible."

"I'll see what I can do." Jake left the room.

"Drew, the dean said that he wanted to talk to you as soon you were able. I'm supposed to call him."

"You have to wait until I talk to Ben, Mom. Okay?"

"Were you supposed to be in that lab? The dean said the professor wasn't there. Is that true?"

He lowered his chin, something he couldn't help doing anytime his mother caught him doing something he wasn't supposed to. It started when he was four, and now even at twenty he couldn't help it.

"It's true, the professor wasn't there." He hesitated. He didn't dare tell her everything, at least not yet. "We were trying to help the professor. He's missing."

"Missing? What's going on, Drew?" Her voice was filled with anxiety.

"I'm not sure, Mom. Really. I need some time to sort things out."

There was a soft knock on the door.

"Hello?"

Drew recognized Sydney's voice. It was the nicest sound he had heard yet.

"May I come in?" Her gentle tone soothed his aching head.

"Hey, Sydney, come in." Drew smiled, happy for the interruption to change the subject.

"I don't want to interrupt anything," Sydney said from the doorway.

"No, no." Drew's mother let loose of his hand. "Please come in. I'm Drew's mom, Kathryn."

Drew could tell by the tone of his mother's voice that she was pleased to see Sydney. He was quite sure that she was already jumping to conclusions.

"Hi, Mrs. Carter. I'm Sydney Carlyle. I heard Drew was in the physics lab accident and wanted to see if he was okay."

"He's doing all right. The doctor says he will have to stay in the hospital at least a couple of days to make sure there's no infection."

Drew could tell his mom had turned back toward him by the direction of her voice.

"Drew, you didn't tell me that you had such a lovely friend at school."

"We're just...well..."

"We're just friends, Mrs. Carter. Drew was nice enough to go to a Bible study with me a few weeks ago," Sydney finished for Drew, although not in the way he had hoped.

"Oh." His mom looked from him to Sydney. "I can see there's a lot that Drew hasn't told me. I'll leave you two and go check on Jake and Ben."

"You don't have to leave—" Drew started but stopped when he heard her footsteps retreating. He waited until she was clear of the door. There were a few seconds of awkward silence. It had been weeks since he'd last seen Sydney at the coffee shop.

"Thanks for coming to see me." Drew couldn't tell where Sydney was. She was the most soft-footed person to enter his room yet.

"I was concerned when I heard how serious the accident was. There are rumors flying all over Facebook." She came to stand beside Drew's bed, on his left. "Are you really okay, Drew?"

He smiled because of the pleasure he took in hearing her soothing voice. He had always loved listening to her talk, not because of what she said, but rather how she said it. And now it seemed so much more delightful. Why?

"I'm doing all right." He reached up and touched the bandage around his eyes. "Sounds like I won't be using these much anymore though."

Why did he say that? Was he looking for sympathy? He wished he could take it back.

He felt the soft touch of Sydney's hand on his own. In a strange but wonderful way, it warmed his whole body.

"I'm so sorry, Drew."

"It'll all work out. I'll cope." He tried to sound less vulnerable. "Might make school a little challenging though."

"Can I pray for you?"

"Sydney, after what I've seen, I don't think prayer is going to help one bit."

"Why not?"

Such innocence in that question. Drew didn't want to hurt her feelings. After all, she had made the effort to come and see him. "If you want to pray, then be my guest."

He felt her fingers touch his bandaged eyes. Her little finger gently rested on his right cheek, and it once again soothed him.

"Dear heavenly Father. If there is any sin in my heart, please forgive me."

Drew frowned. That was a strange way to start a prayer. How could someone as sweet as Sydney have any sin? She'd better start over and begin with *his* sins.

"I come before You on behalf of Drew. You know his condition. You know his pain. You know his heart. Please, Lord God, heal him completely. Heal his eyes that he might see again. Heal his heart that he might believe in You. Heal his spirit that You might live in him. You are the mighty healer. You are the merciful and the forgiver. You are the beginning and the end. Thank You for hearing my prayer. In Jesus' name, amen."

It was a short, strange prayer, but for all that...

It affected him.

She left her hand on his eyes a bit longer and continued to whisper another prayer. He could feel her breath on his cheek and felt the closeness of her body. From her little finger, warmth flowed across his face and into his eyes. The ache from his eyes dissipated. She continued in quiet prayer until all the pain was gone. When she removed her hand, he just lay still and enjoyed the peace that he felt, ignoring the question nagging at the corner of his mind. He took a deep breath. *The pain reliever must have just kicked in.*

Yes, that was it.

"Your mother seems like a sweet lady."

"Yeah, she's pretty amazing." Drew smiled. "She'd have to be to put up with me for twenty years." He pictured Sydney's face and could imagine her delightful smile framed by a perfect complexion.

"Was that your dad I passed in the hall on the way here?"

"No. He's just a good family friend. My dad passed when I was twelve." There it was again, the sense that he was somehow fishing for sympathy. He hated being weak. "Jake is a great guy...really helped out my mom and me through the years. He took me camping for weeks every summer."

"Sounds like quite a friend. Where did you go camping?"

"Every summer was a different place. Alaska, Glacier National Park, the Badlands, the Mojave Desert, the Everglades, Tenne—"

"The Mojave Desert? The *Everglades*?"

Drew laughed as he imagined the surprised look on her face. He wished he could see it. "Yeah. These weren't your typical camping trips. Jake was Special Forces, and he doesn't believe in having normal fun."

"How horrible!"

"Actually I loved it. Jake taught me a lot of things. I think I could survive just about anywhere if I had to."

"Hmm. Well, when things get bad, I'm calling you then." Sydney giggled.

Drew loved it, but stiffened when he heard commotion near the door. "Sounds like an army coming." He turned his head slightly so his right ear could hear a little better.

He felt Sydney back away a little.

"I should be on my way."

"You don't have to go." Drew liked having her near.

"I'm meeting a friend at the Blend in fifteen minutes. You take care, Drew Carter."

She went to the door.

"Sydney."

"Yes?"

Her voice was just the right volume, but too far away, and he already missed her. "Thanks for coming to see me."

"I'll be praying for you."

Drew heard a short, polite exchange between his mother, Jake, and Sydney outside his room, but someone else had entered.

"Hey there. How are you feeling?"

"Ben!" Drew almost jumped out of the bed. "What's going on? What happened?"

Ben sat in the chair next to his bed. "We made quite a mess." His low voice was somber.

"The lab?"

"Pretty much destroyed. I told the dean it was all my fault."

"That's not true, Ben. I had just as much—"

"Drew, I am the one with access. I am—or was—Dr. Waseem's assistant. I am the one who told you about his research. It's my fault, and I'm sorry I got you into this."

Drew knew there wasn't much point in arguing. "How much trouble are you in?"

"Possible expulsion."

"*What?* Did you explain what we were doing?"

"I tried, but I think that it only made it worse," Ben said.

"Well, when Dr. Waseem shows up, he'll stand up for you," Drew said, grasping for some hope.

There was a long pause.

"He did show up, Drew. He's dead. They found his car at the bottom of an embankment smashed into a tree."

Drew didn't know what to say. His mind went wild with speculation. What was happening? He sat up and leaned forward. "When?"

"They discovered his car last night. I found out this morning." Ben's words were emotionless, but Drew felt the pain radiate from him.

"I...I'm sorry." Very few people had earned Ben's respect and admiration like Dr. Waseem. The man was more than a teacher and a mentor to Ben. He was an icon of everything Ben hoped to be one day. Now...

Everything important to Ben had been wiped away in a day.

"They say his brakes went out." Ben's voice held an edge of skepticism.

There was a long silence. Drew knew Ben's mind must have been filled with theories and conjecture for hours. He sounded tired.

"That equipment should have never exploded like that," Ben said. "It doesn't make sense, and neither does the professor's accident."

Drew didn't dare speak. Everything that Ben had suspected was true. Although Drew couldn't quite come to terms with thinking of the invisible man he saw through the LASOK as an alien, he had to admit he was at the very least an invader of some sort, whether of this world or of another. What if the invader he saw was standing in the room with them right now? Was anyone safe? Would he and Ben be the next "accidents"? How much power did the invader or invaders have over them already?

"What did you see through the LASOK, Drew? Tell me it wasn't all for nothing."

Drew felt the blood coursing through his veins. He heard Ben's breathing. He opened his mouth, but nothing came out.

"She sure is a sweet girl, Drew." His mother spoke too loudly as she and Jake entered the room. "When did you meet her?"

"In high school."

"Have you taken her on a date?"

"Mom, I'm not really her...type, I guess you could say." Drew gave a crooked smile.

His mother engaged Ben in chitchat, and Drew knew it was her way of trying to help him feel better. Jake stayed silent through most of the conversation. Drew knew he was watching, analyzing, and absorbing the situation. His ability to discern danger was uncanny, and Drew was quite certain that he knew something more was happening.

After fifteen minutes, the nurse showed up to take Ben back to his room. He was to be released today. Drew put his hand up for Ben to take, just like he had done three years ago when he reached out to the geeky statistician lying on the cafeteria floor. Ben took his hand, and Drew quickly pulled him in close until he could feel his friend's breath on his right shoulder. His mouth was nearly touching Ben's ear. In words more quiet than a whisper he spoke so no one could hear.

"You were right—be careful!"

He felt Ben freeze. The exchange was simple, but the meaning was colossal. Ben exhaled, and Drew could sense his friend's relief and anxiety. How could two college students convince the world of the existence of invisible invaders, whoever they were? It sounded absolutely ludicrous, and yet Drew knew what he saw.

Would anyone besides Ben ever believe him?

11

MISSING A FRIEND

The next few weeks did not go well. Ben was expelled from the university and fell into deep depression. With no one to defend him and everyone to blame him, his chances of getting into graduate school at another university were nil.

Drew was released from the hospital and returned home to recover. When the bandages came off, he opened his eyes to precisely the world that the doctors said he would...one of utter darkness.

Drew would have to learn how to live life as a blind man.

He had no choice but to withdraw from the university. Once he settled back into his home with his mother and came to accept the reality of his condition, depression set in for him as well. He spent most of his time holed up in his bedroom. He tried to talk to Ben multiple times, but his friend had closed off the world.

One afternoon, while Drew's mom was still at work, Ben's father and mother showed up at Drew's home asking if he knew where Ben was or where he might go.

Ben was missing.

Drew sickened with worry.

After a short exchange and a few questions, Drew tried to offer some hope.

"I'm sure he just needs time to sort things out. He'll show up soon." But as much as he tried to encourage them, his heart was heavy. There was every possibility that something very serious had befallen his friend.

Drew closed the door behind Ben's parents and felt his way to the couch. He sat down and waited. He was next. He was the only one left now who knew the secret of the invader's existence. It was just a matter of time.

With each passing day, he became more and more frustrated, confused, angry, and afraid. To speak of what he knew could mean instant death, or worse, the death or peril of his mother. He hourly weighed this risk with the incredibly slim chance that someone with any ability to do something would believe him. He considered all the possible outcomes and always came up despondent and hopeless. He imagined that Ben had also been tormented by the same agonizing mental exercise in futility.

In the end, the only response was silence.

Drew came to consider his blindness as a gift. He didn't have to look over his shoulder or gaze at dark corners every waking minute, unlike what he imagined Ben was doing. After days of weary waiting for some bizarre tragedy, he decided to focus on dealing with his blindness just to keep from going mad. He began spending time in the backyard, near the trees that bordered their property. His mother would walk him to a place under a sprawling oak, where he liked to listen to the sounds of nature. It was his first attempt at trying to reconnect with the world.

One afternoon, as he leaned against the large trunk, his ears picked up the soft crunch of grass beneath shoes. It was obvious the intruder was trying to be stealthy, and it unnerved Drew. If he was in danger, he wouldn't have a chance to escape.

"Who's there?" The footsteps came faster, and Drew's heart began to race. "Who's there?" he said louder as he moved to a crouching position.

"Don't cause such a commotion!"

"Ben?" Drew tilted his head to make sure he had identified the voice correctly.

"Yes, it's me... Be quiet. No one can know I'm here. I've been waiting for two days to talk to you."

Drew smiled, joyful that his friend was still alive. "Where have you been? What's going on?"

"Just lean back against the tree and look like nothing is happening."

Drew relaxed and obeyed.

"I don't have a lot of time. I've been gathering some supplies and am leaving Rivercrest."

"But your parents are worried sick. What are you doing?"

A few seconds of silence passed until Drew wondered if Ben was still there. His voice finally came again, low and nervous.

"I know they are, but first you have to tell me everything you saw."

All the dread and fear Drew had been dealing with swept back on him. "I...I don't think it's safe, Ben."

Silence.

"Weird things are happening." Ben's voice was grave now. "I think they're after me."

Ben sounded scared, and Drew didn't blame him.

Drew didn't dare reveal what he knew—the invader might be standing and listening to every word he was speaking, but he also couldn't leave his friend in such a confused and paranoid state. Ben's survival might depend on what Drew told him. He had to risk it.

"It's very real, Ben. We are in danger. The man I saw was one vicious-looking dude. I thought he had killed you. The worst of it is that I think he knows we were onto him."

"He was a man?"

"Yes...no, not really. There was something unearthly about him. I've never seen anyone like him before."

"How many were there?" Ben asked, his voice trembling.

"I only saw one, but we should assume there are more."

"Weapons?"

Drew realized that even in his frightened state, Ben's logical mind still ruled his emotions, and he was trying to get as much information as fast as possible.

Drew hesitated because he knew how absurd his answer was going to sound.

"He was dressed in black clothing and wore a trench coat. He carried a…a sword on his back."

"A sword? That doesn't make any sense. Beings from another world with that kind of cloaking technology would not use such archaic weapons."

"Yes, but it seemed as though it was more than a sword. Like it could affect things the way he wanted it to."

"What do you mean?"

"Ben, I saw him plunge the sword right through you. Did you feel anything?"

"Uh…no…I don't think so."

"Well, that was exactly the same moment when the LASOK overloaded and exploded." Even as Drew said it, it sounded absurd. "I don't know, it could just be coincidence—it all happened so fast."

Ben said nothing. Drew knew he was processing the new information. "That's another thing, Ben."

"What?"

"Fast… This guy was incredibly fast. If this invader is from another world, the planet he comes from must have a much higher gravity, because when I saw him move toward you, he nearly flew across the room. It was a blur, and then he was there. I've never seen anything living move that fast."

There was no response from Ben, then…

"I'm sorry about your eyes, Drew."

"I'm sorry about your expulsion. What are you going to do?"

"Disappear—heck, I don't even know if I *can* disappear. I can't even leave a note for my parents, and you can't tell them either."

Drew understood the frustration and strain in his voice all too well. If it weren't for his blindness, Drew would do the exact same thing.

"Have you considered telling someone?" But Drew knew the answer.

"All the proof is gone, including the pictures. Who would believe me? Besides, you're the one who saw it. It's just hearsay from me. You can't tell anyone because you can't defend yourself or your mom." Ben hesitated. "I'm sorry, Drew, but I think we are both in real danger…and our parents."

Drew knew what Ben was trying to say. "Don't you worry about me. Since I'm blind and don't understand the experiment like you do, I may not be in as much danger as you." Drew considered asking where he could find Ben but knew that was a foolish thing to ask. Besides, even if he knew where Ben was, Drew could never follow him. If Ben came up with a plan, Drew would have to wait for his friend to come to him.

"The wilderness might be a safe place," Drew ventured.

Ben snorted. "I don't have super survival skills like you do. They wouldn't even have to try and get rid of me. I'd be dead in a week from my own folly. No…I need technology. That's my area of expertise."

Drew caught the subtle hint.

"Do you remember my last science fair project when I conducted research on the possibility of finding alien life on other planets?"

Drew smiled. He had teased Ben mercilessly about the project, but his research was so perfectly thorough and scientific that it had won him a trip to the International Science and Engineering Fair.

"Yeah, I remember. I guess I owe you an apology."

"Not really, I just wanted to say thanks for the help."

Drew didn't know what to say. He couldn't remember giving Ben any help whatsoever. If anything, he had been more of a hindrance. Was Ben being sarcastic?

"I'm not—"

"I have to go. You be careful, Drew."

"You be careful too, Ben. Watch your back."

It was a strange end to a strange conversation.

JAKE REARRANGED HIS SCHEDULE so that he could stay close to Drew and his mom for a few weeks. Though Drew was trying to adapt and not be a burden to his mother, he knew it was taking a toll on her. Jake's presence was more for his mother's sake than his own, and Drew was glad for it. Though he was steeped in self-pity, he felt bad for his mother. He tried to cheer up for her sake, but the mountain was too big to crawl out from under.

Jake tried to talk to Drew and get him to open up. A dozen times, Drew almost confided in his mentor, but the vision of the alien stayed his tongue. He wasn't willing to risk putting Jake or his mother at risk.

Drew checked with Ben's parents a couple of times after their visit, just to see if he had made contact with them, but he hadn't. He wanted to comfort them somehow, but he had promised Ben. When the police investigator showed up to ask Drew questions about Ben, he knew that Ben—or the invader—had been successful.

Ben had indeed disappeared.

There were times Drew suspected the worst, and it made him afraid.

In spite of his blindness, Drew continued to be surprised at his heightened sensitivity to sound, touch, taste, and smell. In the hospital he'd thought it was due to the medication they put him on, but once the meds wore off, the heightened sensitivity not only remained but increased. Did eyesight dull the other senses this much?

After some experimentation, he came to the conclusion that the accident had done more than just blind him. Something had changed. Both his mother and Jake noticed it too and were amazed by Drew's perception of what was happening around him.

One Saturday afternoon, two months after the accident, Drew's mother insisted on taking him to their favorite mountain lake for a picnic. After hours of cajoling, Drew acquiesced just to be done with the pleading. He knew she was trying to break him out of his melancholy, but the struggle was so much deeper than dealing with the loss of sight.

Jake joined them, and by midafternoon they were enjoying the cool, fresh air and warm sunshine of what Drew knew was a beautiful day. Being there caused him to miss his eyesight more than ever, but his other senses went wild with the stimulation of nature and its life. The rustling leaves, the crunch of pine needles, the song of the birds, the smell of evergreen, the velvet touch of forest moss, and the delicate push of air on his cheeks were just a few of Drew's vivid sensations. He had never realized how alive the world was until he was blind.

"Aren't you glad you got out of that dingy bedroom of yours?" his mother said with a delighted sigh.

Drew tried to smile but failed. "Yes, Mom. As usual, you were right. It's good to be here."

For a few minutes, Drew forgot about the threat on his life by the invader. But then the fear returned. Was he more or less vulnerable being out and away from civilization?

Though there was nothing gourmet about the fried chicken, beans, and potato salad, the meal tasted wonderful. After eating, they walked down to the lake. Drew held onto his mother's arm and adapted to walking on irregular ground with a guide. Their feet shuffled the stones beneath, rearranging their placement. The gentle lap of miniature waves licked the shoreline. Drew heard Jake pause, then wind up and release a stone. Drew counted.

"Six skips and a slide."

"How do you do that?" Jake sounded amazed. "You actually heard each skip?"

"It's strange. I can almost hear the earth breathing."

"That's rather poetic for a math and finance major," his mother said. Drew heard the smile in her voice.

He turned his face to her and froze. Something flashed across his eyes.

"What is it, Drew?" She sounded alarmed.

He turned his head right and left…and then saw it again. One white flash crossed his eyes. He held up his hand in what he thought was the direction it came from.

"What is there?" he asked, pointing.

"It's the reflection of the sun off the lake water," his mother replied.

Drew's heart skipped a beat. He kept moving his head back and forth, hoping for one more flash. It was the first light he had seen in two months. He blinked many times, and then it happened a third time. "I…I *see* it."

His mother let loose a startled cry. Drew felt her touch his cheek.

"What do you see, Drew?" Jake asked.

"I think I see flashes of light. I haven't seen anything but blackness until just now."

"Oh, Drew," his mother said.

He tried for a long time to see the flashes again, but there were no more. He felt teased, but a twinge of hope crept into his mind.

Drew's mom took him to the hospital the next day, where the ophthalmologist looked at his eyes.

"Residual visual optic nerve activity" is what the doctor called it after examining Drew's eyes. The doctor took Drew's mom out of the room, into the hallway. "He's just going to have to accept the fact that he will never see again."

The man spoke in a hushed voice, but Drew heard every word.

The drive home was silent, and once there, Drew retreated to his bedroom. He fell to his bed and allowed his depression to sink him into sleep. He dreamed of better days—days with his dad playing catch with the football. His dreams were still full of color and light, but no matter what images he saw, there was always a dark shadow where it shouldn't have been. It gnawed at his consciousness until he awoke from the fitful sleep. He stumbled out of bed and felt his way to the door. When he opened it, the rush of air drawn in by the door filled his nostrils with the usual smells, plus one more—one that lifted his spirits. He made his way down the hallway to the living room.

"Sydney Carlyle."

"Hi, Drew!" Her delightful voice enticed a weak smile.

"Now that's not something we see very often," his mother said from the far side of the room.

Drew brushed his bed-head hair back, hoping it wasn't too disheveled.

"Sydney came by to see how you were doing," his mother said.

Drew made his way to the couch, which he knew was empty based on the placement of the two voices.

"Home on break?" Drew assumed that spring must be about now.

"Yes," Sydney replied. "I got home yesterday. How are you doing, Drew?"

"I'm doing great. Why wouldn't I be? I'm blind, I've dropped out of school, and my best friend is missing."

"Drew!"

At his mother's scolding tone, Drew hung his head. He was always grumpy after sleeping, but the weeks of depression had apparently caused him to lose any sense of civility.

"I'm sorry, Sydney. It's been a rough few weeks." Drew heard his mother take a deep breath.

"You don't need to apologize. I can't imagine how hard it's been for you."

"Sydney, would you like something to drink?" his mom asked. "Iced tea, Coke, water?"

"Yes, please. A glass of tea would be wonderful."

Drew's mother exited the living room, and he could hear her preparing a couple of drinks. He knew she would take longer than needed. He heard Sydney rise up from the cushioned chair she was sitting in and walk toward him. She sat down on the couch next to him, her perfume drifting delightfully to his nostrils. He loved that smell. Her hand touched his forearm, sending synaptic shock waves to every part of his body. He resisted the urge to pull back from the sensory overload.

"I'm sorry this has been so difficult."

Drew wanted to thank her, to tell her how much she meant to him, but there was no possible future together for them now. With or without this Jesus she always talked about, he figured blindness trumped anything.

He shook his head. "Why are you here, Sydney? I don't need people feeling sorry for me."

She pulled back her hand. The synaptic shock wave lingered, then subsided. It made him sad, but it was something that had to be done.

"I'm here because I care about you."

"Like you might care about a wounded puppy?" It felt mean, but he didn't care anymore. Might as well end it now.

"No, like I care about a lost soul. A soul who needs purpose and life that only Jesus can give." Sydney's voice broke.

Now Drew felt bad. Why did a girl's tears have so much influence over guys? It wasn't fair.

"Sydney, I'm going to be honest and tell you right now that there is no way that you are going to convince me that some god is in control and loves anyone down here…especially now. This world is a mess, and I've seen too much, literally, to believe in that baloney."

"I know that may be how it seems to you, but all things work together for good to them that love God."

"What's that supposed to mean? That all of this is for my own good? For Ben's good?"

"God can use tragedy to bring about good, Drew. I believe that one day you will see that and understand it."

"What I understand is that Ben has disappeared and I am blind and miserable. No good can come from that."

Just then his mom returned with drinks for all of them. They were forced into trivial conversation. He wanted it to end so he could get something to eat. When Drew and his mom escorted Sydney to the door, she turned to Drew and gave him a quick hug.

"I will always be praying for you," she whispered.

Drew said nothing and was happy to be done with the visit. The girl he once thought he'd like to date had become an enigma to him, one that left him feeling uneasy and confused whenever he encountered her.

He heard his mother open the door for Sydney, and a bright light flashed across his eyes again, except there was a darkened outline where he thought Sydney would be. This one hurt. He winced.

Residual visual optic nerve activity…yeah right!

DREW CONTINUED TO EXPERIENCE bright flashes of light, and the more they occurred, the more they hurt. Darkened outlines of doors, windows, and people now accompanied every flash of light. He didn't dare hope to fully regain his eyesight, but seeing anything rather than utter darkness was encouraging. He decided to keep the changes in his sight to himself. Anything to avoid seeing that depressing ophthalmologist again. After a few weeks passed and the darkened outlines cleared somewhat, the bright flashes stopped. Instead, dull, milky images danced in his vision, reflecting actual movement. It was then that he realized the truth:

He was recovering at least some of his vision.

He dared not hope just yet, for if this was as good as it was going to get, he would still be classified as legally blind.

Four months out of the hospital, Drew questioned his own memory. Why was he still alive? If this invader or whatever he was had any power at all, why hadn't he taken Drew out? The fact that he was still alive caused him to doubt everything he had experienced. Had he actually seen a man in the LASOK viewer? Drew found himself again in a mental exercise of futility. He came to three possible conclusions.

First, if there was an invader, the invader didn't consider Drew a threat because the LASOK and most of the professor's research had been destroyed. There was nothing that Drew, by himself, could do about it.

Second, the invader didn't realize that Drew had seen him.

Third, Drew had dreamed the whole thing up. After all, it was only a ten-second glimpse, and the image of the man was fading with each passing day.

One Saturday morning, Drew awoke to the delightful sounds and smells of pancakes, sausage, and potatoes cooking in the kitchen. It was something his mother had done every Saturday since Drew could remember. He realized it was her attempt at compensating for the cold cereal breakfasts that often made up the week because of her work schedule.

He rubbed his eyes, hoping he would be spared the headache that had become common for him since the accident. He opened his eyes and held his breath. Warm yellow light bathed his vision, and it did not cause him pain—at least, not at first. He turned his head toward the window, and his room filled his vision—*all* of his room.

Drew didn't know what to do. Was he still dreaming? He reached down to pinch his leg. Nope...no dream, yet impossible. He just lay still, looking at everything he'd thought he would never see again. The image wasn't perfectly clear, and strange floaters drifted across his vision, but none of that bothered him.

He could see!

He slowly sat up and let his feet come to rest on the cool floor, afraid that some sudden movement or blink of an eye would make him lose his sight again. He looked around the room and smiled. It was cleaner than he ever re-membered it. His mother had made sure to keep everything in its place so he could find it. He stood up and reached for the wall near the headboard. The world swayed around him and then stabilized.

"Impossible!"

Just then his bedroom door opened.

"Hey, sleepyhead, breakfast is— Oh, you're already up."

Drew turned and looked at his mother.

"Mom."

"Yes." She stilled, as though she sensed something was different.

Drew's mouth curled into wide smile. "You look beautiful today."

His mother's mouth dropped open, and hope filled her eyes. She pushed the door open wider with one hand while the other held a spatula at her side.

"Drew?" She moved her head from left to right to see if he was tracking her.

"Yes...I see you."

She dropped the spatula and covered her mouth with both hands. Tears filled her eyes. Drew walked toward her, being careful not to lose his balance. She grabbed his arms and looked deep into his eyes.

"How—how can it be?"

Drew shook his head. "I don't know, Mom. It's not perfect, but I can see."

She wiped the tears from her eyes and hugged Drew with all her strength, then looked back at his face and touched his cheek, just like she had done ever since he could remember.

Drew explained what had been happening over the past few weeks, and she scolded him for not saying something sooner. When she insisted on taking him back to the doctor, he refused.

"I'm done with Dr. Fletcher. He obviously doesn't know what he's talking about...at least in my case."

"Then let's find a different doctor."

"No, Mom. I just want to let it be...please." He added the "please," but he was not going, and she got the message.

"Okay, but if the headaches get bad, you have to promise to let me take you in."

Drew nodded, but they would have to get really bad before that happened. Then Drew realized he didn't dare let anybody else know he had regained his sight. There was no way of telling just how vast the invaders' network of observation was. Once they learned that Drew could see again, he and his mother would be high-priority targets.

"Mom, I need to ask you not to tell anybody about this. Okay?"

"Why on earth not?"

"Because I don't want the attention, and it may not last. Let's just keep it between us...just for now."

She scrutinized him. "All right. I suppose that would be better until we find out how you do with it."

"Promise?" Ever since he was a little boy, he knew that if he could get her to promise something, earth would have to move out of its orbit before she would break it.

"I promise."

"I want to tell Jake the next time he comes. It would be a cool surprise." Maybe he'd call Jake... No, that wouldn't be safe. Did the invaders monitor phones? At this point he had to assume they monitored and knew everything.

She smiled. "I want to be there when you tell him."

"Deal." Drew breathed a sigh of relief.

As the day wore on, Drew's vision deteriorated, which discouraged him no small measure, and to make things worse, a massive headache that emanated from his eyes put him down about three in the afternoon. Ibuprofen helped only slightly, and so the rest of his day was spent in his bedroom with the shades drawn. The next morning brought new hope, however, for his headache was gone and his vision was better than the day before.

And so it went for the next few weeks, until his vision no longer was strained by the end of the day. He did have to learn how to manage his headaches, however. The brighter the day, the more affected he was by them, but even an overcast day strained his eyes and might spark a headache. He discovered that sunglasses helped immensely, so anytime he was outside, the shades were on. Although still daily burdened by the knowledge of Ben's disappearance and the threat of the unknown attacker, his mood improved. As his eyesight returned,

Drew wondered if he would lose the heightened sensitivity of his other senses, but that was not the case. Now that his vision was back, everything around him seemed more intense. His visual acuity continued to improve until he was certain his eyesight was even better than it was before the accident, which made no sense to him because he had always had 20-20 vision.

Then he realized that not only could he see better, he could see quicker. If he concentrated, he could focus on a fly in flight and see it as clearly as if it were sitting still on the table. Such concentration always triggered a headache though. The longer the concentration, the more severe the headache, so he did not use this ability often. When the headaches hit him, he would retreat to the darkness of his room, although even that was different now. Nothing seemed truly dark anymore. The pitch-black, moonless nights Drew remembered had somehow been transformed into a soft, glowing gray-lit landscape.

With his senses heightened, the rest of his body responded in an accelerated way. Once while his mother was placing a pot of chili on the supper table, she bumped Drew's full glass of water, and it tipped. He reacted so quickly that only a few drops spilled out as he righted the glass. That in itself was not so remarkable. What *was* remarkable was that he wasn't even looking at the glass when it happened. The sound of the colliding dishes generated a shock wave of synaptic impulses, and he simply reacted. The moment almost froze in time for him, and he could have drawn a perfect picture of the shape of the water as it neared the rim of the glass.

After supper he went online and took a reaction-time test. His first attempt was off the chart, with a reaction time of 26 milliseconds—fifteen times faster than the average human! He tested himself a dozen times to confirm it. His last reaction time came in at 19.9 milliseconds. He stared at the blinking number, one question running over and over in his mind...

What was happening to him?

12

EYES OF ANOTHER WORLD

Living with heightened senses was fascinating at first, but it soon became an extreme nuisance. Drew found it difficult to do the simplest of tasks without being distracted by every sight, sound, smell, and tremor around him. Sleep escaped him until he learned how to cope with the hypersensitivity. It took a few weeks, but Drew discovered that through concentration, he could numb his senses to a degree. But any loud sound or sudden movement often triggered an avalanche of stimuli, and it took hours to recover some normalcy.

It was late spring, and Drew's restored eyesight brought not only new hope but also new danger. Drew considered looking for Ben. If his brilliant friend had devised a plan, Drew could now be an integral part of it. But the fact that he could see again also meant that Drew would be a threat that the invader might eliminate. A twinge of paranoia lingered in the corner of his mind as he considered his new options. Did the invader already know that he had regained his sight? How long until he became a target too? He would have to be careful.

Drew hadn't gone to town since his accident and especially since regaining his sight. There were two reasons, not the least of which was that if he had any chance of staying off the radar of the invaders, it would be in the solitude of his home. The other reason was not as strategic. Rumors about the incident at college would be rampant, and he was in no mood to deal with them. Sydney was the only person who had come to see him since he was hurt. Additionally, the stigma under which he had left high school would never die. He had no desire to face any of his old nemeses again. College had been such a welcome reprieve from his past at Rivercrest High that when he came back during breaks, he rarely left his house. The one exception he made was the twenty-four-hour fitness center on Second, and he was very selective about the timing of his workouts there.

One night, sleep evaded him, and he decided to make use of the time rather than toss and turn all night. At 3:00 a.m. he drove to the gym and dived into an intense workout. Even though he worked harder than he could ever remember, he felt like he could still do more. His energy seemed limitless, but after three hours, he finished up and decided to stop by the FoodMart to pick up a few groceries before heading home.

Drew stepped out of his car into the parking lot, where just eight other vehicles were parked. Dawn was beginning to break as the morning rays painted a few scattered clouds on the horizon in a brilliant pink-and-orange hue. He soaked up the visual feast. He would never take his sight—or the wondrous things to be seen—for granted again. He could not remember the sky ever looking so alive before. He almost expected to hear the sunlight and wondered what such a thing might sound like.

Drew walked toward the grocery store and considered putting on his sunglasses. Though the morning light wasn't yet bright enough to spark a headache, the fluorescent lights inside the store most certainly would. The sliding doors swished open, and he felt the familiar twinge of pain behind his eyes just before he set his sunglasses in place. He picked up a basket and headed for the orange juice, smiling at an elderly woman as he passed. He grabbed a quart of juice and a gallon of milk, then made his way toward the registers at the front of the store. The pizzas in the frozen foods aisle caught his attention, so he opened the glass door and looked over the selection. Something gnawed at his mind...

That's weird—

Sudden chills flowed up and down his body as his eyes caught the reflection of the aisle to his right in the glass door. Terror froze him as he focused on the ghost of an image.

The invader.

His large, dark frame was unmistakable. Drew didn't dare turn to see if the reflection was real or purely his imagination. His heart beat harder and faster than it had during his three-hour workout. His senses escalated, and he struggled to control them. Foggy condensation on the glass door blurred the image until it disappeared. The freezer cold spilled onto his body, adding to the intensity of the chills that raised goose bumps on his arms and legs. The door was opened to his left, which meant that whatever he saw was at the end of the aisle to his right, near the back of the store.

He willed himself to close the door, then stared at it, seeing his own reflection in the dissolving fog inside the compartment, fully expecting to see another ghost looking over his shoulder, but all he saw was his own terrified image. He forced himself to turn and look to the right, but no one was there. He started to breathe again but could not yet move.

Was he going mad?

Though the image had been brief, it was without a doubt similar to the figure he saw through the LASOK. *How is that possible?*

"Can I help you?"

The voice shattered Drew's delicate state of mind, and he nearly dropped the basket of milk and juice. He spun around to see the store's assistant manager looking at him.

"No. No thank you," Drew muttered.

"We have pizza pockets and Pizza Rolls further down if you're looking for those." The man nodded in the direction that Drew did not want to go.

"Uh, thanks." Drew looked to his right once more.

Still nothing.

The basket in his hand felt like it weighed two hundred pounds, and the gravity pulled him into the earth. The assistant manager walked merrily toward the end of the aisle, and Drew envied his ignorance. Drew forced his heavy legs to move toward the registers, wanting desperately to be home and back in the security of his bedroom.

Two registers were open, one of them occupied by the elderly woman he had seen earlier. He stepped toward the open register, all the while wondering what had just happened. Just when he considered attributing his experience to "residual visual optic nerve activity," the reality of his world changed in an instant and forever.

A massive figure walked from behind Drew, nearly bumping into his left shoulder as he passed. Drew stepped back, shock searing through him, as the invader walked past the register clerk, the corners of his black trench coat flapping with each stride. The invader was nearly seven feet tall.

"I can help you, sir," the young red-headed clerk said with a smile on her face. She looked right through the passing invader.

Drew struggled to contain himself, grateful the invader's back was to him. The same unearthly sensation he had felt back in the lab many months earlier filled his soul. He glanced at the clerk and then back at the invader. The huge man walked another twenty feet to the front of the store, which was lined with large glass windows, and stopped. His head turned right and left as though he were looking for someone. Though Drew had not seen the man's face, he was nearly certain this was a different invader. Which confirmed that there was more than one on the planet.

Drew eyed the handle of the sinister sword strapped across the invader's back.

"Sir?" the clerk questioned.

Drew couldn't take his eyes off the invader's back. He wanted to run... hide...be away from whatever it was he thought he was seeing.

This is impossible!

"Sir?" the clerk said louder.

At that, the invader turned around and stared at Drew. His heart nearly stopped beating as he tried to recover himself. He turned to the clerk. "Uh, yes, I thought I'd forgotten something."

He set the basket on the black conveyor, not daring to look toward the invader. He would live or die by how he reacted in the next few moments. He fumbled for his wallet and realized that his hands were shaking as he tried to remove a ten-dollar bill.

"Are you okay?" The clerk spoke in a hushed voice.

"Yes...yes. I'm fine." Drew managed a weak smile.

He finished paying and bagged the milk and the juice, then stood with his back to the front of the store, trying to gather the courage to turn and face his nightmare. The clerk watched him closely and then turned to help another customer. Drew took a deep breath, lifted his two bags, and turned to exit the store.

The invader was still there, near the door on the right side. He was well within the range of the motion detector that would open the sliding doors, but they stayed closed, as unaware of the invader's presence as was the store clerk.

Though his car was closer to the doors on the right, Drew chose to exit the store via the doors on the left. He moved that direction, and then his fragile composure shattered again. Through the window, Drew saw two more invaders approaching! They walked right through the door of the grocery store to his right, as if there were no door at all. Drew blinked hard. Had he seen correctly? One of the newcomers looked toward Drew, and he quickened his pace so he could turn away and not be tempted to look their direction.

He exited the store and hurried to his car. He had to drive past the storefront to exit the parking lot, and he couldn't resist looking once more toward the invaders' meeting place. They were still there, and it was quite obvious that the first invader he had seen was giving orders to the other two. Then the leader's eyes fell on Drew as he drove by, and for one brief moment, there was an eerie exchange between them.

Drew was almost certain the invader knew he knew. It frightened him to the bone. He accelerated his Mustang, and all the way home, Drew's mind was filled with bizarre thoughts and questions. Whatever had just happened, there were only two possible explanations. Either Drew was going mad...

Or he could see into the hidden world of the invaders...

Without the LASOK.

Drew pulled into his driveway and scanned around him. Had the invaders followed him home? How could he have been so stupid as to come straight home? He should have made sure he eluded them first. Fear welled up within him, and it reminded him of the time when he was ten years old and had spent the night at a friend's house. They stayed up late and watched a creepy movie, which then kept him awake all night wondering if the monster from the movie was going to crash through the window and get him.

That same fear threatened his sanity now. He suppressed the desire to run to his bedroom, lock the door, and hide under the covers of his bed. But Jake had trained him to deal with fear—fear of heights, fear of water, fear of an unseen enemy, and fear of death. But this…

This fear felt different.

Nothing Jake taught him had prepared him for something like this.

Nevertheless, he had to do something to get on top of his emotions and deal with the situation. He tried to implement Jake's teaching. *"Deep breath, be a machine, respond, react, predict, do the job. Failure is not an option, but plan for it to eliminate fear. You are more capable than what you think you are."*

Slowly Drew reined in his emotions and climbed above his fear. Twice he felt it clawing its way back toward him, but he beat it down.

"Tactical scan—move forward." Drew used all three mirrors on the car first, then reached to the backseat to grab his bag and get a complete scan of the front area of their home.

Clear.

His senses were in hyper mode, and he knew he was going to pay for it with a massive headache. He opened his car door and stood up, maintaining a casual demeanor as his senses caught every movement, sound, and smell within a hundred yards. It was like watching a movie at half speed.

His enhanced observation abilities restored his confidence and determination to own this moment and his reaction to it. He walked toward his home while looking at reflections off his mother's minivan and the house windows. He felt the crunch of gravel beneath his feet, the radiant sun on his arms and neck, and the molecules of air being pushed aside as he walked. Ants, birds, grass, squirrel, distant car, exhaust fumes, evergreen, train horn—no threat. Drew entered his home and turned to shut the door, half expecting to see one of the invaders walk right through it, but nothing happened.

"Drew…you're up early." His mother poked her head out from the kitchen. "You look beat. Are you okay?" She came to check his forehead.

"Yeah, I'm good. Just had a tough workout."

He felt the beginning of the headache and knew the crash was coming.

"Want some breakfast?" she asked. "I can whip up some pancakes."

Drew needed food and ibuprofen fast.

"That's okay. Got any leftover egg bake?"

"Sure." She came closer to study him. "Sure you're okay?"

"Yep, just starving and tired." Drew shot her a quick smile so she would leave.

Drew reviewed what had just happened at the grocery store, trying to remember every detail. Suddenly his confidence shattered as he realized that, in spite of his hypersenses, the invaders hadn't made a single sound that Drew could hear. Everything they did happened in absolute silence. Of his five senses, only one could transcend into their dimension of existence: his eyes. It made sense, though. The LASOK was designed to see into the invaders' dimension, nothing else. But sight alone was not enough to detect the approach of such an enemy. And why, if they weren't of any use to him in this area, were his other senses heightened? What did they accomplish except to bring on these painful headaches?

Drew was having a hard time thinking or focusing. This headache was getting bad. He went to the kitchen to grab the plate out of the microwave and wolf down the egg bake, followed by three ibuprofen tablets with some water. Then he retreated to the dark of his room, hoping that the pain wouldn't last all day. He focused on relaxing his body and then the muscles in his eyes.

It helped.

But his mind wouldn't stop buzzing... *Was* he going crazy? He'd seen movies of people, some of them very famous and intelligent, who experienced hallucinations. How real were they to those people? Drew had never been so unnerved or scared in his life. If he wasn't crazy, then these invaders were real. And if they were invisible to humans, how extensive was their power? Could they read his thoughts...or perhaps even control them?

He closed his eyes...

If only he could close out the fear as well.

13

BETRAYED!

Over the next couple of weeks, Drew reevaluated everything—his knowledge of the invaders, their purpose, his abilities and vulnerabilities... everything. It occupied his thoughts every minute of every day. He came to two conclusions. First, now that he could see them, he'd be able to speak of them in secret and know that they hadn't heard the conversation. Some semblance of secrecy was at least possible. Second, Ben was the key to formulating a plan to counter the invaders.

Drew had to find Ben.

He tried to act as normal as possible, but his mother noticed that something was up. When she tried to talk to him, he attributed any oddities she might have seen in his behavior to his uncertainty about his future, emphasizing a desire to return to college and pick up where he left off. Drew was quite certain she didn't buy it, so he tried all the more to act as normal as possible, even though he was acutely aware of a silent global invasion of aliens probably trying to take over the human race.

Before long, Jake contacted Drew to arrange a short weekender trip to the Flint Hills, and Drew knew his mother had asked Jake to do it. Still, it would be good to get away.

Jake took a Friday off, and they arrived in the Flint Hills by three in the afternoon. Drew filled his lungs with the fresh air and felt some of his burden lift. He scanned the area, but there was no sight of the invaders. Maybe the wilderness offered a measure of safety as opposed to being in close proximity to the city. Once camp was set, Drew had an idea.

"Hey, Jake. How about we forget survival training and go straight to combat?"

"Okay. What're you looking for?"

"Hand to hand."

"With or without weapons?"

"Knife for you, nothing for me."

"You're feeling pretty confident for a man who's just got his eyes back," Jake said with a smile.

"It's been a while. I need to come back hard."

Jake pulled his MK3 Navy combat knife out of its sheath and stuck it in a nearby tree; then he dug in his bag and replaced it with a dull-bladed training knife. He inked the cutting edge.

"Sure you're ready for this?"

Drew just nodded, and Jake came at him less than a second later. Drew hadn't learned to control his hypersenses and reactions yet. There were times it felt like they were controlling him. He reacted with the speed of a cat, retreating to a safe distance from the knife and allowing the initial attack to complete its motion.

Clear…control…counter…

Jake's training on weapons defense came flooding back. Drew initiated his first aikido move, jamming Jake's knife arm and controlling his elbow. He rotated his hips ninety degrees to Jake and performed a wrist throw, which put Jake on the ground. He locked his wrist and took the knife. It was over in less than three seconds. Drew checked his hands and arms—no ink.

He gave Jake a lift up. "You don't have to play dumb. I'm a big boy now."

Jake looked rather stunned. He didn't respond to the comment; he just came again. And the end result was the same, except Jake ended up with a long ink mark across his chest. Drew helped him up again.

"Where have you been practicing and with whom?" Jake rubbed his arm.

That's when it hit Drew. Jake had given him his best. Drew felt a little bad for having bested him so soundly.

"I…um…haven't been. You're it."

"Well, I recognize the moves, but"—Jake shook his head—"never seem 'em used quite like that."

Drew knelt down and wiped the ink off the blade, then flipped it around and handed it to Jake. "Sorry."

"Are you kidding?" Jake took the knife. "I couldn't be more proud. The day the student beats the instructor is a day to celebrate." Jake put an arm on Drew's shoulder. "It's the goal. Well done."

They decided to do some tactical target shooting. Drew loved his Springfield .40-caliber XDM—the perfect balance between versatility and power. Sixteen rounds in the magazine plus one in the chamber, smaller than a .45 but with as much impact. Drew couldn't convince himself to buy anything else.

Jake's choice was always the M45 Colt 1911. "The stopping power of .45 is just too important," he told Drew, but it didn't change his mind.

Drew hadn't shot since last summer, when he and Jake took their last trip. He missed shooting and was excited for the practice he would get today. He leveled his XDM at the target, took a breath, released half, and gently squeezed the trigger while maintaining a firm sixty-forty grip high on the tang.

His first shot sent him into sensory overload.

He actually heard the firing pin impact the round's primer, and the concussion that followed was overwhelming. The sound exploded through his hearing protection as if he wasn't wearing anything. The recoil in his hands felt like someone blasted a hammer into his right palm. The smell of gunpowder sent his olfactory senses into overdrive, and he could taste it in his mouth. His vision was the only sense that hadn't been adversely affected because he shut his eyes when the first tidal wave of input hit him. It was so overpowering! How would he ever get past it to shoot?

Of course, his shot went way wide of the target.

"You okay?" Jake studied him.

Drew lowered his pistol. "I'm not sure. I need a moment." He checked his earplugs to make sure they were seated properly and readied himself to try another round. This time he was expecting the concussion and was able to keep his eyes open. At trigger squeeze, every sense ramped up again, and Drew saw things happen as if a high-speed camera had captured the moment. For a fraction of a second, he saw the back end of the bullet exit through the orange flame plume at the end of the barrel. The shock wave rippled through the smoke, and his round pierced the center of the target an eternity later.

"Nice shot. Looks like you've got a bead on the target now."

Drew focused again and emptied his magazine, forming a tight two-inch pattern in the chest of the target.

"Wow" was Jake's only response.

Jake set him up to force shots from behind trees, standing, kneeling, lying down, and moving. Nearly every shot was tight. When they stopped, Jake took an extra minute to look over the targets. He glanced over at Drew.

"That's as good as I've ever seen, and I've seen a lot." He waited for some reaction from Drew, but Drew just nodded and set to cleaning his weapon.

They finished up, made a fire, and cooked supper.

"Drew, what's going on?" Jake asked after a silent meal. "Something's changed. I've seen men experience stress, but what I'm seeing in you is unusual. I know you've been through a lot—can't imagine what it's been like, but your mom is concerned."

"Are you?"

"I don't know. Should I be?"

It was dusk, but Drew could still see well. He made a three-sixty scan, then started trying to relax his eye muscles before the approaching headache overtook him.

"There's no one around for miles. Why did you do that?"

Drew could fool his mother most of the time, but he could never fool Jake, especially when it came to identifying somebody looking for a threat—big red flag. He looked at Jake and realized that if there was anyone in the world besides Ben who he could trust, it would be Jake.

"Jake, you've trained me to be calm, objective, and calculated, and I've tried hard to take all of your instruction to heart. And by the way, I could never express to you how grateful I am. You've been…well, a father to me."

Jake's gaze dropped to the ground. Drew had never said anything like that to Jake, and it was long overdue. Jake seemed moved.

"You ever known me to be prone to a wild imagination?"

Jake looked up. His eyes were warm. "Of course not, Drew."

Drew took a deep breath.

"That accident at the university left me with some very interesting side effects…and abilities."

Drew watched Jake's eyes for some response, but Jake just waited. He never interrupted a man and never cut an explanation short. Neither did he make any conclusions until he'd heard everything. Normally Drew appreciated this about him, but this time, he wished he could get a read before he went too far.

"I can hear things, feel things, smell things, and see things like never before. You're right, something's changed. You should be able to tell that by what we just did."

Jake nodded. That was good.

"This is going to sound extremely bizarre, but I can see…" Drew bit his lower lip. The next few words he spoke could change everything, and he couldn't quite force the words out. He restarted.

"When you were on mission, did you ever come into a situation where you knew the enemy was near but you just couldn't ID him?"

"Often."

"Then, all of a sudden, even though you might have been looking right at him, you could see him and you wondered why you couldn't see him before?"

"Kandahar…it was frightful," Jake said with a distant gaze.

"That's what we have right here…in America…in Rivercrest, and I'm sure everywhere."

"We've always had domestic enemies, Drew. The tough ones are those we can't see, but it's nothing to be paranoid about. You can't live like that. The fear will eat you up."

"Exactly." Drew knew he couldn't turn back now, and Jake wouldn't understand unless he told him everything. "The lab that Ben was working at with Dr. Waseem had a device that was designed to accelerate light. What very few people knew was that the doctor's ultimate goal was to see into another dimension."

At that, Jake smiled.

"I saw into that dimension."

Jake's smile slowly vanished, and his eyes narrowed.

"And the accident, by some freakish way, has allowed me to continue to see into that dimension." Drew waited, watching Jake's every minuscule reaction.

He was silent for a long moment. "The enemies you're talking about are from another dimension…and you can see them?"

Great. Jake sounded like he thought Drew was nuts.

"I know it sounds crazy, and you are the only person alive I can trust now. We have enemies that are fierce and powerful. Who knows how long they've been here or what they are capable of, but one thing is for sure, they are our enemies."

Jake held up his hand. "Drew…stop! Listen to yourself and get a grip." He glared at Drew, then softened his stare and sighed. "I know many good men that have struggled after some pretty traumatic things have happened, and you've been through a lot these last couple of years."

Drew's heart sank. If Jake didn't believe him, he was truly alone. Now he had to act better than he'd ever acted before. He hung his head and rubbed his neck.

"I'm sorry, Jake. Lately my thoughts have been a mess." He rubbed his eyes and face with his hands. "Especially since Ben disappeared. I'm not sleeping well, and when I do sleep, my dreams are pretty vivid. Perhaps that has something to do with all of this." He looked up at Jake. "I'm so tired, and my head hurts again."

Jake's face softened. "Get some rest. Let's take it light tomorrow and just relax."

"That sounds really good. Coming here has already helped…I can tell."

He forced a smile and hoped Jake couldn't see the lie behind it.

The next day and a half that Drew and Jake spent in the Hills, Drew forced himself to believe it was all a bad dream. Sunday evening when they returned to Rivercrest, he felt like he had covered some of his error. He asked Jake not to say anything to his mom but didn't get a firm promise from him.

WEDNESDAY MORNING, DREW WENT to work out. When he pulled up to the house, he recognized Jake's car but an unfamiliar vehicle was parked next to it. As he entered the front door, his mother greeted him, and Drew became suspicious.

"Hi, Drew." His mother put her arm through his. "I would like you to meet someone."

Drew took off his sunglasses and frowned. "What's going on, Mom?"

She escorted him from the foyer into the living room. Jake was sitting on the couch, and across from him was a middle-aged man wearing narrow glasses. Except for a little hair near the back of his head, he was bald. A synthetic smile seemed pasted on his pale face. He stood up as Kathryn and Drew entered the room.

"Drew, this is Dr. Fisher."

Drew shot a quick glance toward Jake, but he averted his eyes to Dr. Fisher. Something wasn't right. Jake always looked him straight in the eye, except when he felt like he couldn't tell Drew something. Drew's defenses snapped on.

"Hi, Drew. It is a pleasure to meet you." Dr. Fisher's voice dipped and rose in a way that disgusted Drew. The man stepped forward and stuck out his hand.

Drew hesitated, then extended his hand. Dr. Fisher's hand was soft and malleable, the kind Drew hated and couldn't wait to withdraw from.

"Are you an eye doctor?"

Dr. Fisher's condescending smile set Drew's teeth on edge. "Not exactly. Please sit down. I'd like to talk to you for a few minutes, if you don't mind."

Drew did mind. "What's going on, Mom?"

"Please…sit down." Dr. Fisher motioned to a chair near him. Drew's mother averted her eyes from Drew too and took her place next to Jake.

Drew sat down, analyzing the threat and his escape.

"I understand you are on the mend from quite an accident," Dr. Fisher said with another insincere smile. "Your mother tells me you're making a remarkable recovery—especially your eyes. How are you feeling?"

"Fine." Drew turned his full attention on Dr. Fisher. His eyes narrowed. "What kind of a doctor are you?"

"The kind that wants to help you, Drew. Can you tell me when your vision was restored?"

Drew felt like a prisoner being interrogated for information he didn't want to give. His answers were cautious and hesitant. The first few questions seemed harmless enough, but each time he glanced toward his mother and Jake, they would either look to the doctor or attempt a weak smile. Whatever was going on, he had lost them as allies. Drew played along for fifteen minutes of innocuous questioning, and then his suspicions were validated.

"So you are seeing very well with your eyes now, and you haven't had them checked. Why not?" Dr. Fisher asked.

"Because I'm tired of bad news. I guess I don't trust doctors. After all, I was supposed to be blind for life, and yet, there you are." Drew motioned toward him with his hand.

Dr. Fisher nodded as if to agree with him. He looked all around the room. "Do you see everything in this room?"

"Yes."

"Do you see things in the room that shouldn't be here?" Dr. Fisher's eyes became probing sensors, evaluating every move Drew made.

Drew glared at his mother and then at Jake. He had been betrayed. He knew exactly what had happened. Jake had shared Drew's story with his mother, and they both thought he needed psychiatric help. He clenched his teeth as he fought to keep control of his anger.

"Yes, I do see something that doesn't belong in this room," Drew said with a strained voice. "You!" He stood up. "And me!"

Drew glared at Jake. "I trusted you." He turned and made his way to the door.

"Drew!" Jake yelled, but Drew did not stop.

He opened the door and slammed it behind him. Anger seethed within as he threw his Mustang in reverse. Rocks and gravel peppered the cars in front of him as his tires spun and his roaring engine shot him backward away from his home. He whipped the steering wheel to the left, which slingshot the front of his car one hundred eighty degrees. Before the front end came to rest, Drew snapped the stick into first gear and the wheels spun forward. The acceleration felt good, and the direction felt even better.

Drew had to leave home soon, but he had hoped it would be under better circumstances. This betrayal by Jake and his mother struck deep into his heart. Logically he knew he shouldn't blame them, but he did. If they wouldn't believe him, then no one on earth would either.

He began formulating a plan—a plan that would give him answers and evidence, for there were many questions. Could he evade these invaders? How much, if at all, did they track individual humans? He assumed their biggest concern would be with people of power and influence, which made him grateful to be a nobody. At least he didn't seem to be on their radar yet. Did the invaders have human conspirators who knew what was happening? There was so much to learn if he was going to survive. He figured it was inevitable that the invaders would eventually discover that he could see them… Perhaps they already knew. Drew shivered.

He drove to the place that had become a favorite for him and Jake. It was a lush green rise overlooking a small, still pond nestled in the hills of Kansas. Tall trees cradled the ground to the east and south. For some reason, when the sadness of losing his father pressed in on him, this was the place that made him feel whole, at least for a little while. It was his favorite place to think and to be alone. It was here that Drew evaluated his options.

The first option he considered was to disappear into the wilderness, away from the madness that he had discovered. With the skills Jake had taught him, he knew he could survive. But Jake had also taught him to take his course and cast it forward to see where it would land. Isolationism would not solve anything, and although Drew might have temporary peace, he knew a time would come when he would regret it. He eliminated that option.

The second option was to continue on in Rivercrest as if nothing had changed, but with what he could see, he would never be able to pretend life was normal. It was what he was trying to do now, and he was miserable. That left only one other option…

The third option was by far the riskiest and most dangerous. He would disappear into the mass of humanity with the intention of studying and learning as much about the invaders as possible while formulating a plan of counterattack. He needed to be where the invaders were, at least more than there were in Rivercrest. He also needed to find Ben. With Ben's knowledge of the LASOK and Drew's ability to see the invaders, they might just come up with a way of identifying and proving their existence to the rest of the world. It was a long shot, he knew, but at least it made sense, and it gave him something to occupy his mind. If it was at all possible, Drew knew he needed to disappear from both the invaders and traceable humanity.

As he wrestled with and tried to embrace the inevitable, Drew heard the soft crunch of grass behind him and estimated that the man approaching him was still fifty feet away. At thirty feet, he felt the man's first footstep in the ground beneath him.

"I can't believe you betrayed me, Jake." Drew didn't turn around. Only Jake knew of this place.

Jake abandoned his silent approach, walked next to Drew, and sat down beside him.

"I know that's what it looks like to you, Drew, but I didn't betray you." Jake picked up a small stone and threw it at a tree squirrel. "Your mother is concerned about you. If I hadn't told her what you told me, I would have betrayed *her*."

Drew shook his head. Jake would never have arranged for a shrink to evaluate him like that. His mother had set it up, probably with Jake petitioning against it.

"So do you think I'm crazy, like my mom thinks I am?"

Jake hesitated. "No, I don't think you're crazy. I've seen crazy and you're not it, but to some you sure sound like it. You have to admit, it's a stretch and your mother just wants to help you. You've been through a lot, Drew. You can't blame her for wondering if you are…well, coping properly."

Drew lowered his head. "Yeah. I suppose you're right."

Drew looked over at Jake, who had that very serious countenance that told Drew he was about to teach him something important.

"Listen, wherever you're going…whatever you're planning to do…remember everything I've taught you. You are going to need all of it…and more."

Drew nodded. "I figured you knew I was going to have to leave. You're not going to try and stop me?"

Jake laughed. "Nope. I've taught you too well for that. Not sure I'd be very successful anyway. Do you remember what I taught you about dropping off the grid?"

Drew raised an eyebrow. "Why would you ask that?"

"Because in spite of that nice acting job a few days ago, I think you believe what you told me, and that leaves you no choice."

Jake allowed a slight smile to cross his lips.

"It's what I would do." Jake put a hand on Drew's shoulder. "If you need help, you know how to find me. Just promise me you will find a way to let me know what's going on."

Drew wasn't sure how he could do that just yet, so he didn't respond. "When I'm gone, what are you going to tell my mom?"

"Not sure yet. I'll think of something. It's going to be hard on her. You'd better figure out a way to say good-bye without saying good-bye."

Jake reached into his pocket and pulled out a wad of folded bills.

"Here. It's about thirty-six hundred dollars. It's not much but should get you to where you're going." Jake looked at Drew for some confirmation, but he gave him none.

"You sure?"

Jake just pushed the money toward him.

"Thanks, Jake. I'll repay you, I promise."

"Here's something else I took the liberty of making for you." Jake handed Drew a card. It was a Minnesota driver's license for Ryan Johnson, but it was Drew's picture. Ryan was his father's name, and Johnson was his mother's maiden name. It would be easy for him to remember. Drew examined the card—it looked authentic, but the birth date and ID were not his.

Drew looked up at Jake.

"Sometimes my clients require an extra measure of protection while they are traveling to hide their identity. This will help you where you are going as long as it is stateside. Beyond that, you're on your own, and I wouldn't recommend it."

Drew nodded his thanks; then they both looked into the distant beauty of the land. When it felt like it was time to leave, Jake moved to get up.

"Hey, Jake. My mom's been asked out by more guys than I can count."

This comment made Jake fidget. "Yeah, I'm sure she has." Jake stood up. Drew followed.

"She's never gone out with any of them...ever."

Jake shot Drew a puzzled look.

"Good grief, Jake, if you wait any longer you might as well go off the grid with me."

Jake turned away. "I...I promised your dad I'd take care of her, not date her. It feels like I'd be...dishonoring him." He rubbed the back of his neck. Drew had never seen him so uncomfortable. "Besides, Kathryn is...well...she deserves better than me."

"You have honored my dad for eight years. Don't you think he would want his best friend to date her rather than some random guy?"

It felt a little strange talking to Jake like this about his mother, but over the past year, their relationship had shifted. The word *friend* defined what was between them now. Even still, Drew sensed he had said enough.

They walked in silence back toward their cars. Jake looked across the hood of his Charger.

"Hey," Jake called out.

Drew looked up.

"Thanks."

Drew gave a quick nod, then settled into his Mustang and drove for home. His excursion to the hills had used up the whole day. The setting sun nested between two hills on the horizon, the last of its glowing rim disappearing. He looked at his phone and saw twelve missed calls and multiple texts...all from his mother. He felt bad. When he pulled up to the driveway, his mother ran out to the car with tears in her eyes. Drew jumped out and gave his mom a long hug.

"I'm sorry, Drew." She wiped her eyes, then touched his cheek. "I should have talked to you about Dr. Fisher before asking him to come."

"It's okay, Mom. I understand. I just needed some time to sort things out. I'm sorry too."

They walked arm in arm back to the house, and she fixed a delicious meal as Drew set the table. Mother and son sat, ate, talked, laughed, and cried together.

"Mom, you have been so strong through the years. I don't know how you've done it, but I know you did it for me." Drew looked across the table at his beautiful mother. A lone candle flickered between them. "Dad would be proud. Thank you."

Flame-reflected tears trickled down her cheeks. "You remind me a lot of him," she said with a gentle laugh. "He would be so proud of the man you've become, and so am I."

A lump formed in his throat. Did all sons long to hear that from their fathers? He thought of Jake and what a friend he'd been to them both.

"Jake's been good to us." Drew smiled through his emotions.

"Yes…yes he has. He's a good man."

"Next to Dad, there's none better out there." His mother tilted her head and narrowed her eyes. Drew just smiled. "Their friendship must have been deep."

She nodded, then became lost to some distant memory. "Like the brothers they never had."

Drew grew somber. His mother reached for her glass, and Drew made a quick scan of as much of the house as he could see from where he was sitting before she looked back at him. "I'm worried about Ben, Mom. I know he's out there, and he needs help."

There, the seed was planted, the explanation given. It would be enough. His mother's eyes saddened, but she nodded as she set her glass down.

"I can't imagine what more you could do that the police haven't already done, but when you're ready, I'll help you."

What his mom would not understand when he left was that he was doing it as much to protect her as to find Ben. He was convinced that once the invaders understood who he was and what he was trying to do, he and everybody around him would be in danger.

"I love you, Mom."

"I love you too, Drew."

14

THE INVADER WAR

The next morning, when his mother left to teach, Drew grabbed the last few things he thought he would need, including his .40-caliber XDM handgun and four boxes of ammunition. He then drove to the bank and withdrew the twelve hundred thirty-six dollars left in his account. He sat in the bank parking lot with nothing left to do but leave. He knew what his first move should be, but there was something inside him that compelled him to make one visit before he dropped off the grid.

He set his direction east toward Drayle University. The six-hour drive gave him time to think. He hadn't yet figured out how to go about searching for Ben. Drew had thought about his last conversation with Ben a hundred times, hoping to find some clue as to where Ben might go. As he replayed that conversation in his mind one more time, a realization struck—Ben told him where to start looking! He had thanked Drew for helping him on his science fair project, but Drew hadn't helped at all. That comment was no mistake.

Drew looked at the baseball cap lying on the seat next to him, a gift that Ben brought back from that trip. Drew picked it up and smiled at the bright-orange C on the front of the hat.

He parked his 67' Mustang in the visitor's parking lot near the south end of the Drayle University campus. He stood up and stretched to get the blood flowing to his legs and arms again as he looked around at the towering dorms and university facilities. Coming here wasn't the smartest move. After all, this was where it all began. But two things pulled him back here: the physics lab and Sydney.

He needed closure with both.

He slipped his baseball cap on his head, threw his backpack over his shoulder, and walked toward the physics building, trying to look as casual as the rest of the students on campus. Nearly eight months had passed since the accident, but it seemed as though it had happened yesterday. Outside the building was a large construction dumpster with a vinyl chute going through one of the windows in the second-story lab, which was still under renovation. It was amazing how slow new building and renovation projects seemed to go.

Drew kept the brim of his hat low on his brow and his sunglasses in place as he walked by the lab and across the street to the union. The events of that Friday night replayed in his mind, step by step, to the time he went unconscious.

Did it really happen?

He went through the front doors of the union and then turned and leaned against the entrance sidewall as if he were waiting for someone. The scene in front of him was the same as the picture Ben had shown him months earlier. He took a deep breath and looked across the street to the physics lab. He didn't believe in fate or destiny, but he couldn't deny the strange and compelling feeling that there was a purpose to all of this.

He reached into his pocket, pulled out his new prepaid cell phone, and dialed Sydney's number. After three rings, she answered.

"Hello?"

"Hi, Sydney."

"Who is this?"

Something caught the corner of Drew's eye, and he turned. A dark wisp of something disappeared up the stairs leading into the main foyer of the student union. Almost as if a shadow appeared and then disappeared with the flash of a camera. Whatever it was, it was gone. Drew ran up the stairs and scanned the large room filled with tables, chairs, students, and computers.

Nothing.

"Who is this?"

Drew heard the faint voice coming from the forgotten cell phone in his hand. "Sydney...it's me...Drew."

"Drew? How...how are you?"

"I'm good. I'm wondering if you have a few minutes to talk."

"Of course. I'm getting ready to go to class, but I can talk on the way. And we can talk more later if you like."

"Is there a place we can meet?" Drew looked around. Still nothing.

"Meet?" Sydney sounded confused. "Are you on campus?" Excitement lifted her voice.

"Yes."

"I've got two classes back to back right now. Can we meet after that? How long will you be here?"

Drew hesitated. It would delay him at least three hours. It was too long. "That's okay. I need to be moving on. I'll catch you another day." But he knew it was a lie.

"Wait...I'd really like to see you. Is someone with you?"

Drew frowned. Was he picking up an echo on his phone? No, the sound was coming from the mix of voices in the student union. Drew scanned the union and saw Sydney trying to load her backpack with one hand while holding her cell phone with the other.

"No...I'm alone." He started walking toward her.

"But how are you able to..."

By now he was just a few feet away. He clicked his phone off. "Get around?"

Sydney spun on the spot, dropping her phone onto the couch by her book bag. "Drew!" She reached for him as he walked toward her. With his sunglasses still on, he couldn't help the tease that entered his mind. He kept walking until he bumped into the back of the couch.

"Here." Sydney grabbed his arm. She ushered him around to the front of the couch, holding on to him... He liked that. He grabbed her hand as she helped him sit.

"How on earth did you get up those stairs by yourself? Who dropped you off?"

Drew smiled and pretended to gaze to the right of her head. "I managed." He still held her hand, and she seemed fine with it. Probably because she thought he was impaired. "How have you been, Syd?"

She smiled. "My little sister calls me that."

She looked so beautiful. He knew he shouldn't have come to see her, but he couldn't help it. His mission off the grid could last years, and he wanted to soak up every detail of her face into his memory.

"I'm fine, but how are you, Drew? What are you doing here?"

"Well, that's a long story, but the main reason I am here is to apologize to you…in person."

"Drew, you don't have to—"

"Yes, I do." He squeezed her hand a little tighter. "I was a real jerk when you came to visit me. You were trying to be nice, and I…well, I'm sorry. You're an awesome girl, and I had no right to treat you like that."

He watched her out of the corner of his eye. She lowered her head and appeared quite moved. Now he was starting to feel like a jerk again.

"Hey, I know you have to go so—"

"No." She put her other hand on top of Drew's. "I'm going to skip this class… I want to talk to you."

"You sure?"

"Positive."

"Even if I were to tell you that I haven't been completely honest with you?"

Sydney frowned. She stared at him in silence.

"Not about the apology. I really am sorry, and am again." He shook his head. "Oh, never mind."

He reached up with his free hand and removed his sunglasses, then looked straight into her eyes. Sydney's face transformed from confusion to elation and back to confusion again. She lifted one hand and waved it in front of his eyes. He lifted his hand and waved back.

"Hi there."

"How… I thought… This is *incredible*!"

Drew laughed. He loved the expression on her face. She looked down and realized she was still holding his hand.

"You are a jerk!" She withdrew her hand, but her smile didn't diminish. "What happened? Can you really see?"

Drew nodded. "Will you forgive me? Again?"

Sydney still looked stunned and ignored his question. "How? Did the doctors find something to help you?"

Drew told her the story of his recovery, leaving out any references to the invaders. They talked for almost an hour, and Drew was glad he had stopped to see her. The warmth of their conversation delighted him. Sydney had a test in her next class, so it was time to leave. He walked her to her class, which was on the second floor of Bisimee Hall. At the doorway, she seemed hesitant to leave. This time he would be the one to walk away.

"It was good to see you, Syd," Drew said with a crooked smile.

"You too, Drew." She reached out and touched his arm, and though he had learned to control his sensitivity to most things, Sydney's touch was something else. Hundreds of synaptic waves flowed up and down his arm.

"It's probably going to be a while before I see you again, so you take care, okay?" Drew nodded.

"Next break, when I get back to Rivercrest, maybe we can get a cup of coffee."

Drew raised an eyebrow. "I thought that was something you didn't want to do."

Sydney looked away. "Yeah…I know, but I've been praying, and I am convinced that God hasn't given up on you. And I haven't either. In fact, I think God has big plans for you."

Drew smiled. If she wanted to believe in fairy tales, that was all right by him, as long as he had a chance with her.

"I'll look forward to that coffee," he said, knowing full well it would never happen. The ache returned to his heart with surprising force, but there was no way out. The momentum of his life was gathering.

Drew walked away from Sydney's class wondering if he would ever see her again. He made his way toward the stairway and descended to the platform of the first half of the flight of stairs leading to the main floor. He was in a mix of a dozen or so students and turned to walk down the second half of the flight of stairs.

That's when he saw them.

Two massive alien warriors walked through the double doors into the building, swords drawn. The students strolled by them, headed to their next classes in complete ignorance. Drew froze, and the guy behind him slammed into his back. The student cursed, but Drew paid him no attention. His eyes were fixated on the warriors at the bottom of the stairwell.

They were looking for something...or someone. The hatred in their eyes spewed out onto the crowd of unsuspecting students. Drew's senses peaked and his mind began registering every sight and sound around him. A young man entered the doorway and stood next to the warriors. He looked human, but there was something different about him. The man turned his head from side to side, but there was a delay in his face as he turned, almost as if he had two faces and one lagged behind the other. It was a strange and deathly trio—two alien warriors and one two-faced human. Was this how an alien could take complete control of a human? Dread built within him as he realized what was happening. One of the warriors spoke something to the man, and he opened his coat to reveal a semiautomatic MP5 submachine gun with at least six thirty-two-round 9 mm clips.

Drew jumped back and screamed for the students to go back. Within seconds, there was absolute panic as the air exploded with the concussion of 9 mm rounds being fired. Shouts and screams sounded all around him. When he saw three students collapse at the bottom of the stairs, he turned and pushed the students behind him back up the stairs.

"Go back! Go *back*!"

Time slowed down as Drew's mind and senses accelerated to a level he had never experienced before. He watched as a string of bullets tore into the wall at his left. His mind registered snapshots of the bullets in their trajectory. He reached down to help a girl below him climb back up the stairs. She screamed and collapsed as Drew pulled her upward.

He glanced up and saw the two warriors standing guard over the man as he sprayed bullets into terrorized students as fast as the semiautomatic action of the rifle allowed. The malevolence on his face matched that of the alien warriors guarding him. Then one of the warriors turned and rushed back out through the front doors. Drew only got a glimpse, but it looked as though two more alien warriors were approaching with swords drawn. Somehow they looked different. Drew's attention fell back to the gunman. For one moment, the man looked right at Drew, and it sent chills up and down his spine. The man brought the MP5 to bear on Drew, and Drew pulled the girl clear just as another burst of bullets tore into the concrete stairs beside them. Drew and seven other students made it to the second floor, but the girl he was helping had been shot in the leg and was hysterical.

"We have to tell everyone up here to get out of the building. Tell them to take the south stairs!" Drew shouted, but only two guys and one girl heard him. The other four were already running down the hall. Drew lifted the girl in his arms and ran toward Sydney's classroom. He burst into the room, ignoring the professor's initial exclamations of protest.

"There's a gunman on the first floor. Take the south stairs and get out of the building *now*!"

The blood from the girl's wound was all the evidence needed to convince everyone in the classroom. Drew walked toward the two closest male students. "You two—take her and get out quickly!"

Drew scanned the room for Sydney and motioned for her to come to him. He realized the two students were stunned and had not yet moved. He set the girl beside them.

"Move!"

They jumped up, and each took one of the girl's arms and supported her over their shoulders. Then they rushed toward the exit as dozens of students followed.

"I'll check to make sure the hall is clear first." Drew pushed his way to the front of the doorway. He carefully opened the door to a corridor that was rising to alarm. There was no sign of the gunman yet, but Drew could hear screams below him and more 9 mm rounds echoing throughout the building. The pause in gunfire told him the gunman was reloading.

"Go!"

The first few students, including the two carrying the injured girl, rushed through the doorway, but then students at the back pushed and a bottleneck formed.

"Don't push!" the professor yelled at the students near the back.

Twenty of the thirty-four students had made it into the hall when the gunshots resumed and the terror increased. Drew could tell that the gunman was at the top of the stairs now.

"Go back. He's in the hallway!" But two more students bolted out into the open anyway.

Crack…crack…crack!

Drew saw one of the students fall as he pushed the remaining twelve students, including Sydney, back into the classroom. He looked at Sydney, and the absolute terror on her face was painful to see. It made Drew angry…angry that someone could cause such fear in the hearts of innocent people. He hated these invaders. Could it be— Was everything bad that had ever happened in the earth their doing?

"We must stay calm and we'll get through this," he said.

"What about the window?" one student suggested.

"It will be at least a twelve-foot jump, but it's worth a try…if we have time." Drew looked at the professor. He was a short, balding man, but he kept his wits about him.

"We need to block the door to give the students more time," the professor said.

Drew nodded. He turned to the remaining students. "Try the window— I'll work on the door. If we run out of time, get to the back of the room and stay low."

The only thing movable in the entire room was one table near the front. They quickly turned it on its side and put it across the doorway.

"Stay clear of the door," Drew said as he and the professor each held the ends of the table near the wall and crouched low to the floor. Drew realized that Sydney had stayed with him. She crouched down beside him.

"Drew."

At the quiver in her voice, Drew put a hand to her cheek. "I'm going to get you out of this."

Sydney nodded, then flinched as a fresh burst of gunshots rang out near their doorway.

"The windows don't open!" one student shouted in near panic across the room.

There wasn't enough time.

"Get to the back," Drew said.

Sydney ran to the back with the other students and slunk down behind the seats that were bolted to the floor.

No one but Drew saw what happened next, and it frightened him in the worst of ways. The alien warrior protecting the gunman walked right through the door and into the classroom. The solid door gave marginal resistance, but that was all. Drew couldn't help but stare at him. The alien was massive and stood nearly seven feet tall. His grisly sword drawn, he scanned the room with a scowl on his face. When his gaze fell on Drew, Drew looked away toward the professor and held up his finger to his lips, hoping to hide his ability to see into this secret dimension of the alien. He chanced a look back toward the alien, and this time, there was no hiding the fact that he could see him. Their eyes locked for a moment, and fear gripped Drew. A fear rivaled only by the terror he felt the first time he saw an alien. Then it dawned on him.

What if...

The aliens and the gunman might be here for one reason: to kill Drew.

But how did they know he was here? And they did all this for one person? His heart sank as he considered all the innocent people dying because of the aliens' hunt for him. He thought of Sydney cowering at the back of the room, waiting to die...all because of him. He knew at that moment that he could never hide from these beings.

Drew slowly stood and looked straight into the alien's eyes. They were very dark...black, in fact. There was no iris of color to soften the harsh gaze. Surprise flashed across the alien's face, followed by a fierce contempt and absolute hatred.

"What are you doing?" the professor cried out.

Drew saw the alien's lips move as though he were barking out a command. Drew heard nothing, but it was evident that someone else had. The door handle turned and pushed against the table barricade. Drew fell to the floor and resumed his position against the table. Seconds later, splinters flew as five rounds exploded through the door. Drew and the professor held their ground as the gunman tried to push his way through the door, screaming obscenities. The alien warrior thrust the tip of his blade into the floor between the door and the table and forced the table away from the door with each push of the gunman. Drew was astonished that the same sword that just moments earlier had passed through the door was now able to force the table to move.

Drew pushed with all his might but to no avail. The force of the invisible alien combined with the gunman was too great. Just as the gunman was bringing the barrel of his 9 mm to bear, Drew saw a flash of light burst through the window. At first he wondered if the police had thrown concussion grenades into the classroom, but that was not the case. He chanced a quick look and was astounded yet again at what he saw.

Another alien warrior with sword drawn had charged into the room from the outer wall and stood just as tall, just as fierce, and just as massive as the one helping the gunman, but there was a different air about him. He was dressed in a white thigh-length coat and a close-fit mock T-shirt. The mix of his ancient weapon and his modern apparel was paradoxical. Was this alien the commander of this assault team?

No sooner had this white-dressed alien arrived than the dark alien warrior reached into his trench coat and pulled out a Glock 21 .45-caliber semiautomatic pistol while yanking his sword out of the floor and away from the door. This released the force on the table, and it slammed onto the barrel of the gunman's weapon just as he fired three rounds into the classroom. The professor screamed and grabbed his leg. Drew stared, stunned.

These two aliens were not allies, but enemies.

The white-dressed warrior reacted with blazing speed, and in the next few seconds, Drew witnessed a one-on-one duel beyond any human experience.

The light warrior rushed…no *flew* toward the dark warrior, his sword leading the way. But in that fraction of a moment, the dark warrior aimed and squeezed off two rounds.

Drew's mouth fell open when he watched the light warrior deflect the first bullet with the flat of his sword and then tilt his chest just enough to dodge the second bullet. Now both warriors' swords were out of position, and the aliens collided with devastating force. They slammed into the wall, and this time it was as solid for them as it was for Drew. He could not understand the apparent change in material states from one moment to the next. It was a bizarre and unearthly duel.

In the fray that followed, the light warrior dislodged the gun from the dark warrior's grip, and it flew across the floor. Drew watched in amazement as the weapon slowly dissolved in greenish wisps of vapor until it disappeared from sight. Drew thought how much it looked like dry ice sublimating. The dark warrior drove a powerful fist into the light warrior's chest, which threw him back and away about five feet. Both warriors brought their swords to bear on each other in a blaze of flashing steel.

Sound exploded in Drew's ear and forced his attention back to the world of humans. The professor was trying to crawl away from the gunman's aim through the crack in the door. Once the professor moved, the gunman slammed his body up against the door and forced his way into the room. Drew tried to gain his feet, but the door hit him hard and he stumbled backward. He recovered and stood up, only to see the gunman's darkened eyes glaring at him. A twisted, evil smile was on his double face, and he reveled in the moment of terror he was causing his captives.

Drew stepped backward, but there was no escape.

He had seen countless movies of aliens inhabiting humans, but never in his wildest dreams did he think it was possible. Ben had believed it, and now so did Drew. Without movement, the features of the alien inside this man aligned closely with the man's. His hands, face, legs—every part of him had a very slight double image. There was a darkness in the windows of this inhabited man's eyes that forced Drew to admit the existence of a universal evil.

A few feet to the gunman's right, the silent duel between alien warriors continued. Drew allowed one momentary glance that direction just in time to see the light warrior parry a thrust, then counter with a slice across the dark warrior's right shoulder. It tore open his coat, and blood oozed through his garment. The dark warrior recoiled. Simultaneously the gunman aimed his MP5 straight at Drew's chest, now ten feet away.

"No!"

Sydney's scream came from the back of the room. Drew saw the gunman's finger tighten as he squeezed the trigger. Once again, Drew's senses flew into overdrive, and he heard the trigger mechanism release. But at the exact same moment, the light warrior's blade sliced through the submachine gun. The firing pin jammed a fraction of an inch before hitting the primer on the next round.

Time froze, and Drew stood paralyzed by the knowledge that his execution had been delayed. He knew what he should do, but his arms and legs felt locked in amber resin. Jake had taught him to react instantly when his life was on the line, but never had he faced something like this outside of his training. He watched as the MP5 fell to the ground in slow motion and then again as the gunman pulled out of a holster the same Glock 21 handgun that the alien warrior had fired just seconds earlier. It made no sense! None of this did.

"Drew!"

Sydney's shout was long and slow, but it shook him from his paralysis. By now the gunman was just lifting the barrel of the pistol to Drew's chest. Drew launched himself toward the gunman, hoping to cover the ten feet between them before he got a shot off, but it was not to be. Drew saw the man's finger tighten once again, and this time the saving alien warrior was too far and too encumbered with his fight to do anything. Before the gun fired, Drew knew exactly what path the bullet would fly. He dropped his right shoulder just as the gun began its recoil. He felt and heard the bullet whiz past his right ear and then heard the deafening explosion of the shot. He dived the last four feet toward the man. He could smell the burned powder from the barrel as he passed. Drew heard another shot go off, but it coincided with the powerful impact of his shoulder into the man's abdomen. Drew slammed the man up against the front wall of the classroom, and his head hit the wall with a thump.

Drew scrambled for control over the man, but it was not necessary—the gunman was unconscious. The alien inside him, however, was not. The being was writhing about as if trying to force his unconscious host to rise up. It unnerved Drew to no end. He grabbed the gun and aimed it at the man, not sure whether to pull the trigger. He chanced a quick look over his shoulder just in time to see the light alien thrust his sword through the dark alien's chest. Blood spilled from the wound, and the alien fell to the floor.

Drew felt like he was in some bizarre science fiction movie, and he wanted it to stop, but the oddity continued. As the dark warrior clutched his chest and gasped, his body dissolved just like the gun, but this time, the wisps of green vapor fell down through the floor. Everything about him dissolved, including his spilled blood, until there was nothing.

Drew shook his head and refocused on the gunman and his writhing invader. What should he do? Just then the white-dressed alien came and knelt down over the gunman. There was a brief and obviously contrary verbal exchange, and then the light warrior slammed his fist into the head of the gunman...and the alien. The gunman's body jerked, and both he and the alien invader became perfectly still. The light alien warrior turned his head and looked up at Drew. Drew forced himself not to look into his eyes but continued to stare at the face of the unconscious gunman. The moment hung forever. The light alien tilted his head, and Drew knew he suspected something.

Though Drew dared not look directly at his face, the alien's gaze was different than that of his fallen enemy. His pale-blue eyes were just as piercing as the black eyes of the dark alien, but not as terrifying. Just when Drew felt he could take it no more, the alien fell through the floor and disappeared.

Did he know?

"You'd better put that gun down before the police get here or they might shoot you instead," the professor said from the corner by the door.

Drew realized that the professor was exactly right, but he didn't dare release the gun...not yet. No one here saw what he saw in the man.

"Get something to tie this guy up," Drew yelled over his shoulder to the other students. Slowly—much too slowly—the students came forward to help. Sydney was one of the first. Two guys found a belt to tie the gunman's hands.

Sydney touched Drew's back. "Are you okay?"

"Yes...see if you can help the professor. Somebody else call 911 and tell them what happened so they don't come storming in and shoot somebody."

He could hear one of the girls trying to explain the events to the 911 operator, but she was having a hard time keeping her composure.

Drew heard heavy footsteps coming down the hallway.

"They're coming. Is he secure?"

"Yeah," one of the students replied.

"Everybody sit down at the far wall—now." When everyone was ready, Drew motioned for Sydney to sit at the end, and he sat next to her. He released the magazine from the gun and slid the gun along the floor to the back of the room.

"Put your hands up with your palms out so they can see they are empty." Drew took a deep breath, closed his eyes, and lowered his head. His eyes and head hurt. It felt like a massive headache was coming on strong.

What just happened? There was so much to process...so much to think about. He reasoned that if any of this had anything to do with him, the people he cared about were in real danger, and his plan to leave had come none to soon.

He felt Sydney lean against him.

He turned and looked at her. "How are you doing?"

"I was so scared, Drew. Praise God you didn't get shot." Her voice trembled.

Drew didn't respond. He was captivated by a subtle bluish glow dancing close to and all around her body. Were his eyes playing tricks on him? It was almost as though some sort of living plasma emanated from the pores of her skin, but there was nothing he had ever seen before that he could compare it to. He reached over and touched her cheek with the back of his hand, and the glow wrapped around his fingers but stayed close to her cheek.

"Remarkable..." He spoke without thinking.

"I know. He was watching over you." Sydney leaned into his touch. Whether it was her fear or something else that had made her soften toward him, it didn't matter—it was going to be hard to leave her. And yet, he was being catapulted out of her life again. It seemed that every possible force in the universe was working to keep them apart.

"I'm not going back to Rivercrest, Sydney."

She looked at him, her eyes wide and questioning.

"I'm leaving, and I don't know when I'll be back." Drew withdrew his hand. "I'm going to find Ben, but no one can know where I'm at."

"I don't understand… Why?"

"It's complicated, but it has to do with things like this." Drew motioned toward the chaos that had just happened. He reached into his pocket and pulled out the keys to his Mustang.

"They're going to have the campus on lockdown, and I have to leave without being identified."

Sydney looked scared and concerned.

"Please just trust me." He took her hand and put his keys in her palm. "I need you to take my car."

"No, Drew…I won't—"

"Please, Sydney. I need you to do this for me. When they open campus up, get it off campus and back home. Please?"

Sydney nodded. "What is going on, Drew?"

Drew wanted to tell her…wanted to open her eyes and convince her of the truth, of the foolishness of her religious beliefs, but it was impossible.

"You're an amazing girl, and I hope that one day I can explain it all to you, but for now I just have to disappear."

"Disappear? How will I find you?"

He touched her cheek once more. There would be no finding him. Just then the door flew open and smashed into the table that was still partially obstructing its swing. Six SWAT team members exploded into the room shouting for everyone to keep their hands where they could see them. The professor quickly explained the situation, and the tension diffused.

Outside, emergency personnel were everywhere. Police were taking testimonies from the uninjured, and the EMTs were treating the injured. News crews were interviewing anyone who would talk to them. Parents and friends of students began showing up as well as hundreds of curious bystanders. In all the chaos, Drew slipped into the crowd and slowly lost himself in the confusion. Planning his exit from the crowd, he glanced back toward Bisimee Hall and spotted three dark invaders in deep discussion near the entrance. One of the three appeared to have authority, just as the one he had first seen back in Rivercrest. He seemed angry and began barking commands. The sight of him made Drew quiver. Drew exited the crowd on the far side away from the invaders and navigated through vehicles and buildings.

The campus was on lockdown just as he had suspected. All the roads leading in and out were barricaded, and police were in the process of blocking foot traffic. It took twenty minutes for him to find a way off campus without being seen. He called for a taxi and was driven to the bus station. He needed to leave town fast, and the next bus to Chicago didn't leave for another five hours. He checked routes and then paid cash for a ticket to Des Moines, Iowa, under his pseudonym, Ryan Johnson.

The bus would leave in a little over an hour, and it would at least get him out of town and in the right direction. Because he was early, he was the sole occupant of the station. He sat down far enough away so that he could see the entire room and both the entrances and the exits. He pulled the back off his cell phone and popped the battery out—no more texts or calls. His head pounded in the wake of the adrenaline rush. He was exhausted, but he could not sleep. There was too much to think about—so many questions and nowhere, or no one, to turn to for answers. He pulled the bottle of ibuprofen out of his backpack and swallowed three, then chased them with some water from his water bottle. He returned the water and ibuprofen to his pack, grateful that he had thought to wear his backpack when he left his car. He had his money, ID, a change of clothes, some granola bars, and a few survival items that Jake had told him to carry at all times. There were many things he would have to replace or do without, including his gun. Losing the bulk of his supplies at the beginning of the mission was not good. At least he had the essentials.

He leaned his heavy head back against the cold, hard bricks of the station and closed his eyes. Visions of invaders with swords and guns filled his mind. Although he was sure these beings were from another world, he wasn't convinced they were actually aliens. Just…invaders.

He replayed the horrific scene from Drayle, trying hard to remember every little detail.

"Mommy, look at me!"

At the little girl's squeaky voice, Drew opened his eyes just wide enough to see that a woman and her little girl had entered the station. The little girl's ebony face was framed by black curly hair with pigtails tied up with pink ribbons. She was balancing on a narrow brick ledge that bordered a handicap ramp leading up to the exit door on the far side of the large waiting room. Twenty feet away, her mother was talking to the attendant at the ticket window.

Drew took a deep, relaxing breath. Thank goodness Sydney was okay, but so many had lost their lives in the attack. It weighed heavy on his heart.

Drew was about to close his eyes again, but then his heart jolted as he saw a man with a hooded sweatshirt and dark glasses enter the station door to his right. Although he looked threatening, it was the large, dark figure that walked through the closing doors behind him that caused Drew's senses to ramp up.

Not again.

The invader whispered into the hooded man's ear, and he looked toward the little girl. The mother was deep in conversation with the attendant and was not yet aware of the potential danger. Drew sat up and glared at the man. Why would an invader bother with such trivial things as a little girl if they were working toward world domination?

The hooded man took a few steps toward the girl, and the invader smiled a wretched, evil smile. Drew shuddered and his heart pounded. He had the vantage point to study the chiseled face of the invader more completely than any other he had seen. The invader's black eyes were likes holes into an empty abyss, and his sickening grin caused Drew to wonder at the darkness within the heart of this invader.

Drew stood, but just then, from behind him, another invader flew into the room with sword drawn. This invader looked similar to the one who had helped Drew at the university just a few hours ago. His cream-colored cloak did little to hide his taut, bulging muscles. He positioned himself between the little girl and the dark invader, who reached for his sword but didn't draw. Instead he backed away without losing his evil grin. Drew wondered at the scene between the dark and light invaders and realized that the hooded man was still moving toward the little girl, who had now walked far enough up the ledge that she was no longer in view of her mother. The light invader turned and looked at the little girl. His countenance was both fierce and anxious.

Drew started walking toward the scene. His approach was to the left and behind the hooded man. The light invader glared at both of the approaching men, and Drew tried to look beyond him to the girl. He quickened his pace to try to catch up to the hooded man, but he was going to be too late.

"Be careful, little girl!" Drew called out when the hooded man was just five feet away from her. Drew was another five feet behind him. Drew's call startled the hooded man, and he jerked about to look at Drew. At the same time, the light invader swung his sword toward the man's feet. He tripped and fell forward. When he put an arm out to stop his fall, a knife that had been concealed in his hand and sleeve went sliding across the floor.

He hit the hard tile with a thump, then rolled toward the knife. At the same time, the dark invader drew his sword lightning fast and flew toward the light invader for an attack. Drew ran to the little girl and grabbed her hand. She screamed. The light invader took a dangerous split-second glance toward Drew in between two sword cuts and looked as though he was going to abandon the dark invader to come after him.

"Let's go see your mom." Drew kept an eye on the fleeing hooded man.

"Charity!" the woman screamed from the ticket counter, and began running toward them. The little girl wiggled her hand loose from Drew and ran for her mother. The woman's face was filled with terror and anger. Drew saw the dark invader retreat and follow after the hooded man.

Drew held up his hands. "There was a man with a knife, ma'am. I was just trying to help."

She swooped the girl, who was now crying, up in her arms. "I'm going to call the police!"

In his peripheral vision, Drew saw the light invader sheathe his sword, cross his arms, and stare at him.

Drew backed up. "I was just trying to help," Drew pleaded, pointing in the direction that the man had fled, but there was no one there. The woman hurried back to the office ticket window and began pointing and talking. Drew went to his backpack and considered making a run for it. No matter what he did, he could not get a break. He had seconds to decide. He calculated the risks and came to the conclusion that if he got detained by the police and then connected to the university shooting, it would all be over. Even if he was released, he figured every alien invader, both good and bad, would know of him and of his location.

He looked to see what the woman was doing and noticed that the light invader was whispering to the little girl.

Drew threw his backpack over his shoulder and started making his way toward the exit. The woman looked toward him, and it seemed as though another scene was about to unfold. He quickened his pace. The light invader was still beside the little girl, but he was just watching now. The woman looked much less hysterical as she put the little girl on the ground and held her hand. They started walking to intercept Drew, and he wasn't sure what to do. He reached the door.

"Mister?" the woman called out.

Drew stopped with his hand on the door.

"I'm very sorry. I was just scared for my daughter."

Drew didn't relax. He still wasn't sure if he should stay or go.

"The ticket office said you bought a ticket to Des Moines, and Charity said that the man with the knife was scary. I figure you must be telling the truth."

Drew relaxed and took a breath. "I'm just glad she's okay." He smiled at the little girl.

"I guess I'm just a little on edge with the school shooting and all. This is getting to be a crazy world."

Drew focused on the invader behind the woman while appearing to look at her. "Isn't that the truth."

The three of them sat down and talked as the station began filling with people. Drew was in the most awkward of situations, with the light invader standing nearby—he simply wouldn't leave—and Drew suspected he was waiting to find out information about him. It took every bit of his concentration to ignore the hulking form as he asked Charity what the name of her puppy was. He kept asking questions so he wouldn't have to answer any about himself.

About thirty minutes later, a bus arrived with Charity's grandpa. Drew watched the family talk briefly, and then the man came to shake Drew's hand and thank him. As they left the station, Charity turned and waved at him, and he waved back. Strangely the light invader left with them.

Drew breathed a sigh of relief.

He boarded his bus and tried to lose himself in the far back corner seat. The ibuprofen took the edge off, but he was left to fight through the dull ache that remained. There was so much to process—so much to think about. Could the light invaders be trusted? They were obviously at war with the dark invaders, but why? Would mankind be any better off if they won the war? Wouldn't humans still be conquered? Did the hooded man and the little girl actually hear the whispers of the invaders?

Drew struggled to put the pieces of this crazy puzzle together. So far, however, none of the pieces fit. He looked out the window, thankful he would soon be moving away from the chaos. He could smell the diesel from the bus's engine as the last few passengers climbed the steps into the cabin. Drew leaned his head against the window's cold glass, and he started to feel his body relax.

He closed his eyes and heard the bus driver make his destination call. When he opened his eyes, condensation from his breath had collected on the window around his face...

But it did not completely obscure the two ominous dark forms standing just outside the bus.

15

ESCAPE AND EVASION

A lump formed in Drew's throat. He had seen both of these invaders before. He wiped the condensation away from the bus window to see more clearly. One of the invaders was the one who had tried to manipulate the hooded man into kidnapping or harming Charity. The other was bigger, darker, and more ominous.

Although he couldn't be sure, Drew believed him to be the commanding invader he had seen at the university outside Bisimee Hall. His skin crawled as he looked at the black-eyed invader he decided to dub "Kurgan," after a brutal enemy in some old movie he had seen.

Kurgan was listening carefully to whatever the first invader was telling him. Drew wanted to scream to the bus driver to leave, but he'd only draw attention to himself. The driver moved as if he had all day long. The doors closed as the lesser invader pointed first to the station and then to the bus. The commanding invader lifted his gaze to the bus, and Drew recoiled from the window. He stopped breathing and froze. Had they connected him to the two tragedies he helped avert? How could he hide from such beings if they were onto him?

Drew watched, horror creeping through him, as the lesser invader materialized through the bus doors and scanned its interior, studying each unsuspecting passenger. Drew ducked behind the seat in front of him and untied his shoe, then slowly began tying it. He looked forward through his eyebrows, watching the aisle for any movement. The first large black studded boot set down in the aisle to his left, and Drew could imagine the sound would have been heavy and dark. The other boot stepped up beside the first, and Drew felt like throwing up.

The invader was waiting for him.

There was no escape.

There was no hiding.

The bus lurched forward, and Drew noticed that the invader stepped slightly forward to balance himself. Drew made a mental note that the laws of momentum and gravity still applied to the invaders, at least to some degree. Drew finished tying his shoe and decided to continue to play ignorant. He straightened and didn't glance toward the invader, but instead took his coat and bunched it into the corner behind his head. He leaned against it and closed his eyes, trying hard to convince himself that this was just a bad dream. Would the invader hear or even see his racing heart? Or perhaps—the unthinkable—could he read Drew's mind?

Ten long, agonizing minutes clicked by, and Drew could almost feel the dark presence near him. The front-right wheel of the bus hit a bump in the road, and Drew used the jerking motion as an excuse to rouse himself from his act of slumber. He looked first out the window, then scanned left through the inner cabin of the bus until he saw the menacing form of the invader still standing…staring…waiting just two feet away.

At any moment, Drew expected a grisly blade to cut through his body, or a serial killer to start shooting people on the bus, or the engine to explode into flames, but the agony continued in a dull, aching glare of torture. Drew forced a deep breath into his lungs, then chose to stare out the window, away from the invader. If he was to die, then so be it. Perhaps he was still there because he didn't know what he was looking for. Drew's mind raced with a hundred bizarre possibilities. The mile markers ticked by as he replayed every fraction of every moment that had transpired both at the university and back at the bus station. And then he did it again…and again…and again, mostly to distract himself from his unwelcome and menacing observer, but also to learn and to remember.

And so the journey continued, with Drew always under the watching glare of the dark invader. One thing was for certain—if he survived the trip, he could not continue on to Chicago, at least not yet. Searching for Ben with his enemy seeing his every move would destroy his mission before it began. He had to hide his final destination from the invaders at all cost. What should he do?

"When facing an enemy, first control your area of engagement."

Jake's words whispered through him, and he knew what he needed to do.

By the time the bus stopped in Des Moines, Iowa, Drew had a plan. He found the ticket window and purchased another ticket to Duluth, Minnesota. An hour and a half later, Drew was back on a bus heading north. The night wore on, as did the ever-glaring gaze and presence of the dark invader. Fatigue tore at him mercilessly.

Somewhere in the night, Drew found exhaustion a companion enough to let him sleep a couple of hours despite the invader. By early morning, he was in Duluth and hitchhiking a ride north into the Superior National Forest. The thick pine, fir, and mountain ash forests welcomed Drew like old friends. The Boundary Waters in the Superior National Forest was one of Jake and Drew's favorite places to camp. And it was the easiest environment in which to survive, as long as the temperatures didn't get too subzero.

The forest's nearly four million acres of woods and lakes was the perfect place to lose himself from humanity.

He stopped at a shop near the park border and picked up a few more survival essentials, including a map of the forest. Three days after the Drayle University incident, Drew was deep in the wooded wilderness of northern Minnesota. Though it was late spring and the weather was still a little cool, Drew was happy to be there.

All through the journey, the invader watched and waited. At first it was eerie, but Drew learned to cope. And then he realized this might even prove to be beneficial. It could allow him the opportunity to study his enemy up close and personal. His biggest concern was whether he would survive if the invader decided to attack him in some way. He was still unsure about how such an attack might happen. So far it seemed to be through other humans or by apparent natural events. Perhaps, since he could see his enemy and his actions, he could avoid such events. Only time would tell, but the cost of failure might be his very life.

Drew hiked another three days north toward the Canadian border and set up a camp in the most secluded and isolated area he could find near one of the larger lakes. He continued his act of ignorance toward the invader, taking mental note of every action and inaction he observed. Drew put his survival skills to use. He had to admit that at first it was a little uncomfortable not being able to rely on Jake, but within a week, his confidence grew as he realized just how perfectly Jake had prepared him. Fresh water was not a problem, and the mild climate made shelter a cinch. The forest was abundant in plant and animal food, so he settled into the game of wait and watch.

As the days became weeks, Drew thought often of the angst he must have caused his mother. He tried not to think about it too much. At least she had Jake with her to help her deal with it.

Don't drop your guard, Jake, and take care of her.

By the third week Drew still hadn't fallen to some evil scheme of the invader. In fact, the invader seemed more agitated and annoyed as the days wore on. Seeing a massive dark invader so irritated was unnerving, to say the least. Drew guessed that the reason he hadn't yet been attacked was because the invader was restricted by orders of observation only.

One afternoon while he was sunning on a large boulder on the shore of the lake, the invader paced back and forth and then began screaming at Drew; at least that's what it appeared to be. At one point he came to within inches of Drew's face, and something changed. Drew could feel anxiety rise, and thoughts that did not seem his own pierced his mind. Fear welled up, and bizarre thoughts of suicide entered his mind. He shook his head and ran his fingers through his lengthy hair and beard, but it didn't help.

The invader continued his raging bursts of assault on him, and Drew wanted to run away, but he knew it would be pointless. He stood up and paced back and forth on the massive boulder overhanging the lake's shoreline. The internal turmoil the invader was causing confused and angered Drew. Was this how they controlled the fate of mankind?

When Drew thought he couldn't take it anymore and he feared he couldn't hide the fact that he could see the invader any longer, he did the only thing he could think of: he jumped into the icy-cold water of the lake. The shock of the cold on his heightened senses freed him from the mental and emotional turmoil caused by the invader. He figured it would be a brief reprieve once the invader followed him, but that was not to be. The invader's ranting continued with even greater vigor—but he didn't enter the water. Drew swam a hundred yards along the shoreline in an attempt to warm his body with exertion, and when his skin became too numb to continue, he moved toward the shore.

The invader finally stopped his silent attack, but fury was upon his face. Drew expected the onslaught to start again, but as he waded through the shallow water, he pretended to be preoccupied with an odd-shaped rock a few feet from the bank. Though his feet were numb, his experiment was too valuable to quit just yet. He stayed offshore long enough to convince himself that the invader wouldn't enter the water.

How bizarre.

And what intriguing and incredibly valuable information.

Drew built a large fire and dried himself and his clothes in its warmth while eating a delicious meal of dried rabbit and pine-needle soup made from the fresh light-colored tips of a budding pine tree. He flavored the soup with some wild honey he had recovered from a hive. The meal and this newly discovered information delighted him. He tilted the tin bowl to finish off the last bit of soup and felt something change. There was a lifting of a dark burden. He lowered the tin bowl—

The invader was gone.

Drew was careful not to come to conclusions and was also careful not to become too intent on searching for the invader, just in case the creature was watching him from afar. Instead, he forced himself to continue his usual routine.

To Drew's dismay, less than an hour later the invader was back. That night Drew lay awake into the wee hours of the night, thinking and plotting.

The next day, there was marked change in the invader's actions. The brute was no longer just an observer—he became a tormentor. It started out with little episodes of frustration—multiple ant bites, spilled water can, collapsing leg of his shelter, and getting treed by a curious black bear—all the direct result of the invader's actions and influence. Clearly, the invader was attempting to encourage Drew to move on to his final destination.

That's when Drew decided to take an expedition west along the shore of the lake, but it was so big that he could not circumnavigate the lake in a day. He spotted a small river that spilled into the lake on the southeastern edge. At the mouth of the river, jagged rocks jutted out of the shallow water. It was here that Drew discovered a treasure.

From somewhere upstream, an old makeshift raft had been lodged onto the rocks. It would require extensive repair, but it would do. Drew began patching up the raft, and it agitated the invader to no end, who made every task a frustrating one. By noon of the next day, Drew made his maiden voyage out onto the peaceful calm waters of the lake...without an enemy at his side to torment him. Drew loved it, and the voyage solidified his recent discovery about the invader—he would not go into the water. What Drew wasn't certain about was whether this would hold true for all invaders or just this particular one. At the very least, he could use this information to his immediate advantage. New plans formed in his mind, and for the first time in weeks, Drew became hopeful that his mission might not yet have failed.

He continued his voyage using a long steering pole and a makeshift paddle and navigated across the lake back to his camp. When he arrived, his everpresent invader was waiting, scowling, and cursing. When Drew gathered wood that night, the invader drew his sword and caused him to stumble over an exposed root of a large tree. When Drew caught himself on the trunk, his hand was pierced by a sharp twig, which coincided with a quick slice of the grisly sword. The wound was deeper and worse than it should have been.

Next he dealt with a couple of wasp stings. He was quite miserable that night, but the knowledge that he had frustrated his enemy was consolation. Surely the dark invader could do worse than a small cut and a couple of wasp stings. What was he waiting for?

Over the next few days, Drew put rafting into his routine, and he noticed a pattern by the invader. Each time Drew came back to camp, the invader was gone for a while, but he always returned. Drew lengthened his time out in the raft each day until he had conditioned the invader to disappear for over two hours. He also made sure to take his pack with various items for his excursions. When the routine was established, he was ready to make his move.

Drew woke up early and trapped a couple of tree squirrels to cook for lunch; then he prepared his camp as though he would return for lunch, packed his bag, and set out onto the lake on his raft. He navigated straight into the middle, but this time he continued across to the opposite southern shore. At first he acted as though he was just extending the day's excursion by prepping the raft for a return voyage. Once he felt certain that he was alone, he cut the ropes holding the raft together and dismantled it. He took the extra time needed to hide all evidence of the raft components.

And then he ran.

He ran for ten minutes straight into the woods and stopped. When he was sure he was alone, he changed his direction ninety degrees and set a running pace that he could handle for the next hour. Still no invader. He rested ten minutes, then ran another hour.

Drew pushed himself to near exhaustion over the course of the day trying to put as much distance as possible between himself and the invader. He had seen how fast these invaders moved, and there was no way to know how much territory he could cover. At one point Drew collapsed beneath the cool shade of a large pine tree, his muscles screaming for him to stop.

"Get up, Carter. You only have one shot at making this work." He huffed between breaths. "Get *up*!"

If the invader did find him, he was sure that dark sword would be used for more than just pricking his hand.

Drew also reminded himself that every step away from the camp exponentially increased the area the invader would have to search, so he pushed his body until it was too dark to see the terrain.

Finally, he fell under the cover of some thick brush and slept until morning. He ate a quick breakfast and rehydrated himself, then set out again. This time he went at a pace that he could keep up all day without exhausting himself and in a direction that would take him to a small town to the west. Drew disciplined himself not to rush his escape, even if it took an extra week.

It was a long and arduous trek, but Drew never saw the invader again. Ten days later, Drew found a dumpy motel south of the forest in which to rest and clean up. He kept his hair longer than he liked and decided to keep the beard but trimmed it close. He thought about dying his hair as an extra measure but decided his new look was enough. It certainly was different than he'd ever looked before. It wouldn't fool an invader close up, but it might from a distance.

Without a credit card, Drew couldn't rent a car, and he didn't want to go back through Duluth, so he hitchhiked his way to Grand Rapids, Minnesota, and eventually made it to Minneapolis. From there he rode a bus to Chicago.

The skyline of the Windy City was a beautiful sight. There would be invaders...lots of them, but if there was one thing Drew had learned these last six weeks, it was that the invaders were not all knowing or all powerful. They had limitations—some that Drew didn't have. As frustrating as the time lost was, it encouraged Drew.

He had evaded an invader!

16

OFF THE GRID

There was something compelling about the city of Chicago, but as with every city, along with the glamor came the grunge. Those with money could insulate themselves from the dirty, desperate people who lived at the fringes of their wealth. And though it was tempting for Drew to stay suburban, he had learned from Jake that the best camouflage was in the dirt, grass, and muck. That was why the Rangers and the SEALs were so effective. They operated in places most people didn't even want to look.

In Chicago, these places were the ghettos and the slums.

It was easy to drop off the grid into the wilderness and survive, but the city would be much different, since Drew was sure the invaders were drawn to the hubs of humanity. As much as he wanted to stay off the enemy's radar, his mission was not just to disappear but to find Ben. Search and rescue while staying off the grid would be very difficult. He had to be careful, methodical, and thorough.

Drew got off the bus late in the night at the Greyhound terminal not far from downtown Chicago. A few blocks west of the station he found a cheap hotel and crashed. He slept the rest of the night and far into the afternoon of the next day. When he awoke, he downed a couple of granola bars and some water and clicked on the television. He surfed until he came across a news station doing a recap on the shooting at Drayle University, which had sparked a renewed effort by antigun lobbyists to propose a ban on semiautomatic handguns. The memory of the tragedy became fresh again as he heard the reporter state that nine students had died and seven more had been seriously wounded.

They replayed some of the interviews with the students—shock, disbelief, and tears filled the eyes and faces of the students. Drew's heart sank as he remembered that day. Had he caused it? Were the invaders targeting him, or was he just caught up in a coincidental mass shooting? Why were the invaders fighting each other? All the hundreds of unanswered questions came rushing back. After an hour of fruitless effort to make sense of what had happened that horrific day, Drew pulled out his computer and deleted his Facebook and Twitter accounts and every other web account he could remember.

The disappearance of Drew Carter was complete.

As far as he could tell, neither the human grid nor the invader grid could pinpoint him now. His mind then turned to Ben. He web searched for the building where Ben's International Science and Engineering Fair would have been held two years ago and found the Chicago Tech Center. Good.

That would be his starting point.

Jake had prepared him for wilderness, not the urban jungle, but he figured some of the same techniques with modification would still make sense and work. He located a few possible apartment buildings less than a mile from the Tech Center where he might be able to find a cheap place to stay. After many hours of searching, plotting, and planning, the enormity of the job depressed him—millions of people, hundreds of thousands of buildings and businesses, and no idea where to begin. His money was limited, so finding a source of income would become important soon. He figured he could make it two months before he had to earn income locally to sustain himself.

He mentally prepared himself to be in this for the long haul...potentially years.

He closed his laptop and leaned his head back, feeling like he alone was carrying the burden of the world on his shoulders. But no. Ben was somewhere out there, and he probably felt the same way. Two were better than one.

Do what it takes to find him, and then you have a fighting chance.

His stomach rumbled, but he was too tired to leave the room and too cautious to order out. He found some dried apples and another granola bar in his pack, devoured them, and dozed off.

WHEN MORNING BROKE on the Chicago skyline, Drew was well rested and on the street, heading toward one of the apartment buildings he had found in his Internet search yesterday. The crisp morning air bit at his cheeks, but he didn't mind. With the morning came a sense of hope, and his spirit was somewhat renewed. Drew walked south, occasionally taking a moment to catch the gleaming sunbeams streaming through the towering cityscape a mile or so to his left. He stopped in a bakery and bought a muffin and an orange juice for breakfast.

The first two apartments he checked out were unlivable. The third was certainly not the Hilton, but at least it was furnished and clean enough so that he wasn't worried about catching a disease. It was a second-floor apartment in a depressed but clean neighborhood. All the doors and windows had iron bars across them, which seemed so unnecessary in the bright morning light with birds singing and the leaves of the boulevard trees budding with new life.

Evidently the nighttime would paint a different scene for the neighborhood.

Here, the buildings were all two to three stories tall and built so close to each other that only a narrow sidewalk separated them. To the east was a small grocery store, and one block south there was a small park with playground equipment for children and picnic tables surrounded by trees.

The landlord, Mr. Dench, was a gruff old man who spoke in broken sentences.

It took Drew a few minutes to adjust before he could understand him.

"Rent the first erry mawnth. Late...you out. Got it?"

Drew nodded.

He paid his deposit and first month's rent in advance, then set out on his search, reminding himself to stop by the grocery store on his way back from the city.

After fifteen minutes of brisk walking through outlying neighborhoods of the city, Drew found himself standing in front of the Chicago Tech Center. The stone and glass building towered above him, an icon symbolizing the enormous task that lay before him. He half expected Ben to walk up and greet him after all he had risked and sacrificed to get there. But it didn't happened.

Drew took a deep breath. He'd taken only one small step on a very long journey. If only he knew where to begin. Was Ben even alive? Drew fought the weight of the futility of his task.

The buildings and streets bustled with activity as the business of the afternoon moved onward. Drew's stomach growled, and he knew he needed something more substantial than a muffin to sustain him. He ordered a couple slices of pizza from an Italian pizzeria on the corner and then sat at an outside table. As he ate, he watched people.

He was amazed at how important everyone thought their lives were as they scurried to and fro. Did they have any idea what was at stake? Drew watched as a well-dressed man carrying a briefcase left an office building a little farther up the street. Drew's heart skipped a beat when he saw a dark invader materialize through the glass door behind the man, who turned and walked along the mirrored glass walls of the building. The invader followed close behind, constantly speaking into the man's ear.

As the invader continued his assault on the man's mind, Drew saw bitterness and anger rise up within him. When he was directly across from Drew, the man stopped and looked up at the building from which he had come. Drew watched in astonishment as the invader removed his leather glove and reached sharpened fingernails into the man's chest and gripped his heart. Some imperceptible curse left the man's lips, and when he turned to go, Drew saw the man's countenance was full of rage. The invader followed behind him with a constant onslaught of malicious influence.

Drew watched people and invaders for the rest of the afternoon. Here in the city, the presence of the invaders was much more significant. He'd been right in assuming that they would be more concentrated in heavier populated areas. He practiced controlling his reactions to seeing invaders and also his ability to watch them without being obvious. Their tactics were still a complete enigma, but then, it was difficult to understand the tactics of a general just by watching a few troops. The invaders were militaristic, which meant there had to be a chain of command, and at the top…a commander.

Drew shuddered to think of it.

The invaders he saw were likely at the bottom of the command line, but they were plenty fierce and terrifying. He couldn't image what the visage of the commander might hold.

He meandered through the downtown streets and saw many similar instances of invader-human interaction. Once, he even saw a disheveled man with two faces, similar to what he'd seen in the gunman who attacked the campus at Drayle.

How and why would an invader take over a human like that? Did the human know the invader was in him? It was like a scene out of some bizarre science-fiction body-snatcher movie.

Farther up the street, but too far to make out any details, he was sure he saw another brief but violent encounter between a light and a dark invader.

The world spun around him, and he saw, heard, smelled, and felt every detail of humanity like never before, both the good and the bad. He watched and heard the coarse exchange between a taxicab driver and a passenger, saw a teenager shoplift a video game, watched as a man helped a woman pick up a bundle of dropped mail, saw a businessman exchange money for drugs with a dealer in an alley—and every little detail with every encounter. In many of the encounters, he knew what was going to happen just by watching the faces and eyes of the people involved. He was seeing the world and humanity as it wasn't meant to be seen…but why? Was he supposed to do something about it? When the invaders were involved in the encounters, bad things happened unless a light invader interceded. Of course, Drew noticed that most people didn't need help being rude or deceptive.

It was odd, though. Drew didn't see many children. When he did, there always was a light invader nearby. Were children more vulnerable to the attacks of the dark invaders? Were the light invaders trying to protect the future of humanity by guarding children?

As Drew pondered all he saw, he came upon a startling yet comforting conclusion. None of the invaders in the city noticed that he could see them.

That brought no small amount of encouragement. So he could—and perhaps already had—dropped off the grid of both humans and invaders. If that was the case, it would make his search for Ben far easier.

OVER THE COURSE OF the next two weeks, Drew searched shops, restaurants, and office complexes block by block using the Tech Center as the epicenter of his search. He learned that by tapping into his heightened senses, he could watch a busy room and scan every person in it in seconds. And yet, despite his abilities, he still felt like he was looking for a needle in a haystack.

One day as Drew was scanning the inside of a department store, he spotted two invaders talking with each other. Drew maneuvered behind a clothes rack and watched as one of the invaders pointed to a young woman at one of the checkout counters. The other invader sneered and disappeared through the wall in a flash. Drew considered moving on but could not bring himself to abandon the girl. Something bad was in store for her, of that he was sure. He pretended to browse through the clothes. She came toward Drew, and the invader followed close behind.

"Can I help you?" Her white-blond hair draped around her shoulders, and her makeup was model perfect. She was a pretty girl of about nineteen.

"No thanks. Just looking." Drew smiled, working hard to ignore the massive dark figure lurking over her shoulder. His hypersenses kicked in—he couldn't stop them this close to an invader.

"If you need any help, just ask," she offered with a returning smile.

She turned to leave, and he risked a panning glance across the face of the invader but wished he hadn't. The large black pupils pierced him with contempt. Drew fought the urge to run. He looked toward the retreating girl, and as he did, the invader leaned close to Drew. He resisted the temptation to recoil. If he gave away his cover to one invader in Chicago, it could mean the end of his search for Ben. He stayed still as the invader whispered something in his ear.

Strange and unnatural feelings about the girl rose up within him. Just then she turned around and saw Drew staring at her. He saw subtle evidence of concern in her eyes. He averted his gaze and moved to a different department, away from the invader. He found a bench and sat down. His breathing was heavy and his heart was pounding. Once again, an invader had influenced his mind. This one was darker and more powerful. How could an invader have the ability to influence his emotions and thoughts like that? How far did the invaders' powers over a man go?

Once Drew regained control of his emotions, he stood and, from a distance, reacquired the girl in the clothing department. Thirty minutes passed, but nothing happened, despite the invader's gawking presence. Just as Drew was about to leave, he saw the second invader enter from the outside. Beside him was a young man in obvious emotional distress. The invader was whispering poison into the man's mind. He spotted the girl and kept his distance, but the invader kept working on him. Drew wanted to leave but knew he couldn't. If he helped her, he risked being exposed to the invaders. But if he didn't, guilt would haunt him. He was a prisoner of his father's call to honor and his own conscience.

After another twenty-five minutes, the girl was relieved by another worker. Drew checked his watch. It was twelve o'clock, and the girl was taking her lunch break. She walked toward the entrance that connected the department store with a mall hallway at the back, where there was a food court. Drew quickened his pace to parallel her, while keeping an eye on the man following behind.

The girl stopped and spoke briefly to another coworker. As she did, she glanced toward Drew and spotted him looking at her again. This time she looked alarmed, even frightened. Drew turned about and started walking in the opposite direction to the front of the store and the entrance that led outside. How could he have been so careless? How in the world would he be able to avoid the invisible invaders if he couldn't keep his cover from an unassuming cashier?

He was at the door and was about to leave when he realized no matter what she thought, he couldn't leave her. He retraced his steps, and by the time he returned, the woman and the trailing man were gone. He quickly made his way into the food court and scanned the area. There were hundreds of people, and the sound was deafening for Drew. He changed vantage points twice until he spotted her. She had just purchased a tray of Chinese food and was making her way to a small table on the side of the eating area.

This time Drew was careful to position himself far enough away and to the back of her so she couldn't see him. Then he spotted the young man coming her way, his hands in his sweatshirt pockets. The invader was still working him, and his emotional distress was now replaced with bitter anger. Drew moved in closer—senses ramping up. The man swung his leg over the chair and sat down, startling the girl. He smiled a malevolent smile, and the girl's pleasant face transformed to alarm and anger. She looked around as if for a way to escape. Drew grabbed an empty cup off an abandoned table and sat down kitty-cornered from the girl and the man.

"I told you to stay away!" the girl said sternly. "We're through, Dex."

"No…no, we're not." The man's voice rattled…on the verge of losing control. "We're through when I say we're through. You can't leave me, not now, not ever."

"You're sick and you're tripped out again. I don't know why I ever went out with you. Leave me alone, or I'll call the cops."

Drew watched the man's hands out of the corner of his eye. The man's right hand was gripping something in his pocket. If it was a gun, it was a small caliber, but Drew bet against it. The girl grabbed her food and drink and was about to get up.

"You're not leaving," Dex said.

"Watch me," the girl replied as she stood up.

"Sit down!" Dex spoke through clenched teeth. "Or you'll regret it."

The girl froze. The invader was now smiling. Drew scanned the courtyard and spotted a security guard, but the second invader whispered something into the guard's ear and he disappeared down an adjoining hallway.

"I mean it, Trish. Sit down!"

Drew couldn't see her entire face, but what he did see indicated absolute fear. She sat down.

"You need help, Dex. Seriously."

"No…all I need is you. Tell me you won't leave, and I'll take care of you forever."

The girl just stared at him.

The invader reached into Dex's chest from behind, and Dex's face filled with fury. He reached across the table with his left hand and grabbed the girl's right arm. He stood up, moved to stand beside her, and lifted her out of her chair.

"Well, if I can't have you, no one will!"

Drew stood up and came to the table. He positioned himself, his feet apart, weight slightly forward, and hands ready. The man's right hand was still clutching something in his pocket; his left hand squeezed Trish's upper arm so tight that the skin around his fingers turned red. Drew looked at Trish and saw the terror in her eyes. For one brief moment she looked confused as she recognized Drew. Almost imperceptibly she shook her head back and forth. Her eyes darted to her captor's coat. Behind Dex, the invader's countenance filled with rage. He called out for the other invader.

Drew risked a glance toward the distant dark invader. He had turned to come, but at the same instant, a light invader streaked in from behind a nearby wall with his brilliant white sword drawn. There was something familiar about the light invader. Drew refocused on the man and the girl.

"Hey, dude, why don't you just relax and let the girl go. I don't think she's done with her food yet."

"Get lost!" Beads of sweat formed on Dex's forehead, and his pupils were dilated. This wasn't going to end well.

Just then Trish tried to yank her arm from his grip, but it didn't work. She screamed as Dex whipped out a four-inch switchblade, extending the blade as he did so. Drew blocked Dex's first thrust with his left forearm, simultaneously punching Dex on the left side of his rib cage with his right fist. Dex released his grip on Trish as he recoiled from Drew's forceful blow. Drew slid his left hand down to grab Dex's wrist before he could pull back his knife hand and strike again. Drew's next move was so quick it surprised even him. He grabbed Dex's throat with his right hand, turned, and flipped him over his hip and onto the ground. Dex hit the tile with a thud. Screams and shouts rose up from the surrounding tables. Dex was conscious but dazed. Drew slammed Dex's hand into the tile until the knife flew across the floor three feet away. Drew flipped him over onto his stomach and yanked both hands behind his back.

"Somebody get security!" Drew shouted.

Within a couple of minutes, two security guards came and handcuffed Dex. When they stood him up, he began cursing and shouting at Trish, at Drew, and at the security guards. The guards had their hands full, but one of them turned to Drew and the girl.

"We'll need to talk to you. Stay right here and we'll be back in a few minutes."

They both nodded. Drew was glad he couldn't hear the vile curses that came from the lips of the invaders.

Drew turned to Trish as the security guards escorted Dex away from the food court. "You okay?"

"Yeah...I guess." Her arms were wrapped around her stomach. "Thanks. I think he would have killed me if you hadn't helped." Her lips trembled. "And I thought *you* were the creeper...sorry."

"Hey, I get it. I'm just glad everything turned out." Drew gave her a quick smile. "Stay away from guys like that, okay?" He turned to go.

"Hey, where are you going? They want to talk to us." She seemed afraid to be left alone again.

"You'll be okay. You tell them what happened. I have to go."

"You...you were watching me. How did you know?"

"I saw him come in, and he didn't look right. The way he was watching you I figured you might be in trouble."

He tried to leave again, but she stepped in front of him. It was a plea not to leave her.

"What's your name?"

Drew looked to where the security guards had disappeared. His time was running short. He scanned the room and realized that the invaders had left, including the mysterious light invader. Had he been helped again? He put a hand on the girl's shoulder.

"I promise you are going to be okay now." He walked her over to a table and sat her down. He looked her right in the eyes and smiled. It helped her.

Drew left the food court down the hallway opposite the direction the guards had gone. Once he was a couple of blocks away, he found a place to eat and recovered himself. The encounter left him facing a new burden…a new responsibility. The words he had spoken to Ben years earlier echoed in his mind…words from his father.

"It's wrong to do nothing when you have the power to do something."

17

THE GUARDIAN

As the days turned to weeks, Drew had to fight the urge to call or write or e-mail his mother or Jake. How he missed them! Loneliness was now a constant companion, and any time he saw something that reminded him of home, the ache in his heart grew. He despised this unchosen mission that had trapped him, that had made him a prisoner and separated him from the only part of his life that he loved. And yet...

Each time he came to the precipice of giving up, he remembered Ben and the invaders hunting him. The code of loyalty flowing in his blood and the training and example he had received from Jake would not release him to apathy, so he pressed onward.

Drew continued his search for Ben, but soon he realized there was not enough precision or purpose in his method, so he reevaluated. Ben would have to have a job. Without an identity, he would be limited. It would be tech related but blue collar. Ben was famous for fixing computers both during high school and during college, so Drew reasoned he would resort to that which he already knew and did well.

Computer repair shops. That's where he needed to look.

On his way home one evening, Drew walked through an alley and spotted a smashed, discarded computer. An idea brought a smile to his face. Within a couple of minutes, he had the cover off and the hard drive removed. It was an old system, because the hard drive was only 120 gigabytes. It didn't matter to Drew; he just needed the prop. He tucked it in his backpack and went on his way.

Back in his room, Drew took the outer case off the hard drive and dragged one of the heads across the top platter, damaging both the head and the platter. He scratched and broke open a couple of circuit lines that looked important as an added measure. He was ready.

Drew did an Internet search for computer repair shops in Chicago, and his enthusiasm faded. Hundreds of little red dots peppered the map around the Chicago area, and hundreds more were spread out west and up and down Lake Michigan. It would take months or even longer.

He dropped his head into his hands. Was it worth it? Was it even possible? He wanted to go home. It had only been two months, but he was already weary of it. He closed his laptop and clicked on the television, hoping to numb his aching head. The news was reporting on the atrocities happening to innocent people in Sudan, eastern Burma, the Democratic Republic of the Congo, Syria, and other nations throughout the world.

Drew changed the channel. Another story on a kidnapping in New York. He changed the channel again. A story about the rise of human trafficking, not only in third-world countries but in America too. On and on the stories went, and Drew saw the plots of the invaders unfold. He had glimpsed just a few minor incidents, but he could imagine what was happening globally on a grand scale. What would the world be like without the influence of the invaders? Anger welled up within him. He and he alone knew what was happening. *"It's wrong to do nothing when you have the power to do something!"* His own words shouted at him.

"If it takes me twenty years, I will find Ben."

Ben held the key. In his mind was the answer to revealing the invaders to the world, but he needed help. Drew found his resolve in the atrocities happening at the hands of the dark invaders. He would not fail...*could* not fail!

He left his apartment and walked to the grocery store. It was a little after nine and he knew the neighborhood got rough as the dark of night overtook the day, but he didn't care. His anger for the invaders seethed within. He passed by an alley and heard a ruckus.

"Please, stop" was all he heard between thumps and groans.

Drew ran toward a group of teenage gangbangers who were kicking and beating a homeless man. The man's grocery cart was tipped on its side, and its contents spilled all over the alley.

"Hey!" Drew counted four teens. "Leave him alone!"

Two of the teens saw Drew and ran. The other two looked at Drew and scowled.

"Make us, jerk!" said one.

The other teen moved to put Drew between them. The old man was rolling on the ground, moaning.

"What's wrong with you? He's got nothing you want." Drew's senses peaked.

"Yeah…but it's fun," the leader said. "And smashing your face is going to be just as much fun."

They both attacked at once. Drew did a quick spinning back kick on the closest attacker and landed a heel squarely across the teen's face. The gangbanger fell to the ground spitting blood and cursing. The other teen backed up, then pulled out a knife. Drew squared off, and the teen came at him. Drew deflected the knife, sidestepped, and made a powerful blow to the back of the attacker's elbow. The teen screamed and ran off cradling his injured arm. Drew looked back at the other teen, who had gained his feet. He was pointing a pocket .380 auto at Drew's chest.

The moment paused and Drew saw, heard, and felt everything, including the powerful adrenaline filling his veins. His heart beat twice so hard it felt like it flipped in his chest. Fear gripped his mind, and he told himself to react in spite of it. He saw the skin on the teen's trigger finger flatten, then heard the firing pin slide forward. Drew aligned the sights of the gun and knew he was a dead man. Still, he acted.

He spun his torso to the left as the concussion of the exploding round blasted past his ears and echoed off the brick walls of the buildings lining the alley. Microseconds later, searing pain ripped through his right shoulder. The sound of a second round trailed the first, and Drew was hoping that the natural kick of the gun up and to the left of the single-handed shooter would buy him just enough space to survive the trajectory of the next bullet. He heard the bullet whiz past his right ear, but his twisting maneuver coupled with the impact of the .380 round into his shoulder caused him to stumble and fall to the ground. He rolled to an attack posture, but it wasn't necessary. The shooter was running down the alley, away from his victims.

Drew reached for his shoulder and felt warm blood oozing from the wound. More than a graze but less than full penetration, it was going to require attention...something he didn't want. He went to the old man, who was trying to sit upright. His white beard on his black skin was a dramatic contrast. Red blood stained the right side of this cheek.

"Are you all right, sir?"

"You my gawdian angel, aren't you?"

The man slurred his words, but Drew couldn't tell if he was drunk or just hurting badly. "No, I'm just a friend. We need some help."

The man pointed to his cart. "I need my possessions. Did they steal my possessions?"

He seemed to like the word.

"No, it's all here." Drew tried to help the man stand, but the man was hurting too much and Drew's right arm reverberated with pain each time he tried to use it.

The old man clutched his ribs and groaned. "Take me to Emmanuel."

"Is that a clinic or something?"

"Reverend Ray Branson...he'll hep me. Thank you, gawdian...thank you." The old man wheezed and nearly fell over.

Drew caught him. "Where is Reverend Ray?"

"Two blocks over...Emmanuel Church."

It finally clicked. Drew had seen the gray block church once before but given it no attention. Now he realized what the man was talking about. Drew grabbed the old man's cart and tried to use it as a walker for him, but he refused to leave his "possessions" in the alley. Drew repressed his frustration and pain and gathered the man's things and put them back in the cart. Then he had the man hang onto the cart with one hand and placed the man's other arm around Drew's shoulder.

Together they shuffled along while Drew tried to bear as much weight for the man as possible. Blood was trickling down Drew's arm and dripping from his elbow. The body odor from the man was almost more than Drew could take, especially with his nose in overdrive. It took forever, but they made it. Drew tried the door, but it was locked.

"'Round the back," the old man said. He was almost spent and about to collapse.

Drew found another door that led to an adjoining apartment. He knocked. It took some time, but they were rewarded with a door that cracked open.

A middle-aged man peeked out. When he saw the old man, the door opened wide. "Jeremiah, what have you gotten yourself into?" He was a handsome black man with friendly eyes behind wire-rimmed glasses.

"Oh, Reverend Ray, I was 'bout to die, but the Lord sent me a gawdian angel to save me."

"Some teens were beating him up in the alley a few blocks over," Drew piped in.

"That would be the Dragons. That lousy gang is spreading its territory," the reverend said, shaking his head. "Jeremiah, what are you doing in an alley this time of night? You should be in the shelter!" Reverend Ray clearly cared about the man. "Bring him in—" Reverend Ray's eyes opened wide as he saw Drew's blood-soaked shirt for the first time. "You're hurt too!"

"It's just a graze."

"Looks more than that. We need to get you to a hospital."

"No...I can't do that." Drew readied to leave.

Reverend Ray scrutinized him. "Let's take a look at it; then we'll decide."

Drew helped get Jeremiah into Reverend Ray's home. Just past the entryway, Drew heard footsteps.

"What is it, Dad?" A slender girl of about fourteen came into the room. Her eyes opened wide when she saw Jeremiah and Drew, both blood-stained.

"Go get your mother, Shana," Reverend Ray said.

"Bullets went right through him, Reverend. You shoulda seen it."

The reverend looked at Drew. "Yes, that's what bullets do, Jeremiah."

"Shoulda killed him, Reverend. Two bullets that close...shoulda killed him."

Drew shook his head. "The kid was a bad shot. We're just lucky."

"Oh, son…luck has nothing to do with it," the reverend said. "God was watching over you."

Drew opened his mouth, then decided against saying anything.

Reverend Ray's wife, Nicole, and daughter helped get Jeremiah cleaned up and bandaged on their couch while Ray helped Drew at their kitchen table. The reverend's little boy, Micah, ran for supplies any time his mother or father called for it. Once Drew's wound was cleaned, it didn't look as bad as it felt, and he convinced Reverend Ray that he would be okay.

"We still need to report this to the police." Reverend Ray reached for his phone.

"Please don't, sir."

Reverend Ray's eyes narrowed. "Are you in trouble, son?"

Drew took a deep breath, trying to relax from the pain and rush of the night. "I swear to you, Reverend, that I have done nothing wrong or illegal."

Reverend Ray sat back in his chair, fingering his phone while considering Drew. "But you're running…or hiding from something."

Drew felt the weight of his mission fall hard on him again. His shoulders drooped. "You could say that, but it's not the authorities…not exactly." He could see by the reverend's face that he was not very convinced. Drew made a quick scan of the home, at least as much as he could see. "I just need to lie low for a while. It's hard to explain."

"Try me," the reverend said with a forced smile. "I'm a good listener."

"I…I can't, sir, but please believe me when I say that all I'm trying to do is help people."

Micah ran from the couch to the kitchen, taken up in all the excitement. He grabbed his daddy's hand. "Jeremiah's going to tell the story, Daddy. Come on!"

"Okay, Micah. Let's go hear the story," Reverend Ray said with a sideways glance toward Drew.

Jeremiah regaled them with the story—and with a great deal of exaggeration…or maybe not so much—but it sure sounded like it to everyone in the room except Micah. His eyes got bigger and bigger. When it was over, Micah came to Drew and poked him.

"Are you really a guardian angel?"

Drew laughed and patted him on the shoulder. "If angels exist, I don't think they bleed." Drew massaged his shoulder. "It wasn't quite as cool as Jeremiah made it sound." He gave the boy a wink and stood to leave. "I need to be going."

"We can't let you go without feeding you," Reverend Ray said. "Shana's made some delicious soup."

Nicole insisted and so did Shana and Micah. Drew was trapped, at least for a little while. They ate at the table while Reverend Ray sat on the couch and fed Jeremiah a bowl. When the old man dozed off, the reverend joined them at the table.

Drew learned that Reverend Ray not only pastored the Emmanuel Church, but his family ran a soup kitchen each day for the homeless in the neighborhood. The church pews had been replaced with chairs that could be rearranged to accommodate the kitchen during the week and then set back up for church on Sunday. All four of the Bransons helped run the kitchen, with aid from various volunteer groups and outlying churches that had a heart to minister to the inner city.

The Bransons were beautiful people, and Drew wondered why the invaders didn't seem to have a dark influence on them like they did on so many others. Did their religious and superstitious beliefs make them less vulnerable somehow? Perhaps their devotion to doing good to their fellow man made it harder for the invaders to break them down. It was an interesting line of reasoning that Drew was going to have to explore in greater depth.

When they asked for his name, Drew offered *Ryan* instead.

Reverend Ray looked straight into his eyes and seemed to read his thoughts. "Whatever you're running from or looking for, son, there are answers."

If only he knew how true that was.

By the time Drew was ready to leave, Shana could hardly pull her little brother away from him.

"I think you have a new best friend." Shana smiled bashfully.

Drew gave Micah a fist bump, which made the boy smile from ear to ear.

Reverend Ray and his wife walked him to the door. "Thanks for helping Jeremiah. You did a brave and good thing tonight."

"Couldn't just walk by."

"Neither could the Samaritan," Ray said. "And Jesus bragged on him."

What in the world did that mean? Drew wondered.

"Once you're healed up, would you be interested in giving us a hand at the soup kitchen from time to time?" Ray asked. "We could always use a man who's got a heart for the needy."

How should he respond to that? He'd never find Ben while working in a soup kitchen in a church, but how could he refuse the good work of such good people? Isn't that what his end goal was, even if this was on a much smaller scale?

"I'll see what I can do," Drew replied.

Drew made his way home. The groceries would have to wait until tomorrow. He heard sirens in the distance and shouting from farther down the street. It was so big...so impossible. He walked up the eight concrete steps to the apartment doorway. Something white flashed out of the corner of his eye. He looked to the edge of his apartment building...

But whatever had been there was gone.

18

MR. LEE

Drew's wound was healing quickly. Two days later, he felt good enough to set out in the morning with renewed determination and a map that he printed from a cheap printer he'd picked up at OfficeMart. Once again he used the Tech Center as his point of reference and worked his way out, visiting computer repair shops with his damaged hard drive. Only someone with Ben's skill and expertise could recover data from the drive, and every store had "the expert," so he insisted on talking to the technician who would be working on it at each store. Once in the back room, and after determining that Ben was not working there, Drew would ask for an approximate cost to recover the data and then say he'd changed his mind, that it wasn't worth it after all.

Each day Drew journeyed from repair shop to repair shop, eliminating the little red dots one by one, and each night he ventured out into the night, looking to help one more person. As his escapades of help became more daring, he edged closer to the limits of his abilities and the risks became greater, especially when guns were involved.

On numerous occasions, Drew received the timely help of one or two light invaders. Though he dared never look them in the face, he was sure they were the same ones each time.

One of them in particular seemed powerful and skilled and carried an air of authority. Drew referred to him as Wallace, after the great Sir William Wallace. He wondered why such an invader would be involved in the petty affairs of the people of this ghetto, but then again, much of what the invaders did, both light and dark, didn't make much sense to him. He came to believe that the light invaders' war against the dark invaders was somehow motivated by more than a desire to rule and conquer humanity. But why they would help him help others was still a mystery.

Deep in the recesses of his mind, he wondered if he could contact them. It would be a bold and risky move. He would need time to consider it, but for now he was just glad to have them on his side from time to time.

One day, Drew stopped in to check on Reverend Ray and his family. They were operating their soup kitchen, and Micah and Shana pleaded with him to help, so he decided to pitch in for a couple of hours. When it was over, he realized as he left that helping out there gave him a satisfaction as deep as protecting someone from a crime.

"I'm hearing things," Reverend Ray said to him when they were alone cleaning up the kitchen.

"Yeah?" What could the reverend be referring to?

"Folks around here been talking…about the Guardian. That's what they call him anyway."

Drew swallowed. He didn't want attention, so he just stayed silent. Of course, it didn't seem to fool Reverend Ray, who somehow knew things without being told.

"You be careful, Ryan. There's a limit to what even the best can do. Won't be long before this Guardian will have the attention of the local gang. They don't like vigilantes."

Drew nodded.

"I'll be praying for you."

Drew smiled, reminded of Sydney. Oh, how he missed her.

As he walked home, he decided to make working at the soup kitchen a weekly event.

A FEW DAYS LATER, Drew took stock. His money was dwindling, so it was time to find work. He applied for a job delivering takeout food for a small Korean restaurant a few blocks from Chicago's city center.

"You don't have car, you can't deliver!" Mr. Lee, the store owner said. He looked to Drew to be a shrewd businessman.

Drew didn't leave. It would be the perfect job, because he could stop at computer repair shops near his deliveries and kill two birds with one stone. "What if I can save up to buy a car, can I deliver on foot or bicycle until then?"

Mr. Lee laughed. "Too slow. No car, no job." His face became stern. "Good-bye." When he waved Drew out of his office, Drew noticed that Mr. Lee's forearms were muscular and well defined. He scanned the office and saw a martial arts certificate lying on a pile of papers on the shelf behind him.

Drew got up to leave, but at the door he stopped. "Mr. Lee."

The man just grunted.

"I'll spar you for the job."

At that Mr. Lee looked up from the bills he was working on. "You do not want to do that."

Something told Drew that Mr. Lee might be more than just another black belt. "I need the job, and I might surprise you."

Mr. Lee stared hard at Drew; then without warning he threw his pencil, like a bullet, toward him. Drew snatched the pencil out of the air just inches before it hit his chest. He walked back to the desk and handed it to Mr. Lee.

"Ahhhh." Mr. Lee's eyes sparkled. "Tae kwon do?"

"Yes, and some karate, aikido, and jujitsu."

"What degree?"

Drew shook his head. "Nothing formal. I don't have a belt."

Mr. Lee squinted and pursed his lips. He seemed disappointed, although it was difficult to read him. He stood, and as he did, he transformed from humble restaurant owner to Eastern warrior...the kind to fear. "If you spar with me, you might get hurt."

"I might get better, and I need that as much as I need a job."

Mr. Lee opened his desk drawer and handed Drew a card. "Tonight, eight thirty."

Drew looked at the simple card: Lee's Tae Kwon Do.

"You spar; then I decide if you get job."

Drew smiled and bowed, then left.

DREW FINISHED THE DAY by checking off six more computer repair shops. At eight twenty-five he was standing in front of Mr. Lee's Tae Kwon Do. He entered to see a class working on their patterns. Mr. Lee watched as another instructor walked between the nine students as they worked. Drew had never learned patterns, but evidently it taught consistent and fundamental technique. He waited for the class to end. Within fifteen minutes, only Mr. Lee, Drew, and the other instructor remained. The instructor became busy with preparing the school for the next day. Mr. Lee came to Drew and stood before him. The Roman numeral VII was embroidered at the end of his black belt...

Mr. Lee was a master.

Drew swallowed. Maybe he should withdraw his challenge.

"Where is your gi?" Master Lee asked.

"My what?"

"Never mind. Why you learn tae kwon do?"

Drew had never thought about it before. "Ah...I guess because my mentor thought I might need it someday."

"To fight someone?"

"To defend myself...and others."

Master Lee didn't seem satisfied. "We learn tae kwon do so we do not have to fight."

Drew thought about that for a moment. It was a different philosophy than the Special Forces philosophy. "There are innocent people who do not know how to fight. I learn to fight for them."

Master Lee squinted and frowned. After a long ten seconds, he broke his glare. "Mr. Chi!"

The other instructor appeared before them. Mr. Chi looked a little older than Drew and had two stripes on his black belt—a second degree. Drew had no idea what to expect based on the degree of black belt, for he didn't know where Jake's skill level might fall. For all he knew, he was a novice, but he doubted it.

"Spar with Mr. Ryan," Master Lee commanded.

Mr. Chi's eyes widened, and he made a quick assessment of Drew in his

T-shirt and jeans. He questioned Master Lee with his eyes, but Master Lee just stepped back and crossed his arms.

"Strike him," he commanded.

Mr. Chi bowed and took up a sparring stance. Drew followed suit. He could feel his senses kick in as he watched and evaluated his opponent. The first strike came, and Drew deflected and sidestepped but did not counter. Then came a side kick, but that too was deflected. After three more mild attacks, it became apparent that Mr. Chi would hold back no more.

Drew prepared himself and became absorbed in the fight. He met each blow and kick without a single one landing on his body. Mr. Chi's frustration mounted, and he attacked with more force and intensity until Drew saw the perfect opportunity to strike. He ducked beneath a roundhouse kick, then countered with a spinning wheel kick that struck Mr. Chi square in the chest.

"Break!" Master Lee stepped between them. "You are dismissed, Mr. Chi. Thank you."

Mr. Chi looked frustrated and a bit humiliated. He wasn't ready to stop just yet. Drew bowed low to honor him, and Mr. Chi responded likewise.

Master Lee stepped in front of Drew. "You are"—Master Lee seemed to search his vocabulary for the right word—"unrefined. But very quick. No kicking. Block my strikes."

Drew readied himself for the first blow, and it came much faster and stronger than anything from Mr. Chi. It startled him. The strikes continued, and Drew's reactions kicked into overdrive. Fists, forearms, and elbows moved in a blur between them. Drew had never had to move so fast for so long. After deflecting thirty-some strikes, he was becoming weary. Master Lee finished with a knife hand strike to Drew's neck. As the strike came in, Drew did not block but instead grabbed Master Lee's wrist. Master Lee stopped and stared deep into Drew's eyes. Drew released his grip, stepped back, and bowed.

"You are unusual, Mr. Ryan. I will train you, and you will fight for me in tournament."

"No, Master Lee. I will not fight in any tournaments."

Master Lee resumed his disappointed frown. Apparently he was not used to being told no. "What you want, Mr. Ryan?"

Drew smiled. "I want a job, sir."

Master Lee shook his head. "You must train. To not train is waste. I will train you, then decide on tournament." Master Lee nodded as if Drew had agreed. "Three nights each week." He turned away.

Drew dropped his gaze to the floor. "I can't pay."

"Train first, pay later." Master Lee seemed annoyed.

"What about the job, Master Lee?"

By now Master Lee was walking away, toward the back of the gym. He grunted some incoherent Korean words and shook his head. "Eight o'clock. If late, you fired."

"Thank you, sir!" This was better than he had hoped for. A strange thought came to mind. "Master Lee. There is one thing I need to learn first."

Master Lee stopped and looked back at Drew.

"I need to learn how to dodge bullets."

Master Lee's stoic face broke into a wide grin. "Ha! You funny boy, Mr. Ryan." He walked to the back of his gym, shaking his head and mumbling and laughing to himself.

19

DODGING BULLETS

Drew began delivering Korean food on a bicycle he had found for cheap. But after a few days, when Drew arrived at work one morning, Master Lee threw his keys at Drew.

"You too slow. Buy gas and do not wreck car."

Drew was ecstatic. Now he could cover much more territory in his search for Ben.

The first few classes Drew attended with Master Lee were spent testing the extent of his abilities. Drew came to appreciate the martial arts genius of Master Lee. The man was much more than a seventh-degree black belt. He was an analyzer of personality and human potential. Some of the things he had Drew do didn't make sense, at least not at first, but Drew began looking forward to his training because it stretched him beyond anything he had ever experienced. After each session, Master Lee appeared more somber than usual. At the end of the second week, Master Lee came to Drew in the silence and solitude of his empty gym.

"I will not train you anymore," Master Lee said flatly.

Drew was perplexed. What had he done wrong? "Why, Master Lee? I'm learning so much from you."

Master Lee squinted with a fierce look. He pointed a finger at Drew's chest. "What you are, no one has ever been or should be. I think darkness follows you."

Drew's mouth opened, but he didn't know how to respond. How could

Master Lee have known? How much dared Drew reveal? He scanned the gym. "Master Lee, you are right."

At that, Master Lee pulled back his hand and straightened his shoulders. He waited.

Drew struggled for the right words. "Darkness does follow me and is indeed already here."

Master Lee's eyes widened ever so slightly.

"But I am here to fight the darkness, and not just for me, but for everyone. If I am to survive and help many people, I need your help to discover and perfect my abilities."

Master Lee stared at Drew, still as a stone statue. Drew knew that he was considering every shred of information, piece by piece, in a logical way. And then his eyes softened and a decision was made. At that moment, something changed between them. Master Lee had discovered and confirmed something supernatural. He nodded, and Drew could see understanding in his instructor's gaze.

"Master Lee...no one can know...ever."

In that instant, the magnitude of Drew's mission became Master Lee's, and Drew could tell that the severity and sober realization of what was at stake penetrated his instructor's understanding. From that day on, Drew's training became singularly purposeful. No martial arts instructor in the world had ever had to train such a man as Drew, and as Drew was stretched to his limits, so was Master Lee. Both teacher and student became obsessed in the challenge of it, and Drew's abilities transcended that of mortal men.

As Drew's skills improved, he became challenged with keeping his identity and mission secret while trying to help people against the devastating attacks of the invaders and those they influenced. Such as the local gang. Everyone in this area of the city knew all too well how fierce the Dragons were. Even the police were hesitant to venture into their territory.

Drew couldn't understand the invaders' tactics, except that they always caused chaos and discord among humans. He caught glimpses of a command structure and realized that in the ghettos of Chicago, only the minions were working. Perhaps that was why he was able to stay under their radar. On the scale of influencing humanity, Drew was nothing, and he needed to keep it that way as long as possible.

It wasn't long into Drew's training when Master Lee implemented what he called the suk dahl, or in Drew's words, bullet dodging. At first it involved a high-speed airsoft pistol, but when Drew proved proficient, Master Lee elevated his training with chest and face protection, rubber bullets, and a Glock 21 handgun.

After discovering just how painful rubber bullets were, even with protection, his senses needed no goading to ramp up to full capacity. Through the suk dahl training, Drew discovered that his best results came when he was close enough to focus on the aim of the gun and move his body the instant before the trigger was pulled. Inside of twenty feet, if he waited until the round exploded, he was not quick enough to dodge the bullet. Outside of forty feet, his eyes could not pick up the bullet or predict the sight picture until it was too late. He learned those margins well and practiced until he had mastered the technique.

On that day, Master Lee seemed stunned.

When Drew received his first paycheck, he tried to pay Master Lee for some of the lessons, but his teacher refused.

"What I have seen, and learned, cannot be purchased." He looked at Drew with eyes of wonderment. "You are here for a purpose, Mr. Ryan... Use your life wisely."

DREW KEPT VOLUNTEERING each week at Emmanuel Church and became friends with Reverend Ray. One week Drew came to the church and noticed a blue fifteen-passenger van parked out front. Two light invaders stood guard near the front of the church. It wasn't unusual for a light invader to be near the premises of the church, but this seemed a little out of the ordinary. These were two that Drew had never seen before. He entered the church to discover the food-serving line was occupied by smiling young people. Ray met him at the door near the front of the church with a grin that was bigger than usual.

"Ryan! It's good to see you. Look at how the Lord is working here today!" He motioned to the college-aged helpers.

"What's up, Reverend?"

"Campus Ministries from Drayle University is here this week to teach vacation Bible school for the neighborhood and wanted to help with the soup kitchen in the evenings."

Drayle? Could it be…

Drew's heart skipped a beat as he saw his beautiful Sydney walk out from the kitchen carrying a pan of food. Her hair was tied up in the back with a few strands dangling near her temples. She looked so content and joyful in her work. Seeing her warmed him from the inside out. It took every ounce of control not to run to her.

"Come on, I'll introduce you to them." Ray pulled on Drew's arm. "I've already told them about you."

"No, I can't. I've got some things I need to take care of."

Ray looked disappointed. He turned and faced Drew. "God is working on you, Ryan, but I'm not going to push you and neither will they. They're wonderful kids, and I know they'd love to meet you."

Drew watched as Sydney exchanged the food tray and smiled at a little old woman in the line. Even from one hundred feet away he loved her smile…he missed her smile.

"Thanks, Reverend, but I really can't."

Ray's eyes saddened. "Okay, Ryan. If that's what you want."

Drew huffed. It wasn't at all what he wanted, but it had to be. Reverend Ray turned to leave. "Reverend."

"Yes?"

"How long will they be here?"

"Three more days."

"Any idea where they are staying?"

"I heard them say the Travel Host, downtown Chicago."

Drew nodded. "Thanks." He took one more look at Sydney and realized she was looking his way. He turned and left. It hurt.

Drew walked away from the church, but after one block he stopped. He looked up at the darkening sky that was threatening rain. He was compelled to go back, so he retraced his steps and sat down on the steps of an apartment building across the street, watching.

The light invaders were still there.

Drew evaluated over and over again the risk of contacting Sydney, and though his heart pleaded to do so, all logic and reason forbade it. He had already nearly caused her death. She was safest away from him, and yet…he couldn't bring himself to leave his watchful perch.

The late day disappeared into night as Emmanuel Church finished its duty to a few blocks of the hungry and poor of Chicago. Drew told himself that if he could see Sydney just one more time, he would be released and could let her go. As the night blackened, dark invaders appeared with shady human companions. The two light invaders took note and drew their swords. They were alert and ready, as if expecting an attack. Apparently the presence of the students at the church was causing a heightened level of invader activity.

Drew leaned forward. Two…three…four dark invaders lurked nearby. The light invaders stood back to back with swords drawn. Drew felt his pulse quicken and his senses heighten. Why?

Reverend Ray opened the door and took a moment to speak with the college ministry leader. Distant thunder echoed off the walls of the shops and apartments that lined the street. That was when the invaders attacked. Drew stood, chills flowing up and down his spine. All four dark invaders came at the van in a blur. The two light invaders met them head on, each one slicing and countering the onslaught from the vicious dark warriors. Their movements were so quick that Drew had a hard time following them.

One dark invader jumped on top of the van and came down at one of the light invaders from fifteen feet above, brandishing both a grisly sword and a handgun. The light invader made one quick slice that found its mark deep in an opponent's chest, then turned, dodged two rounds, and used the brick wall of the church to launch himself at the dark invader attacking from above. His sword deflected another round before the two massive warriors collided midair and crashed to the ground in a fury of steel and blows. The other light invader caught a slice off his left shoulder, his red blood staining the blade of his ruthless opponent. Now wounded and facing two fierce attackers, his fate looked desperate.

Drew started to move toward the battle not knowing what he could do but unable to remain still at the terrible sight of it. Just then a white flash flew from behind him toward the battle…another light invader—

It was Wallace!

He sped toward the light invader who was in retreat and fighting for his life, now up against the brick wall of the church and desperate. Wallace changed his angle toward the van, where one of the students was just opening the back door. Wallace planted his foot against the opening door, which the student seemed to have to pull a little harder to open, and launched himself toward the dark invader executing a final, killing blow on the failing light invader. With one wide, arcing slice, Wallace's blade cut clear through the dark invader. The evil body began dissolving into wisps of green vapor that fell down into the earth.

Now the dark invaders were outnumbered, and it looked as though the battle might be over. Drew watched as one of the dark invaders yelled out in desperation. Whatever he said, Wallace looked concerned. Rather than taking on another duel, he turned and scanned up and down the street.

A car horn bellowed from Drew's right. He had walked into the street, gawking at the ferocious fight that was happening all around the unsuspecting college students. Drew jumped back onto the curb as a car whizzed past him, the driver cursing obscenities as he went. The students began piling into the van. Drew saw Sydney exit the church at the same time that Wallace caught sight of something dreadful and prepared himself. Drew followed his gaze, and what he saw shook him to the very core of his humanity.

The battle at Emmanuel Church was far from over.

20

BATTLE OF THE BEAST

Drew stood, frozen, as a creature from a graphic horror film appeared from behind a building just fifty feet away. The fanged beast larger than a horse came charging up the street, its mouth snarling, its blood-red eyes flashing. Part grizzly, part wolf, part dragon, this creature invoked terror in Drew's heart unlike anything he had ever experienced. And yet Wallace stood firm and resolute in his defense of the students.

The other dark invaders continued their attack as Wallace drew a short blade to accompany his gleaming white sword against the unearthly beast of destruction. With yet thirty feet to close, the grotesque beast launched into the air for a chilling, powerful lunge at the light invaders.

Wallace did not retreat nor wait. He catapulted himself toward the beast, diving and twisting his body so that he flew just beneath the attacking monster. The beast struck viciously at him from above with powerful four-inch claws, but Wallace's long blade found its mark first, slicing deep into the creature's underbelly as he passed below. The creature screamed at the same moment that a lightning bolt exploded above them in deafening thunder.

Drew vaguely heard the startled scream of one of the girls entering the van. The tail of the beast swung downward, pounding into Wallace from the side. The impact loosed his grip on the sword, and it skidded out of reach along the pavement. Strangely, this weapon did not dissolve. Wallace hit the ground and rolled to a crouching position, his short blade at the ready, while drawing an FN Five-Seven handgun from a side holster.

The beast slammed into the ground and fell up against the van. It jostled, but Drew couldn't tell if it was from the beast or the students jockeying for seats inside. In the middle of the street, Wallace attacked first this time, before the beast could orient itself. Blood dripped from the deep gash in the beast to the asphalt street, and Drew was shocked that it was still alive. Wallace charged, emptying the twenty-round magazine into its head and chest, but its effect seemed minimal. Just as he reached the creature, it lashed out with its grisly talons and struck him across the chest, tearing open his coat and skin with four deep gashes. Wallace flew like a rag doll up against the brick wall of the church, then fell to the concrete in a heap.

Drew stepped back into the street toward the church, watching helplessly as the beast moved toward a stunned and shaken Wallace, who let the empty gun fall beside him to take a double-handed grip on his short blade. The FN dissolved away. Wallace rose up to one knee but seemed too dazed to fight. The beast lunged once more, but Drew could tell its wounds were taking a toll. Just as the razor-sharp teeth were about to snap closed on Wallace, he leaped upward in a spinning, twisting maneuver that brought him down on the back of the beast. He sank his sword deep into its thick black hide. It cried out once more, then fell and dissolved to green nothingness.

Wallace fell to the ground through the dissolving mist. The gashes across his chest looked painful and even fatal for a normal man. Once the other two dark invaders saw the death of their beast, they retreated, but not before one of them managed to slice his sword through the left front tire of the van as he went. And they did not retreat far. Drew could hear the faint hiss of escaping air.

Reverend Ray smiled and waved as the van drove off; then he went back into the church and closed and locked the doors. Drew watched two dark invaders join with three more to follow the van. He turned to look at Wallace, who gave orders to the one light invader who had not been injured. That invader took off after the van. Wallace looked toward Drew, and Drew didn't pretend he couldn't see him.

Too much had happened…too much to ignore.

He looked into Wallace's eyes for the first time. Tousles of black hair hung down toward penetrating pale-blue eyes that nearly glowed in the night. There was pain and concern in them. They were ancient eyes that caused Drew to tremble. It was an eerie moment. Drew broke his gaze and looked at the retreating van with the light invader following close behind. Some of the dark invaders had caught up to the van and were riding on the ceiling. Drew took one more glance toward Wallace and saw him subtly shake his head. Drew knew what that meant, but Sydney was in that van.

This night of tragedy was far from over.

Were they after Sydney specifically? It almost seemed so. He bolted down the sidewalk after the van. By the sound of the air he had heard escaping the tire, they wouldn't make it more than three or four blocks.

Drew ran as fast as he could, but the van quickly outdistanced him. Up ahead, he saw them turn left toward the highway and directly into six blocks of some of the worst gang-infested areas of Chicago. Drew forced his legs to run faster. Long minutes passed before Drew reached the corner where the van had turned.

Three blocks ahead, he could see the van pulled off to the right of the road. His lungs hurt, but what he saw next made him push even harder. Up ahead, a number of dark invaders were conversing in the street, and two low riders were pulling into positions at the front and rear of the van. Drew whipped out his phone and dialed 911 to report a crime in progress. He gave the address and hung up, hoping it would be enough to get the police there but also fearing they would be too late.

Drew sprinted down an alleyway and then between two buildings toward the sidewalk, where the gang members had accosted the students. He stayed in the shadows, needing to discover what was going down.

Five gang members surrounded the van. By their colors and markings he recognized them as Dragons. They had the students, who looked terrified, lined up against the van. Sydney was in the middle of the group. The light invader was nowhere to be found, but three dark invaders were pacing and whispering into the Dragons' ears.

"Wallets and purses...now! Cell phones too...all of them," he heard the gang leader say.

"I've already called the police," the ministry leader said. "Please don't hurt anyone."

The gang leader sneered and glared at him face to face, just inches away. The man was trying to be brave, but his darting eyes and sweating brow betrayed him. He was a clean-shaven man in his early thirties. Spiked dark hair, glasses, soft hands, and pale skin told Drew the man was not a fighter. *Just be quiet…*

"That's not phat, busta. Police be scared here 'cause this our turf." The Dragon smiled. "No help comin'. You be in our turf, you pay." His sickening smile twisted into an evil sneer. He jammed his gun into the ministry leader's temple and shouted just inches away from the man's face, "So shut up!"

At least one other Dragon had a gun, and several had knives. The odds were bad…very bad. If all the Dragons took was the students' money, he would let it go. It would mean the least possible threat to the students.

"Don't hide nothin' or you'll get stuck…get it?" The Dragon leader's arms were tattooed with snakes, dragons, knives, and skulls from both shoulders to his wrists. Some cryptic words were tattooed up his neck to his temple and across his forehead. A blue skullcap covered his shaven head. He had piercings on his face, lips, and ears. And he was the one that a dark invader worked on relentlessly.

Drew saw Sydney lower her head, and knew she was praying. He pitied her—if she could see what he saw, she wouldn't waste her time. A dark invader whispered to one of the Dragons, and he pushed Sydney up against the van.

"Yo…eyes on us, dime."

Two Dragons collected the wallets and purses and threw them into the car parked behind the van.

"Very nice, kiddies." The leader smiled, then turned to the two who had collected the valuables. "Get it to the dome."

They jumped in their car as the Dragon leader turned back to the students. "Back in the van."

The ministry leader tried to step aside and let the students in before him, but a Dragon shoved him.

"Get in!"

The students began piling back in the van, but the Dragon leader pulled Sydney and another girl out of the line.

"You two dimes be with me."

One of the students just ahead of Sydney turned around. "No!"

The leader smashed the grip of his handgun into the student's head, slamming him up against the side of the van. "Stupid reaker!"

Drew couldn't wait any longer.

He pulled his hood over his head, stepped out onto the sidewalk, and started walking toward the van. He was just twenty feet away when the Dragon leader shoved the bleeding male student into the van. Drew closed the distance as quickly as he dared. There was enough commotion for him to get within just a few feet of the ruckus before one of the Dragons saw him and pointed a gun at his face.

"Be gone, stupid!"

Drew saw the dark invaders move to his rear, readying their swords. Light invaders must be advancing too.

He lowered his head and held up his hands. The gun was inches from his face, so his hands bracketed each side. He didn't hesitate. With one lightning move, he snapped both hands inward, his right hand landing just behind the Dragon's wrist and his left hand grabbing the gun. He twisted his hand to the inside, toward his open grip, and before the Dragon knew what had happened, Drew took the gun from him.

Drew spun inward toward the Dragon, slamming his left elbow into the gang member's temple, knocking him out cold. As the man fell, Drew pulled the slide of the .45 ACP to expel one round and chamber another to verify its load. The cocking was complete by the time the unconscious Dragon hit the pavement.

Drew evaluated his next threat. The Dragon with the knife was closest at just five feet to his right, while the leader was behind and to the left, near the van—and the two girls. Both men turned on Drew, the leader bringing his gun to bear. Drew's mind and body accelerated as he considered his options. Dodge? Shoot? Strike? Predicting the ricochet and potential shrapnel fly-out from shooting the Dragon's gun was too difficult, especially with Sydney so close.

The risk was too great. He was close enough to see, predict, and dodge one bullet if that was all he concentrated on, but if the Dragon shot three or four rounds in quick succession, he would be in trouble.

He stopped and focused on the Dragon leader fifteen feet away, watching his trigger finger. The Dragon with the knife froze when he saw that Drew was armed.

"Hey…that's…that's the Guardian!" The Dragon with the knife took two steps back.

"Leave!" Drew said.

He saw the decision made in the Dragon leader's eyes before his finger even moved. Drew dodged, the primer fired and the bullet whizzed past his right shoulder, almost in slow motion. He heard screams in the van and from the girl beside Sydney; then he saw a flash of swords to his left but stayed his attention on his own world. The Dragon with the knife actually dropped his weapon and backed away, his hands up as he turned and ran. The Dragon leader turned to grab Sydney as a shield. The only thing that could cover the distance in time was a bullet, so Drew pinpointed the Dragon's shoulder socket and fired just as the Dragon squeezed off another round. This bullet traveled in slow motion too, but with his concentration on aiming, Drew couldn't predict or move in time to avoid the Dragon's shot. The spinning hollow point was moving directly at his heart and there was nothing he could do about it. With all his might he twisted, but his muscles simply were not as fast as his mind. Fear swallowed him as the bullet reached out to take his life, but in the final fraction of a second, something flashed.

A white steel blade swung from above to intercept the bullet.

Drew watched as the slug deflected at just enough of an angle to nick his sweatshirt, but that was all. Wallace completed his twisting dive, landing on his feet next to the building near the sidewalk. Life shattered back to full speed. He heard the scream of the gang leader as his gun fell to the sidewalk. The Dragon backed away toward his car, clutching his shoulder and shouting an endless string of obscenities.

Drew grabbed Sydney and pulled her back toward the van as the man stumbled into his car and screeched down the street. Drew caught a glimpse of

Wallace as he staggered toward the narrow walkway that led to the alley. Sirens came from up the street.

"Is it you?"

The hushed and frightened question came from Sydney. Drew leaned her up against the van, then lifted the other girl off the sidewalk and into the van. He wiped the grip of the gun he was holding and was about to throw it into the gutter—if by some chance the police tracked him down and he was in possession of a gun, no excuses would save him. Still, what if the Dragons came back? He weighed the risks, then lifted his sweatshirt and tucked the .45 in his belt, at the back, and covered it. He came to Sydney and held her face.

"Drew…it's you." Tears pooled in her eyes and she was trembling.

"Don't tell them it was me. Promise me!"

Sydney nodded. The sirens were almost on them. She reached for him, but he slipped away. He dashed back between the buildings and into the alley. Flashing red lights reflected down the narrow walkway behind him. Drew ran, looking up and down the darkened lane. Across the way, just twenty feet to his right, Wallace was leaning heavily on one arm against a brick wall. His other hand cradled the deep gash in his chest. Drew approached, not sure what consequences would result from such an action. But this was the second time this invader had saved his life. Did he dare approach this warrior of another realm?

Wallace peered at Drew through dark eyebrows, and Drew stopped, afraid to come closer. Then Wallace turned and leaned his shoulder against the wall and sank to his knees. He grimaced as he lowered his head. Tousles of sweat-soaked black hair hung over his brows.

Down the alley, Drew could see two dark invaders lurking in the shadows. They were focused on Wallace, apparently not sure whether to attack or run. Their swords were drawn, and their apprehensive approach told Drew that this light warrior was feared, even when wounded. Drew looked for help and protection from other light invaders, but there were none to be seen.

The sirens grew louder, then stopped—the police were in the street, just on the other side of the building. Flashing red and blue lights reflected into the dim alleyway. Drew went to Wallace and knelt down on one knee before him. Thunder crackled across the sky, and Drew felt the first minuscule drops of rain. Wallace looked at Drew with fierce, pained eyes. What was he thinking? Drew reached out and tried to touch his shoulder, but his hand passed right through him. He watched Wallace's lips move in silence.

"I can't hear you," Drew said.

Wallace grimaced again, but this time he clenched his teeth, closed his eyes, and looked as if he might pass out…but he did not. What happened next rocked Drew's world.

Miniature flames of blue licked at Wallace's face, torso, arms, and legs. His entire body glowed, and then…he materialized into the world of humans. Drew's heart raced. Shivers covered his entire body as he beheld the physical form of an invading warrior, just inches away.

"You must go before they find you." Wallace's voice was deep and commanding, though laced with pain.

"How can I help you?"

Wallace lifted his head and glared at Drew. He looked down the alley at the approaching invaders. Drew followed his gaze. Just thirty feet away, they looked as though they were ready to strike, although they seemed concerned with the sky above them. Were they looking for other light invaders to jump them from above?

"You saved my life. I'll help you fight them."

Wallace shook his head. "You are not protected. They will destroy you." He winced again. "Weapon," he whispered.

Drew looked at the bloodied short sword still in Wallace's grip. He didn't understand.

"Yours."

Drew grabbed the .45 and held it out for him. Wallace reached for the gun, and the moment he touched it, an exact copy of the Sig Sauer pistol fell to the ground beside him…a copy in the invaders' realm. Wallace dropped his hand to cover it, and Drew gawked. Could they replicate *everything* from this world into their dimension? Drew heard movement between the buildings. In one swift and powerful move, Wallace grabbed Drew's shirt just below his neck and pulled him to within inches of his face.

"Now, *go*!" He pushed Drew away.

Large drops of rain splashed on the pavement around them. When Drew heard the voices of policemen, he scrambled to his feet. He glanced up the alley, but the dark invaders had left. Wallace fell to his side and then onto his back, the bleeding gashes across his chest open to the sky above. Wisps of blue enveloped him once again, and he translated back into the realm of invaders. He grasped both the short sword and the .45 in his hands. Drew turned to leave, but something caught his eye. Every drop of rain that pounded into Wallace's wounds sizzled and evaporated into steam. Wallace winced in excruciating pain, but he did not try to stop it.

The voices grew louder, forcing Drew to run. At the end of the alley, Drew stuffed the .45 back into his belt and turned to see Wallace's fate. Another light invader stepped through the brick wall and knelt down beside his injured commander. Wallace dropped his sword and grabbed his comrade's hand, screaming silently. Drew looked up toward the sky, now saturated with water droplets.

Flashlight beams broke through into the alley, and Drew ducked around the corner of an apartment building and sprinted as fast as his legs would carry him. His mind raced wild with questions. Did Wallace die? Why would a light invader risk so much to save his life? Had the invaders pinpointed Sydney as a target and somehow connected her to him?

He ran three more blocks, until he was sure he was clear of any searches, then slowed his pace. He found a dark corner to lean into to catch his breath, and all that had just happened swept over him, overwhelming him. The aftereffects of a full adrenaline rush took their toll—his arms and legs ached. He stayed still for a long while, numb from the night's bizarre events. Just when Drew thought he could place one more piece into the puzzle...

Another three appeared.

IMPOSSIBLE LOVE

The next day, Drew went to the church, hoping to see the usual activity, but instead he saw that the churchyard was full of children—and the Drayle University students. The same students who had endured being terrorized by the Dragons last night!

They were playing games with the children and teaching them. Drew shook his head. What courage…or foolishness. He noticed that Sydney would look up from time to time and search around them.

She was looking for him.

Perhaps the most unusual activity he saw was in the invader realm. Drew counted thirteen light invaders standing guard. He had never seen so many at one time. The incident last night must have triggered some sort of alert up their chain of command.

After work that night Drew caught a cab to the Travel Host Hotel. He smiled at the young woman at the front desk. "Can you tell Sydney Carlyle she has a visitor?"

She made the call, then nodded. "I've given her the message."

Drew stepped over to the television at the far end of the lobby, but in just a few seconds, he heard a door open and close. He looked up at the balcony that fed the stairway down into the lobby. Sydney appeared at the railing, halting her run just long enough to look down and confirm that it was Drew. His heart skipped a beat as he saw her gazing down at him.

She resumed her run down the stairs and into the lobby. Drew wasn't sure just how to greet her, but she chose it for him. She embraced him with a long hug, and he held her. All the stomach butterflies he'd felt before swelled within him again, but multiplied four times, and he dreaded what was coming next. She released him and stepped back, a little embarrassed.

"How is it possible that you were there to save me again?"

Drew scanned the area. "We can't talk here, Sydney. Can you walk with me?"

She nodded. They walked across the street to a twenty-four-hour breakfast restaurant and found a booth in the back corner of one of the dining areas. Drew sat so he could see the entrance and the lobby, although he knew that meant very little when facing an enemy that could appear through the wall behind him at any second.

He looked across at Sydney and smiled. "It's so good to see you."

Sydney's eyes gleamed. "You too, Drew." Her smile faded. "What is going on? I want to hug you and slap you all at the same time." She shook her head.

"Slap me? Why?"

"Because I got arrested by the FBI because of you!" Fire sparked in her eyes.

"What? How?"

"When I went to pick up your car at the university like you asked me to, FBI agents rushed in on me and put me up against the car—at gunpoint!"

Drew sat back against the booth bench. "How did they know?"

"Evidently they checked all the plates on the cars and searched any that weren't registered with the campus. When they searched yours, they found a handgun. When I showed up, they were waiting for me. Once they connected me with being in the classroom with you, everything went nuts, and they started asking me all kinds of crazy questions. They held me for hours. I had to tell them everything. I thought I was going to go to prison the way they were talking. It was the testimony of the professor that convinced them to let me go, but they're looking for you, Drew." Sydney tilted her head to the side. "What is going on?" It was a question, a plea, and a command.

Drew rubbed his eyes and leaned forward. "I'm so sorry, Sydney. I should never have asked that of you." He looked at her and saw the anxiety and confusion in her beautiful eyes. Her only crime was getting to know him. For a moment he considered telling her everything, but he knew she wouldn't believe him. The FBI had probably told her to report any contact she had with him. He imagined her telling them that he believed aliens had invaded earth, and cringed. He couldn't do that to her. But perhaps he could give her enough truth without sounding crazy. He took a deep breath and slowly exhaled.

"It all started with the lab accident." Drew watched her eyes to see if she was questioning the truth of his story. "Dr. Waseem was conducting research on accelerating light, which has some far-reaching scientific and military implications. He received a grant from the government even when most scientists and physicists thought his work was absurd." He paused to see if Sydney was still with him. "That's the first red flag. Ben was his number-one assistant, and he came to me the day Dr. Waseem was killed and told me that the professor's experiment was successful. Ben was scared, Sydney, because he suspected foul play in Dr. Waseem's death. I mean, not only did the doctor die under questionable circumstances but the entire lab, including all the research, was completely destroyed."

Sydney's brow furrowed. "But you and Ben were there, Drew. How does that have anything to do with it being a suspicious event?"

Drew looked down at the table. Just how far did he dare involve her? He looked back up at her. "Because I saw someone else there too. Someone who wasn't supposed to be there."

"Who? Who was it?"

Drew shook his head. "I don't know. I only got a glimpse of him just before I went blind, but Ben and I both think whoever it was had everything to do with Dr. Waseem's death. I don't think this guy or the people he works for had any idea that Ben knew as much as he did about Waseem's research, or Ben would have been killed too."

Drew let Sydney think about what he said for a minute. "There's something else I've never told anyone."

Sydney leaned forward. She was hanging on his every word.

"I talked to Ben a couple of days after he disappeared. He told me they, whoever 'they' are, were after him. Sydney, he was scared for his life. That's why he disappeared, and I don't know if the FBI, the CIA, or even the MIB are the ones that are after him, but now it looks like they're after me too."

"You need to get help. What about the police, or at least Jake?"

"The police already investigated Dr. Waseem's death. They won't believe me. And whoever is behind this will be watching my family, including Jake. There's no one, Sydney. I'm in this alone."

"So why Chicago? Why are you hiding here?"

"I'm not just hiding. I'm searching…for Ben, just like I told you at Drayle. I believe Ben is here, and if I can find him, we have a chance of proving this whole story. Think about it—why else would they be after Ben? He hasn't done anything."

Sydney sat back against the booth seat. She looked stunned, as if she was trying to absorb this governmental conspiracy theory. Drew felt sorry for her. If she knew just how bizarre it *really* was, she would flip on him and the FBI would be at his door before midnight. He had to keep her tracking with what the world considered reality.

"It's hard to believe, Drew… I mean, it's just a little crazy." Her eyes yearned for some sort of proof, some tangible evidence that what he was saying was true so that she could justify keeping quiet.

"I know the FBI has asked you to tell them if you have any contact with me."

Sydney's gaze dropped to the table, and her countenance fell in utter sadness.

He reached across the table and covered her hand with his own. "That's why I tried so hard, once I saw you, to keep my presence here a secret. I didn't want to put you in a compromising situation or bring any more danger to you, but I couldn't let that gang hurt you either. Do you see my dilemma?"

"You saved my life…again. How do you… How can you survive such things? You moved so fast it almost seems impossible."

"Once I understood the danger I would be facing, I started training with a seventh-degree black belt. He's very good… I owe him a lot." He hoped she would buy that for now. "You guys drove into the Dragons' turf. That's a bad place to go through, let alone break down. I've had encounters with them before, and I'm sure it won't be the last. They don't like me much." He offered a sheepish grin.

She looked at his hand covering her own. "Thank you...for saving us." She put her hand on top of his, then looked up at him. "All I have ever seen from you, Drew, is a guy who wants to do what is right. I know what I saw at Drayle, and I know what I saw last night." She looked him straight in the eye. "I choose to believe you."

Drew sighed in relief. "Thank you. You have no idea how good it feels to have someone believe you."

"Actually I do. And perhaps one day you will believe *me*."

Drew cocked his head to the side, not sure what she was implying.

"I've prayed for you every day since your accident back in Rivercrest. Now, more than ever, you are going to need prayer. God has His hand on you, Drew, but I'm scared for you."

"I can take care of myself, Syd."

"You can't dodge bullets, Drew!" Sydney's glare revealed her passion.

Drew loved that she was concerned for him. "Speaking of bullets, what I want to know is, after last night, how come you and your friends are still in Chicago? Don't you realize how dangerous it is here?"

"We know the risks, but someone needs to share Jesus Christ with these people."

Drew stared at her. How could he be so drawn to a girl who was so deceived and confused about life? "I can't for the life of me figure out what drives you, Sydney."

Her eyes sparkled. "What drives me is my love for God and for people. The time is short, the harvest is ready, and the laborers are few."

Drew shook his head, smiling. "Girl...you say the strangest things. As happy as I am to see you, I wish you had never come to Chicago." He glanced out the window and thought he saw something move. "You need to leave."

She looked at him in an almost condescending way. "Drew, I didn't come here to find you, and I didn't come here for me." Her voice was confident and cool. "I came here because I was called by God."

Drew smirked.

"I know you don't believe in God, but that doesn't change the fact that He is in control."

That's what she meant when she talked about him not believing her—he didn't believe her in regard to God and Christianity. But in light of all the injustice he had seen over the past months, of the dark invaders and the havoc they were wreaking on humanity, how could he believe in God? It frustrated him not to be able to show her the truth.

"Well, if God's in control, then He's not doing a very good job. Besides, it looked to me like you all needed some protecting last night."

Sydney shook her head. "My protection is in following God's will. The fact of the matter is, Drew, that you are the one who needs protecting. You are the one who is in danger."

Drew looked at her for a moment and had the strangest feeling that she might know more than she was letting on. "What do you mean?"

Sydney looked deep into his eyes. He saw a fire in her eyes that burned from an ancient wisdom. "There are forces at work in this world that most people don't know of."

Drew's skin tingled and the hairs stood straight on the back of his neck. Did she know of the invaders? Was it possible she had known all along? Had she been playing him all this time?

"How do you know this?"

"Because God's Word says so. And unless you put your faith in Jesus Christ, you are in grave eternal peril, Drew."

Drew sighed. More spiritual mumbo jumbo. He shook his head. "So God wants you and your friends to risk your lives in the ghettos of Chicago so homeless people can have a bowl of soup. Is that right?"

"It's so much more than that, Drew. We're here to teach the homeless and as many children that we can about the truth of God. To show them how to love and trust in Him and to show them how to win eternal life through Jesus Christ. There is no mission greater than this." Sydney's passion for her faith was admirable, Drew had to admit.

"Sydney, I've been living in the ghettos for the past six months. Every night I go out and rescue people, stop crimes, and try to help the police put criminals behind bars." He shook his head. "It seems so hopeless. There's too much… darkness. It would take an army of vigilantes to make a difference in just one city."

Sydney's soft and gentle lips curled into a broad smile.

"What are you smiling about?"

"You're not that far away, Drew. I believe you will one day see the truth."

"And one day so will you," he said with a returning smile. Drew glanced out the window—and his blood turned cold. Four dark invaders were talking in the parking lot. The one giving orders…

Was Kurgan.

22

A MISSION FOR TWO

As dark as every dark invader was, there was something deeper about Kurgan's darkness. Drew hadn't seen him since the incident at the bus station. Were they looking for him...or for Sydney? Either way she and Drew were in trouble. If Kurgan was as much of a commander as he looked, and if he connected Drew to Kansas, it would mean the end of his search for Ben. It felt like a noose being tightened around his neck.

"What's wrong, Drew?"

Drew turned to look at Sydney, trying to control his rising dread. "We need to go now."

Sydney thought for a moment and then gathered her things.

As they walked to the exit, Drew whispered in her ear. "I want you to go into the bathroom while I pay. When you come out, walk directly out of the restaurant and toward the hotel. Understand?"

Sydney nodded. She looked around for some threat.

"Don't look around. I won't be far from you. Okay?"

She looked up at him, her eyes filled with concern.

Drew stood in line behind two other people waiting to pay, when he saw one of the invaders materialize through the wall where they had been sitting. He looked up at the security camera monitor, which was divided into four screens—two showing the outside of the building and two showing each half of the dining room. None of them revealed any sign of a seven-foot, darkly dressed warrior brandishing a sword on his back, but there he was, right in the middle of the camera's field of view.

The invader scanned the tables in the room and then began walking toward the restaurant lobby. Drew stepped beside and ahead of the man and woman in front of him and slapped a twenty down on the counter to cover his ticket. Then he slipped into the opposite side of the restaurant, where there were multiple privacy walls and booths to give customers a more secluded feel. He maneuvered to the back of the restaurant, watching the invader's search pattern, and stepped into the kitchen.

"Oh…I'm sorry. I was looking for the bathroom." He tried to look embarrassed.

The cook pointed to a door on the other side of the kitchen without looking up. Drew crossed the kitchen and exited, ending up back on the side of the restaurant where they had been sitting and where the invader had already searched. Drew grabbed a menu, sat back down in their booth, and watched. Sydney stepped out of the bathroom and headed toward the exit just as the invader was returning from his search of the other side of the restaurant. Drew's heart accelerated as Sydney walked straight at the invader, unaware of the darkness glowering at her. Drew searched the nearby humans to see if any of them were under the influence of the invaders, but the invader turned away and continued his search by entering the hallway to the bathrooms.

Drew made his way to the lobby and exited twenty feet behind Sydney. He scanned the parking lot but didn't see any sign of the other invaders.

So…Sydney was clean. He was definitely the one the invaders were after, but had she inadvertently brought Kurgan here? After all, the invaders wouldn't have ignored the attention brought on her by being detained and questioned by the FBI. Drew needed to distance himself from her, not only for his sake but for hers. He diverted his walk so that he entered the lobby of the hotel a few minutes after Sydney, then confirmed that neither of them were being followed. Inside, Sydney sat staring at an empty fireplace.

Drew sat down beside her, and she didn't move. He didn't know what to tell her. She had to think he was paranoid, just like his mother had thought.

Drew reached into his pocket and pulled out an envelope addressed to his mother.

"Unless you think mailing a letter will get you in trouble with the FBI, will you do one last favor for me?"

Sydney turned her head and stared at him…expressionless.

I've said too much…pushed too far. He couldn't take the thought that she viewed him as a crazy man. He turned away and started to return the envelope to his pocket. "It's okay, it's not that impor—"

He felt her warm hand cover his. "Of course. Where do you want me to mail it from?"

Drew looked back at her, the sadness in her eyes melted him. He loved and hated to love her. "You *are* intelligent, Syd. From the campus post office on Drayle University in a couple of weeks. I've been out of contact with my mom for months and I'm sure she is sick with worry. Thanks."

Sydney slipped the envelope from his hand and stood up. Drew rose with her. He could tell she knew exactly what he needed from her—distance. She looked up into his eyes with a visage as serious as ever he had seen from her.

"You stay alive," she whispered.

Drew smiled at her, then opened his mouth to tell her he would be fine, but she pressed her fingers against his lips. Somehow, she understood the gravity of his mission, or perhaps it was that she understood how serious he knew it was. Whatever the case, she would not be placated by meaningless words of affirmation. She turned and walked away from him, and it reminded him of high school. Every time she did it though, his heart fell further into her arms.

Two days later, Drew felt great relief and great sadness when the campus ministry van left Chicago. For the few days Sydney had been there, the darkness of a dreary city dissipated and the burden of his mission seemed lighter.

BY WINTER, Drew had worked his way through thirty percent of the computer repair shops in the Chicago area. He'd covered all of downtown Chicago and a three-mile radius out from the Chicago Tech Center. He looked at his map and despaired as he realized that those were the easy ones. With every radial mile farther out, the distances became much greater and the density of repair shops diminished. He would have to cover more ground to reach fewer shops.

He was tired of bicycles, ramen noodles, invaders, and gangs. He threw the map across his musty apartment and wallowed in self-pity. He rubbed his eyes and decided to go to the one place that lifted his spirits, despite it being filled with homeless needy people.

Drew walked into Emmanuel Church and was greeted with a warm hug by Reverend Ray. Micah came running and jumped at Drew, who caught him and swung him upside down, threatening to drop him on his head.

"You're here early today, Ryan," Ray said with a smile. "The kitchen doesn't open for another hour."

"Yeah, I know. I just thought, well…"

"Hey, we're always glad to see you, son, and always glad to have your help."

"Save anybody last night?" Micah asked with big eyes and a smile as wide as his face could handle.

Drew grabbed him and swung him on his back. "I don't know what you're talking about, M."

Drew and Ray walked toward the kitchen as Micah rode piggyback.

"We have another helper tonight," Ray said with a sly smile.

"Yeah?"

"A volunteer from the university."

"She's cool. I told her all about the Guardian," said Micah.

Drew flipped Micah over his shoulder and set him on the ground. "Micah…I told you not to tell stories like that. You're going to get me in trouble."

"Let me introduce you," Ray said as they stepped through the doorway.

Drew froze in his tracks. There, adorned in an Emmanuel Church cook's apron, stood Sydney. She looked up from the soup she was stirring and smiled a knowing smile.

"Sydney Carlyle, I'd like you to meet Ryan. But don't ask him his last name 'cause he's kind of a mysterious fellow."

Drew stared, dumbfounded, as Sydney wiped her hands on her apron and came to meet him. She held out her hand and tilted her head.

"I'm pleased to meet you, Ryan Somebody."

Drew slowly stuck out his hand and gawked.

"I do believe you've made him speechless, missy," Ray said.

"I…I'm pleased to meet you too." Drew struggled with the shock wave of sensation emanating from his hand, an effect he could control from everyone's touch but hers. "What brings you to Chicago?" he asked with an edge in his voice he couldn't help.

"I've heard such great things about the University of Illinois that I transferred and am going to school here this next semester." She gave him the most delightful smile.

Drew once again was speechless.

"How long you gonna hold her hand?" Micah stared at their entwined hands, his nose scrunched up.

Drew jerked his hand back. "How nice." He forced a smile. Joy and anger wrestled inside him.

"Sydney helped us earlier this summer and now wants to volunteer on a regular basis," Nicole said as she and Shana entered the kitchen. "We are so glad to have you."

Drew was forced to play his "Ryan" role in a way he never wanted to, and Sydney enjoyed it way too much. He played ignorant for the rest of the evening, and despite finding himself wanting to work beside her as much as possible, an observation at which Reverend Ray and his family couldn't help but chuckle, he couldn't wait to berate Sydney for her foolishness.

He got his chance when she drove to his apartment after their work at Emmanuel was finished. "What are you doing, Syd?" Drew closed the door after her.

She looked around at the moldy walls and tattered gold curtains, ignoring his rebuke. "I love what you've done with the place."

At the wry comment, Drew turned away. For all her discernment, she didn't seem to understand at all what was at stake. He turned back, grabbed her arm. "I'm serious, what do you think you're doing?"

She spun to face him, eyes blazing. "I'm here to help you." She crossed her arms. "And you *need* my help."

Drew clenched his teeth. "You don't understand." He turned around and walked away, partly because of his frustration, but also to give him the opportunity to do a quick scan. "Your presence could jeopardize what I'm trying to do."

"How so?"

"The FBI is probably monitoring you. If they find me, the search for Ben is over, and so is any hope of finding out the truth about Dr. Waseem and his research."

"It's been months. I don't think they're watching me anymore, and even if they are, I'm completely justified in being here."

"How do you figure?"

"My mission trip earlier this summer had nothing to do with you, and I'm rooming with my cousin who has been at UIC for the past two years. But in spite of that, we'll just have to be careful."

Sydney walked toward Drew. "Besides, you can't do this alone."

She was right, and he knew it. The ground he needed to cover to find Ben was too much for one guy. His limited access to Master Lee's car was not enough, and he couldn't even register for a car of his own without showing up on the grid. Maybe…she was exactly what he needed to accomplish the mission. Then he thought of the danger to her and shook his head.

"It's too dangerous, Sydney." He turned and put a hand on her shoulder. "I won't let you. You must go back to Kansas."

She closed her eyes. When she opened them, he could see a peace inside her that Drew had never felt himself. *Where does that come from?*

She put a hand on his arm. "Drew, I care about you…a lot. And my heart is so torn I can hardly stand it, which is why I just about didn't come. But there is a voice inside me that would not let me stay in Kansas. Never in my life have I been so sure about hearing God's voice and calling on my life as I am right now, even though I'm not sure why He has me here. Maybe it's you, maybe not. But whether you accept my help or not, I am going to school at the University of Illinois, and I am going to volunteer at Emmanuel Church." She lifted his hand from her shoulder and released it. "But you also need to know something else. I cannot love you, and I will not love you while you remain unsaved." She squinted at him. "So don't get any ideas."

Drew stood staring at the most amazing girl he had ever met. So close and yet so untouchable. For the first time in his life, he was glad for this imaginary God of hers. He took a deep breath and gave in.

He looked down at the floor and then back up at her. "I didn't know if you really believed me."

"I wouldn't be here if I didn't. What do we need to do?"

"Come here." He brought her to the small table in the kitchen area. He opened up the map and began explaining his process for finding Ben. Within an hour, they had a dual attack plan for covering the computer shops. They also planned to find a cheap car that she would buy and register so that Drew could drive and cover more ground.

Drew felt new life flowing into him as he saw the probable success of the plan increasing tenfold. When Sydney stood at the door, ready to return to her dorm on campus, Drew felt it necessary for one more warning.

"Listen, I have become an expert at identifying"—he hesitated—"agents. You must act as though they can see you and hear you at all times. Cell phone calls between us can only be used in emergency. Whoever we are dealing with has resources and weapons beyond anything you can imagine. One wrong move, Sydney, and this all ends in a moment. Do you understand?"

Sydney nodded. "I'll be careful."

Drew closed the door behind her and lowered his head. He hoped he hadn't just bought her a ticket to tragedy.

A DESPERATE MOVE

Drew bought a beat-up 1999 Grand Prix for five hundred dollars from a friend of Reverend Ray's. The car was falling apart inside and out, but the engine still purred like a kitten, and that was all that Drew needed. Mr. Lee was thrilled he didn't have to loan Drew his car for the longer deliveries and gave him a raise.

Drew and Sydney used Emmanuel's soup kitchen as a rendezvous point each week to share and compare information. After their work serving in the kitchen was done, they would meet in a room in the church that Reverend Ray had converted to a small chapel for people who wanted to worship in private. For some reason, Drew felt like it was as safe from dark invaders here as in the middle of the ocean.

It turned out to be the perfect place since Drew rarely saw a dark invader on the church grounds. After three weeks of searching for Ben, Sydney and Drew had covered more computer repair shops together than he had covered in two months. Despite their efficiency, they still had no leads.

The Bransons all seemed delighted with the apparent friendship developing between Ryan and Sydney. However, Drew learned from Sydney that Reverend Ray had found an opportunity to counsel her to be careful because of Ryan's mysterious background and about being in a relationship with an unbeliever. She thanked him and assured him she would be careful and not compromise her faith. She told Drew that she and Reverend Ray had agreed to pray for Drew's protection and salvation every day.

Had Drew not known the truth about the invaders in their world, he probably would have felt annoyed by their piety, but instead he just felt sorry for them in their foolishness.

One week, Drew watched Sydney as she served the homeless and spent time at the tables talking with them. The joy radiating from her seemed contagious, spilling out onto each person she talked to. She was doing much more than just being cheerful, though. He overheard her telling one desperate young woman who seemed to be tripped out on crack that Jesus loved her and if she would come to Him, He would forgive her sins and create a new life for her. And on that day, in that church, Drew came to a convicting conclusion.

Sydney really did love God and really did love people.

He helped at Emmanuel because it felt good to do so. His reason was based in selfishness. She helped at Emmanuel because she actually loved those homeless people. It was a humbling realization because Drew knew he couldn't be like her. There was something she had that he didn't. Something that allowed her to function the way she did, and he marveled at it.

Afterward, they walked down one of the church hallways toward the chapel together.

"I feel like we are being dishonest with Reverend Ray and his family," Sydney said.

"I know, me too. I promise I'll tell him as soon as I feel it's safe for him and his family to know. Keeping them in the dark is also protection for them, okay?"

Sydney hesitated, then nodded.

"So, what have you got?" Drew asked.

"I checked out twelve more this week but got nothing." Sydney frowned.

"Well, we still have over two hundred and fifty to go, so we won't know until we finish with the last one. How are you holding up? Any suspicious contacts?"

"No. Although there are always some students on campus that look suspicious to me." Sydney grinned.

"Really?" Masquerading as a college student would be the perfect cover for an FBI agent.

"No…I'm kidding." Sydney's smile faded. "This whole thing has really changed you, Drew. You hardly smile anymore."

She was right, but how could all this *not* change him? If she knew what he saw, it would change her too. "I'm sorry." He sighed. "You're right… I'll try to smile more."

Sydney flashed a weak smile. "How about you, any contacts?"

Drew thought about the invaders he saw every day and night. "No… No FBI, as far as I can tell. But that doesn't mean they're not there. Please be careful."

She nodded. "I guess we'd better get going."

Drew hated that he could spend only a few minutes with her each week, but the less they were together, the safer she would be.

She stood and went to the door and then turned. "Hey, there is one shop that wanted to help me. The guy said he'd do it for free."

Drew smiled at that. He could imagine some geek in a back room happy to help a cute girl with her computer problem. "While he was looking at the disk, he asked me out."

"I'll bet he did," Drew said with a smirk.

"Yeah…when I told him I was doing this for my boyfriend, he handed the hard drive back to me and said the disks were too damaged to recover."

"Boyfriend, huh?" Drew raised an eyebrow.

"Well…you are a friend and you are a boy… It gets me out of a lot of fixes." Sydney winked, and Drew's heart missed a beat.

"And you are telling me this because?"

"When I was leaving, he said that there was a shop on Thirty-Sixth that had a guy who could help me. I didn't have time to get there today, but I thought maybe you might want to check it out."

"Hey, that's promising. I'll check it out first chance I get tomorrow."

Sydney reached for the door, but Drew held it closed. She looked up with eyes that melted him, and he wished for a different life.

"I don't know how to thank you, Syd."

Sydney smiled at him with her eyes. "I do."

"Name it—lunch…dinner…of course it would have to be private because of the—"

"Come to church with me on Sunday. Pastor Worthington is amazing. He's very logical, and I think you'd enjoy him."

Oh, great. Now he felt trapped. "Don't you think the FBI, if they are watching you, might think that church would be a perfect place to keep an eye on you?"

"I'll pray for extra protection." Sydney smiled as she turned and opened the door. She was so disarming and impossible to refuse… Still, he'd have to think that one through before he committed.

Work was long the next day, and none of his delivery routes took him out far enough to cover any new repair shops, so he had to wait until his shift was over. He zipped to Thirty-Sixth at four thirty and asked to speak to the tech. Drew waited five hopeful minutes, but a heavyset dude with scraggily hair and thick, black-framed glasses came to the counter. Drew's heart sank.

"T'sup?" he said as he leaned on the counter. The smell of Dr Pepper and barbecue potato chips permeated the space between them.

Drew put the hard drive on the counter. "I've got data on this that I need to get off, but the drive doesn't work."

The tech picked it up and squinted as he looked it over. He removed the cover to expose the disks. "Yeah…you've got a problem. The heads have damaged at least one platter. Can't help you." He set the drive down and turned to leave.

"But another shop told me you could help. Is there someone else that might work here who could do it?"

"Dang it, Lenny… I *told* him to quit sending people here. The only dude I know of that could have helped you quit three weeks ago. Sorry, man, you're out of luck."

"Someone quit? Hey, this is really, really important. Can you tell me where I can find him?" Drew struggled to curb his rising excitement.

"Not really. Some suit walked in all mad because the tech guys at his company couldn't fix his iPad. Two days later, Chider had it fixed."

"Chider?"

"Yeah…Chider Anderson. Turns out the guy with the iPad actually owned the company. He asked Chider if he knew anything about networks and then offered him a job on the spot at double his salary…right in front me—that arrogant jerk!"

Drew whipped out a twenty. "It's yours if you can remember the name of the company."

The tech smiled. He reached for the twenty and took it. "Hey, Sherry," he called over his shoulder at the receptionist. "The suit that stole Chider from us. What company was he with?"

"How should I know?"

"Look it up!" The tech rolled his eyes at Drew and mouthed the word *ditz*. She huffed and started clicking with her mouse. "Donovan Chambers."

"W-h-a-t c-o-m-p-a-n-y?" The tech spoke loud and slow.

"I d-o-n'-t k-n-o-w," the girl sassed back even louder and slower. "He paid with a personal credit card…sheesh!"

"That'll work." Drew held up his hand. "Thanks, you saved my life."

The tech shrugged and turned to go back to his sanctuary. Through the doorway Drew saw shelves of disassembled computers, laptops, and monitors. It looked like a techno rat's nest. To each his own…

Drew started walking away, then paused. "Hey…just so I can recognize him, what does Chider look like?"

"I don't know…like every other tech geek, I guess. Straight brown hair and eyes with dark rings beneath."

Drew nodded. Could be.

"Just a warning," the guy called back. "Chider's a genius, but he's a little off and way paranoid if you know what I mean."

Drew nodded. That didn't eliminate many tech geeks, but it certainly included Ben. That was something.

That night, Drew searched the net for Donovan Chambers and came up with only three hits. One was Reliance Office Suites, a high-end office rental corporation that provided phone, Internet, tech support, computers, and even receptionists and secretaries, if needed. They were located on West Randolph. Drew closed his laptop.

"Please let this be Ben."

It almost sounded like a prayer and Drew shook his head. Sydney must be rubbing off on him.

Drew found it difficult to sleep that night. After lying with eyes wide open for two hours, he rolled out of bed, powered up his laptop, and began planning rendezvous points and alternates. At 2 a.m. anticipation gave way to fatigue, and he fell asleep for a few short hours.

Later that morning at six, Drew drove into downtown Chicago and found an open parking spot in a pay-per-day lot five blocks from the Reliance Office Suites building. It was the next closest parking to the garage right across the street, which he felt was a little too close for comfort in case he had to make a getaway on foot. He needed his car safe and accessible.

He walked five blocks south and then purchased a newspaper from a stand across the street from the Reliance building. A small grassy courtyard diagonal from the building made a perfect vantage point to see the building's entrances. It was a classy twelve-story building with a balanced mix of Renaissance and modern architecture. At seven o'clock the city hummed with activity. Drew called Mr. Lee and told him he couldn't work for the next two days. He didn't know Korean, but he was pretty sure that some of the things Mr. Lee uttered as he hung up the phone weren't very complimentary.

At seven forty-five Drew saw some interesting activity…from the dark invaders. One took up a lookout position at the corner of the Reliance building while another waited across the street near a parking garage. One block to the east, a bus stopped and unloaded a crowd of people. Drew was evaluating every person who came into view. As the crowd dispersed in three different directions, he was tasked with validating each of the men. One man stuck out, for there was a dark invader following close behind him. If his destination was the Reliance building, he would pass just across the street from Drew. Drew ignored every other person because the man's gait was familiar. He didn't dare hope, and yet couldn't help it. Months of searching…months of evasion…could this be it?

The man was walking in front of another man and two women, all headed west toward the Reliance building. The collar of the man's coat was pulled up high around his neck, but with each step closer, Drew became more and more hopeful and yet anxious. Certainly he was a target of at least one of the dark invaders, whether for reconnaissance or assassination, he did not know.

The man walked to the stoplight directly across the street from the courtyard Drew was in and pushed the crossing button. Then he did something most people wouldn't do: he turned and looked all around him while he waited for the Walk signal. As his gaze passed through the courtyard, Drew saw his face—and nearly shouted.

There stood Benjamin Berg.

Drew bit his lip, trying hard to remain a nameless, faceless figure in the distance. Relief, joy, and fear swallowed him. He forced himself to stay calm as he watched Ben step into the street—and then a start jolted through him.

He'd lost track of the invader in front of the building.

Drew scanned the area and found him. He had jumped onto a car approaching the intersection Ben was now crossing. With sword drawn, the invader sliced through the roof of the vehicle and held the blade across the driver's eyes. Another invader now buffeted Ben with his sword, shielding Ben's eyes from the oncoming car—which was not slowing.

Drew stood, shivers flowing up and down his body as he watched his friend's impending death. Had he searched for so long to be just seconds too late? The oncoming car careened toward Ben, who seemed oblivious of any danger.

Drew ran onto the sidewalk and screamed at the same time that one of the women behind Ben shrieked, but the warnings were too late. Just as Ben was about to be struck by the car, a man behind him grabbed his coat and yanked him backward. The car whizzed past Ben, missing him by fractions of an inch. Drew saw the dark invaders curse while the man and two women gathered around Ben to see if he was okay.

Drew stopped and turned away, hoping he hadn't given away his position to the invaders. If he had, all would be in vain. He disappeared into a small drugstore and hurried to the back. He found his way to the storage room, where he bumped into a stocker. Drew didn't dare look behind him.

"Is there a back door?"

"You're not supposed to be back here," the man said.

Drew ignored him and kept moving until he spotted the exit. He opened the door into the alley and pressed on. He dodged between two buildings and onto an adjoining street, where he meshed into a crowd of people. At a crosswalk, waiting for a light, he took a chance to scan. As he turned to glance behind him, an invader glared at him just inches away—at least that's what Drew thought until he realized that it was a Goth complete with a dozen piercings, white skin, black and purple makeup, and white pupil contacts.

Drew jumped and the Goth just smiled. Drew breathed a sigh of relief as he realized there was no sign of any real invaders. He started making his way back to the Reliance building, circling the block kitty-cornered to the Reliance block six times...pacing and thinking.

What should he do now? Ben was a target for assassination and might not make it through the day—the dark invaders had obviously figured out his importance. Drew had to make contact with Ben, but without exposing himself to the invaders. If they figured out that he was in Chicago and had found Ben, he could only imagine what kind of forces would be brought against both of them. Neither would survive, that was sure.

After two hours of considering his options, Drew was ready. He had to save Ben now, if it wasn't already too late.

24

SAVING BEN

Drew waited until he was certain there were no dark invaders outside the Reliance building, then walked past the entrance a couple of times to get a view of the inside through the large glass windows that lined the front of the building. When he was convinced the lobby was clear, he entered. The neomodern lobby and reception desk contrasted the exterior architecture and yet was quite appealing. Drew scanned as he approached the receptionist. She was a perfect complement to the décor with her black bobbed hair and sleek, straight-fitting business dress.

"Can I help you?" she asked with a pasted smile.

"Yes, I am a close friend of one of your employees…a Mr. Chider Anderson?"

"Yes, he's one of our computer technicians. Would you like me to call him?"

"No, that's all right. I don't want to bother him now, but I was hoping to catch him for lunch. Could I write a note and have you pass it on to him?"

She handed him a piece of paper, and he wrote, *I'm in town and was wondering if you wanted to buy me lunch in exchange for the help I gave you years ago on your science project. Charley's Deli—11:00.* He folded the paper twice, wrote *Chider* on the outside, and handed it to the receptionist.

"Thanks."

Drew had never heard of a computer technician dying while fixing a computer, although anything was possible when conditions and events were manipulated by the dark invaders. He figured if the invaders were going to make another attempt on Ben's life, it would be when he was outside and in the open, where they would have unlimited access to people and machinery. There was a slim chance that a break in Ben's routine might throw them off. Knowing Ben, Drew figured he wouldn't normally leave for lunch, so the invaders might not even track him until after work.

At 10:45, Drew positioned himself on the second floor of the parking garage that faced the Reliance building. At 10:50, he watched Ben exit and walk west. Initially Drew was elated that no dark invaders were in sight, but when Ben reached the corner of the building, one came through the brick wall beside him. The invader looked perturbed as he whispered into Ben's ear. Ben stopped and looked around him in all directions. He glanced back at the entrance to the building, turned around, and started walking back. At the doorway, he stopped again, even though the invader was relentless in trying to influence him.

Ben rubbed his hand across his eyes and forehead, then went back onto the sidewalk and retraced his steps to the end of the block. Despite the constant buffeting of the invader, Ben continued onward.

The dark invader scowled and flew south across the street to pass right below Drew, through the main level of the parking garage. By the urgency of his movement, Drew suspected he was going to report this change in Ben's routine. It was a break Drew hadn't expected, and odds were that the window of opportunity wouldn't last long.

He ran down the garage staircase and onto the street. Ben stood at the intersection across the street, waiting. Even though the Walk light was green, he wouldn't cross. Four lanes of moving traffic separated Drew from Ben. The seconds ticked by, and the window was closing. The dark invader would soon return, and when he did, others would be with him to finish what they had started earlier—the termination of Ben's life.

A man stepped around Ben and started across the crosswalk. Ben looked both ways four times, then followed close behind the man. Drew turned and ran parallel to Ben across his side of the street. He then turned and waited for the light so he could get on the same side as Ben. He watched as Ben stepped up onto the curb and proceeded down the street. Drew considered darting through the traffic, but it was too thick to take the risk. The yellow light seemed to take hours to turn. Drew looked south, down the street behind him. He caught sight of distant movement but couldn't be sure what it was.

Cars slowed and stopped as the yellow light finally changed. Drew dashed into the street, narrowly missing one car that was trying to skim through the intersection. He cut the corner and ran to catch up to Ben, who was now fifty feet up the sidewalk. Drew took one more glance down the street to the south and saw the movement again, this time much closer.

They were coming.

Drew sprinted ahead, losing line of sight of the attacking invaders because of the building across the street. He had less than ten seconds to either make contact with Ben or disappear before the invaders spotted him. He had no choice. He had to abort. He was just a few feet behind Ben when he decided to veer off and away. He looked across the street, where the invaders would appear in just a few seconds.

Had he just set up his long-lost friend to be killed?

Right beside him a taxi driver honked his horn to get the traffic ahead of him moving, and Drew reacted. He moved forward and grabbed Ben's arm. "Ben, it's me, Drew—get in the cab now!"

Ben jerked away, but Drew didn't let go. He pulled Ben to the cab and reached for the door as it started to move forward. Ben resisted at first, then just froze.

"Drew?"

Drew saw a flash at the corner of the Reliance building. It was an invader just materializing through a bus in the street. Drew grabbed Ben's waist and the back of his head, bent him over, and threw him into the cab, then jumped in behind him and slammed the door shut.

"Stay down!" Drew kept his hand firmly on Ben's head.

"Anywhere, fast—please!" Ben said to the cab driver, who didn't seem the least alarmed at what might appear to be an abduction.

The cab lurched forward as Drew pulled his hood over his head. Out of the corner of his eye and through his sunglasses, he saw three dark invaders searching the sidewalk up and down the Reliance building block. Drew's heart raced. Maybe, by some freak chance, they wouldn't think to check the cab.

The cab driver made a swift lane change, putting the bus ahead between them and the searching invaders. He made a couple of turns and headed north. Every second that passed was a moment of relief.

Ben tried to lift his head, but Drew wouldn't let him. "Not yet, Ben."

"Drew? Is it really you?"

"It is, my friend. Just hang on for a couple of minutes."

"Cars aren't safe."

"We don't have much of a choice right now, Ben." He continued to scan for invaders. The cab driver raced away from the Reliance building. After a few minutes of dodging traffic and avoiding red lights, and when Drew was sure they were in the clear, he let Ben sit up.

He looked at Drew with wide eyes. "Oh man! It's good to see you!" He gave Drew a quick one-armed hug.

"It's good to see you too, Ben. I wondered if I would ever find you." Drew couldn't hold back a broad smile.

"How is it possible that I'm being abducted by a blind man? I thought the doctors said you would be blind for life." Ben waved his hand back and forth while looking into Drew's eyes as if he were inspecting some new technology.

"I guess doctors don't know everything." Drew shrugged.

Just then the cab pulled over to the curb.

"How's this?" the cabby asked without turning around.

Drew realized that the parking lot his car was in was just across the street. He looked in the rearview mirror and saw the cabby staring back at him. Drew got the strange sensation that often came over him when he was near an invader. He fully expected to see a gun in his face followed by a barrage of bullets. Drew looked at the back of the man's head to see if he could make out a double image, but he couldn't. But something in his eyes looked familiar...

Drew held the man's gaze. "How much?"

"No charge today," the cabby said. "Got a pickup in three minutes, so be on your way."

Drew reached for the door without taking his eyes off the cabby. He made sure Ben was out of the cab before he was, and as soon as they closed the door, the cab drove off and turned a corner. They stepped up onto the curb. Drew did a quick three-sixty scan to check for invaders and saw none, but there were too many buildings close by to be sure.

Ben frowned when he saw Drew make his scan. "You have to live like you don't know they're there." He began shaking his head, then quickly looked behind him and back again. "Otherwise it will drive you mad...I know."

Drew furrowed his eyebrows. *Like you don't know they're there?* He grabbed Ben's arm. "Come on. My car's just over there."

Ben shook his head again. "Cars aren't safe. Most transportation isn't safe. I figured that out quickly." Ben's speech accelerated with each word. "Power stations, large equipment, airports, subways... I've got a list. Do you want to see it?"

Drew eyed Ben. Something was out of place. "Are you all right?"

He looked at Drew a bit wild eyed. As if catching his mental breath, Ben calmed down. "Yes, I'm all right."

Paranoia was really tightening its grip around Ben. Unfortunately, much of his paranoia was justified. After all, he had just experienced an attempt on his life by the dark invaders. Ben needed help, and Drew knew just how to give it.

"Come with me, Ben. I promise it will be safe."

"There's no such thing as safe." Ben glanced over Drew's shoulder.

"Yes, there is." Drew kept his voice confident, and he looked Ben straight in the eye. "Come on."

Ben finally got in the car with him, and they drove north out of Chicago about twenty miles, until they reached Winnetka. He rented a canoe at an outdoor shop on a local resort lake. It was no small feat to keep Ben's mind occupied throughout the journey, but Drew kept asking questions that helped Ben focus on things unrelated to the invaders. Drew set their course for the middle of the lake. After twenty minutes of rowing, Drew stopped, scanned all about them, and finally looked across the length of the canoe toward Ben.

"Water is safe. I haven't figured out why just yet, but"—Drew scanned once more—"we're safe here."

"You know as well as I do that there is no place safe from them," Ben said. "This is pointless. It's all pointless. My life is pointless. We're just sitting here waiting to die."

"Keep your voice down. They can hear very well."

Ben looked at Drew and smirked.

"Ben, let me finish telling you what happened before you start asking a bunch of questions."

Ben stared at Drew with a blank expression and then nodded.

Drew did another quick scan. "When my vision came back, I discovered that...I could still see them."

Ben's eyes opened wide. As the full impact of Drew's statement settled into his brain, excitement built in his eyes—excitement that he struggled to contain.

Drew held up his hand. "At first I couldn't believe it myself. Once I started to see images, it took many days for my vision to clear. Then one day in River-crest, I saw one, an alien—I call them invaders—just like the one in the lab. I couldn't believe it. At first I thought I had gone insane, but everything was too real to be my imagination. I watched and then realized he didn't know I could see him. That is my one and only defense, that they don't know I can see them. I have to protect that or I'm a dead man."

Drew scanned again. "I knew I had to find you. You were the only one who would believe me. I needed someone I could trust...someone who knew I wasn't crazy. I've spent the last six months looking for you so that we could have this conversation."

Ben's eyes became red.

Drew fought tears himself. "There are places that are safe, Ben...if we are careful. Do you believe me?"

Ben's gaze fell to the floor of the canoe, almost as if he were looking for something. "Is it possible?"

Drew slowly nodded. "I swear it."

"The lens of your eyes… Somehow the plasma coupled with your body's electrical energy must be able to excite the photons entering your eyes. But the plasma is no longer—"

Ben started to stand up and come to Drew, but the canoe wobbled left and right at the uneven weight caused by the movement.

"Whoa! Sit down."

Ben sat. "I need to see your eyes."

"Not now. We've got more important issues to discuss."

Ben let loose of his scientific analysis of Drew's ability to see the invaders, at least temporarily. He smiled. "It's incredible. Can you really see them… I mean, *really* see them clearly?"

"As clearly as you are sitting there in front of me. It's rather…disturbing actually," Drew said with a frown.

"What have you learned? How much do you know about them?"

"Not nearly enough and certainly not even a fraction compared to what they know about us. There are many of them—thousands at least. This isn't just an alien visitation." Drew hesitated. "It's an all-out invasion. That's why I call them invaders."

Ben sat back in a daze. "It makes perfect sense."

"What do you mean?"

"Think about it. What better way to take over a world than without the inhabitants even knowing it's happening? If an alien race has cloaking technology, it would be the perfect invasion."

Drew nodded. "You're right. But their ability to cloak themselves goes beyond just being invisible."

"How so?"

"They can walk through walls and doors. It's like they are in some interdimensional state. What I don't get is how come they can see us but we can't see them. Oh yeah, I can't hear them at all. It's like watching a silent movie."

"Of course…the LASOK dealt only with light. I wonder how sound is transmitted in their dimension?"

Drew could see Ben's genius mind already contemplating a whole new set of experiments and theories.

Ben refocused on Drew. "Aliens from another dimension…fascinating… and unbelievable. How do they interact with our dimension, and what are they hoping to gain?"

"I haven't figured that all out yet, but they can affect the outcome of naturally occurring phenomena. Like make a tire go flat to cause an accident or maybe weaken a support in a bridge to cause it to collapse."

"Or cause a plasma generator to overload and burn down an entire research lab," Ben added sardonically.

"Yeah…or that. It's usually the small things though. They do what they do in such a way that people would never suspect the event has been tampered with. They are extremely careful and crafty that way."

Drew could tell that Ben was soaking up every word, analyzing all of this new data. "Are they trying to take over or destroy us?"

"I don't know, but they definitely cause a lot of damage. I can't quite figure out their motive. It seems as though they are causing chaos so that we don't advance. Perhaps they've been trying to keep humanity from gaining the technology to detect their presence, which would certainly make Dr. Waseem and us a big target."

Drew let Ben soak the new information up for a minute as he took time to sweep the area once more. When he looked back at his friend, Ben was staring at the floor of the canoe, shaking his head.

"What is it?"

Ben looked straight at him. "Imagine where we would be if they hadn't been messing with our future for…decades…centuries…millennia?"

Drew nodded.

"Imagine what is happening in our government," Ben continued, "in governments all over the world. I'll bet they're messing with all of the world's leaders."

"Here's the kicker, Ben."

Ben waited, anticipating Drew's next words.

"The invaders—they're not all bad."

Ben cocked his head to the side.

"These invaders are at war with each other. Some are trying to destroy us and some are trying to help us. It's the craziest thing you can ever imagine. They all have swords, but any weapon is an option for them. The battles I've seen…" Drew shook his head, momentarily lost in the memories of the ferocious duels between the good and bad invaders.

"You mean—" Ben started, then stopped, apparently considering his next words carefully. "So what you are telling me is that these aliens from another dimension have invaded our planet and are fighting each other to see who will rule." Ben crossed his arms. "That's what you're saying."

"Hey…you're the one who got me into this mess to start with. I'm just telling it like it is. I thought you were all gung-ho on this alien stuff."

Ben rubbed his forehead with his fingertips. "I know…I know. It's what I've always suspected and more. It's like the Autobots and the Decepticons… Neo and Agent Smith…Obi-Wan and Darth Vader… It's like every epic fantasy or science fiction story ever imagined…but it's actually happening. I can't get my mind around it. It's like—"

Drew finished for him. "Like subconsciously we know something is happening but can't quite put our finger on it, so we replicate it in our stories."

Ben pointed at Drew. "Yes! Yes, that's it! We know, don't we? Mankind knows!"

"Yes, I think so. But not enough to change it."

Ben's eyes were wild. "What about spaceships or portal terminals or other alien technology? Have you seen anything like that?"

Drew shook his head. "No…nothing. I've only seen them run…or rather fly across the ground. They move so fast it's hard to tell."

"How did they get here?"

Drew shrugged. "I don't know. Maybe they've been here for thousands of years…maybe they're marooned here…who could know?"

Ben's eyes saddened. "Do you think we're the only humans in the entire world who know what's happening?"

Drew took a deep breath and considered. "How could anyone know without the LASOK?"

Ben looked out across the peaceful lake, toward shore. "Maybe, but what if there's an underground group of people who...somehow know. What if we could find them?"

That thought had never occurred to Drew, and now it was his turn to ponder this new perspective. "How could we even look for such a group, if they even existed, without sounding or looking mad? There are a lot of wackos out there."

"What about the CIA or the FBI or some secret government organization with letters we've never heard of?"

Drew nodded. "Yeah...it would have to be someone with access to some serious technology. Maybe there's a way to detect the aliens without actually seeing them..." Drew looked away.

"What is it, Drew? What aren't you telling me?"

"The FBI...they're looking for me."

"What?" Ben whisper-shouted. "The FBI?"

Drew nodded. He told his friend about the incident at Drayle University, and Ben listened in stunned silence.

Drew shook his head. "It's hard to watch all this destruction without trying to do something about it."

"I can only imagine. But what can you do anyway?"

Drew looked sideways at Ben, not sure if he wanted to tell him about his other special abilities, but he could see that Ben was already waiting for something more. "There were some side effects that came with the accident."

"Like?" Ben looked impatient.

"Like I can see, hear, feel, and smell things in our dimension that I never could before. And I can move quicker. Everything seems to be...accelerated... improved."

Ben laughed. "So you're like some superhero or something?"

"Hardly. I don't know what I am, but I don't want it. I wish I could just be normal and ignore all of this. My whole life has been cursed!"

"Hey...I've been hiding out in the dark, waiting for them to get me at any moment. You want to talk about cursed? I think I was starting to go crazy!"

Drew stared at his friend and realized just how true that was. He was even now questioning if Ben had stepped off the ledge a bit. Unlike Ben, at least he had a way of fighting back.

"There are times when I think the invaders suspect me. At least one of them does." Drew shivered as he thought of Kurgan.

"Why swords? You did say swords, right?" Ben asked out of the blue.

"Yeah...but they can use anything that's in our world too. Knives, axes, clubs, guns...although nothing big, for some reason."

"So they can use guns, but they use swords? I don't get it. Why don't they use guns all the time? It doesn't make any sense."

"I wondered that too until I realized that they are fast enough to dodge bullets...at least usually. There's only one handgun that seems to give them trouble, the FN Five-Seven."

"I have no idea what that is."

"It's a handgun used by the Secret Service. The muzzle velocity is over two thousand feet per second. That's probably why they have a hard time dodging those bullets. Maybe that's the limit of their speed. It doesn't matter though. Once the bullet leaves the gun, the shooter has no control over it, but the tip of a sword is always under an invader's control. Invaders are so fast that I think the tips of their swords fly faster than our bullets...even an FN Five-Seven."

"Yeah, but what about longer range, when a sword won't do? Why not use guns?"

"They do occasionally, but the longer the range, the more time they have to dodge the bullet. They seem able to see every little detail, including a bullet in flight. I've seen a light invader dodge and deflect bullets with his sword until he cut the attacker down from three feet. This is a battle like our world has never seen."

Ben let out a low whistle. "I've imagined a lot, but never anything like that."

Drew and Ben both fell silent as they considered all that had been said. Drew scanned again, then looked at Ben. His face said it all. He looked worried, tired, and afraid.

"Hey, we're not alone anymore, Ben. We may be the only two in seven billion people who know what's going on, but we have each other now, and we need a plan," Drew said with conviction. "A plan that will give us purpose and direction."

This helped Ben a little. "Agreed."

"The way I see it, we need help, and to get help, we need people to believe us, and to get people to believe us, we need evidence."

"What kind of evidence?"

"The same kind that made us believers." Drew looked straight at Ben.

His friend's lips turned upward. "I know where you're going with this, and I've given it a lot of thought, Drew." Excitement spilled from his eyes. "It's one of the reasons I chose Chicago: availability of resources and technology. I think I could do it. I knew Dr. Waseem's work better than anybody, even the grad students. I've been studying and have re-created many of the notes and schematics." Ben's countenance lowered. "But it would take space, time, and a lot of money."

Drew's eyes narrowed. "Yes, it would, and it would have to all be done in secret."

Ben nodded.

"Time, we have, even if it takes ten years. You start looking for the space, and I'll see what I can do about the money. I haven't explored all the benefits of seeing interdimensionally just yet. Perhaps there's a way to leverage some funds."

It seemed impossible, and yet, hope revived them. Drew could see the wheels turning in Ben's mind once again. He smiled...

Ben was back.

25

THE PLAN

Drew started to paddle the canoe.

"Hey, I'm not done. I have a million questions. We can't go back yet," Ben said.

"I know. We might look a little funny just sitting still in the middle of the water. Ben, we need an MO."

"A what?"

"A method of operation—rules that we operate under and never break."

"Like what? Stay away from cars?"

"No. Like rule number one: when we aren't here, we can never talk about the invaders. Don't think you can fool them; they are extremely intelligent. I'm certain they can't read minds, but if they can spy on someone without them knowing it, they wouldn't need to."

"Okay. Agreed. What else?"

"Rule number two: from this moment on, you can never go back to any place in Chicago that you've already been."

"What? Why? Why me and not you?"

"First, I can see them and you can't. Second, you've been targeted, Ben. That close call this morning at the intersection? That was them."

Ben's face went white. "I *knew* it! Stuff like that has been happening for the last week. I knew they were onto me, but I couldn't do anything about it. So you were there? You saw it?"

"Yes. Two invaders were manipulating people to try to kill you. I had to find a way to get you away from them without suspecting me."

Ben swallowed hard. "If it hadn't been for that guy behind me I wouldn't be here right now."

Chills went up and down Drew's spine. The eyes of the cabby—*that's* where Drew had seen them before. It was the same guy! Was he human? Was he part of some secret group that knew what was happening, trying to protect Ben too? Possibilities flew through his mind.

"What about my job? My apartment?"

"You can never go back, Ben. You have to change everything. They know what's important to you, and they'll be waiting."

Ben put his head in his hands. "I have to have my notebooks and computers. Without them, it can't be done."

"Can't be done? You said you were re-creating the doc's work. Can't you just do it again?"

Ben frowned at Drew. "One of the hard drives on my server is a complete backup of Dr. Waseem's work. He asked me to do it as a secondary backup. The university didn't know I had it, and when it looked like there was foul play, I kept it a secret. My notes and schematics are derived from the information on that hard drive. Without that data, we don't have a chance."

"It's going to be dangerous, Ben. The risk is great."

Ben thought for a moment and then shook his head. "I have to have them if we are going to pull this off."

Drew took a deep breath. "I'll think about it and see what we can do. Maybe we can stage a theft or something."

Ben seemed satisfied with that, at least for now. "Rule number three?"

"No one else knows until we have positive proof."

Ben gazed out toward the shore. "Yeah...we definitely need proof."

Drew laughed. "Your previous boss didn't buy it, huh?"

Ben just stared back. "Anything else?"

"Not now. We may need to modify our MO as we proceed, but that should keep us safe for now. You, we can make completely disappear. For me,

I think I can use Sydney's ID for what I'm going to do to raise funds. If not, how are you at forging fake IDs?"

"How do you think I became Chider Anderson? Wait…did I hear you say Sydney…*your* Sydney?"

Drew nodded.

"Oh man! Drew, what are you thinking? What about rule number three, huh?"

"She doesn't know about the invaders. She thinks this is all about a conspiracy to keep Dr. Waseem's research under wraps and that the FBI might be involved. She knows they're looking for me and thinks they're the only ones we're hiding from. It's a good cover."

"Not good, Drew. Not good."

"Listen, she came to me, and quite frankly if she hadn't, you'd probably be dead right now. She's the one that found the lead that led me to you."

Ben's eyes widened. "Really? She helped you find me?"

"Yes. Without her it would have taken me months longer to find you. From the way those invaders were coming after you, I don't think you would have made it."

Ben bit his lower lip. "Okay, so I owe her my life… I got it."

"My biggest concern about Sydney is making her a target. At least you knew they were after you. She doesn't have a clue what's happening and who to be afraid of."

Ben nodded. "We'll have to be careful." He got really quiet. "The next time you see her, tell her thanks, okay?"

"Sure."

"Hey, what about my bank account and my money?"

"We're going to have to leave it. It's the first place they'll look for you, and if they can cloak themselves, I'm sure they're smart enough to trace bank wires. When we get you hooked back up online with your computers, you're going to have to be careful to the extreme. Can you remain electronically anonymous for your research?"

Ben nodded. "Yeah, I can."

Both of them fell silent, and Drew just let the canoe drift for a few minutes. What lay before them seemed impossible. It felt like they were fighting every evil villain that ever existed *and* as if they were going up against the FBI, CIA, KGB, and the Mossad, all at the same time.

"So where should I go?" Ben broke their solemn silence. "Do we leave Chicago?"

"I'd like to. These invaders seem to have certain regions of responsibility. I was being tracked in Kansas until I broke loose and disappeared in Chicago. However, there is one invader I've seen both in Kansas and in Chicago." Drew paused. "I don't want to cross paths with him again… I think he's one of the commanders. The other invaders all fear him."

"Where to then?"

"The problem is, Sydney's my connection with the grid, and she's got a perfect alibi for being here. She's going to UIC and doing mission work at a church in the ghetto. Right now she doesn't suspect the invaders, and the invaders don't suspect her. The hitch with Sydney is that the FBI may be watching her."

"Oh…well, if it's only the FBI," Ben said in his old dry humor.

Drew smiled. "If I can avoid the invaders, I can avoid the FBI. We need Sydney, and therefore we are going to have to stay near Chicago. Let's put you up way out in the burbs…preferably near water. How much space will you need to re-create Dr. Waseem's work?"

"Fifteen hundred square feet minimum, with a ten-foot ceiling. Stable power and the fastest broadband we can find. Oh…and a bed."

"You want to sleep in the lab?"

"We want this to happen as fast as possible, don't we?"

Drew nodded. "You got it."

"So where are we going to get the money for all this?"

"Do you remember the mock investments I played with in high school and my freshman year at Drayle?"

Ben smiled. "You did well, but we're talking millions, Drew. I just can't see it happening."

Drew looked at the inside of their aluminum canoe.

"Ben, do you see these rivets around the rim of our canoe?"

"Yeah."

"Count them."

"What? Why?"

"Just count them. Go."

Drew focused and swept his eyes around the entire rim. "Stop. How far did you get?"

"Twenty-three. What does this have to do with anything?"

"There are four hundred and sixteen rivets."

Ben stared at him. "How did you do that?"

"I can see things and evaluate them in seconds. I don't know how I can do it, I just can." He smiled. "And the Chicago Mercantile Exchange is sitting right under our noses."

Ben thought for moment, then squinted. "Do you think you can do it for real?"

"We're going to find out. How much money is it going to take?"

"Dr. Waseem had six million in grants."

Drew shook his head. "Even on my best investments I didn't get close to that, and we'll be using most of the earnings to buy equipment instead of reinvesting. Give me a number that's realistic."

"Well, a lot of the money was used up in his initial research. I won't have to repeat that. And I think I can find used equipment that will do just as well as what he bought." Ben squinted as he did some quick calculations. "Some of that equipment is way expensive, Drew. I'd need two million...one point five at the very least."

Drew nodded. "That's going to take some time, but we can build as we go."

"How come you haven't hit the exchange already?"

"It's too exposed. I couldn't risk it while I was looking for you, but now I don't see that we have any other choice."

The two men looked at each other across the canoe.

"You ready for this?" Drew asked.

Ben clenched his jaw. "I can't wait!"

Drew smiled.

"Thanks for finding me, Drew."

"Hey, we stand by each other, remember? No matter what happens."

Drew didn't know what the future held. Didn't know if they'd succeed. But he did know one thing that gave him hope…

He was no longer alone in his mission.

Drew and Ben found an apartment north of Chicago, not far from the resort lake where they had devised the plan. Drew left Ben with some cash and a promise to return with his notebooks and computers, although he wasn't quite sure how to pull that off without blowing his cover. It might be the one string in the web that, if tripped, would bring the spiders after them in full force.

THE NEXT MORNING, Drew drove to Ben's old apartment and conducted surveillance from a safe distance. The monotonous task was interrupted frequently by dark invaders who were doing more than just passing by. They were looking and waiting. Drew aborted any thoughts of recovering Ben's work, for at least a few days—until the invader activity around the building diminished.

Drew's next stop was the Chicago Mercantile Exchange. His delivery shift at Mr. Lee's didn't start until ten, so when trading commenced at eight thirty, he watched the trading floor come alive. Although he observed from the fourth-floor viewing area, he felt the pulse of the exchange as if it were a living creature. The ticker screens streamed instantaneous stock information that Drew absorbed as he scanned the pit. The open outcry trades escalated the excitement that Drew felt as he became lost in a world few understood. His mind raced as he analyzed thousands of potential buys and sells. Any experienced trader would consider him a fool to try to jump into the heart of such a beast, but Drew was not dissuaded, for they could not see what he saw. Two hours passed before Drew could detach himself from the hypnotizing throb of the pit.

"You late, Mr. Ryan!" Mr. Lee's gaze was fierce. He stuck his finger into Drew's chest. "First you not show up, now you late. You fired!"

"I'm sorry, Master Lee. I was helping a friend," he said with a bow. Extreme politeness and humility were the only way to win Mr. Lee over.

"Awck!" Mr. Lee waved his hand in the air. "Deliver orders now!"

"Mr. Lee, I must tell you that this is my last week. I have to take care of some other business."

"You can't quit. I need you to deliver orders."

"But you were just going to fire me," Drew said with smile.

"That different. You still owe me for lessons. You no quit," he said with a nod.

Drew stepped close to Mr. Lee. "I owe you much, Mr. Lee. Thank you." He bowed again.

When he straightened, Mr. Lee was Master Lee for a moment. "The honor was mine, Mr. Ryan." He bowed his head. "When you leave, you be careful."

Drew found it difficult to finish the day out for Mr. Lee, as his thoughts kept returning to the plan to re-create the LASOK. It felt so good to know that Ben was alive and safe. He almost called Sydney but decided to wait until Friday when he would see her at Emmanuel.

OVER THE NEXT COUPLE of days, Drew began making plans for his entrance into the exchange. He made a couple of trips out to Ben to keep him updated as well. On Friday at the church, he worked beside Sydney, serving the homeless.

"I found him!" Drew whispered into Sydney's ear as she served a bowl of soup.

"What? Really? How is he?"

Drew scanned the room and handed her another empty bowl.

"He's fine. They were zeroing in on him though, so I had to help him disappear again. You saved his life, Sydney. He said to say thanks."

Sydney handed the filled bowl to an old man with no teeth, then set the ladle down and turned to look at Drew.

"I am so happy, Drew." She reached up and hugged him.

"Oh man!" The cry of disgust came from behind them. "I hope you aren't gonna start kissing now."

"Hey, Micah, you know me better than that. Besides, Sydney would never let that happen." Drew winked her way.

"Good!" Micah turned to deliver a plate of rolls to the end of the counter.

Later in the chapel, Drew explained to Sydney the plan he and Ben had formulated...without the details of the invaders.

"You actually saw these guys come after him? How did you get him away?"

"It's a long story that I can tell you later. The important thing is that we have a plan to re-create the LASOK. We have to do it in secrecy. I may need some help from you, Syd."

"As long as it's legal, I'm in."

"What if the FBI is involved in trying to cover up Dr. Waseem's death? What if the government is trying to steal his research?"

Sydney fell silent for a moment. "Are you asking me this because what you're going to do is illegal?"

Drew held up his hands. "No. That's not why I'm asking you this. But when does 'right' supersede 'legal'? If there is a connection between those who are trying to cover up Dr. Waseem's death and now trying to kill Ben, and the FBI, how far would you go for the truth?"

Sydney's gaze fell to the floor. Her sadness was hard for him to see, but she needed to know what she might be getting into.

"I don't know, Drew. I'll need to rely on the Lord for wisdom when the time comes." She gave a confident nod. "Rebuilding the LASOK sounds expensive. How are you going to fund it? Dr. Waseem had the university and grants. I don't think delivering Korean takeout is going to get you very far."

"You're right. I think I can build some capital by investing in the exchange. But I'm going to need to lease a membership, cover some fees, and have some seed money for my first investment."

"How much will that all cost, and how much do you have?"

"It's going to take about six thousand to get us started. Ben had three thousand saved, but we don't dare touch it—they'll be watching his account. I have about eighteen hundred."

He considered sending her to Rivercrest to get some cash from Jake, but there was no way of knowing if an invader might be watching his home and follow her back.

Sydney was lost in contemplation. "I've got thirty-five hundred you can have."

"No, Sydney, I can't take your money. Playing the mercantile exchange is almost like gambling. It's too risky, and I know you need that money for college."

Sydney reached out and touched his arm. "You need this, and I can take out another student loan in the meantime. Besides, what I'm giving you is just a loan, and I charge high interest. I expect full payment back."

Drew thought for moment. The deposit and first-month's rent for Ben's apartment took a good chunk of his funds, and he simply didn't have access to any other money.

"Are you sure about this?" He looked deep into her eyes for any sign of hesitation.

"Yes. Where and when should we meet so I can give you the money?"

"Tomorrow I'm going to try and recover Ben's notes and computers and get them to him. How would you feel about being a lookout when I go in?"

"I can do that. I'll bring the money at nine o'clock and pick you up then."

"It's a date." Drew allowed a sly grin.

She smiled back. "No, it's not."

They stood up to leave.

"Syd, it could be dangerous tomorrow."

"I know." She said it without batting an eye, then walked out the door.

26

A SECOND CHANCE

Drew and Sydney drove around Ben's apartment building numerous times, then watched from a safe distance for over an hour. When Drew didn't see any invader activity, he left Sydney waiting in the car and walked into the building. His senses were peaked. He hated taking this risk, but Ben was convinced it was necessary.

Ben's apartment was on the third floor of the six-story building. Drew felt in his pocket for the key that Ben had given him, but when he went to insert it in the lock, the door was already open. The hair on the back of his neck stood straight. He stepped inside. It was a simple one bedroom with a kitchenette and a living room to his left. A narrow hallway led to the bedroom on his right, where the door was open just a crack.

Drew took silent steps down the hallway and peered in through the small slit between the door and the frame. His stomach rose into his throat when he saw a dark invader inside. He froze. This close, even the slightest of movements would give him away. Drew swallowed and wondered if even that might be too loud. He dared to continue watching, for the invader was turned away from the doorway so that Drew could see his back, his left shoulder, and a portion of the left side of his face. The invader was bent over and looking at Ben's notebook on the desk just below the window against the far wall. Although the notebook was closed, the invader fingered the book so that its pages turned, but they were pages that existed only in the invader realm. The actual notebook remained closed and lying still on the desk.

The invader seemed to read everything he saw in mere seconds, and when he reached the end of the book, he lifted his hand and the pages dissolved away. He stood straight and turned just enough so that Drew could see the rest of his face. That's when Drew regretted allowing Ben to convince him to come here.

It was Kurgan.

He scowled as he scanned the room. Drew pulled back just enough so that he wouldn't be seen when the dark invader's gaze passed by. He didn't dare step back. After five long seconds, he peered back into the room just in time to see two more dark invaders falling through the ceiling to stand at attention before Kurgan. He barked out orders and pointed out to the street below.

Was it Sydney? Had they found her? This escapade was transforming into a nightmare. Just as Drew was about to attempt to retreat, the two dark invaders fell through the floor and Kurgan jumped up through the ceiling.

Drew scanned behind him, then opened the door to the bedroom and bolted inside. He grabbed the notebook on the desk, plus the two that were in a drawer below and stuffed them into his backpack. He looked for Ben's laptop, but it was gone. The server sat humming on the floor, a deep-blue light glowing from the top. Drew unplugged it and yanked it out from beside the desk. He pressed the button to open the case and then took a quick scan around the room, his heart racing. He located the three hard drives and unplugged the power and SATA cables to each, then dismounted them from the drive racks. He shoved them into the backpack and zipped it closed.

After stepping quickly to the door, Drew looked down the hallway to the kitchen area. Clear. Every second that ticked by this close to Kurgan could mean the end of everything. He struggled to keep calm and think straight. Drew ran to the door of the apartment and scanned down the hallway. The stairwell was at the far end. Just as Drew started to step out, he saw Kurgan fall through the hallway ceiling and land twenty feet away, sword drawn and battle on his face.

Drew jerked back. He was trapped! He turned and nearly collapsed from fear, for toe to toe with him was a light invader, sword drawn and ready. He looked angry and concerned. His eyes were the same eyes of the cab driver earlier that week. He pointed to the bedroom and spoke. Although Drew heard nothing, he knew what the invader said.

"Get out!" The silent words were powerful...frightening...final.

Drew ran to the bedroom and shut the door. As if that would stop them.

He went to the window, opened it, and looked down. Just below him was a small metal and concrete balcony for an apartment on the second floor. He slipped his other arm through the backpack strap and stepped out onto the ledge. He fell eight feet to the floor of the balcony, smacking his shin on the barbecue grill near the wall. He then straddled the railing and knelt down to hang onto two of the black iron spindles. He dropped the three feet to the ground and dodged to the back of the apartment building, hoping against hope that he had not been seen. He sprinted down the alley, making his way back to Sydney's car. When he came up from the opposite direction he had left and opened the car door, Sydney jumped.

"Good grief, Drew, you scared me to dea—" She stopped when she saw his face. "What happened?"

Drew couldn't take his eyes off the apartment building. "Let's go. Head south quickly!"

Sydney pulled into the street, and Drew turned to look over the seat, out the rear window. Dread filled his heart. He saw the light invader falling backward out from the wall of Ben's apartment. Kurgan burst through the wall after him, a two-handed grip on the handle of his sword, which was raised above his head, its razor-edged tip plummeting downward toward the falling light invader.

"No!" Drew couldn't hold back the cry as the light invader smashed into the pavement below. Just fractions of a second later, Kurgan's blade, with all of the invader's weight and the force of a three-story fall, pierced the light invader, clear to the hilt. Kurgan landed on one foot and one knee beside the light invader's body. He seemed to relish the few seconds of agonizing pain the light invader felt before his body dissolved into a vapor and floated upward.

The terror of the encounter left Drew's eyes watery.

Sydney touched his arm. "Are you okay? I didn't see anything or anyone. What happened?"

Drew couldn't speak. He just shook his head and looked at the backpack at his feet.

"It had better be worth it, Ben," he said softly, then bit his lip and closed his eyes as his mind unwillingly replayed what he had just seen. For the rest of the drive, other than giving Sydney a few directions, he sat in silence and stared out the window, mourning the death of a good invader who had sacrificed his life to save Drew.

Thirty-five minutes later, Drew and Sydney pulled into the parking lot at Ben's new apartment. Still numb, Drew forced himself to scan the premises before entering the building and climbing the stairs to the second floor.

"Did you get it?" Ben asked at the door before they had even stepped inside.

Drew held the backpack out.

Ben unzipped the bag as Drew and Sydney walked through the door. "You're my hero, man, my Captain America!"

Drew just walked over to the living room window and stared out.

"Hey, Sydney, good to see you."

"Hi, Ben. Glad to see you're okay."

Ben looked from Drew to Sydney. "What's up with him?"

"I don't know. Something happened back there, but he won't tell me."

"Oh."

Sydney and Ben talked a few minutes, but soon Ben was lost in his notebooks, reviewing every little detail from the first to the last page of each. Sydney came to stand beside Drew and stare out the window with him. "Did somebody get hurt back there?"

Drew nodded.

"Are you in trouble?"

"No. He was trying to help me. An agent took him out."

Sydney covered her mouth. "Drew, you have to tell someone. If people are dying, this is getting too serious...too deep."

Drew turned and looked at Sydney. "People dying is what started this in the first place."

"What are you going to do?"

"I'm going to make his death count for something." Drew turned and looked at Ben. "I need a complete ID set for Ryan Cooper. Enough to get me a bank account and a membership on the mercantile exchange."

"I can have it by Wednesday," Ben said without looking up from his notes. "Have you got the money you need?"

Drew looked down at Sydney, and she nodded. "Yeah, we have enough to get a start."

"Good. The first thing I'm going to need is a computer to access these hard drives," Ben said.

After a couple of hours discussing the details of their plan, Drew and Sydney drove back to Chicago. When they pulled up to Drew's apartment, Drew hesitated.

"If you want out, now's the time, Sydney. I don't know how bad it's going to get."

"I'm okay." She touched his arm. "Are you?"

Drew reached for the door handle. "I will be. The less contact you have with me, the safer you'll be." He sounded cold, and she looked hurt. He softened his tone and forced a smile. "Thanks...thanks for everything."

She nodded and he left.

DREW DEVOTED THE FIRST part of the week studying up on the exchange, learning the outcry hand signals, and reviewing stock prices for recent past trades. He spent hours reading market reports, bulletins, and articles on managing risk at the exchange. He refreshed his knowledge of chart patterns and saw nuances in the data that he had never seen before. He practiced on historical prices and was able to predict buy and sell points that would return four and five times the investment. However, his plan was to ease into the market carefully, with very little risk, to prove to himself that his new abilities to analyze and predict price moves were not ill placed.

It was good timing for Drew to lie low anyway, knowing that the invaders would be looking for anything that would lead them to Ben.

Wednesday afternoon, Drew picked up his ID set from Ben and opened an account at the CME, the Chicago Mercantile Exchange, and was able to lease a membership to operate as a floor trader for two thousand dollars. Thursday, Drew spent the entire day on the floor watching, learning, and running his own mock investments. There were times he stood in the middle of the pit and felt the exchange breathing around him. He could see the trends in the markets as well as he could see bullets flying from a gun. It was uncanny.

He restrained himself from trading for one week, looking for just the right buy at just the right time. His first trade was for soybeans, and he turned a seven-hundred-dollar profit. The next day that he traded, he gained twelve hundred. He saw bigger opportunities, but he disciplined himself to stay small and low risk, slowly building his pool of funds. After one week he had turned his initial two thousand dollars into five. And then five into fifteen, then fifteen into thirty.

Each week Drew learned more and gained more. Three times he lost, but within a couple of hours he'd recovered and moved on. His first withdrawal was to repay Sydney, with interest, then to pay rent for a building that Ben had located for the lab. The first equipment purchases for the LASOK followed shortly thereafter. He fed Ben money each week while being careful not to bleed off too much and thus limit his trading capabilities. After six weeks, their plan was in motion and functioning well.

Drew found himself in a position to improve his living conditions, but he could not bring himself to abandon Reverend Ray and his family or the people of the neighborhood he had fought and defended so many times before. He moved to a cleaner apartment that was still within walking distance of Emmanuel Church and began making anonymous donations to the soup kitchen ministry. It allowed Reverend Ray to expand the work so they could feed more homeless each week. Drew continued to volunteer on Fridays, but his friendship with Sydney seemed strained, and he didn't know why.

ONE SATURDAY, SYDNEY JOINED Drew to visit the LASOK lab. When they entered, Ben was busy calibrating a piece of test equipment.

"Hi, guys. Welcome to the world of light acceleration."

Drew was amazed at how Ben's energy seemed limitless when he was working on a project, and this one was the mother of all projects. How few hours of sleep was Ben functioning on?

"Drew, I'm coming to a standstill until I get the funds for that electron microscope."

"How much do you need?"

"Well, I found a used one on eBay for twelve thousand, but I don't think the specs are quite there. We'd better plan on forty to fifty thousand and get it right the first time."

Drew thought for a moment, calculating how much from the account he could release without impeding his buying power for future trades. "I should be able to have it to you by Thursday. Will that work?"

Ben hesitated. "With shipping time, that puts me out another two weeks."

"Okay, I'll shoot for Tuesday, but that will depend on Monday's trading, so I can't promise anything."

"Deal," Ben said with as big a grin as Drew had ever seen.

"So how's this going to work?" Sydney looked at a bench full of strange equipment and gadgets.

"Uh-oh." Drew sat down. "You'd better ask for the short version." He started perusing one of Ben's notebooks and did not pay much attention to the physics lesson Sydney was about to receive.

Ben didn't look up from his work as he talked. "The concept is simple, but the implementation is extremely complex. Basically, we take light and pass it through a series of electrically excited lenses to accelerate it."

Sydney frowned. "Why?"

Ben made a final adjustment on his oscilloscope. "So we can see into another dimensio—" Ben's eyes widened as he realized what he'd just said.

Drew looked up. The silence that followed was as loud as an exploding bomb.

Sydney raised an eyebrow and looked toward Drew.

"Ben's pulling your leg, Syd." Drew gave her a quick smile. "The ramifications for accelerating light in the physics world are huge. It would rock the scientific community in a way that hasn't happened since Einstein proposed the theory of relativity."

"Yeah." Ben became preoccupied with another piece of equipment at the far end of the bench.

"I see," Sydney said, but Drew knew she didn't buy the cover.

Sydney was very quiet after that except for when she tried to ask Ben a few more questions, but he did everything he could to avoid her. When they left, she walked to the car in silence. Drew closed the door and dreaded getting in with her. There was nothing he could say that was going to appease her or convince her. If she suspected that he had been lying to her, there would be no telling what might happen.

He walked around the car and got in the driver's seat. He put the keys in the ignition but didn't turn the engine on. He turned to look at her at the same time that she turned to look at him. Her arms were crossed, and there was a seething anger boiling in her eyes that he had never seen before. It actually scared him.

"Ben wasn't kidding, was he? He really believes he's building a machine that can see into another dimension, doesn't he?" She didn't wait for Drew to respond. She knew the answer. "Is he crazy?"

Drew didn't respond. There was no way *to* respond. Once she realized he believed it too, everything would come tumbling down. And if he lost her trust, she'd have no reason not to call the FBI. With them involved...

The only light he would see would be through a small window in a prison cell.

27

FUGITIVE

Sydney held Drew's gaze. "In high school I heard stories about Berg but never believed them...not until now." She eyed Drew. "Has he messed you up too? How much of all this is some big science fiction fantasy that the two of you are living? Tell me, Drew, are you crazy too?"

"No, Sydney." He reached over to touch her arm.

"Don't touch me! I drove by Ben's old apartment after I dropped you off that night that you said somebody died."

Drew was stunned. Had she been suspicious of him that long?

"There were no police cars, no emergency vehicles, nothing in the paper about a man dying. Nothing, Drew...nothing!" She started to break down.

"I...I..."

"The only thing I know for certain, Drew, is that the FBI is looking for you, and I could go to prison for not telling them where you are." Tears fell down her cheeks, and Drew's heart broke.

"I risked everything, and you lied to me. How long have you been lying to me, Drew? How long?"

"I haven't lied to you, Sydney."

Anger and sorrow mixed with tears poured out of her soul. She reached for the door handle to get out of the car, but Drew grabbed her arm.

"Let me go!"

"Please, Sydney, just listen and I'll explain. Please."

"Let *go* of my arm!"

"Okay, I'm going to let go, but before I do, I want you to remember the day I stepped in front of a crazy man with a gun at Drayle to save your life. And I want you to remember the day I fought three gang members to keep you from being kidnapped and very possibly murdered."

Drew relaxed his grip on her arm and hoped she wouldn't bolt from the car. She remained still, with her head bowed. When she looked over at him, he felt like he had ripped her heart in two and betrayed the one and only girl in the world that he loved.

"Sydney, I am not crazy, and I did not lie to you. Everything I told you was absolutely true. I promise. But there are things I didn't tell you, for your own protection."

Sydney sat perfectly still...waiting. How long would she listen? He had to choose his words carefully.

"Everything I told you—Dr. Waseem's death, somebody sabotaging the lab, Ben being targeted—it's all true. What I didn't tell you is what else happened in the lab that night."

Drew tried to read Sydney's expression, but all he saw were drying tears and a broken heart. He took a deep breath. There was no way around this except with the complete truth.

"The LASOK experiment worked. I saw it work. I was the one who was looking through the lens when the light was accelerated." Drew rubbed his mouth and jaw as he remembered that fateful night. "I did see someone... someone who wasn't supposed to be there. I saw him as plain as I am seeing you. But when I looked at the exact spot with my own eyes, he wasn't there. I looked again through the LASOK, and he came at us. That's when the lab exploded."

Drew rubbed his eyes, then turned in his seat to face Sydney better. "Please believe me, Sydney. I know it sounds crazy, but I know what I saw. You can imagine why I didn't dare tell you or anyone else. Later, after the accident, I tried to tell Jake, and he and my mother nearly put me in the nut house."

Drew lowered his head. He was tired. Tired of being chased...tired of hiding...tired of being afraid to tell people the truth.

"I know what I saw. And it's not over, because when my eyesight came back, I could still see them. That lab experiment changed me forever, and now I live with this curse. Whoever these beings are"—Drew looked at the lab through the front window—"they don't want this experiment to work, and they will kill Ben, me, and anyone else who gets in their way."

Drew looked at Sydney, and she averted her gaze, lowering her head to stare at the floorboard.

It was over—there was no reason not to say everything now.

"I know I'm not supposed to love you, but I do... I can't help it. The last thing I ever wanted to do was to hurt you, Sydney. I've protected you and begged you to go away because I didn't want you to get hurt. If you don't believe anything else I've said, I hope you will at least believe that."

They sat in silence a long while.

"Please take me home." Sydney spoke without looking up.

Drew started the car and drove toward UIC. Nothing else was said, and when she got out of the car, Drew let her go without saying a word.

THAT NIGHT WHILE DREW was sleeping, the FBI broke into his apartment, handcuffed him, and hauled him away in a black car with smoked windows. Just before they started interrogating him, he woke up to discover he was still lying in his own bed back in his apartment. The blue LED of his clock glowed a 5:23, and he knew his sleep was done.

Why hadn't they come for him? He went to the window and looked out at the street below. The lone lamppost in front of his apartment building fought to push back the darkness that surrounded it on all sides. He felt like a lone lamppost, trying to hang on until morning.

Drew dressed, walked down the stairs, and exited the building. He stood underneath the lamppost and stared up at the light. He didn't want to try to disappear again. He didn't want to start over again.

He walked back toward his old neighborhood and found himself standing before the doors of Reverend Ray's church. Why had he come here? He went to the corner and looked toward Ray's home. A soft white glow emanated from one of the windows, and he went toward it. He stood for five minutes at the door before he gently knocked. After a minute, the door opened.

"Ryan, come in. I was just praying for you. Is everything okay?"

Drew forced a weak smile. "I'm sorry to bother you at this hour, but I saw a light on and, well..."

Ray grabbed his arm and pulled him inside. "Come in here, son. I thought God woke me up to prepare a few more notes for my sermon this morning, but I can see it was for more than that."

Amazing the way Christians could take the simplest of coincidences and try to wrap them with God. This morning he didn't care though. Ray brought him into the kitchen, where the smell of fresh coffee triggered memories and emotions that took him back home with his mom. He ached to see her again.

Ray poured them each a cup of coffee and sat down opposite Drew. Drew held the warm cup in his hands, watching the swirling black liquid settle.

"What's on your mind, Ryan?" Ray set his glasses on the brim of his nose. He crossed his hands in front of him and waited.

"That's not my name."

Ray smiled. "I know."

Drew looked up from his coffee cup into Reverend Ray's warm gaze. He knew? "My name is Drew...Drew Carter. I didn't want to lie to you, Reverend, but...there are...people after me, and I don't want you or your family to get hurt because of me."

"What did you do, son?"

Drew shook his head. "It's a long story, and that's not why I'm here. I don't have anybody to talk to and—" Maybe he shouldn't have knocked on the door, but he'd gone too far now to stop. "And I don't know what to do. Sydney thinks I've betrayed her. I think I've lost her. I guess I didn't realize just how much she meant to me."

Ray looked down at his hands and then back up at Drew. "Sydney is an amazing girl, Drew. Besides whatever it is that just happened between you two, do you understand why she can't have a close relationship with you?"

Drew nodded. "Yeah, she's told me. Without Jesus, I'll never be good enough."

Ray smiled and shook his head. "You're right, but not in the way you're thinking. Listen, I can't begin to imagine what it is you are running from, but I do know this: you are a good man with a good heart. If even half the stories I've heard are only half true, about how the Guardian has helped the people in this neighborhood, then you are as good a man as I have ever known."

Drew shook his head. "I just try to help people, that's all."

"I know it. Here's the thing, Drew. As good a man as you are, and as good as the things are that you've done, you still aren't good enough. But I'm not talking about for Sydney. I'm talking about for God."

Drew didn't know how to respond to that.

"The Lord will judge you not on your good works, Drew, but on your faith in Him. If you don't believe in Him, all the good works in the world won't get you into heaven, because the Bible says that all have sinned and fall short of His glory. That includes you. Jesus was the only man who ever lived who was 'good enough,' and that's because He was without sin. When He died on the cross, He died for all of us. He sacrificed Himself for you, Drew. And because you don't yet belong to God, Sydney can't belong to you. Does that make sense?"

Drew looked at Ray in silence. This sounded a lot like the John 3:16 verse that Sydney had written on his hand so long ago. He remembered searching for the verse on the Internet and reading something about God loving the world so much that he gave His Son so people would not perish. Ray made sense, but there was still a mountain of logic, reasoning, and scientific evidence that Drew could not ignore. And yet...

In that mountain, Drew realized for the first time in his life that scientific evidence and logic could not explain good and evil. In the last two years, he'd seen people, and invaders for that matter, do a lot of good and bad things. And if seeing into the invader realm convinced him of anything, it was that evil was real.

So what made the leader of the Dragons want to kill, molest, and steal, and what made Sydney want to feed and help the homeless? What made Kurgan want to destroy all that was good, and what made Wallace and the other light invaders fight and even sacrifice themselves to save others? There was indeed a dark and a light in the souls of people, and scientific evidence and evolution could not explain it.

The questions and new understanding gnawed at his mind, but he suppressed them to think about later.

"Ray, I know you mean well, and I have come to love you and your family. But I see the world in a way that no one else does, and the Bible just doesn't explain what I see."

Ray smiled warmly. "Are you sure, Drew? How do you know if you haven't read it? What do you see that the Bible can't explain?"

Drew hung his head. He couldn't bear having another friend think he had gone crazy. He had confided in those closest to him, and they didn't believe him. It was clear no one would ever believe him. Ben *had* to succeed, that was all there was to it. He looked up at Ray.

"Please tell Sydney that I...I'm sorry and that I hope her life is everything she hopes it will be."

Ray's smile faded and his eyes saddened. "You can't keep running, Drew. There was a man in the Bible who tried to run from God, and it didn't turn out well for him. Why don't you stop and look up. That's what Sydney is hoping for...praying for."

"You've been good to me, Reverend. I must move on or I'm afraid I will bring danger to you too."

Ray looked at Drew, then nodded. The two men stood and walked to the door. Ray stopped and put a hand on Drew's shoulder.

"I need to tell you something. Jeremiah told me he heard that the Dragons have targeted you. Evidently you've interfered with their operation and territory too much, and they plan to take you out. It's probably a good time for you to move on anyway. Be careful, son."

"I will. I promise. You be careful too, Reverend. This neighborhood is still a tough one."

Ray opened the door, and the chilly morning air rushed at them. "I'll be praying for you, Drew. Always."

Drew smiled and gave Ray a hug. "Say good-bye to Micah and Shana for me, okay?"

"Of course."

DREW LEFT EMMANUEL CHURCH and drove to the lab to talk to Ben. He entered, and his senses kicked in—the lab was unusually quiet and dark. He drew his .45 from his concealed holster and began searching the area.

"What are you doing here?"

At the voice from the dark corner near the back, Drew jumped. "Ben? What's going on?" Drew clicked on the lights.

"I do get to sleep a couple hours each day, don't I?" Ben squinted and covered his eyes. "What are you doing here?"

Drew relaxed and took a deep breath, holstering his .45. He pulled up a chair next to Ben's bed in the corner. "We've got problems, Mr. Genius."

Ben rubbed his eyes and face, then ran his hands through his bed-head hair. "More than you know."

"Why? What's going on?"

Ben looked at Drew and huffed. "Dr. Waseem's final calculation, the one that enabled the LASOK to accelerate light, I can't resolve it."

"What does that mean?"

"Apparently he never entered that last calculation in his notes onto the computer. It was only in his notebook."

"And that was destroyed in the lab fire."

Ben pointed at Drew. "Bingo."

"You're smart, Ben, you'll figure it out."

Ben shook his head. "It might take months...years... I may never figure it out. It's the final missing mathematical piece. Without that final calculation, when the electron microscope comes in, it might as well be a huge paperweight."

Drew scanned, then frowned. Might as well dump all the bad news at once. "Sydney knows everything, and she doesn't believe me. I think we're in big trouble."

Ben sat up. "What kind of trouble?"

"FBI trouble."

Ben's gaze went across the entire lab and back to Drew. "I told you she would be a problem!" Ben's voice raised. "Why didn't you abide by your own rules?"

"You were the one who told her we were trying to see into another dimension. Why didn't you watch your mouth?"

Ben's eyes glared. He stood up and began pacing. He rubbed the back of his neck with his right hand. "Come on, Drew…what are we supposed to do now? This is your fault. I told you she was going to be a problem from the very beginning!"

Drew stood up too and walked away, his anger rising. He came back and pointed a finger at Ben's chest.

"Just remember that without Sydney, you'd be dead and we wouldn't be having this conversation right now!"

Ben and Drew stared at each other, anger spewing out of their eyes. Then Drew remembered the younger Ben, who sat silently next to him on cold fall days eating a sack lunch when the world was scorning him. Drew dropped his gaze.

"I'm sorry, Ben. You're right. I should have been more careful. I think she suspected me long before you even said anything."

Ben's shoulders slumped. He shook his head. "I'm sorry too. Sometimes my mouth just disconnects from my brain and things come out before I know what I'm saying."

"Well, I guess we both could have been a little more careful." Drew walked to the coffee maker and began making a pot of coffee.

"The FBI is after you, not me. Why don't you just disappear again and I'll press on with the LASOK?"

"Because if Sydney does turn me in to the FBI, they will at least come and talk to you. If they come here, so will the dark invaders. If the dark invaders come, you're done."

Ben just shook his head. "Do you know how long it will take to move this stuff? How many weeks we will lose?"

"It's worse than that, my friend. We may not have *time* to move this equipment. In fact, we shouldn't even be here right now. The FBI could show up at any minute. Taking time to move this isn't an option."

At that, Ben hung his head. They had come so far...done so much. This was indeed a major setback.

"Can't you try and talk to Sydney? See if she's thinking about turning you in?"

"Yeah, I'm going to try, but last night she wouldn't talk to me or even look at me. She's really upset, Ben...and confused. I thought I'd better give you a heads-up before I tried again though. I think we need to get you out of here until we get a better idea of what's going down. We'd better think about implementing plan B at the alternate location."

Ben nodded. "Give me ten minutes to get my notes and hard drives."

"Sure." Drew watched the black liquid in the coffee maker dribble into the glass pot. He waited until there was enough for a cup and then robbed the pot of its strong contents.

Twenty minutes later, Drew dropped Ben off at a hotel a few miles from the lab.

"What about the exchange?" Ben asked. "We still need that electron microscope."

"It all depends on Sydney. I don't dare hit the pit or touch that account until I know where she's at. Meanwhile, you keep working on Waseem's equation."

"You know it. What else would I do?"

Drew smiled. Of course that's what he would do...that's *all* he would do until he got it.

Drew didn't dare contact Sydney directly. Her cell phone would be monitored by the Feds. There was only one way of getting a message to her without blowing his cover—he would have to find her and follow her. On a Sunday morning, there was only one place where she would be.

Church.

Drew couldn't remember the church, but he remembered the pastor's name—Pastor Worthington. He searched and found him at New Life Church, just north of the Kennedy Expressway. It looked like a large church, which was both good and bad. It would be difficult to ID Sydney in such a large crowd, but it would also be easier for him to blend in if the Feds were looking for him by watching her. Sydney went to a ten o'clock service—he knew that because she had invited him before. The timing was good—he still had thirty minutes to recon the area.

DREW ARRIVED AT NEW LIFE Church at 9:40. He drove through the parking lot for a few minutes, scanning and watching for both invaders and federal agents. He spotted a dozen light invaders, which made sense to him. Very few of the churchgoing people would willingly be influenced by dark invaders, but with such a high concentration of people, the light invader force would make sure of their protection. He wondered what a football stadium filled with thirty thousand people would look like in the invader realm.

Drew parked, and in the thick of hundreds of cars he started walking toward the church. It was a massive building with one huge section that Drew guessed was the sanctuary. The rest of the building sprawled out over fifty thousand square feet. He figured thousands of people would be attending each service in a church of this size, and he was once again amazed at the folly of so many gullible people. They were all looking for answers, and he was the only one who had them.

He walked past two light invaders who were talking and watching each person who went by. Drew ignored them and entered the lobby, hoping to disappear into the throng of people inside, but he was greeted near the door by an older couple with broad smiles and warm handshakes.

"Welcome to New Life Church. Are you attending for the first time?" the older gentleman asked as he grasped Drew's hand a little too long.

"Ah…no." Better to avoid any sort of newcomers' attention.

"Well, thank you for worshiping with us today," the man said with a twinkle in his eye. He then turned to the couple coming up behind Drew.

Drew scanned the area looking for any stakeouts. He hadn't been in a church since his grandmother's funeral in South Carolina. That one seemed so cold and stuffy. New Life was different. Despite it being a church and way too large, there was a warmth and friendliness here that he had never felt before. They even had a coffee shop. Drew ordered up a cappuccino and tried to pay, but the pretty young teenage girl held up a hand.

"No need to pay. Donations only." She smiled and pointed to an oak box at the end of the counter.

"Thanks." Drew dropped a five into the box, then found a corner table to sit at and continue scanning. He forced his senses into high gear so he could cover as many people as possible. The large foyer could easily hold eight hundred people, although Drew figured there were a little more than half that at the moment. He hadn't seen Sydney yet, but he did lay eyes on one man who looked suspicious. There was an air about him that Drew recognized—the air of a man who knew how to handle himself and a weapon. The man was scanning just as Drew was. When he turned to the right, Drew saw the subtle bulge off his right hip, indicating he was carrying. Drew was about to abandon his cappuccino and make a break for the door, but he was afraid it would be too obvious now.

The man continued turning, and Drew hesitated. Then he saw a name tag on his left lapel with the word *Security* below the man's name. Drew waited, taking the risk to let the man's gaze pass through him. It did, and he didn't even hesitate.

Drew breathed a sigh of relief. He looked past the man, then froze once more. Sydney was on the far side of the room in a mix of three girls and four guys…and was staring right at him. He felt stupid. With all his powers of observation, he had been scoped by Sydney first. She was smiling and laughing with the others, but Drew could tell something was wrong. She broke eye contact with him and started chatting with the girl next to her. Then she started to dig in her purse as if she were looking for something and finally shook her head in disgust. She spoke briefly to the girl next to her, and the girl nodded and handed her phone to Sydney. Sydney dialed on the phone, and a few seconds later Drew's phone vibrated, indicating he had received a text. Sydney put the phone to her ear and began talking and laughing as if she were having a great conversation with a friend.

Drew scanned the room again but came up empty. The text could only be from Sydney or Ben. If it was Sydney, Drew would be impressed. He pulled the phone from his pocket just enough to see the screen.

agnts near not sfe

Drew spun away from the table in the opposite direction and cautiously slipped through a group of people coming in through the side door. He glanced over his shoulder, and that's when he saw him. Thirty feet behind and a little off to the side was a short, balding man with the same air about him as the security guard, but he was not security. He was searching the crowd and hadn't yet made Drew. He saw the man speak into his sleeve and knew there had to be other FBI agents nearby.

Just ahead, a dark-haired younger man was entering from outside and Drew could see FBI written all over his face. Drew ducked into a bathroom to his left and went to a sink to pretend to wash his hands. There weren't any dark invaders in the church, but if they knew the Feds were onto Drew, they wouldn't be far away. Drew waited fourteen seconds, the time he calculated it would take for the younger agent to pass by the bathroom door. No one entered the bathroom, so he went back to the door, cracked it open, and saw the agent walk past.

Drew didn't wait—he slipped out and continued to the side door, away from the two agents inside. Once outside, he dashed between parked cars to find his beater Grand Prix and exited the parking lot. His heart was pounding hard, and he was sweating profusely. That was too close, but it did tell him one thing: Sydney had not ratted him out. Despite such a close call, Drew was elated. It meant more than just the possible continuation of their mission—it meant that Sydney was still with him.

He wasn't sure which made him happier.

Twenty-five minutes later he was back with Ben at the hotel.

"They know you're here—in Chicago!" Ben paused in his pacing. "We can't stay here. We have to leave now!"

Drew leaned up against the desk. "I know, but we don't know what Sydney has told them, if anything. By the way she was acting and the text she sent me, I think she's still with us."

"But she's hot— Ah...you know what I mean."

Drew stifled a laugh. "Yeah, there'll be no contacting her in any way, that's for sure, and there is no longer any reason to stay in Chicago." The words dragged Drew's heart into the mire. "But if we can wait until tomorrow night, we can rent a truck and load up most of the equipment, and I can make one more day of trading on the exchange. We're going to need money to start someplace new, and I am on the verge of a couple of huge payouts."

Ben sat down on the bed. Both men thought long about the risk involved and the time lost if they jumped ship without any prep.

"It's your call, Drew. If you think it's worth the risk, then I'm game. I would hate to start over again."

Drew nodded. "We'll rent a truck first thing in the morning; then you start packing. I'll hit the exchange, try to get out early, and help you with the last few larger pieces of equipment."

"Okay." Ben nodded.

DREW AND BEN SPENT the night in the hotel room and were awake by the time the Monday morning sun hit the Chicago skyline. By nine o'clock, they were at the lab, and Ben began dismantling and loading. Drew decided to abandon his apartment just in case and instead bought a new set of trading clothes at a department store before he hit the exchange. He knew it was dangerous—extremely dangerous—but he had over sixty-five thousand in his account and was on the verge of turning that into two hundred thousand today. It would get Ben close to the minimum he needed to finish the LASOK project.

Drew entered the pit and scanned for an hour. It caused him to miss one of his promising trades, so he abandoned caution and began trading like a man who had no tomorrow. He felt the economic heartbeat of the pit and let the endless sea of numbers massage his intuition. By two o'clock he was at one hundred eighty thousand dollars. Twenty minutes before the exchange closed, Drew took the biggest risk he had ever taken, and it paid off.

He sold his stock in feeder cattle at 167 and finished with an account balance of $234,000. It would be enough to set up a lab and purchase all the remaining equipment in some small, remote city away from the masses and the invaders. Now Drew faced the problem of cashing out that amount of money without drawing attention or raising flags. He withdrew just under ten thousand and decided to figure out later how to either transfer or withdraw the money over an extended period of time.

By four thirty, Drew was on his way back to the lab. He hoped that Ben had not been discovered and was relieved when he saw him in the back of the building, struggling to haul some electronic test equipment up the ramp and into the truck. There was a sense of relief that they had made it this far through the day without either of them being discovered.

Or killed.

Forty minutes later, Drew closed the back door to the truck, and Ben locked up the building. All was set.

They met at the door of the truck, and each of them took a deep breath.

"We made it, Ben." Drew smiled.

"I'll feel better when we are hundreds of miles away from Chicago." Apparently Ben couldn't smile quite yet.

It was getting to be dusk, and they planned on driving until midnight to put some distance between them and the threat.

"I'll drive the truck. You follow behind in the Grand Prix," Drew said.

Ben nodded. "Sounds—"

Drew's phone rang, and they both froze.

"Don't answer it, Drew... You know what it means."

Drew pulled the phone out of his pocket. It had never rung before. It was his emergency phone. He stared at it, hating what it might mean and hating what might happen if he didn't answer. Sydney's number stared back at him on the display. He shook his head and clicked the answer button as Ben threw back his head and turned away.

"Yeah." Drew heard one faint, unintelligible whisper, and then the phone went dead.

He pulled the phone away from his head...five bars. Ben turned around and came back.

"Something's wrong."

Just then a text came through: *ray trble drags here.*

Drew looked up at Ben. "I have to go." His heart quickened with each passing second.

"I know. It could be a trap, Drew."

"Yep…but if it's not—" He didn't need to finish. Drew gave Ben the ten thousand dollars and the keys to the truck. "You know where to go and what to do." Drew locked hands with Ben and gave him a hug.

"Yeah." Ben backed away and hung his head. "Drew, you be careful. I can't do this without you."

"I will. I'll rejoin you by tomorrow."

Ben looked at him like he didn't believe him. He nodded and climbed up into the truck. Drew ran to his car, cranked up the engine, and slammed it into drive. He set his direction toward Emmanuel Church.

It would be the longest fifteen-minute drive of his life.

28

INTO THE DRAGON

By the time Drew pulled onto the street in front of Emmanuel Church, he knew the situation was bad. Lights of police cars and an ambulance flashed everywhere. Drew parked his car as close as he dared and hurried toward the scene. He spotted Wallace speaking to two other light invaders, one was bleeding from his left shoulder. They listened gravely as they received their orders, then flew in opposite directions. Wallace turned to look at Drew, his gaze full of fierce anger.

Anger...at Drew. But why?

Drew didn't take time to scan for Feds. An ambulance meant someone was down, and based on Sydney's text, he shuddered to think that it might be her. He got to within thirty feet before a policeman stopped him.

"Back away, sir," the young officer commanded.

Drew leaned around him to see Reverend Ray lying on the sidewalk in a pool of blood. Two EMTs were working on him, and Ray's wife, Nicole, was kneeling beside him in painful anguish. Drew couldn't see Ray's face, so he didn't know if he was dead or alive.

"*No!*" Drew pushed, but the policeman pushed back.

"Sir, you need to back away or I'll have to restrain you."

"Ray!"

Just then, the EMT near Ray's head leaned to the left to get supplies from his bag next to him. Ray turned his head toward Drew and reached out his hand toward him.

"Look," Drew said to the policeman. "He's asking for me."

The policeman turned his head to look at Ray, and Drew was past him in an instant.

"Hey!" the policeman called, but nothing was going to stop him.

Drew ran to Ray and grabbed his hand. Nicole looked desperate. There was a commotion between the EMTs and the policeman.

"I want him here!" Ray sputtered.

The policeman hesitated and then backed away while the EMTs continued to work. The left side of Ray's abdomen was dark red, and the EMTs were working fast.

"Ray...what happened?"

Ray pulled him close so that only Drew could hear. "The Dragons took Shana and Micah, Drew. They want you—" He grimaced. "They said if they see the police coming, they'll kill them."

Drew clenched his teeth. Blood coursed through his veins and his muscles tightened. He had caused this.

Drew looked for Sydney but couldn't see her. "Where's Sydney?"

The EMTs were getting ready to lift Ray onto the stretcher.

"Out of the way," one of them ordered.

"They took her too," Nicole said, her voice choked.

"They caught her texting you. They know she's yours," Ray wheezed.

"One, two, three!" The EMTs lifted Ray onto the stretcher, and he winced.

They raised the stretcher until it locked in the up position, then wheeled it toward the ambulance. Drew would have followed, but a policeman stopped him.

Ray's voice came to Drew over the chaos. "You have to find them, Guardian. You have to save them!"

Nicole grabbed Drew's arm. She seemed torn between wanting to be with Ray and her desperation to find her children. "Find them, Drew... Whatever has happened, you find them!" It was more than a plea.

She turned to enter the ambulance just as Drew felt four strong hands on him all at once. A second later he was facedown with his cheek pressed hard into the asphalt. His senses peaked, and the anger that boiled in his blood accentuated everything. The doors of the ambulance closed.

"God and His mighty angels go with you," he heard Ray's faint voice call out.

"FBI. You're coming with us, Drew Carter."

Drew glanced at the nearest police car. He heard a police captain radioing for a SWAT team and more chatter about the abduction. Drew felt the cold steel of handcuffs tighten around his wrists. The two agents lifted him to his feet and yanked him away from the scene, toward an unmarked car farther down the block.

Drew began racing through his options, but in handcuffs, there weren't many.

"We've been looking for you for a long time, Mr. Carter," the older, balding agent said.

"I have to help, or the Dragons will kill them!"

"Hey!" a policeman called out from behind them. It was the captain.

The agents stopped as the captain caught up with him. "Why are you taking him in? What did he do?"

"He's wanted in connection with the Drayle University shooting in Kansas," the younger agent replied.

The balding agent scowled. "It's federal business, Captain. You've got your own mess to deal with, and if you can't take care of it, we'll be back."

The captain eyed the agent, then looked at Drew. "The reverend's a good man. I heard him call you Guardian. Is that true?"

"Captain, I have to help Ray's family. You know I can."

"Time to go," the balding agent said.

"Wait." The captain barked out the order. "This man has helped a lot of people in this part of the city and aided us in putting a bunch of gangbangers behind bars. You sure you got the right man?"

"You do your job and we'll do ours." With that, the agent spun Drew back around and pushed him toward the car. Drew glanced over his shoulder and saw the captain mouth a few words that didn't look very polite, then turn and jog back to his squad car. Drew's frustration was more than he could bear.

"You guys know that gangs don't abduct people; they kill. If I don't help them, they're going to die. SWAT team or no SWAT team."

"Shut up, Carter."

"The Dragons are armed to the teeth, and they own that area. They want me, and if I don't show, there isn't going to be anything the police can do."

"Well, they'll have to get in line because we wanted you first."

Drew clenched his teeth. He jerked backward, away from the car, but he couldn't break loose from their grip. The agents slammed him onto the trunk of the car.

"You can make this hard, Carter, or you can make this easy."

Drew looked up and saw Wallace glaring at him from the right side of the car. He had never seen the invader quite so fierce.

"Please, help me. I have to save them!" Drew looked into the invader's steely eyes. Wallace eyed the agents and then looked at Drew.

"Carter, you're only going one place, so shut up!" The agent lifted him back to his feet and shoved him onto the sidewalk.

Wallace drew his sword as the younger agent reached for the rear door of the car and pulled it open.

Drew looked at the two Feds. "Nothing personal, guys, but I just can't go with you right now."

The younger, dark-haired agent's brow furrowed. The older agent put his hand on the back of Drew's head just as Drew saw the flash of Wallace's sword out of the corner of his eye.

The handcuffs fell from his wrists.

Before they hit the ground, Drew spun and grabbed the older agent's outstretched upper arm. He used that leverage to slam the agent's head into the car, just aft of the door opening. The concussion knocked the agent out cold.

The younger agent was standing just forward of the open door. He reached inside his jacket for his gun, but Drew side-kicked the door, which slammed into the young agent. He sprawled backward onto the sidewalk. Drew reached down and pulled the gun out of the unconscious agent's holster. He brought it to bear on the fallen agent, who froze, holding his hands clear of his jacket. Drew covered the ground between them as Wallace flew through the nearest building and disappeared.

"Don't do it, Carter." The agent held his gaze. "You don't want to kill a federal agent."

Drew reached into the agent's coat and removed his gun. It was identical to the one he was holding—two FN Five-Sevens. "Turn over...on your face."

The agent obliged, and Drew took a quick look back to the scene in front of the church to make sure none of the officers had seen what had happened.

He handcuffed the agent, then recovered one extra magazine for the FNs from each of the agents. He turned the agent on his back and sat him up.

"For the record, I would never shoot you. I'm one of the good guys, and I'm going after the gang that abducted those people."

"You do this, and we'll come after you in full force."

Drew knelt down, reached into the agent's coat pocket, and pulled out the keys to their car. "Yeah...I expect so. Shouldn't take long to GPS track your car. When you come, just remember that I'm trying to save those people."

The agent frowned. "You weren't in on the shooting at Drayle?"

Drew stopped and looked over his shoulder. A policeman one hundred feet away was looking toward them. The dark of the evening must have been enough to obscure what was happening, because he was slow to respond.

"No." He met and held the agent's gaze. "I'm the one who stopped it."

The agent tilted his head and squinted. Drew stuck one FN in the back of his belt and stuffed the two magazines in the front. He looked at the agent as he stood. "I thought only the Secret Service carried FNs."

The agent hesitated, then shook his head. "I'm going to lose my job over this."

"Sorry, there are people who will lose their lives if I don't help them."

Drew shut the open rear door, stepped over the unconscious agent, and jumped into the car. He fired up the engine, put it in gear, and tore off down the street. One thought encouraged him.

The Dragons had no idea that not only would the police be coming but so would who-knew-how-many FBI agents and tactical teams.

He circled the six city blocks that were the center of the Dragons' domain and parked on the southwest side of their territory. From there he took to foot. He'd ventured into Dragon territory a couple of times before, but the number of dark invaders there was so great he didn't come often. The last time he did so, he'd spotted an abandoned warehouse that seemed to be the focus of a lot of the dark invader activity.

That must be the Dragons' hideout…their dome.

Word must be out that something was going down, because the streets were abandoned except for the Dragons on lookout at the street corners. Drew scanned two blocks down the road…

A host of dark invaders moved toward the warehouse.

No doubt about it. This was more than just a human event.

Drew kept to the shadows and alleys until he was just one block from the warehouse. He counted thirty-two dark invaders gathered in front of the warehouse, all with swords drawn—and more kept showing up. In the middle stood the fierce and ominous Kurgan, pointing and issuing orders to each of his minions. Two and three dark invaders at a time flew in different directions as they received orders. Drew ducked into a walkway between two buildings and leaned up against one of the brick walls.

Would Wallace come, and if so, how many light invaders would join in the fight? He gripped his FN and clenched his teeth. He had to get to Sydney and the children before the Feds or the police arrived or the Dragons would kill them and then scatter like rats.

Drew heard the slide of a Glock as a round was chambered. It came from the dark walkway behind him, twenty-five feet away.

"Don't move, sucker. I'm taking you to Fang."

Drew didn't hesitate. He turned and fired his FN so quickly that the Dragon got only one shot off before Drew's bullet, traveling at twice the speed, exploded into his gun and hand. Drew didn't have to dodge because the .45 round went wide by four inches. The Dragon screamed from the pain of his bleeding hand. Drew ran at him and slammed a flying kick into his chest, putting him flat on the ground. Drew continued on into the alley behind them—the gunshots would bring a dozen gang members this way.

He sprinted up the alley toward the warehouse, scanning and avoiding any human activity. Unfortunately, it was impossible to escape the detection and the speed of the dark invaders—two of them caught up to him in less than two seconds.

No hiding now.

One flew past Drew and stood before him while the other flew toward the front of the warehouse where Kurgan was waiting. Drew stopped, not sure how much a dark invader could do to him directly. Could his sword kill him? Cut him? Drew was scared, and the invader apparently knew it.

He came at Drew with his sword swishing from side to side. The sword tip slammed into a garbage can, which went crashing to the ground at the same time that a cat screeched and bolted from within it. Drew didn't know what to do, but he knew he couldn't fight enemies in both realms at the same time.

Just as he was about to close his eyes and charge forward, two light invaders fell on the pavement on each side of him from the buildings above, their gleaming swords ready. Drew rushed forward as the invaders from the invisible realm collided. The battle between the invaders began. He didn't wait to see the outcome—he knew it would be costly and intense. Drew made it to the southwest corner of the warehouse, where there was one lone door. To his right, more dark invaders were coming, but three light invaders materialized through the wall of a nearby apartment building and intercepted them. From above, a dark invader jumped from the roof and was descending right on top of Drew when Wallace leaped from the lower roof of the building across the alley and smashed into the invader midair. They crashed into the side of the warehouse and fell to the alley below.

Drew couldn't become a spectator—he had to stay focused on his mission. He entered the warehouse and scanned the area. Broken glass from the windows was scattered next to the walls. This part of the warehouse was empty except for a few rusted-out pieces of equipment and a couple of fallen pallet racks. Drew made his way along the outer wall of the warehouse, toward a large inner partition that separated the warehouse in two. Part of the wall was broken down, so he decided to step through it rather than take the doorway that was partially open. If this was indeed the Dragons' dome, it had been way too easy to gain access.

Had to be a trap.

Just as Drew was about to step through to the other section of the warehouse, two invaders locked in deadly combat fell through from the other side and onto the ground, just a few feet away from Drew. The dark invader had one hand around the light invader's neck and a short sword in the other. The light invader gripped the wrist of his enemy's sword hand and clutched the tightening fingers of the dark invader's other powerful hand. The light invader reached to draw his long knife, but he was too late. The dark invader slammed a knee into the light invader's ribs, which caused him to release his hold on the dark invader's sword hand. As fast as lightning strikes, the short sword plummeted into the light invader's chest. After one brief, agonizing grimace, he dissolved into a vapor that floated upward.

The dark invader stood and glared at Drew. Hatred spewed from his black eyes, and then he disappeared back through the wall.

Drew struggled to control his breathing. Good invaders were dying, and he couldn't help but think it was all because of him. Anger seethed. He hated the dark invaders, and he hated gangs and the evil they did. He imagined Sydney, Shana, and Micah cowering in fear, or worse, injured or dead because of the blackened hearts of both dark invaders and gang members.

Something akin to invader fierceness boiled in his soul. His muscles tightened, and his eyes narrowed. He felt the knurled grip of the FN in his right hand and drew the second FN with his left. As evil as this gang was, he didn't want to kill anyone, but he would to save Sydney, Shana, and Micah. As accurately as he could now place his bullets, though, he hoped to spare lives.

But not at the cost of losing the innocent.

He took a deep breath and entered through the hole to the other side.

His eyes adjusted to the dim light of the gang dome. To his left and right were what used to be offices lining a long, twenty-foot-wide hallway. It looked like the corridor ended in another large room, but it might just as well have been ten miles away because Drew was entering a gauntlet of death. Broken desks, chairs, metal shelving, ceiling tiles, and broken drywall littered the hallway, providing both obstacles to navigate and cover behind which to hide. Drew scanned every inch of the hallway, listening, watching, and feeling everything.

Drew heard whispers in the second office to his left…foot shuffles behind some shelving…the safety of a pistol clicking off. Nothing escaped his senses. He placed three Dragons already in the hallway behind various covers and at least two more in the second office. Possibly another farther down in an office to his right.

Something flashed at the far end of the hallway, and Drew caught a glimpse of another invader battle. Drew calculated his path, then exploded into action, not waiting for the Dragons to make the first move.

A hand and a gun appeared above the broken desk on the right, followed by the top of a shaved, tattooed head. The first bullet screamed toward Drew, but he had already moved. He fired his FN, and the bullet tore into the Masonite desktop, just below the gun and to the right of the Dragon's head. The high-velocity round blasted into the Dragon's forearm, sending him screaming against the wall.

Two guns fired fifteen feet behind the first Dragon, but not before Drew saw his attackers. He set his foot at the corner of the floor and the wall, pushed off, and dived onto the desk, sliding and rotating his body so he could land crouched and in firing position.

Crack…crack…crack!

Both FNs launched bullets precisely where Drew had targeted. The hallway exploded into chaos. Nothing in that hallway could stop the Kevlar-penetrating force of the FN bullets, so Drew didn't wait for his targets to show once he pinpointed their positions. Muzzles flashed and bullets filled the air. A gunman appeared in a doorway to his left. Drew pulled his right FN off target, fired beneath his left arm, and covered the original target with his left FN. Both guns fired at the same time as Drew moved, dodged, covered, and advanced.

Thirty-five seconds later, Drew stood at the end of the hallway, six Dragons moaning and bleeding behind him.

He knelt down next to the last Dragon, who was cowering in the corner, cradling an injured gun hand.

"Where are they?"

The Dragon sneered and cursed. "Fang's gonna kill you!"

Drew stood and approached the end of the hallway, smelling the darkness of humanity before he saw it. He used the corner of the wall as cover to look into the Dragons' lair—and what he saw stopped him cold.

The room was over one hundred feet square, with a railing along a second floor that looked down from the far two walls. Drew pinpointed seventeen more Dragons, five with guns, the rest with knives and other weapons. But what had him frozen in his tracks was the other realm.

Dark invaders were everywhere.

Drew counted twenty-three at various positions, both on the main floor and on the railing. The entire room dripped with evil. Drew missed them at first, but then he caught the glowing red eyes in the far corner of the warehouse, beneath the railing. The lurking, black form of a dark invader beast...poised to pounce and kill. Though smaller than the beast he had seen in the attack at Emmanuel Church, it was no less fearsome. Deep-set eyes, razor-sharp talons, and dozens of sharp spines along its matted, furry back sent shivers through Drew.

The Dragons had decorated their lair with images of dragons, snakes, and skeletons. Graffiti wallpapered the perimeter with the Dragons' markings. Crusty beds, cots, couches, and other makeshift furniture, along with televisions and other electronics, were scattered throughout, transforming the inside of the warehouse into a bizarre and eerie dark lair of reprobate humans.

Near the center stood a man every bit as evil looking as an invader—perhaps more so. Drew saw the double image of the man's face interlaced with piercings through his eyebrows, ears, lips, and cheeks. Tattoos covered most of his exposed skin. But none of that frightened Drew as much as what surrounded the man.

Sydney, Shana, and Micah stood in front of him as a human shield. A dragon on each side held them in place. They looked unharmed, but terror filled their eyes. And Drew knew, deep in his soul...

He faced the worst of all possible situations.

29

SECRET AGENT OF THE INVADER REALM

Guardian!"

Drew didn't respond to the Dragon leader's call. His mind raced for a solution, but to no avail. The only reason Sydney and the kids were alive was so they could be used as leverage against Drew. He couldn't take all the Dragons down, that was certain, but he could take out Fang. He was the key. And it worked in Drew's favor that many of the Dragons had heard the stories of the Guardian... They feared him.

Drew calculated a dozen different scenarios, but each one ended in disaster. To save the hostages' lives, Drew would have to give himself up. His life and Fang's life were the bartering chips. If he played them right, Sydney, Shana, and Micah might live.

He leaned up against the wall, closed his eyes...and nodded.

So be it.

He did a tactical reload, exchanging his half-spent magazines for full ones, then stepped out into the room and raised both FNs at Fang. Drew strode toward him and his captives.

Twenty feet into his journey, the gang leader stepped up behind Sydney and put a knife to her throat. "How many do you want me to kill before you stop?"

Drew halted but did not lower his guns. He scanned the room again, verifying the positions and armament of the other Dragons. The remaining five guns were all pointed at him. Impossible to dodge bullets from all of them.

"Harm any one of them, Fang, and I promise...you will die."

Fang smiled, seeming to enjoy the drama of the moment. "You not be human, are you, Guardian?" Fang's gaze looked right through Drew. "You be sent to destroy me, aren't you?"

Drew had no response. He'd expected creepy, cruel, and dark—but he wasn't prepared for crazy.

"How great be your powers, Guardian? Are you stronger than my allies?" Fang lifted his hand to the balcony. Drew bet every human there thought Fang was talking about his fellow gang members, but Drew knew he meant much more than that.

Drew had twenty rounds in each of his FNs, with another nineteen in the magazines at his belt...*if* he had time to reload. Fang would have to go first, then the Dragons with guns, then the dragon guards next to the hostages. He calculated his moves and predicted the position of the Dragons' reactions, plotting to the second where he would have to place each shot. Only one thing stopped him: the uncertain outcome of the hostages.

Once bullets and weapons started flying, he couldn't protect Sydney, Shana, and Micah. Not from this distance. They looked at him with eyes that hoped and feared at the same time.

"What do you want, Fang?"

"I want you, Guardian."

"I'm here. Let them go, and I'm yours."

Fang sneered. "Drop the guns, and I let them go."

The dark invaders had drawn their swords. Many whispered into the Dragons' ears. Drew's only option was to make the first move. That would give him the split-second advantage he needed. He tensed, ready to act—

The dark and hulking form of Kurgan stepped through, from the front of the building, into the Dragon's lair.

The dark invaders paused to watch their commander approach. Vile hatred spewed from his eyes as he glared at Drew and then Sydney and the children. He looked up at his warriors of destruction...waiting to give the command that would unleash their terror. Then he spoke, and Fang's head tilted, as if he too could hear the voice of his dark master.

Fang smiled. "You can't escape, Guardian. I am the master of my domain, and no matter how good you are, you will die!"

"And so will you, unless you release them now!" Drew took two steps forward to punctuate his words.

Fang's eyes widened—a flash of fear. He stepped farther behind Sydney and pressed the knife against her throat. "It is nothin' to kill them, Guardian! Drop the guns, and I'll let them go."

Drew didn't trust Fang for one fraction of one second, but he didn't have a choice. Fang could kill one of the three and still have leverage. Drew had pushed as far as he dared.

He knelt down and raised his voice for all to hear. "You know I'm not human, Fang. You double-cross me, and I will return to hunt you and every last member of the Dragons until no one survives!"

The two guards holding the hostages glanced toward Fang. Drew figured many of the Dragons were having the same response. Some had seen Drew do impossible things. Undoubtedly, they'd told exaggerated stories to save face. All of that now worked to Drew's advantage.

He set his guns down on the ground and slowly stood, listening, watching, feeling every move, whisper, and footstep. His mind saw the entire warehouse like a chessboard, locating every piece and calculating a dozen moves and outcomes with each passing second. Standing resolute in the legendary fear he had created, he glared first at the guards and then at Fang. Three large Dragons closed in, two with knives and one with brass knuckles. Drew had disrespected the gang. A bullet would be too merciful. His death would come through brutal beating.

Drew didn't flinch. He pointed at Fang. "Is your word meaningless, Fang? Remember my warning!" He glared at the approaching Dragons. They stopped a few feet from him and looked to Fang for their orders.

Fang tilted his head from side to side, as if trying to decide which ice cream flavor he should pick. Kurgan walked behind Fang and began speaking to the invader inside him. Fang smiled as his eyes became black with darkness.

This was not going to end well.

Where were the light invaders? Were there too many dark invaders for them to even try to help? Drew prepared himself for the worst, calculating the method and the time it would take to recover the FNs, but then—something strange happened.

Sydney lowered her head, and wisps of bluish plasma swirled around her. Like suspended flames of a pure blue fire, the essence licked at the space around her and reached out to encompass Micah and Shana. Drew wasn't the only one to notice. Kurgan turned and recoiled, covering his face from whatever it was that now engulfed the hostages.

Kurgan backed away, and so did other nearby dark invaders, all cursing and hiding their eyes. Drew thought he had seen all that this unearthly realm contained, but this was something new—and it emanated from Sydney! Once before he had wondered if she was more than she let on, but now he knew it to be true. In some unfathomable way, Sydney had discovered a weapon against the dark invaders.

But how?

As her bluish aura continued, the influence of the invaders over their human pawns vanished. Fang frowned and looked around, as if abandoned in his evil plot.

Drew stepped forward. "Release them, Fang! I'm the one you want, not them."

Fang looked left and right, confused and distracted as the blue plasma flame swelled. His double-faced invader turned away and screamed. Fang nodded to the two Dragons keeping the hostages in place, and they let Sydney and the children go.

"Leave the building, Sydney!" Drew made his tone as commanding as he could.

Sydney gazed at Drew through the protecting flames of blue. She bit her lip. Clearly, she knew she had to get Micah and Shana to safety—and that to do so, she'd have to abandon Drew to an execution.

She led the children toward the doors at the front of the building. The dark invaders hid from the burning flames surrounding them. Kurgan recovered enough to roar his rage, both at Drew and now even more so at Sydney. He screamed at the invaders nearest Sydney, Shana, and Micah, and they tried to attack. Fang must have heard it too, for his blackened gaze returned, and he shook himself.

"Stop them!"

Two Dragons with switchblades intercepted them before they reached the door, and Sydney looked toward Drew, with Shana and Micah clinging to her side and fear swallowing them. Drew's anger reached a crescendo. Only he could hear the distant approach of sirens, but it would be too late. Five minutes might just as well be five hours when facing the guns and knives of a ruthless gang.

"Now you die, Guardian!" Fang raised his fist in the air.

Kurgan came to stand before Drew and sneered. Drew raised his head as the massive dark invader lifted his sword above his head to strike him down. The three Dragons stood ready to close in on him, each one with an accompanying dark invader ready to amplify their power and their speed. At least five guns stood ready if by some fluke the Dragons' intent on beating Drew to death failed.

Time stopped as Fang relished his power over the one who had dared stand against him and his Dragons.

In that moment—that moment of ending, of impossible odds and seemingly certain outcome—the invader realm erupted.

More than twenty light invaders burst through the roof of the warehouse, swords drawn and weapons firing as they charged into battle with the enemies of good. Wallace led the assault.

The invader inside Fang looked up and screamed, and so did Fang. *"Kill* him!"

Even as the dark invaders abandoned their earthly charges to engage in deadly combat with the light invaders, the three Dragons descended on Drew. He exploded into action with a spinning back kick that landed square across the closest knife attacker's jaw. The Dragon's head snapped to the left, and he dropped, unconscious, to the ground.

Wallace struck down two of the dark invaders nearest Fang, and Kurgan flew to engage him. The warehouse became a blur of battle in the invader realm as Drew's combat instincts kicked into overdrive. He had to get to Sydney and the children!

Drew sidestepped the first punch from the brass knuckles, grabbed the Dragon's wrist, and pounded a powerful front kick into his attacker's chest. As the attacker doubled over, Drew used the movement and the momentum to throw him into the third Dragon, who was making a knife thrust at Drew. The blade cut into the thrown Dragon's shoulder, and the two stumbled back and away from Drew.

Two light invaders focused exclusively on the Dragons—and their accompanying invaders—who had intercepted Sydney, Shana, and Micah. Then Sydney's blue fire reached out for the light invaders and imbued them with extra power. Their ferocity was frightening. After just three quick but powerful cuts, one dark invader turned to green vapor and the other retreated with a severe wound to his sword arm. One light invader sliced through the nearest Dragon's arm, and the man yelled and clutched his arm as his knife fell to his feet. He cradled his arm and backed away.

Drew dived and rolled toward the FNs lying just five feet away. The concrete around him shattered in spraying pieces of cement and white dust. Bullets ricocheted upward, zinging off in multiple directions. As Drew rolled, both hands found and curled around the grips of the waiting FNs. In near stop-motion framing, Drew came up on one knee, perfectly aligned for his first shot.

Target, front sight, squeeze, reacquire, repeat.

Both guns unleashed five rounds of revenge in less than two seconds. The entire gang froze at the sight of the Guardian in the middle of their lair holding weapons that none could fight against. But the invader realm still screamed with action.

Wallace was engaged in a deadly duel with Kurgan. Drew had seen many invader battles, but none as fierce as between these two warriors from this ancient realm. Swords flashed in a blur as they flew across the warehouse and off the walls, each trying to gain the positional advantage needed for a microsecond breach in the other's defense.

Drew turned his focus on the Dragon still standing between Sydney and the children and the door to escape. He brought his right FN to bear on him, and fear filled the Dragon's face.

"Run!"

At Drew's shout, the Dragon cowered and withdrew. The light invader guided Sydney, Shana, and Micah toward the door, defending them with his sword as they went.

Drew caught movement out of the corner of his eye. Behind Fang, Drew saw the hideous monster of fur and scales charging Wallace's backside. Every other light invader was engaged in battle and unable to help...

Drew knew, deep within, that Wallace would not survive. And there was nothing he could do to help.

Sirens filled the air outside the warehouse, and the Dragons scurried toward their escape routes.

"Behind you!" Drew screamed to Wallace.

As futile as it seemed, Drew charged toward Fang, unloading a continuous stream of jacketed lead from both guns into the air above him, directly at the attacking beast.

Wallace diverted a thrust from Kurgan just in time to see the beast lunging. He was impossibly out of position to effect any damaging cut to the beast, let alone recover in time to keep Kurgan's blade at bay.

Wallace's end was inevitable.

But the protecting light invader was more than just powerful, he was a tactical master. He parried Kurgan's blade outward and upward, then passed the steel of his own sword into the path of Drew's stream of bullets. Instantly, each one translated into the solid reality of Wallace's realm. Thirty-five high-velocity bullets burrowed into the thick hide of the pouncing beast. Death enveloped the monster in a green vapor that spilled forward around Kurgan and Wallace's ferocious duel.

Kurgan turned his head away to protect his eyes, and Wallace used it to his advantage, arcing his sword around in a brilliant flash of speed and cutting through Kurgan's chest and abdomen. Kurgan turned back, eyes bulging in anger and disbelief, but it was only for a moment—for he too dissolved into green nothingness that fell into the earth.

Fang fell to the concrete floor and crawled away toward the back of the warehouse. Kurgan's defeat turned the tide of the invader realm battle, and the dark invaders either retreated or were quickly dispensed.

Drew stood numb. What did it all mean? The police and the FBI were coming, but there was nowhere to run.

Wallace gave quick commands. One of the light invaders that Drew had seen a couple of times before came to Wallace, looked toward Drew, and exchanged what seemed to be serious words with him. Wallace's stern reply didn't seem to sit well with his comrade, but he turned and left. The warehouse emptied of all humans and invaders.

All but Drew and Wallace.

30

THE FINAL ENCOUNTER

The clatter of equipment and boots of law enforcement sounded just outside the front door as Wallace turned toward Drew and stepped forward. Drew swallowed hard, for the warrior looked as though he might not yet be done with battle.

As Wallace came, he stepped through arcing blue flames, out of the invader realm and into the world of humans. Drew's skin crawled as the massive invader approached and stopped just a few feet away, glaring down at him. Wallace raised his sword—then sheathed it and placed his hands on his hips. He looked frustrated, angry, and hesitant.

Drew had been part of saving his life, but he felt like he was being judged for crimes he couldn't understand.

"I am Validus." Wallace's voice boomed like thunder.

A thousand questions raced through Drew's mind, but only one escaped his lips. "Where do you come from?"

The warrior's steely eyes pierced Drew to the heart. "You had better figure that out quickly, for you are in grave danger. They know who you are, and they are coming for you. They are *all* coming for you."

All? Was the LASOK that important?

"Why...why me?"

Validus hesitated. "There are things of which I cannot speak, but the answers you seek are near. Beware, Drew Carter." Validus turned and took two steps, translating back into the invader realm just as the front warehouse door blasted open.

"Drop your weapons!"

Within seconds, Drew was surrounded by men in bulletproof vests emblazoned with FBI—and with an entire arsenal. After another face-plant into the concrete, Drew was handcuffed and whisked out the front of the warehouse toward one of five black SUVs.

"Drew!"

At Sydney's scream, he looked and saw her straining to see him as she stood on her tiptoes. She peered over the roof of one of the other vehicles. It was impossible to read the expression on her face—relief, joy, shock, concern, angst?

"Sydney!" he called back.

She was being encouraged to get in the vehicle but with much less force than Drew was experiencing. The door opened before him, and two agents reached for his head to place him inside.

"I know what's happening to you!" Sydney screamed. "You're seeing—"

"Watch your head, Carter." One of the agents bent Drew's head low, sat him down, and closed the door.

The sounds of the world muffled to silence in the bulletproof glass of the FBI SUV. Visions of both realms washed across his mind, but one event stood above the rest...

Sydney Carlyle, wrapped in blue-plasma fire, battling the dark invaders and the Dragons in a way he could never do.

He had scoffed and ridiculed her for years. Could he be the fool after all? If she had that kind of power, why would the dark invaders come after him? Drew shook his head.

When would this freakish dream ever end?

ꙮ

VALIDUS WALKED THROUGH the warehouse walls and into the alley behind.

Tren was waiting for him. "Never before has an angel spoken as you have to an unbeliever."

Validus looked at Tren and considered the warning. "You're right, but never before have the forces of the Fallen rallied so fiercely to destroy one unbelieving man."

Tren gave a slow nod. "What's happening, Validus? Why this man? I've watched him since childhood. I don't understand."

Validus looked up and into the distant stars of the heavens. "I commanded a continent, and now I guard one man." He looked back at Tren. "I don't understand either, but Drew Carter's life must be a pivotal force in both realms, and if we don't figure it out soon, the Fallen may turn the war once again."

Validus filled his lungs with a cleansing, deep breath, the pain in his chest reminding him of just how close he had come to dissolution. The battle to keep Drew Carter alive had been intense. He nearly smiled as he remembered how the man had taken action to save him from Durgank.

Validus directed his gaze back to Tren. "You know what to do."

Tren nodded.

"Very well...then make it so."

"To Elohim's glory," Tren proclaimed.

"To His glory," Validus returned.

Tren flew through the warehouse, and Validus turned south, down the alleyway. There was perhaps one who could make sense of the actions of the Fallen, but there were risks...risks that might cause even the commander of the western continent to hesitate. He had to be careful. Every angel that fell in battle meant the forces of the Fallen would continue to rise, and the peril of humankind could come spiraling to a resetting demise as had happened too many times before. Somehow...someway...Drew Carter was in the epicenter of that spiraling vortex.

And Validus needed to know why.

God has delivered us from the power of darkness and has translated us into the kingdom of His dear Son, in whom we have redemption through His blood, even the forgiveness of sins. He is the creator of the visible and the invisible, whether they be thrones, or dominions, or principalities, or powers. He is before all things, and by Him all things consist, or are held together.

—PARAPHRASE OF COLOSSIANS I

A NOTE FROM CHUCK BLACK

What does Jesus look like? If we don't know what He looks like, should we allow an artist to speculate and paint a representation of Him? I have often gazed upon a painter's rendition of the Lord and known with fair certainty that it was not an accurate depiction of our Savior. Nevertheless, such knowledge did not diminish the inspiration I felt from beholding the fruit of such gifted labor.

In similar fashion, one could ask, what does spiritual warfare look like? The Wars of the Realm trilogy is a speculative work of fiction that I've painstakingly written, not to contradict Scripture in any way but rather to inspire and challenge you to consider the reality of spiritual warfare in a whole new way. Though the story is intense and the liberties taken in regard to speculation are vast, the boundaries are the Bible and the purpose is to inspire men and women to glorify God. The true hope of this tale is found in the final chapters of the series, just as our hope is in the finished work of Jesus Christ, which will culminate in climactic triumph at the end of days.

The Readers Guide explains the biblical framework from which much of the speculation for this novel is derived. I hope you find it informative and helpful in your own investigation of understanding spiritual warfare.

READERS GUIDE

CHAPTER 1

The Sting of Death

Young Drew Carter and his mother experience the pain of losing his father. In 1 Corinthians 15:56, the Bible says that death has a sting, and anyone who has lived through the death of a loved one knows it to be true. But God promises for those who have put their faith in Jesus Christ that there is coming a day when death will no longer be able to sting. That happens on the day of resurrection.

"Death is swallowed up in victory." (1 Corinthians 15:54–58)

Thankfully, those who have a relationship with Christ can look forward to a new body—immortal and not subject to the afflictions of this world. Death itself will be eliminated forever.

And God will wipe away every tear from their eyes." (Revelation 21:4)

A Father to the Fatherless

Although Jake may not be a Christian, he demonstrates a biblical principle by "visit[ing] the fatherless and widows in their affliction" (James 1:27, KJV). As a child of God, He promises that He will take care of you. If He has to move a stranger's heart to help you, He will. Whether or not you have a loving father on this earth, you are not fatherless.

A father of the fatherless…is God in His holy habitation. (Psalm 68:5)

CHAPTER 2

Least of These

Just as Drew defended Benjamin in the cafeteria, we also should follow Jesus' calling to show kindness and respect to those whom society has deemed "the least."

Inasmuch as you did it to one of the least of these… (Matthew 25:40)

Sometimes it takes courage and the willingness to step outside our comfort zone to be kind to "the least of these," but Jesus commands and rewards such action.

Peer Pressure

Drew faced peer pressure by the "cool" athletes to mistreat Benjamin Berg, the school nerd. We all want to be loved and accepted, and it's easy to mistake the high and the rush of giving in to peer pressure for acceptance and love. But it's a false substitute. The only thing that will make you feel loved is actually being loved. Love comes from family, true friends, and most importantly, from Jesus Christ. When you face peer pressure, take a step back and look at it clearly. What are you hoping to get from the experience? A rush? Acceptance? Will it deliver what you think it promises? And if it doesn't deliver, how will you feel when it's all over?

For all that is in the world…is not of the Father but is of the world. (1 John 2:16)

And do not be conformed to this world, but be transformed. (Romans 12:2)

The key to overcoming peer pressure is to remember that the Enemy often uses peer pressure to deceive, manipulate, and tempt us to commit sin. Remember that God's ways are always better and that He truly is faithful in seeing us through the temptation and wants to lavish us with reward and blessing when we are faithful to Him.

God is faithful, by whom you were called into the fellowship. (1 Corinthians 1:9)

Wrong to Do Nothing

Drew tells Ben: "It's wrong to do nothing when you have the power to do something." Drew received this from his father and does not realize it is a biblical principle found in James.

Therefore, to him who knows to do good and does not do it,…it is sin. (James 4:17)

We who have the truth are without excuse when it comes to doing good unto others.

CHAPTER 3

Man's Fascination with Alien Life

The number of books and movies about alien life is growing exponentially. Our culture seems nearly obsessed with the concept. With this much attention and resources dedicated to an industry that has the ability to shape the thought processes of its viewers and readers, a diligent Christian ought to ponder the question, Is there something more to the promotion of alien life than just entertainment or even distraction from God? Could it be that the Enemy of God and the Enemy of God's people is preparing the world for something? The Bible calls for us to be wary and watchful.

Your adversary the devil walks about like a roaring lion. (1 Peter 5:8)

Finally, remember that the stars in heaven were created for one purpose:

The heavens declare the glory of God. (Psalm 19:1)

CHAPTER 4

The Foolishness of the Wise

When speaking of Sydney, Ben makes the statement: "Religion is a crutch for the weak-minded and needy of the world." Satan has used this delusion to support the worldly notions of self-sufficiency and egotism. You may have heard the saying, "There are no atheists in foxholes." Man seems to have the innate sense to cry out to God for help in his hour of need but just as quickly forgets about his need for a Savior when life is going smoothly. The Bible calls this foolishness.

Professing to be wise, they became fools. (Romans 1:22)

The fear of the LORD is the beginning of wisdom. (Proverbs 9:10)

CHAPTER 5

Real Friends

After the accident, when Drew felt as if everyone was against him, Ben stuck by his side. The Bible has a lot to say about the importance of encouragement and counsel from true friends.

But there is a friend who sticks closer than a brother. (Proverbs 18:24)

A friend loves at all times. (Proverbs 17:17)

Real friends are not afraid to say the hard thing.

Faithful are the wounds of a friend. (Proverbs 27:6)

God Cares

Because of his circumstances, Drew believes that God doesn't care about him. Even though life sometimes feels hard or unfair, it is important to remind yourself daily that God loves you. You are important to Him.

Casting all your care upon Him, for He cares for you. (1 Peter 5:7)

For the Son of Man has come to seek and to save that which was lost. (Luke 19:10)

For He Himself has said, "I will never leave you nor forsake you." (Hebrews 13:5)

CHAPTER 6

Light of the World

Drew encounters Sydney at college and realizes that there is something differ-ent about her that he can't describe. What Drew is drawn to is Christ in her and the light that shines from her because of the Holy Spirit. Even though she hasn't specifically spoken of her faith to him, her behavior and words testify loudly. At some point, we must use words to present the gospel, but until the Lord presents that opportunity, the light of our lives should proclaim Him just as clearly.

Let your light so shine before men. (Matthew 5:16)

CHAPTER 7

Witnessing to an Atheist

Sydney invites Drew to a Bible study, where he must face some of the flaws in his own belief system. There are a number of different approaches to take when witnessing to an atheist, but the first question that must be asked is, does he or she have an interest in discovering the truth? The answer to this question determines the approach. People who are antagonistic toward the Bible and Christianity will not usually listen to sound arguments no matter how scientific or factual they may be. Usually it is the demonstration of love and compassion that has an impact on them.

The goodness of God leads you to repentance. (Romans 2:4)

For a person who is an atheist and yet is open to the truth, an apologetics approach is often best. Apologetics is the branch of theology concerned with the defense and rational justification of Christianity. In Drew's case, because of his father's commitment to defending the freedoms of America, the Holy Spirit led Devin to start there. Another effective approach is to start with Creation and the concept of an intelligent designer.

His invisible attributes are clearly seen. (Romans 1:20)

Using Creation as evidence of a creator leads to a logical and systematic progression toward the gospel of Jesus Christ and ultimately salvation: Creation...existence of God...sin...need for the law...need for a Savior. The book of Romans is an excellent place to take a questioning atheist.

For all have sinned and fall short of the glory of God. (Romans 3:23)

As it is written: "There is none righteous, no, not one." (Romans 3:10)

Therefore, just as through one man sin entered the world, and death through sin, and thus death spread to all men, because all sinned. (Romans 5:12)

For the wages of sin is death, but the gift of God is eternal life in Christ Jesus our Lord. (Romans 6:23)

But God demonstrates His own love toward us, in that while we were still sinners, Christ died for us. (Romans 5:8)

That if you confess with your mouth the Lord Jesus and believe in your heart that God has raised Him from the dead, you will be saved. For with the heart one believes unto righteousness, and with the mouth confession is made unto salvation. (Romans 10:9–10)

Whoever calls on the name of the LORD shall be saved. (Romans 10:13)

Irreconcilable Beliefs

Drew discovers just how important and real Sydney's faith is to her. Sydney takes a difficult but uncompromising stand in obeying God's Word and in protecting her heart.

Do not be unequally yoked together with unbelievers. (2 Corinthians 6:14)

Love is a powerful emotion and can cause people to make unwise decisions that have lifelong consequences. Only a disciplined and obedient mind brought under the truth of God's Word can keep one from making foolish decisions dictated by emotion.

CHAPTER 8

Dealing with Fear

Ben is struggling with intense fear because of what he has discovered about the invaders. The Bible says that fear does not come from the Lord; however, there are two kinds of fear: the healthy respectful fear that we should have for God, and the controlling incapacitating fear that comes from Satan.

> God has not given us a spirit of fear, but of power and of love and of a sound mind. (2 Timothy 1:7)

> The fear of the LORD is the beginning of wisdom. (Proverbs 9:10)

It may seem ironic, but the more we fear the Lord, the less we fear the world and the Enemy, and the more courageous and valiant we become.

CHAPTER 9

Alternate Dimensions

When Ben and Drew discover that Dr. Waseem's experiment works, Drew gets a glimpse into a whole new dimension. The concept of alternate dimensions is not new. Physicists have theorized about such realities for many years, and it has been a favorite theme of science fiction since its inception. But actually, God told us about His "alternate dimension" from the beginning: the spiritual world. Ecclesiastes is correct when the preacher states that "there is nothing new under the sun." John 3:6 clearly identifies and separates the two realities: that of the physical world, or "the flesh," and that of the spiritual world. It is interesting to note that secular scientists and physicists don't give the spiritual world as described in the Bible any credence but would rather invent their own. It parallels their resistance to accept the truth of Creation versus that of the big bang theory.

> That which is born of the flesh is flesh, and that which is born of the Spirit is spirit. (John 3:6)

CHAPTER 10

Hope in Tragedy

Drew experienced tragedy when his eyesight was lost in the lab accident. Because we live in a fallen world, we are susceptible to tragedy. Jesus warned us that we would face trials in this life, but He has given us all the tools necessary to overcome them and be victorious in spite of them.

For I know the thoughts that I think toward you, says the LORD. (Jeremiah 29:11)

These things I have spoken to you, that in Me you may have peace. (John 16:33)

CHAPTER 11

Angel Weapons

Drew and Ben discuss the weapons of the invaders. The Bible states that, at the very least, some angels carry swords. Evidence for this is found in the following verses.

He placed...a flaming sword which turned every way, to guard the way. (Genesis 3:24)

He saw the Angel of the LORD standing in the way with His drawn sword. (Numbers 22:31)

David... saw the angel of the LORD..., having in his hand a drawn sword stretched. (1 Chronicles 21:16)

CHAPTER 12

The Spiritual Realm

Drew can see into the "alternate" dimension. The Bible also tells of men who have seen into the spiritual realm and tried to describe it.

The heavens were opened and I saw visions of God. (Ezekiel 1:1)

Daniel records several glimpses into the spiritual realm.

I, Daniel, had seen the vision and was seeking the meaning. (Daniel 8:15–17)

And I, Daniel, alone saw the vision. (Daniel 10:5–9)

Elisha's servant saw the army of God.

The LORD opened the eyes of the young man, and he saw. And behold, the mountain was full of horses and chariots of fire all around Elisha. (2 Kings 6:15–17)

John had a vision of things to come which he describes in the entire book of Revelation.

Immediately I was in the Spirit; and behold, a throne set in heaven, and One sat on the throne. (Revelation 4:1–2)

The spiritual world is more real than our physical world, for it is eternal. Jesus came from heaven to testify of its reality and to show us the way home: heaven.

CHAPTER 13

Betrayal

Drew felt betrayed by Jake and his mother when they arranged for him to meet Dr. Fisher. Betrayal hurts worst when it is done by someone you love. Jesus felt the sting of betrayal too when Judas, one of his closest friends, gave him over to the chief priests to be crucified.

From that time he sought opportunity to betray Him. (Matthew 26:14–16)

Jesus understands every hurt we feel and every temptation we have endured. He is a Savior whom we can turn to even when we feel betrayed.

We do not have a High Priest who cannot sympathize. (Hebrews 4:15)

CHAPTER 14

Spiritual Warfare

Drew begins to understand that there are two factions of invaders that are at war. Although the Bible doesn't give us a lot of details about what spiritual warfare looks like, it is referenced from Genesis to Revelation. The war began when Satan (Lucifer) became prideful and rebelled against God.

How you are fallen from heaven, O Lucifer, son of the morning! (Isaiah 14:12–14)

Many theologians believe that the reference in Revelation 12:4 refers to Lucifer convincing a third of the angels to follow him in his rebellion against God.

His tail drew a third of the stars of heaven. (Revelation 12:3–4)

Satan and his demons seek to destroy all people.

Your adversary the devil walks about like a roaring lion. (1 Peter 5:8)

As children of God, we are called into the battle as well.

We do not wrestle against flesh and blood. (Ephesians 6:10–13)

The Bible is silent on many aspects of spiritual beings and spiritual warfare. For example:
- What might their weapons be?
- Where would demons get weapons if they have them?
- In any war there is a risk of loss. What might be the risk of loss for angelic beings?
- Do angels and demons feel pain?
- Can they be injured?
- Can an angel lose a fight with a demon?

Whatever the answers are to these questions, it is important to know that God has already determined the end of the war. God is victorious, and we will rejoice on that day.

The devil…was cast into the lake of fire and brimstone. (Revelation 20:10)

God will wipe away every tear from their eyes. (Revelation 21:3–4)

CHAPTERS 15–16

The Attack of the Enemy

Drew experiences an attack by a dark invader. It is difficult to say just how vulnerable man is to the attacks of demons, but it appears to range from simply causing distress to taking life. Two biblical examples give us a glimpse into the capabilities of these fallen angels. The first is found in Job 1, when God allows Satan access to Job's family and possessions. All is destroyed, including his sons and daughters. A second example relates to Paul and the attacks of Satan.

A thorn in the flesh was given to me, a messenger of Satan. (2 Corinthians 12:7)

It is important to note that every spiritual attack described in the Bible is subject to the sovereignty of God.

He rules by His power forever; His eyes observe the nations. (Psalm 66:7)

CHAPTERS 17–18

Being a Good Samaritan

Because of his developing abilities, Drew feels compelled to help other people. But we don't need special abilities to help someone in need. Jesus tells a story of a man who helped another who was robbed and beaten. He uses the story of the good Samaritan as a teaching point for us all. Jesus also states that the greatest love a person can demonstrate toward another is by laying his life down for him. This was a foreshadowing of Jesus' great love for us by dying on the cross for our sins.

Greater love has no one than this, than to lay down one's life. (John 15:12–13)

While we were still sinners, Christ died for us. (Romans 5:8)

CHAPTER 19

Enemy of Truth
Drew sees a targeted attack by the dark invaders on the ministry team at Reverend Branson's church. The purpose of demonic attack is to hinder the work of God and the spreading of the gospel of Jesus Christ. Satan and his demons are the enemy of truth, but we should not be discouraged by his attacks because God is with us.

> We are hard-pressed on every side, yet not crushed. (2 Corinthians 4:1–9)

CHAPTER 20

Beasts of the Bible
Drew witnesses the attack of a fearsome beast against the light invaders protecting the church. The Bible contains much symbolism, so it is difficult to make a determination as to whether there is a biblical basis for the existence of such beasts in the spiritual world. However, John declares in the book of Revelation that he was taken up to the third heaven, God's abode, and he describes exactly what he sees. The beast Drew sees is pure speculation, but it is not outside the realm of spiritual possibility when considering the vivid descriptions of the apostle John.

> Out of the smoke locusts came upon the earth.... The shape of the locusts was like horses prepared for battle. (Revelation 9:1–11)

CHAPTER 21

When Bad Things Happen
Sydney tries to help Drew understand a little about God's character and sovereignty, but Drew has a hard time believing her because bad things happen to good people. Drew's logic is flawed because he doesn't understand that there is

evil in the world and sin has changed the nature of mankind and the nature of all of creation.

For we know that the whole creation groans and labors. (Romans 8:22)

Despite all the pain and suffering people experience in this world because of sin, God has a promise for His children. It is a promise that comes from the almighty God who is sovereign in everything.

And we know that all things work together for good. (Romans 8:28)

CHAPTER 22

God's Call

Sydney tells Drew that she is obeying God's call on her life. Sometimes God calls us to do things that don't make sense because we don't see the whole picture. Hearing God's call is the first step. Taking action and following is the next and potentially most frightening. If we want to be vessels through which God can work, we must be willing to say yes and then step out in faith.

I heard the voice of the Lord, saying: "Whom shall I send...?"
(Isaiah 6:8)

CHAPTER 23

The Attack of the Enemy

Drew witnesses an attack on Ben by the dark invaders. See chapters 15 and 16 for further explanation.

CHAPTERS 24–25

Help from Above

Drew and Ben are given help by a mysterious cab driver. Angels do interfere in the affairs of mankind in such ways. Two such biblical examples are Peter receiving help from an angel to escape prison, and two angels helping Lot and his family escape the destruction of Sodom.

> Behold, an angel of the Lord stood by him, and a light shone. (Acts 12:5–10)

> The angels urged Lot to hurry, saying, "Arise, take your wife." (Genesis 19:15–17)

The Secret War

Drew and Ben speculate that mankind subconsciously knows about the secret war between the invaders. Although they haven't yet discovered the truth about who the invaders really are, they are right about this deduction. The theme of good versus evil is central to almost every story told from the beginning of time. That element of story is a shadowy indicator of the truth of the real epic, invisible battle taking place all around us right now. People are so completely drenched by the concept of good battling evil in all of our legends, books, and movies that many do not even realize or consider that its origin lies in the truth of spiritual warfare.

> For we do not wrestle against flesh and blood. (Ephesians 6:12)

CHAPTER 26

Risk of Loss

Drew witnesses the death of an invader. What does spiritual warfare really look like? According to Daniel 10:20, angels do fight with demons. Whenever there is a battle or a war, there is risk of loss for both sides. If this fighting has been going on for thousands of years and a demon has never won a fight, why would they ever try. I think it is fairly safe to speculate that demons have won some fights over the millennia. What happens to an angel when a demon wins the fight is sheer speculation. On this subject the Bible is silent. However, we do know that a defeated demon can be sent to the abyss.

They begged Him that He would not command them to go out into the abyss. (Luke 8:27–33)

This is a dramatic example of the power of Jesus over the forces of darkness. Even a legion of demons feared him and knew they had no power over him. A typical legion in the Roman army of the day was approximately 5,400 soldiers. From this example, "the abyss" indicates a place of imprisonment and may refer to the bottomless pit referred to in Revelation. When Jesus does battle, He never loses!

CHAPTER 27

Deception
When Sydney discovers Drew and Ben's true intentions, she feels deceived. Although Drew did not tell her for her own safety, she still feels betrayed by the deception. Even with the best intentions, deception is never healthy in a relationship. Drew should have told Sydney that there were things he could not tell her for her own safety and to trust him.

He who speaks truth declares righteousness. (Proverbs 12:17)

Good and Evil
As Reverend Ray witnesses to Drew, Drew comes to a dramatic conclusion that refutes secular science and evolution: good and evil exist, and they exist in both dimensions. He witnessed moral acts of good and evil in the physical world and in the spiritual world. Because of that, he struggles with the question, Where does morality, or good and evil, come from? It cannot come from evolution, reason, conscience, human nature, or utilitarianism. Because good and evil are universal, the moral laws that define good and evil must come from a moral commander. Drew was beginning to understand this and had to face the conclusion that his logic was driving toward. Believing in and appealing to morality requires one to believe in or appeal to that moral commander: God.

I command you today to love the LORD your God, to walk in His ways. (Deuteronomy 30:15–16)

CHAPTER 28

Morals and Ethics

Moral laws come from God, and although ethical laws can be derived from the laws of God, they are generated by man for the proper functioning of society. Sometimes people face a dilemma when moral laws come in conflict with ethical laws. Drew makes a difficult decision when he assaults the FBI agents near Reverend Ray's church. Although it was ethically wrong, in his mind it was morally right because lives were at stake. In essence, he was sacrificing himself for the lives of Sydney, Shana, and Micah because he knew it would be an act with dire consequences, possibly costing him his life. Those decisions are the hardest to make. If a man must break an ethical law to accomplish a moral law, he must be willing to accept the consequences. There is an excellent example of this in Joshua, when Rahab lied to the soldiers to protect the two Jewish spies (Joshua 2; 6), and also in Acts, when the High Priest commanded Peter and the apostles not to preach about Jesus.

But Peter…answered and said: "We ought to obey God rather than men." (Acts 5:29)

CHAPTER 29

Demon Possession

Drew again encounters a "double-faced" man similar to the one he faced in chapter 14. We don't know what demon possession might look like in the spiritual world, only that it is real. Biblically, when a demon possess a person, he is controlled by the demon and may even possess certain unusual abilities. Mark 5:3–4 tells of a demon-possessed man having extra strength such that even chains and fetters could not bind him. Acts 16:16 tells of a woman possessed with a spirit of divination or the ability to predict future events. Today there isn't much credence given to the possibility of demon possession, but it is quite certain that the demons have not gone away. Believers in Jesus Christ need have no fear of demon possession because they are filled with the Holy Spirit and the "room" of a person is filled so that it cannot be occupied by an evil spirit (see Matthew 12:43–45). Also, the Bible tells us that God is much greater than any evil spirit, including Satan.

He who is in you is greater than he who is in the world. (1 John 4:4)

The Power of Prayer

Drew witnesses power being wielded against the dark invaders through Sydney, not realizing that it is God working through her prayers. How God uses prayer is a mystery, but Jesus affirms over and over that there is great power in prayer. See Matthew 17:21; Matthew 21:22; Acts 12:5; 1 Corinthians 7:5; Philippians 4:6; and James 5:16 for just a few examples.

The effective, fervent prayer of a righteous man avails much. (James 5:16)

CHAPTER 30

Angels

Drew learns that the name of the angel who has been helping him is Validus. The abilities and the limitations of angels are not clearly defined in Scripture, and there has been much speculation about them. There are a few things we do know about angels, however. For example:

- They have names (Lucifer—Isaiah 14:12; Michael—Jude v. 9; Gabriel—Daniel 9:21).
- They fight (Daniel 10:20).
- They have power to affect things in the physical world (Matthew 28:2; Luke 1:19–22; Revelation 7:2).
- They are not all powerful (Daniel 10:13).
- They are not all knowing (1 Peter 1:12).
- They carry weapons (Numbers 22:23; 1 Chronicles 21:16).

- They can appear to people (Genesis 19:1–3; Hebrews 13:2).
- They deliver God's messages to people (Luke 1:19).
- They eat food (Genesis 19:3).
- At least some have wings (Ezekiel 11:22).
- They are holy (Acts 10:22).
- Children are protected by them (Matthew 18:10).
- At least some, if not all, stand in the presence of God (Luke 1:19).
- They carry the believing souls of people to heaven (Luke 16:22).

Beyond this, almost everything else about angels is speculation.

COMING FALL 2014!

BOOK 2 IN THE

WARS OF THE REALM

SERIES

"A Pilgrim's Progress for the Xbox generation!"
—Dave Jackson, author of the Trailblazer novels

Audio books and original musical sountrack available online at
www.kingdomseries.com

POWERFUL ALLEGORIES
BIBLICAL VALUES

Sir Kendrick and the Castle of Bel Lione
In this first of Chuck Black's companion series to the popular Kingdom series, Sir Kendrick and Sir Duncan are sent to stop a dangerous new order that threatens their mission to serve the King.

Sir Bentley and Holbrook Court
In this second installment in Chuck Black's Knights of Arrethtrae series, readers will be drawn to the action, adventure, and romance of the story of Sir Bentley, an honorable young knight who battles the forces of evil and discovers the power of compassion to overcome the destructiveness of greed.

Sir Dalton and the Shadow Heart
Sir Dalton, a knight in training, is young, well-liked, and a natural leader. He has earned the respect and admiration of his fellow knights, and especially the beautiful Lady Brynn. But to defend the kingdom, Dalton must face the evil Shadow Warrior—this time will he survive?

Lady Carliss and the Waters of Moorue
Determined, smart and a master of both the sword and the bow, Lady Carliss races against time to save Sir Dalton's life, but an evil plot foils her efforts and she must choose between saving him and saving countless others.

Sir Quinlan and the Swords of Valor
Two best friends are called into duty for the Prince, but only one has the courage to follow. Can Quinlan overcome distrust and his own limitations to bring the Valor Knights back together?

Sir Rowan and the Camerian Conquest
The Dark Knight, deceptive and proud, is determined to destroy Cameria from within, but one young man will learn the power of humility and deliver truth to his people.